Meant
FOR ME

by

L. P. Dover

Printed in the United States of America

Meant for Me
A Second Chances Novel

Copyright © 2013 by L. P. Dover
Editor: Melissa Ringsted
Cover Artist: Regina Wamba (Mae I Design)

ISBN-13: 978-1494750961
ISBN-10: 1494750961

Second chances aren't easy to come by these days, but when you get them ... cherish them. One thing I've learned in my years of being in this world is to never be afraid and to always fight for what you want. I know these aren't exactly words of wisdom, but this series, my SECOND CHANCES series, is special to me in so many ways. I'm thankful and forever grateful to each and every one of you that have stuck by me and have let my stories touch your heart. You all gave me my second chance at a new beginning.

–L.P. Dover

I didn't realize how empty my life had been until you slammed the door on my heart. Right then and there I knew I screwed up whatever chance I had to get you back, but I also knew something else ...
something I couldn't deny any longer.
You were meant for me and I was meant for you. If it's a fight you want, it's a fight you're going to get. I will win you back.

–Mason

Prologue

Mason

The silence in the car was deafening. The beat of my heart pounding in my ears was all I could focus on as Claire drove me to the airport with tears streaming down her cheeks.

Claire.

What the fuck had I done? I knew it was a mistake to let things go as far as they did, even though we both promised none of it would mean anything. It was a lie.

My flight back to North Carolina would be departing in three hours, and it would put thousands of miles between us. My life was back in North Carolina with my badge and my gun while hers was in California managing her family's vineyards. I didn't belong there. We were completely different people, but there was a spark in her eyes that drew me to her when I met her through my cousin, Melissa, years ago. It was the same spark that ignited every desire, every hope of being able to touch her just once. One time was all I wanted, or at least that was what I thought.

The spark that I loved so much about Claire wasn't in her blue gaze as I peered over at her from the passenger's seat. She was pissed at me and I couldn't blame her. Hell, if I was her I would've beaten the shit out of me for doing what I did.

My cousin was the reason I was in California in the first place, and if it wasn't for her wedding I wouldn't have stepped foot on this side of the United States. Melissa used to live in North Carolina, too, but she inherited part of the vineyards from Claire's family when Claire's mother died. Brett was her fiancé at the time, and once he had everything squared away with his job they both packed up and moved across the country. They had just gotten married a couple of days ago and were already on their honeymoon in St. Croix … hence, the reason why I had no one else to take me to the airport other than Claire. I could've called a taxi, but Claire insisted on taking me.

I wanted to make things right, but there was nothing I could say that would make up for what I did. I screwed up and let my dick take the reins on my behavior. I couldn't deny the chemistry Claire and I had, especially the sexual tension, and every time she brushed up against me when we danced my cock immediately sprung to attention. It wasn't until later that night—when I found her laying across my bed with nothing but a pink, lacy babydoll that I could see straight through—that I finally gave in to my desire.

I wanted to taste her, to feel her … to finally get her out of my system. What I got was an addiction, and what's worse was that I craved her even now.

We finally passed a sign for the airport indicating we

only had one more mile to go, and I knew I was running out of time. The tension hung heavy in the air as I turned to the blonde haired knockout clenching the steering wheel so tight her knuckles were turning white. She wore a bright pink tank top with exceptionally short denim shorts that showed off her long, tanned legs. She was beautiful.

"What do you want me to say, Claire?" I asked softly, hoping to get something out of her instead of silence. "I told you I was sorry. What can I do to make you talk to me?"

What I did to her was something I would regret for the rest of my life. After a long, wild night of sex, love making, whatever you want to call it, it finally came time to wind down. The look in her eyes when she told me she was falling in love with me would forever stay ingrained in my mind. My reaction would haunt me forever as well.

Being the asshole that I was, I told her I wasn't good enough for her, grabbed my pants off the floor, and left the room. I realized my mistake as soon as I shut the door, but it was too late. The damage had been done. Claire cried for what felt like hours, or maybe it was my misery that made it seem longer. Meanwhile, all I did was sit there, leaning up against the door and listening. I wasn't prepared to hear those words come out of her mouth, and I sure as hell wasn't ready to face her this morning.

Holding her chin defiantly in the air, Claire kept her eyes on the road. However, I couldn't miss the undertone of hurt in her voice when she said, "Look, Mason, I get it. You don't do relationships. I was the one stupid enough to think that after the night we shared things would be different. I guess that's what I get for thinking."

I wanted things to be different between us, to be

something real, except I knew it wouldn't work with the way we lived our lives. Sighing, I tried to reason with her even though I knew it was hopeless, "We would never see each other, Claire. I work long hours and the work that I do is dangerous. You deserve so much better than me. Someone you wouldn't have to worry about all the time."

She pulled up to the airport terminal and put her FJ Cruiser into park before crossing her arms over her chest. Her breasts peeked up over her tank top, and I could see on the mounds of her breasts where the stubble on my chin had rubbed her skin raw. I wanted to kiss her again and tell her everything would be all right, except the look in her eyes when she turned to me let me know I had missed my chance. All I saw was anger … and pain.

Leaning over my seat, she reached for the handle on the door and pressed it down, opening it wide. Closing my eyes, I breathed in her scent—which always smelled like raspberries—as her body brushed up against mine.

"You're going to be late for your flight. It's time for you to go," she snapped.

I reached for her chin to get her to look at me, but she jerked away from my touch. Gritting my teeth, I released a heavy sigh. I slid out of her car and fetched my bags from the trunk. Before I went inside the airport, I leaned into the window of her car and let every ounce of regret I had pour into my words when I apologized, "I really am sorry, Claire. I need you to believe that."

Pursing her lips, she nodded her head and met my gaze head on, narrowing those gorgeous blue eyes in disdain. "Yeah, well … I'm sorry, too. However, there is one thing you were right about in all of this."

Knowing the final blow was coming, I had to ask,

"What exactly would that be?"

A tear escaped the corner of her eye and she hastily wiped it away, ashamed at letting me see her pain. "It would be the part where you said I deserved someone better than you. Before I would've said you were completely wrong, but now … you were absolutely right. Good-bye, Mason."

With those final words, she turned her face away and sped off out of the terminal, never once slowing down or looking back. I had lost her, and after today there was no way she would ever come back to me.

I was a fucking idiot.

Chapter 1

Claire

FOUR MONTHS LATER

"How are things going with Cooper?" Melissa asked, lifting a curious brow when I peered over at her through the vines.

Her wavy, auburn hair was pulled back off her face showing off the glow to her cheeks. She rubbed her swollen belly soothingly, which in a couple of months would be a set of twin boys. She had on her favorite yellow maternity sundress which only added to her motherly glow.

Every day, first thing in the morning, we walked together through the main vineyard to inspect the grapes. It was always so peaceful to hear the birds sing and smell the richness of the land. When I needed to think or get away from life, this was where I retreated to. I always had, even when I was a little girl.

Melissa used to be the wife of my older brother, Daniel, and also a high school biology teacher. Now she was my business partner and friend. Even though mine and

Daniel's family were in California, he moved to North Carolina to go to college and decided he wanted to stay there, pursuing his career as a financial advisor to the elite of Charlotte. They were married for two years until Melissa caught him cheating on her. Soon after that they got divorced, and then things went completely downhill.

When my mother died about a year and a half ago, she left the whole estate and the vineyards to me, but also left Melissa the little Tuscan villa we had on the other side of our land along with the vineyards on that property. Needless to say, my brother didn't like that and thought he deserved the inheritance, especially, since Melissa wasn't family. He failed to realize that she was more family to us than him. Long story short, he made some bad business decisions and tried to steal the vineyards out from under me. When he got caught, he went off the deep end and kidnapped Melissa in a desperate attempt to get her back. He almost had her over the border to Canada when her cousin Mason, who happened to be a Detective Chief Inspector and also an ex-lover of mine, had tracked them down.

Mason ...

Just thinking about him made me angry all over again. I honestly thought he would come to his senses and show up on my doorstep one day, but he never did. Not that I was God's gift to men or anything, but after the night we shared I felt a connection to him and I knew he did, too. What I didn't expect was for him to completely disappear out of my life. In fact, I haven't spoken to him since I dropped him off at the airport. The closest I had come to hearing his voice was when he called Melissa a couple of months ago to tell her Daniel was out of prison, and a free man.

He had hardly spent any time behind bars for what he did to Melissa and to the clients he stole money from. I guess that was the way the world worked these days. It seemed like anyone could get away with anything and not have to be punished for it. My brother tried to contact me soon after I found out he was out of prison, but I told him I no longer had a brother. It was harsh, but I honestly doubted he even cared. Melissa was my family now, not him.

"Claire?" Melissa asked, waving a hand in front of my face. "Are you all right? You blanked out on me there for a second."

Rubbing my eyes with the palm of my hands, I shook my head and sighed. "Yeah, of course I am. I was just thinking about some things. So much has happened in the past year. It's hard to believe that so many bad and terrible things could happen in so short a time."

"You got that right," Melissa agreed with a smile. "However, you never answered my question. How are you and Cooper doing? You seem to be doing well."

Cooper Davis was an old friend of mine from high school who had just moved back to California after being traded from the Dallas Cowboys to be a running back for the Oakland Raiders. He was two years older than me and also the guy I gave my virginity to. I missed him when he went off to college, but I never regretted the time we spent together.

We had a couple of flings over the years when he would come home to visit his family, and when he showed up at my door three months ago telling me he was moving back I knew he was just what I needed to get over Mason. We'd been seeing each other ever since and we'd even talked about moving in together, except I wasn't so sure on that just yet. I loved Cooper, and the sex was amazing with him, but in my heart I knew something was missing. I just hoped I figured out what it was before things got too serious, which I had a feeling they were about to.

Melissa narrowed her gaze, picking up on my hesitation by the concerned look in her eyes, but I smiled over at her and quickly answered, "Actually, Cooper and I are doing really well as a matter of fact. He wanted me to go with him to Texas to watch him play against his old team, but I told him I didn't want to leave you here to manage everything on your own. I'll watch the game on TV tomorrow night."

Melissa scoffed and rolled her eyes. "What am I … fragile? I know how to take care of the vineyards, Claire, and besides, Brett is always here with me. I think you're making up excuses. What's the real reason you didn't want to go?"

We'd finally arrived back to the main house and I took a seat on the wooden bench inside the gazebo, gazing out at the mountains and the long rows of grapes in the distance. Melissa sat down beside me and waved her hand impatiently in front of my face, waiting on my answer. I blew out a shaky breath and blurted out, "I think Cooper is going to propose to me."

Melissa beamed and clapped her hands excitedly. "Oh, Claire, that's great news. Cooper is a wonderful man and we all love him, especially Brett. I think he's Cooper's biggest fan. You two will make a great match. Not to mention he's hot as hell."

Nodding quickly, I bit my lip and averted my gaze. I didn't want her to see my hesitation. Cooper was all I could ever want. He was tall with dark brown hair and the most majestic blue eyes I'd ever seen on anyone. With him being an athlete, his body was well chiseled and basically a haven of perfection. However, there was a part of me that couldn't let go of the past I shared with someone else.

"Claire? That is great news, right?" Melissa asked uncertainly.

When my gaze lifted to hers, her smile vanished completely and was replaced with understanding and sympathy. She knew what was holding me back. Sighing deeply, she wrapped her arms around my neck and held me as close as humanly possible with her protruding belly in the middle of us.

She murmured softly in my ear, "I thought you were over him, Claire. As much as I think you and Mason would've been perfect for each other, I can't help but think that maybe Cooper came into your life at the right moment. Mason has a stubborn head on his shoulders, but if it's meant to be he will come back for you. Just don't miss out on life because he was too stupid to realize what he had in front of him."

After hearing Melissa's words of encouragement, it finally became clear. I had been holding back and letting happiness slip by me. *Not anymore.*

"You know what, Mel, you're right," I claimed wholeheartedly. I pulled back out of her arms so I could look at her. I was not the type of girl to wallow in despair over a man, and I couldn't let Mason hold me back anymore. It was time I started living my life.

With a renewed sense of determination, I looked at Melissa and smiled one last time before rushing out of the gazebo. "Where are you going in such a hurry?" she called, getting slowly to her feet.

Laughing, I looked over my shoulder and shouted, "I'm going to Texas, baby. There's a sexy football player there who needs me. Besides, I think a little spontaneity will do me some good."

It was way past time to move on.

Chapter 2

Mason

TWO DAYS LATER

"Are you sure you want to look at that tonight, man?" Jason asked, standing in the doorway and looking concerned. Except, it was hard to take his concern seriously with him standing there in jeans, a plaid button down shirt, boots, and a large brown cowboy hat. He took trying to be a cowboy seriously and all the guys at the station gave him hell about it.

"Some of the guys are going to Coyote Joe's if you want to come," he offered. "You've been staring at that folder for hours. I think you could use a drink … or twelve."

The way I feel, I could drink a whole fucking keg.

He was right, though. I had been staring at the file for hours, except I couldn't bring myself to look at the contents. I got the call last night as I was driving home from the gym, and needless to say I wasn't expecting what came

7

through the line. A good friend of mine was found murdered; beaten to death and discarded like a piece of trash
on the outskirts of Las Vegas over a week ago. His wife
was still missing and there were no leads as of yet on
where she could be. The thought of what could be happening to her right now made my blood run cold.

Jason took a seat in front of my desk and sighed.
"What do you think could've happened? This makes the
fourth dead fighter in three months. Weren't you part of
that scene a few years ago before you joined the force?
From what I heard you were pretty lethal."

I held the file tightly in my hands and nodded, remembering those days as if it was yesterday. "Yeah, I
started MMA training when I was eighteen, and by the
time I turned twenty-one I was primed and ready to fight. I
was mostly undefeated during my two years of competing,
losing only a couple of matches. I would have made it to
the big time if I didn't drop out."

"Why did you then?" Jason asked curiously. "I don't
think I've ever heard you talk about your fighting. I always
hear it from other people."

"That's because I was a goddamn mess back then
with a head the size of Texas. All I did was fight and fuck,
blowing tons of money on stupid shit. When my mother
was diagnosed with terminal cancer I had no choice but to
come home. I was travelling every week going here and
there, and I refused to get someone else to take care of her.
I gave it all up for her and never went back."

"Do you ever regret your decision?"

"Yes and no," I answered honestly. "Or at least not
the part of leaving it behind to take care of my mother. I
loved fighting, and if I would've lived my life the right

way then I could've made something of myself. I was going down the wrong path and I couldn't see it. I just hate it took her dying to see the real me and what I had become."

Jason sighed heavily and stood, gazing warily down at me. "I understand, brother. The guys and I will be at the bar until later tonight if you still want to join us. If not, we will see you on Monday."

Nodding, I said, "Sounds good, man. Don't do anything stupid tonight."

"Me? Never," he joked incredulously. "I'm always a good boy."

His laugh echoed all the way down the hall, and once I heard the door to the station shut I knew I was alone to look at the file without being interrupted. Taking a deep breath, I lowered my gaze to the papers and slowly began to read. The pictures taken at the scene were horrific. I could barely recognize the man who had mentored me and shown me everything I would ever need to know about professional MMA fighting. I didn't have to read the medical report to know that he had sustained a massive head injury and multiple broken ribs, which I was sure had punctured a lung if not both of them.

His name was Austin Moore and besides being a fighter he also had a dream to open up his own restaurant. He went to culinary school with his brother, and they both had made a promise that one day they would make their dreams come true and open up a family business. Austin loved fighting, but I knew the main reason he worked so hard at it was to win enough money to fulfill the other dream he pursued. He wanted it all and he was so close.

His wife, Summer, was one of the gentlest women I'd ever met and with her being missing for two weeks now the chances of her being alive diminished rapidly. I re-membered the day Austin and I met her very well. He was bummed about my cousin, Melissa, turning him down for a date knowing very well she was seeing someone already, so we trained extra hard and decided to go at it for an hour longer than usual. As soon as we walked out of the gym he wasn't paying attention and bumped right into Summer, making her spill a cup of soda all over the front of her nursing scrubs. She in turn dumped the rest on him and after that they became inseparable.

Two years later, they married and moved away to Virginia where her family lived, and about that time was when I began training on my own and entering fights. I hated not having him in my corner, but once I started mak-ing money I hired another coach and a personal trainer. Austin and I still made sure to keep in touch over the years, calling each other weekly to catch up. I never missed any of his televised fights and he tried on several occasions to get me back into the fighting scene. It was hard to believe he was gone. He was only three years older than me with so much to live for.

Why does bad shit always happen to the good people? Why can't it be the other way around?

The next picture in the file I came to happened to be one of Summer. She was smiling in that big, goofy grin that made Austin melt each time he laid eyes on her. Her bright blonde hair reminded me so much of Claire, as well as the bright blue eyes and the shape of her face. I didn't want to think of how fucked up I would be right now if it was Claire in this situation.

Claire ...

It had been so long since I'd talked to her, but I could

still remember the way her voice would dip lower when she'd speak my name and the way she smelled when she'd walk right by me. I checked on Claire every now and again when I'd call my pregnant cousin to make sure she was doing all right. I later found out that a month after I left she started seeing some professional football player who also happened to be someone she'd been off and on with for years. At first I was pissed, but then I had no reason to be because I was the one who left her. I had no right to get angry over her seeing someone else, but dammit, if it didn't make me want to kick someone's ass.

It was over … it didn't matter anymore.

After about three hours looking thoroughly through the file, there was nothing in it that led to answers. There was no evidence as to who did it or what happened, but with four fighters showing up dead, all being found in the same way—beaten and bloody—there had to be a link somewhere. I just had to find it.

"What kind of trouble did you get into in Vegas, Austin?" I murmured out loud. "You never did anything stupid."

Frustrated, I stacked all the crumpled papers on my desk into a disheveled pile and decided to call it a night. *Maybe I* should *go out to the bar,* I thought. I could sure use the liquor and a nice pair of tits to keep my mind off of shit … off of everything and everyone, including Claire.

Pulling out my phone, I sent a quick text to Jason.

Me: I'm on my way.

Jason's reply was almost instant.
Jason: Hurry the hell up. The chicks are hot tonight.

Grabbing my coat, I turned off the light in my office and made it halfway down the hall before the phone started to ring. My extension wouldn't just ring unless someone really needed or wanted to talk to me. Quickly, I ran back to my office, turned on the light, and reached down for the phone.

"Mason Bradley," I barked hurriedly, throwing my coat on the desk.

"Good evening, Mason, or better yet I should probably say good morning since it's past midnight out there in North Carolina. I wasn't expecting you to answer, but now that I have you on the phone we can get down to business," the man said matter-of-factly.

"Who are you?" I asked.

"My name is Ryan Griffin. I'm the Chief of Police of the Las Vegas PD. I was the one who granted you permission to see Austin Moore's file."

Cautiously, I replied, "I see. Well, thank you for that, but what can I do for you, Mr. Griffin?"

"First off, I want to say I'm sorry for the loss of your friend. When I checked into your background I had no idea you were close friends with Austin until I talked to his family. I also happened to find that not only were you his friend, but you were an impressive MMA fighter as well."

I chuckled halfheartedly. "Yeah, those were the glory days," I muttered. By the way I said that it almost made me sound like I was eighty years old, but really I was only thirty. My fighting days weren't actually that long ago.

"I know what you mean," Ryan replied. "My wife still remembers how I used to look when I was in my twenties and often reminds me of it in hopes I'd get that way again. I haven't seen those days in thirty years. Anyway, forgive my nonsense, I didn't mean to get off track. So back to Austin. His family told me that if anyone knew where he would be fighting in Vegas it would be you, but we already know he had a fight at the MGM Grand Garden Arena. Do you happen to know what else he was doing out there, or why he would get mixed in with a wrong crowd?"

Sighing, I sat down in my chair and leaned over my desk, staring at Austin's file. "No, I have no clue. Austin was always a straight edge guy, never getting into trouble, never got arrested or did drugs. It makes no sense to me."

"When was the last time you spoke to him?" Ryan asked.

I thought back to the last time he called me and realized it was right before he left to go to Vegas. I remembered the way he sounded; so happy and full of life. He had won all of his matches for the past year, except one, and was on his way to making his name into the big times.

"It was about two weeks ago," I told him. "It was right before he left. He always wanted to remind me of his fights so I wouldn't miss them. Have you gotten any leads? Because what I'm seeing in the file isn't getting me anywhere."

The sound of papers shuffling in the background along with Ryan's grumble didn't exactly sound too enthusiastic. "There are some leads that we're considering, but nothing concrete as of yet. Do you remember hearing about this same type of thing happening about four years ago in Ohio?" he asked curiously. "It would've been after you already quit fighting. The only difference is that the deaths were scattered out more."

Yeah, I remember seeing something about those deaths. Thinking back to those killings, I remembered being curious about them just because the men were MMA fighters, but when the cases were closed I moved on and never thought more about it. I knew several fighters who were so hotheaded they would go looking for fights, especially in the bars.

"Yes, I remember that time, but vaguely. I didn't exactly follow too much about it. Have you talked to anybody, possible suspects perhaps?" I asked.

"There's one guy we've spoken to who is a club owner out here and who also hosts his own MMA fights. He's approved to have them and it just so happens all of his stories and alibis are legit. We can't find a single discretion out of the man, so we ruled him out for now. Basically, what we're looking at is an illegal underground fighting ring, and with it being Vegas I'm sure there's some big money involved as well. We need someone on the inside, someone who could get in with no questions asked and someone who already has the knowledge of how the fighting world works." He paused for a second to clear his throat. "Which is where I'm hoping you come in," he finished, sounding hopeful.

"Excuse me? You have got to be kidding me." *What the hell did he want me for?* "What do I have to do with any of this?" I questioned suspiciously. "How am I going to be able to help you?"

Ryan paused for a second and took a deep breath. "Before I go into those details I want you to answer me one question … what lengths would you go through to find your friend's killer? What if there was a way all of this could come to an end with your help, would you do it?"

Closing my eyes, I laid my head on the desk and set the phone down for a second. I would do anything to find out what was going on. I didn't have to think twice about it, but I knew what he was going to ask me to do and it wasn't going to be easy. *In fact, it was most likely going to be one of the most dangerous missions I've ever gone on.*

As soon as I lifted my head and opened my eyes, the image of Austin's broken body flashed in my mind along with the vision of his beautiful wife who had gone missing. It was all the push I needed.

"I'll do it," I answered, putting the phone back to my ear. "I would do anything to bring Austin's killer to justice. Just tell me what I need to do."

Ryan breathed a sigh of relief and filled me in on everything. After our conversation ended at three in the morning, I grabbed Austin's file and headed home to pack.

I had a plane to catch.

Chapter 3

Claire

When I arrived in Dallas, Texas, a couple of days ago to surprise Cooper, it was in the middle of the night when I knocked on his hotel room door. His dark hair was mussed from sleep and his eyes were half open when he answered the door in only a pair of blue, plaid boxers.

I couldn't deny that he looked sexy as hell. Deep in my heart, I honestly felt that with time I would be able to love him the way he loved me, and there was no better time than the present.

The moment he realized it was me, he scooped me up into his arms, and planted a firm kiss to my lips. He didn't ask what I was doing there and he sure as hell didn't let me speak. His lips made sure of that. We spent the rest of the early morning hours making love until it came time for him to get ready for the game the next afternoon. I was afraid he would be too exhausted to play if he didn't get more sleep, but as I watched him run the ball down the field, I was in awe of how wonderful he played. In fact, he played the best I had ever seen him do, scoring three touchdowns, and putting his team in the lead by twenty points.

Now we were in the plane on the way home, slowly descending as the runway came into view. When Cooper took my hand and brought it to his lips, I turned away from the window and met his intense blue gaze. I was glad we were in first class with the bigger seats because with his six foot four frame and muscular build there was no way he could fit in the smaller seats in coach.

Leaning down closer to my ear, he murmured softly, "Thank you for coming out to Dallas, Claire. You have no idea how much it meant to me for you to be there."

I lifted a brow and smiled. "Umm … I think you showed me more than once how much it meant. I was so afraid you were going to play terrible with me keeping you up all night."

Chuckling, he put his arm around me and kissed the top of my head. "If anything, babe, you gave me the energy I needed. You know you've always been my lucky charm. I always play my best when you're around."

"Are you trying to say I need to be at all your games?" I teased, elbowing him in the side.

"I wish you could, but I know you need to stick around until Melissa has her babies. Next season, though, you better be at them all. I'm not taking any more excuses."

Grinning, he lightly grasped my chin and tilted my head back before placing a gentle kiss to my lips. Even though he was an aggressive player on the field, he had always been the most gentle of the men I'd been with. Closing my eyes, I leaned into his touch and deepened the kiss. Taking my hand, Cooper slowly lowered it to his lap where I felt the bulge of his hardening cock straining against his jeans. Smiling, I rubbed my hand against him, making a strangled moan escape his lips.

"Do you see what a simple kiss from you does to me?" he whispered gruffly. "If you keep it up I'm going to have to take you in the bathroom. Personally, I would rather wait until we get to your house. Trying to fit me and you both in that small ass bathroom isn't going to work."

I laughed, taking my hand away from his lap so he could adjust his pants. "I don't think so either, but before you ravish me can you drop me off at Melissa's house for a while so I can check on her? I also wanted to tell her how everything went."

Cooper smirked, his blue gaze sparkling with mischief when he replied, "That sounds good, babe. While you're doing that I might throw us some things together on the grill for dinner. I could eat a fucking horse right now. Although, I think I might stop by my place after I drop you off at Melissa's and then come back by to pick you up. Is that okay?"

I nodded and waved him off. "Oh yeah, that's perfectly fine. Take your time."

I had a lot I wanted to talk to Melissa about anyway.

My phone had died at some point during the trip home so I couldn't call Melissa to tell her I was back in town and coming over. When we pulled into the driveway of my family's Tuscan villa—which was now Melissa's home—I leaned over to kiss Cooper's cheek before getting out of his brand new, black Toyota Tacoma.

Before I shut the door, he smiled mischievously at me, his gaze lingering on my breasts. "You know, I think you look sexy as hell in that shirt. Maybe you should wear it more often."

Shutting the door, I looked down at the fitted Oakland Raiders jersey top then back over to him, rolling my eyes. He had some specially made for me, and also had some made for Melissa and Brett. Mine happened to be made a tad bit different, and it was the first time I'd ever worn it.

"And why should I wear it more often?" I asked sarcastically. "Is it because I have your name across my breasts and a slogan that says that I'm your girl on the back?"

Chuckling, he shrugged his shoulders and said, "Hey, can you blame me? I want people to know that you're mine."

"I think you've accomplished that already, Cooper," I remarked with a smile on my face. "Just come get me when you get done at your place, okay?"

"Will do, babe. It shouldn't be long," he assured me.

I waved good-bye to him as he pulled out of the driveway before walking up the path to the front door. Melissa's villa was my mother's favorite retreat when she was alive, and when Melissa and her husband, Brett, took it over they kept it exactly the same, not changing a single thing.

In a way, though, it was still strange having to knock on the door when for most of my life I could just walk on in. When no one responded to my knock, I rang the doorbell and waited … and waited. I was about to give up and call Cooper to come pick me up when the door finally opened.

"It's about time someone answered the door," I teased as the door opened. My smile vanished when I saw Melissa standing there, her eyes red rimmed and puffy as if she'd been crying.

"Oh my God, are you okay?" I asked, afraid that something was wrong. Taking her hands, I walked into the house, raking my gaze over her body to make sure she wasn't hurt. She looked the same, dressed in a blue maternity dress with her hair in a bundle of red curls on top of her head. "Are the babies all right? Did you fall? Do you need to go to the doctor?"

Melissa blew out a shaky breath and shook her head. "I don't need to go to the doctor. The babies are fine, Claire. I think the pregnancy hormones are making me emotional."

"Really? That's it?" I asked in disbelief. She glanced nervously over her shoulder before turning back to me. "For some reason I don't believe you," I scolded her. "What's going on?"

Nervously, she tried to usher me toward the door and that was when I realized she was trying to get rid of me. *Did she really think I would leave just like that?* She knew me better than that. "Melissa, you can stop pulling me toward the door because I'm not going anywhere until you tell me what's going on," I snapped.

Before she could answer, my gaze caught a movement off to the side of the room. Someone was there, and out of the corner of my eye I realized it sure as hell wasn't Melissa's husband, Brett. *Please, don't let it be who I think it is, please don't let it be ...*

I chanted that over and over in my mind, and even closed my eyes in hopes that it was just my overactive imagination playing tricks on me. *Nope, the figure was still standing there.* Even if I couldn't fully see who it was I had no doubt in my mind I already knew. My heart pounded the same way it always would when that specific person would be near. I had done so well with moving on and now it was shot to hell. The anger I thought I had suppressed over the past few months came flooding right back, rearing its ugly head, but what was even worse was that deep down there was that little ping of excitement of being able to see him again. My traitorous heart had screwed me over again.

Melissa squeezed my hands apologetically and whispered, "I'm so sorry, Claire. I tried to call you."

Closing my eyes, I took in a deep breath before mustering up the courage to face the man who broke my heart. I didn't have to wait long because the moment I opened my eyes it was no longer Melissa standing in front of me, it was Mason. He was dressed in a fitted gray T-shirt and a pair of loose denim jeans that hung low on his hips with his favorite baseball cap covering his dark blond hair. What made it even worse was the way he looked at me with those piercing green eyes. It was the way he looked at me when we made love four months ago, or better yet, when we fucked, since it didn't mean anything to him.

After all this time he had no right to look at me like that. He had no right to even speak to me.

"What are you doing here?" I asked angrily, placing my hands on my hips.

He moved closer and sighed. "I came to see Melissa and to make things right with you," he confessed. "Can we go somewhere and talk … just me and you?"

Incredulously, I laughed in disbelief, thinking it had to be a joke. When he stared at me, with not a touch of a smile, I knew he was being serious. *Out of all the times for him to come back, it had to be now,* I screamed in my mind.

"Mason, you had four months to make things right with me," I hissed. "There's nothing you can do to make up for what you did. I'm sorry, but I have nothing more I want to say to you … ever!"

With those final words, I turned on my heel and stalked out the door.

Chapter 4

Mason

I didn't realize how much she despised me until the moment I stepped into the doorway and Claire saw me, and I saw the outright venom in her eyes. From that look alone I knew she wouldn't take me back, but it wasn't going to stop me from trying. *I came here for a reason and I'm not leaving until I do what I told myself I was going to do.* I was going to put everything on the line.

As I watched Claire turn her back on me and walk away, I had the deepest urge to handcuff her to a chair and *make* her listen to me. However, forcing her would only push her away even more. When I handcuffed her to anything it would be out of mere pleasure, not anger. I was determined to get her back. Rushing out of the house, I grabbed Claire's arm before she could go any further and turned her to face me.

"Let me go, Mason," she ordered through clenched teeth.

Her body was coiled tighter than a snake, but when I

grabbed her other arm and pulled her closer, I could feel the tension in her muscles loosen and she noticed it, too. I wanted to kiss those lips of hers that tasted sweet like honey with the hint of raspberries, and feel her bare skin on my fingers. Seeing her now only reminded me of how stupid I had been to let her go, and now it was too late. *Or was it?*

"Please give me this chance, Claire," I murmured in her ear. "There are so many things I need to tell you. I know you've moved on to someone else, and it's kind of obvious with his name plastered all over your body, but I can't leave here without telling you how I feel." I paused and took a deep breath. "I've missed you, Claire. I missed you the moment you drove away from me at the airport four months ago."

"Why are you doing this now?" she asked incredulously, pulling her arms out of my grasp and crossing them over her chest.

She stepped back, one small step after another, and the further she moved away the further I could feel her slipping away. A tear slid down her cheek and she wiped it away, whispering, "Things are finally going good for me, Mason. I can't have you screwing that up."

Nodding, I lowered my head and blew out a shaky breath. "I understand, and if you're truly happy then what I have to tell you won't matter at all. I have to get this out or I may never get the chance again. Claire, I …"

Unfortunately, that was as far as I'd gotten before the sound of Cooper's truck coming down the long driveway stopped me. *Are you fucking kidding me? When am I ever going to catch a break?* It was perfect timing on his part, but terrible for mine. Skeptically, he glanced from me to

Claire and then settled his gaze on me with a scowl on his face. It was obvious he knew who I was, and if not it was obvious he didn't care for me. Claire glanced nervously behind her, and I knew my moment to tell her how I felt was lost. Would I get a chance to before I left? I had no clue, but I had to try. Before Cooper could get out of his truck, I stepped closer to Claire and let her see the seriousness in my eyes.

"Meet me tonight," I muttered quickly. "You know where."

Past her shoulder I could see Cooper approaching, but she kept her glistening blue eyes my way. If she didn't agree to meet me tonight there was still the possibility I'd never see her again. Any time I went undercover was dangerous and I always had to accept the probability that it could be the last mission I ever went on. It was the way it worked.

"I'm sorry, Mason, but I can't. I can't risk everything just because you show up on my doorstep. If you want my trust or my heart you need to fight for it … you need to earn it. Until you're willing to do that I don't want to see you again," she uttered boldly.

Cooper finally made it to us and put his arm around Claire's shoulders, pulling her into his side. "Everything okay?" he asked, gazing down at her before turning a lethal glare my way.

Claire wrapped her arms around his waist and nodded, smiling up at him. "Yes, everything's fine." Her smile disappeared when she glanced back at me. "I was just telling Mason good-bye."

With those last words she turned her back on me for the second time today while Cooper stayed behind. We

25

both watched her climb into his truck and shut the door, keeping her gaze on anything but us.

"What are you doing here?" Cooper asked angrily, crossing his arms over his chest. He was a couple of inches taller than me, but height never mattered anyway. We were almost identical as far as body size, but I knew without a doubt I could take him in a fight.

"Not that it's any of your business," I replied with a sly grin on my face, "but if you must know I came to visit my cousin."

Cooper scoffed. "Well, whatever the reasons are you better stay away from Claire. I know who you are and what you did to her. However, I guess I should be happy that you were such an idiot because now I have her and you don't. So thank you for that."

"I don't think you'll be thanking me when I get her back," I warned with a smirk on my face. "I let her go once, but it was a mistake I'll never make again. I'll fight for her no matter what it takes. You can count on that."

I was determined to get her back and of that I was certain.

"I still can't believe Austin is gone and Summer's missing," Melissa murmured sadly, catching my attention. I didn't even know she was behind me until she spoke.

"I know, but I'm going to find out what happened to them. I can promise you that," I vowed wholeheartedly, sealing up the envelope in my hand.

For the past two hours I'd done something I never thought I would ever do in my life … I wrote a fucking love letter, and also wrote down everything Melissa would need to know if I didn't make it back alive. When Melissa showed me to the guest bedroom I'd be staying in for the night, I saw the desk in the corner and went straight to it. The whole time I kept thinking how pathetic it all was to write a letter, but I wanted Claire to know how I felt before I left, in case I didn't come back.

"What is that?" Melissa asked, glancing down at the envelope clutched in my hand.

Releasing a heavy sigh, I passed it over to her and said, "It's a letter to Claire, and all the information you will need in case I don't come back. I need you to make sure Claire gets the letter after I leave."

Melissa took the letter and papers cautiously, furrowing a brow. "You're not telling her good-bye, are you? Because so help me God you better come back in one piece after all of this shit."

Seeing my pregnant cousin looking at me like she wanted to kick my ass made me chuckle. She threw a pillow at my head and huffed, "I'm being serious, Mase. This isn't a laughing matter. Fighters are showing up dead and you're going right into the middle of it. Promise me you'll stay safe."

Taking her hand, I pulled her up from the bed and hugged her tight. "I promise I'll be safe, Mel. I know what I'm doing." She sobbed against my chest and I hated that I was causing her pain, but I wanted to see her before I left, and more so I wanted to see Claire.

"All right, Mel, stop crying."

She released the death grip she had around my waist

and looked up at me. "Will you be able to call me when you're out there?"

"Probably not every day, but I'll make sure you know I'm safe, okay?"

She sniffled and blew out a shaky breath before saying, "Okay."

After she left, I shut the door to my room and lay down on the bed, staring at the ceiling. There were so many things running through my mind that I knew I wouldn't be able to sleep if I tried. From the information Ryan's sources had gathered for him there was a man who seemed to be the number one key suspect in the deaths and who was possibly in charge of the illegal underground fighting ring. He sent me over all the information before I left home to come to California. No one had gotten close enough to get the guy's name, but there was one thing that would make him a little easier to spot … he had a dragon tattoo on the right side of his neck and a jagged scar by his left eye.

Finding him wasn't going to be easy, but I had to try.

Chapter 5

Claire

"What do you want to do today, babe?" Cooper asked, entering the kitchen with only a towel wrapped around his waist. "We can drive down to the bay. We haven't done that in a long time."

When he walked by me, he kissed me on the cheek before pouring himself a cup of coffee. Driving to San Francisco was over a two hour drive from my house, and if we stayed down there all day we wouldn't get back until later. From the confrontation Cooper had with Mason yesterday it wouldn't surprise me if he wanted to get me away just so I wouldn't see him. All night I tossed and turned wondering if I'd made a mistake not meeting Mason when I had the chance. For the first time since I'd known him he actually seemed sincere with his plea. *It was too late now.*

However, I couldn't shake the uneasy feeling in my gut saying that I made a horrible mistake in not hearing him out.

Leaning against the counter, Cooper blew the steam away from his cup and took a slow sip, lifting a brow in the process while waiting on my answer. Putting thoughts of Mason aside, I slid our omelets onto the plates and passed Cooper one before answering as excitedly as I could, "Driving to the bay sounds great. After we eat I'll take a shower and get ready to go."

Smiling, he seemed to be appeased at my answer, except deep down I really didn't want to go. My traitorous heart wanted to see Mason again and I felt guilty for even thinking it. After I ate half of my omelet, I couldn't stomach anymore so I took a shower and made sure to stall just a bit by putting my makeup on slowly and fixing my hair. I had to get Mason out of my mind.

"Babe, are you about ready to go?" Cooper called out from the living room. "I thought maybe we could go to lunch at that restaurant you like so much on the way down there."

I slipped on my little white sundress and zipped it up as far as I could get it before grabbing my sandals and joining him in the living room. Dressed in a pair of khaki shorts and a blue polo shirt that hugged his perfectly shaped biceps, I smiled appreciatively at him before turning my back so he could zip me up the rest of the way.

Instead of zipping me up, he did the opposite and lowered it, leaning his head down to kiss my neck. "Or better yet, we could just stay here and make love all day. You look so damn hot right now."

I laughed and smacked his hand when he tried to grab my breast. "Zip me up and let's get out of here. It was your idea to go on this day trip, was it not?"

He groaned and reluctantly zipped up my dress. "Yes, it was, but that was before I saw you in that dress and before I got a raging hard on. I want you so bad right now."

Pushing his hard cock up against my back, he reached up under my dress, trailing his fingers up my thigh and further up to …

Before he could go up any higher, a knock sounded at the door. Grumbling under his breath, Cooper straightened my dress and marched to the door saying under his breath that it better not be Mason. My pulse quickened as I anxiously waited to see who was behind the door, and when Cooper stepped out of the way, Melissa walked in with a frown on her face.

"Can I talk to you for a minute?" she asked, glancing at me warily.

"Of course," I uttered slowly, cautiously. Again, something wasn't right because I could see it in her eyes.

When I joined her at the door, she nodded her head toward outside, indicating she didn't want to talk around Cooper. I shut the door behind me as I followed her out. We walked around to the garden which was full of multi-colored flowers and herbs. The water fountain we both took a seat at had been a recent addition to my flowery escape.

"What's up, Mel? Why do you look so sad?" I asked.

She sniffled and pulled out a thick white envelope she had stowed away in her bag, handing it to me. "I swear, I think I've cried more with being pregnant than I have in my entire life. This is absolutely ridiculous," she sobbed, pointing to the letter in my hand. "It's from Mason. He wrote it last night."

"Really?" I gasped incredulously. I turned the envelope over and slid my finger underneath to break the flap. "What, was he too afraid to bring it to me himself?" I inquired, rolling my eyes. Pulling out the letter, I started to unfold it when Melissa's next words halted me.

"There's a reason he's not here to give it to you, Claire," she muttered sheepishly. "He left this morning."

"What?" I shrieked, dropping the letter on the ground. "He already left to go back home? How can that be? I can't believe he gave up so quickly."

Sighing, Melissa closed her eyes and shook her head. "Claire, he didn't give up on you, but I do think there's some things you need to know."

Usually, I could handle surprises, shocks, and bad news with an open mind. I had to say, I wasn't prepared for what she said next.

The more Melissa explained Mason's mission, the more I grew sick with fear. What made me even more upset was that I didn't find out before he left, or better yet he told Melissa not to tell me. He left the letter, which I had yet to read, and was somewhat nervous to read it. Mason was on his way to Las Vegas, and for a while I had grown to know that city very well.

After recovering from an injury that ruined any chances of a dancing career for me, I lived in Vegas for a while, doing things I knew my family wouldn't be proud of, but I was angry and upset and I needed the outlet. I experimented with drugs a little bit and enjoyed the high it offered, but it only helped temporarily. I didn't stay on that path for long; I finally came to my senses and sought solace in dancing again. Dancing was my savior and I owed it to a very special person from my past … someone I hadn't spoken to in over a year.

I'd seen the news reports on the dead fighters, but I never in my life thought it would ever involve Mason. Yeah, he fought in the ring years ago, but at that point in time I didn't know who he was. I hadn't met him yet. Mason mentioned it to me briefly on one occasion when I went to North Carolina to visit my brother and Melissa when they got married. I had no clue he was on his way to getting a name for himself until he had to drop out to take care of his mother.

He gave up one of his dreams to take care of his family. It just occurred to me that we both had something in common. Mason lost his chance at fame, and I lost mine at a dancing career when I fractured a knee after a biking accident. The day I had to turn down my spot at Julliard was one of the worst moments in my life; hence, the reason I spent months in depression and fled to Vegas to get away. I was twenty-one at the time and just figuring out how the world worked, and that not everyone always got what they wanted. After two whole seasons, I traded my Vegas life in for a business management degree so I could help with my family's vineyard and winery. It was one of the best decisions I ever made.

Mason could be a complete dick, but there was one thing I could definitely say we had in common … we were both loyal. I was loyal to my family and he was loyal to the badge. He was also extremely good at his job, and I saw that first hand when we were all going crazy after my brother kidnapped Melissa. Mason was determined to find her and he did, just like I knew he would have that same determination to find justice in the recent killings.

While Melissa sat quietly beside me, I opened the letter with shaky fingers and took a deep breath before reading the words.

Claire,

By now you already know that I had to leave. I came to California to not only see Melissa, but to see you as well. Telling you all of this in a letter was not what I intended, but I respected your wishes and stayed away, even though deep down I wanted to handcuff your ass to a chair and make you listen to me. You always drove me completely crazy when I would see you on your visits to North Carolina. I wanted you so fucking bad, but I stayed away, not letting my feelings get too strong because I knew it would never work with my job and the distance between us. All of that was just bullshit excuses. I was afraid, afraid to want something so bad and have it be just outside of my reach. But even more I was afraid of not being good enough for you.

Claire, I have never been in love before. Never once have I allowed myself to open up and let someone in like I've wanted to do with you. The night we made love, I told myself that it wouldn't mean anything, knowing very well it would fuck with my mind completely and make me want you even more. When you agreed, I allowed myself to be selfish, to have that one night with you. What I didn't expect was to hear you say you were in love with me. No one has ever said that to me and meant it, but hearing it come from your lips ...

It scared me because I was in love with you, too. I still am. Ever since then I have lived in a bundle of regret and prayed that one day you would forgive me for being the insensitive jackass that I am. Failing has never been an option for me, but I know I failed you. I will spend the rest of my life making it up to you if you'll let me. If I have to fight my way into your heart again I will. All I'm asking for is a second chance, to show you that you were meant for me. I love you, Claire, and I will be back for you. I can promise you that.

  Mason

Tears filled my eyes as I folded the letter back up and slid it into the envelope. "What did it say?" Melissa asked hesitantly.

"It said he loved me," I cried. "And now it's too late for me to do anything about it."

Melissa lifted a brow and smiled. "Why do you think it's too late?"

Glaring at her, I scoffed and said, "Because he's already gone, Mel. Deep down I knew I should've let him talk to me, but I let my pride and ego get in the way."

Melissa pulled out her phone and gazed down at the clock. A little smirk tilted up her lips when she looked back at me, showing me the time. "His flight doesn't leave for another hour. If you're really wanting to do this you still have time, but in doing this you might lose someone else close to your heart. Is it a risk you want to take?" She glanced toward the house where I knew Cooper was still waiting on me. "You need to decide who you want, Claire. I know you don't want to hurt either one of them, but only you can decide."

She placed a gentle hand on my shoulder and squeezed before strolling up the path toward the front of the house. My heart felt like it had been tugged in a thousand different directions and I needed to decide if I wanted to play it safe or take the risk. Playing it safe would be the smart thing to do because I'd spent my whole life taking unnecessary risks and getting burned. However, some of the risks I'd taken were some of the best decisions in my life.

What the hell was I going to do?

Cooper had the door open and was leaning up against it as I approached. He had been my friend and lover off and on for years and had never let me down, always being there when I needed him. Opening his arms, he didn't say a word as I wrapped mine around his waist and sobbed against his chest.

I had to choose.

Chapter 6

Mason

When I woke up in the morning, or better yet when I stopped staring holes in the ceiling, I took a quick run through the vineyards to Claire's house. It was still dark outside with the sign of the sunrise peeking up behind the mountains in the distance. I had hoped there'd be a chance I could catch Claire awake and talk to her, except when I got there all of the lights were off, and of course Cooper's truck was right there in the driveway. That goddamn bastard was there sharing a bed with her when it should've been me. However, being that I was a glutton for punishment, I knew I deserved it. It was just another reminder of how stupid I was to let her go.

Melissa's husband, Brett, dropped me off at the airport because my hormonal cousin couldn't stop crying to be able to see clearly or function for that matter. She was more like a sister to me than anything, but both Brett and I couldn't wait for her to have the twins so she would get back to normal. When I got to the airport, I didn't have long to wait before they let the passengers onto the plane. My early morning run made me a little bit late, and I was surprised I even made it on time.

Before boarding the plane and leaving my life and everyone behind, my phone rang with an incoming call from Melissa. There was no surprise there. Stepping out of line, I accidentally bumped into a little old lady standing behind me and apologized before hastily answering the phone.

"Mel, what's up?" I asked, hoping she was calling to give me news on how Claire took the letter.

Sniffling, she answered, "I wanted to call and tell you to be safe, but I think I've already told you that a million times now, haven't I?"

I chuckled. "Yes, you have, but it's okay. I'm used to your nagging."

"That's true, but somebody has to do it. Oh, by the way, what airline are you flying with?" she asked. "If you don't get the chance to call I want to make sure I can look up your flight to confirm that you made it there safely."

"Uh … let's see," I said, looking down at the ticket in my hand. I knew I was flying Delta, but I didn't know the flight number. "Okay, it's Flight 1063 and I'm with Delta. Is that the only reason why you called? Have you talked to Claire?"

Sighing, her voice sounded a little hesitant when she responded, "Yes, I talked to her and gave her the letter. She's confused right now, so I don't really know what to say other than give her time. I know she cares for you, but it did take you four months to come back. That's messed up, Mase. I would be pretty pissed if Brett did that to me. You're just going to have to accept the consequences with what she decides to do."

Leaning against the wall, I tilted my head back and closed my eyes, hoping that one day the regret would lessen. "I understand," I said. "Thank you for talking to her and giving her the letter. No matter what happens, I needed her to know how I felt."

When I opened my eyes and noticed all the passengers had boarded the plane already, I said a quick goodbye to Melissa and rushed through the terminal. It was going to be a long four hour trip with only one thing on my mind ... Claire.

The old lady I bumped into in the line before taking Melissa's call ended up being the one who sat beside me on the plane. One of her grandsons offered to take her seat beside me, but she shooed him away and said she was perfectly fine since I was so handsome. The grandson chuckled and said he was trying to save *me* during the flight and not the other way around. Apparently, his grandmother liked to talk and talk she did.

Her name was Evelyn, and she was on her way to Vegas for her birthday. She wouldn't tell me how old she was, saying that a true lady never revealed that, but with her short, snow white hair, the posture of her body, and the age of her grandchildren she had to be in her early eighties. I spent the whole flight listening to stories of her and her late husband, and I even caught myself talking about Claire and how I wanted her back. Talking to her made the four hour flight much more bearable.

When we got off the plane, Evelyn walked with me down to the baggage claim while her family trailed along behind us, snickering and laughing until her grandson—who I had learned was named Jacob—came up and took her hand.

"All right, Grandma, it's time to leave the gentleman alone," Jacob said, grinning.

Evelyn smiled up at him and brushed his red hair off his forehead before pinching his cheek. The guy had to be in his late twenties, and obviously the one who paid more attention to his grandmother. What she said next didn't surprise me. "He's my favorite grandson, but don't tell the others," she admitted slyly.

Rolling his eyes, Jacob shook my hand and grinned. "Thank you for humoring her. She doesn't get out too much these days."

"It was my pleasure. I don't have any more living grandparents, so it was nice to spend time with her."

Evelyn smiled and patted my hand, beckoning me to bend down closer to her. She was about five feet tall while I stood over her an extra foot taller. "If your Claire doesn't take you back, sweetie, I will be more than happy to take her place," she uttered, wagging her eyebrows. "You know, I bet if you asked her to marry you she would come back."

"I will surely think about that," I promised her. "Have a wonderful birthday and maybe I will see you in one of the casinos."

She nodded enthusiastically and kissed me on the cheek before her and her family sauntered off. My luggage finally made its round to me so I snatched it up and made sure it was all in one piece. Once I got to the hotel, I was going to drop off my things and head out to scout the places that I was told could lead me in the right direction.

I had a plan forming and I was …

"Hello, Mason," a familiar voice called out from behind me. Immediately, my heart stopped and I froze, not sure if I'd really heard her voice or if I imagined it. It was impossible. There was no way she could be standing behind me.

I turned around slowly, expecting to have just imagined it, but there right in front of me was an angel in a white sundress; her bright blonde hair draping over her shoulders. However, I wouldn't necessarily call her an angel with the way she glared at me with her arms crossed at her chest and a scowl on her face.

It was Claire … and she was pissed. *What the fuck was she doing here?*

Chapter 7

Claire

I watched Mason as he chatted with the elderly woman in the plane; he was so engrossed in her stories that he didn't even know I was there. My name came up a few times in their conversations, but I was too far away to hear exactly what they were talking about. I kept my distance as Mason walked to baggage claim with the lady in tow, and I had to admit it was kind of sweet and not something I ever thought I'd see Mason do, except it still wasn't enough to get me over being pissed at him. He left without saying good-bye, and even if I told him I didn't want to see him he still should've tried.

The old lady and her family finally walked away once they got their luggage, so I walked up behind Mason, arms crossed, and ready to battle. For once he didn't have his baseball cap on and I noticed that his shortly cropped, dark blond hair had grown out just a bit on top and was gelled in messy spikes. His dark denim jeans hung low on his hips, but what caught my attention was the bright red T-shirt that hugged the bulging muscles in his arms, showing off the lower half of the sprawling eagle tattoo he had that covered his shoulder to mid-bicep.

My God, he's gotten bigger in the last few months. Was it bad that all I wanted to do was run my hands over his arms and feel them under my touch? His arms were the most magnificent part of his body and being in them was even more so. *Stop thinking about that, Claire,* I chided myself.

"Hello, Mason," I said, catching him off guard.

His whole body froze, and I swear it took him over a minute to finally turn around. "What the …" Mason began, completely taken unaware. "What are you doing here?"

"Umm … I flew on a plane," I remarked sarcastically.

Mason rolled his eyes and groaned. "No shit, Claire. What I want to know is how is this possible? There's no way you could've been on my flight."

I straightened the bag on my shoulder and nodded, but I was more than happy to tell him how I got past him without him even noticing. "Yes, I *was* on your flight. I snuck by you when you were on the phone with Melissa. I made her call you because I knew it would distract you. I can be smart sometimes you know."

"Son of a bitch," Mason growled, running a hand through his dark blond hair. "I can't believe she told you where I was going."

"Well, it's a lot better knowing instead of reading a good-bye letter wondering when you'd be back," I hissed. "It would've been nice to hear the truth from you, especially if there was a chance I'd never see you again."

Eyes going wide, he stiffened and balled his hands into tight fists when he asked, "What are you talking about?"

He was angry and I knew he'd be angry with Melissa,

but he had to understand why I came. "Mason," I started, my voice low, "Melissa told me what you were doing here. She told me everything. I came because I thought you could use my help."

"Hell no," he thundered, pulling me off to a secluded corner. "I'm not going to put you in harm's way, Claire. Do you even know the kind of people I'm going to be around? You're crazy if you think I'm going to let you anywhere near that shit. My friend's wife is still missing and I know what happens to pretty women like you on the street; I've seen it. I would never forgive myself if anything happened to you."

It was true; he'd seen some horrific and disturbing things being a cop, and I couldn't imagine seeing it up close and personal. He, on the other hand, didn't know I had connections in Vegas. "Nothing is going to happen to me," I promised. "I know my way around Vegas, and I *know* I can help you. You need to hear me out."

His emerald green gaze grew weary as he stared at me, and I knew deep within my heart what he was wondering. He lifted a hand to my cheek, and it took all I had not to lean into his touch, but then he pulled away before he could make contact. I would be lying if I said I wasn't disappointed.

With a heavy sigh, he asked softly, "Is that the only reason why you came … to show me around Vegas? How do you even know your way around here?"

I didn't want to tell him *all* the details of why I spent my time in Vegas, but if it came down to disclosing my past to help him I'd do it in a heartbeat. However, of course, showing him around wasn't the only reason why I came, but I didn't want him to know that just yet. He couldn't expect me to come crawling back to him after just a simple letter. He said he would fight for my heart, and I was sure as hell going to make him.

Straightening the bag on my shoulder, I reached down to grab the handle of my suitcase and smiled. "Oh, you know me, Mason. I'm always up for an adventure. Besides, what kind of person would I be if I knew a way to help you and I didn't? Melissa would never forgive me if something happened to you. Once I help you I'll leave Vegas and go home to my life, simple as that."

Narrowing his gaze, he responded dryly, "What about Cooper? Is he okay with all of this or does he even know you're here alone with me?"

Cooper was furious when I told him what I was doing, and the last thing I wanted to do was lie to him. He deserved more than that and he didn't deserve to be betrayed. It broke my heart when he insisted on reading the letter Mason wrote to me, except deep down I think he knew I still loved Mason anyway. Cooper was the one who always picked me up when I was down and he was always there for me, except for the time I left for Vegas. I shut everyone out at that time. I loved him dearly, but I knew I was never *in* love with him. In time I think it might have happened, but there was something about Mason that stirred every fiber in my soul. However, I wasn't going to let him know any of that yet.

Turning on my heel, I ambled my way toward the exit signs and called out over my shoulder, "Excuse me, but I don't think mine and Cooper's relationship is any of your business. Now come on and let's go. We can't get anything done here."

Mason scowled, but I saw the hint of a smile behind

that scowl. He kept his pace beside me and once we got outside, the heat of the Nevada sun engulfed me. *Holy shit, I forgot about the heat.* It was only May, but it felt like an inferno already; it had to be in the nineties.

Mason swiped the dampened hair off my shoulders and I jumped in response. I wasn't expecting him to touch me like that … so intimate. The heat in my body jacked up another ten degrees and it wasn't on my skin where I grew damp. Leaning close, his breath tickled my neck as he whispered in my ear, "I'm not going to lie to you, Claire. When I turned around and saw you my heart did a fucking flip. I didn't know if I would ever see you again. It killed me to not be able to touch you, and worse it pissed me off seeing you with another man. As much as I don't want to do this, there's something you need to understand—"

A cab pulled up to the curb, interrupting him, so he moved away and spoke to the driver before loading our bags in the trunk. He opened the back door for me, but before I could slip inside, he stepped in the way so he could finish what he was saying. "I don't know how you think you're going to be able to help me other than showing me around, and you have no idea how happy it makes me to be able to talk to you, to touch you. However, my mind isn't going to be swayed. I need you safe, and being with me here is too risky. I need you gone as soon as possible."

I glared at him and was about to tell him he didn't get to make my decisions for me, but he put a finger to my lips and leaned closer, his nose almost touching mine. My breath hitched, and with his lips so close I wanted to close the distance. "I'm sorry for all that I've done and tonight I want nothing more than to make it all up to you in any way you want, but once tomorrow comes I'm sending you on a flight back to California. You mean too much to me."

Little did he know it, but I wasn't going anywhere.

We arrived at the Bellagio, per my request since Mason's former idea of a hotel ended up being the crappiest one in Vegas. Not that I was high maintenance or anything, but staying in that rat hole just wasn't going to do. We'd probably get mugged as soon as we stepped out of the cab.

Mason busied himself with getting our bags out of the trunk while I waltzed inside to see if the hotel had any rooms available. The Bellagio was my favorite hotel out of all the ones on the strip and it was mainly because of the fountain of lights in front of the hotel. Each night they would play music and the water would dance in an extravagant display along with the sound. It brought me peace, it relaxed me, and most importantly it also helped bring me out of my depression.

Memories came flooding back as soon as I entered through the front doors. My eyes immediately went straight to the massive fixture on the ceiling. It had to be one of the most beautiful things I had ever seen. There were over two thousand different colored glass-blown flowers made into an enormous chandelier. It was absolutely breathtaking.

By the time I got to the front desk, I was able to walk right on up to the lady at the counter whose nametag said her name was Laura. She looked to be in her late thirties with her chocolate brown hair pulled back in a sleek ponytail, wearing a silky cream colored blouse and a knee-length brown skirt.

She smiled warmly and greeted me, "Good afternoon, what can I do for you today?"

Pulling out the wallet from my bag, I laid it out on the counter and answered, "I'd like a room, please, preferably one that overlooks the fountain if you have it."

She grinned and typed away on the computer for a few seconds. "Okay, let's see here. It looks like the only fountain view room we have available is in one of our Cypress suites. It's an open floor plan with a king size bed along with a his and her bathroom, but we do have other rooms available if this doesn't suit you."

Out of the corner of my eye, I saw Mason finally come through the front door carrying our bags, starting straight for me. Pulling out my credit card, I handed it to Laura quickly and said, "The Cypress suite sounds perfect. I'd like to book it for two weeks if that's possible."

She nodded and ran my card before giving it back to me. I tucked it back into my wallet and shoved it into my bag just as Mason came up to my side with a scowl on his face.

"Did you just pay for our room?" he muttered incredulously.

Laura handed me the paperwork and the keys with an amused expression on her face as she gazed back and forth between us. I knew he would insist on paying for it so that's why I did it as fast as I could. Mumbling under his breath as we walked off toward the elevator, I tried to take one of my bags from him, but he held on tighter and wouldn't let me grab it.

As soon as we got inside in the elevator, I patted him on the back, hard. "It'll be okay, Mason. If I let you pay for the room we would've ended up with one bed and no view," I teased, trying to get a rise out of him. Yes, I got us a room with one bed, but I didn't want him thinking I did it on purpose. It was probably childish of me to do that, but I wanted to see the way he reacted when I told him we have a room with two beds.

The elevator doors closed and we were off to the Cypress suite on the fourteenth floor, which I knew was going to have the most phenomenal view. "So," Mason began, "you think I would've gotten a room with one bed, huh?"

"Yep, which is why I got one with two," I told him, trying to hide my smirk. "Now that I think about it, maybe I should have gotten two rooms. I might go back down there and do that."

Mason chuckled and turned to face me, a gleam sparkling in his eyes. "Are you afraid of something, Claire? Perhaps maybe afraid of what you might do being in the same bed with me."

"Now why would I be afraid of that? I don't have to worry about it since we'll be in separate beds," I challenged. He stepped closer, but when the elevator doors opened, I rushed out and walked briskly down the hall until we came to our suite. Maybe I should've gotten a room with two beds. The only thing I was afraid of was falling too fast and getting hurt again. He said he wanted me back, but I needed to know for sure he wouldn't leave me the way he did before. It was hard to give value to promises these days.

Mason sidled up to my side, leaning against the wall, and brushed a strand of hair away from my face. My skin tingled where he touched. Softly, he murmured, "Actually, I think I'm the one who's afraid. Sharing a bed with you would be like waving alcohol in front of an alcoholic. The temptation to take a sip of that sweet burn would be too much to bear with it being so close yet so unreachable at the same time. I would have no restraint, and I fear of what that would do to me to have you only to have you go back home to someone else. I meant every word I said in my letter, Claire. Please … give me another chance to show you how much I love you."

My breath hitched in my throat and immediately my eyes misted over with unshed tears. I never thought I would actually hear the words come out of his mouth, but there they were. Mason was not a man of words; he was a man of action. To hear him say such things to me were beyond his comfort level, but he knew that was what I wanted to hear … needed to hear.

Knowing he was taking a risk, he leaned down and kissed my lips gently, unsure of how I was going to take it. I moaned at his touch and opened my lips, inviting him in. More firmly, he cupped my neck, pulling me even closer and slipped his tongue between my lips, tasting me.

"Claire," he whispered, resting his forehead to mine, "what are we doing?"

Smiling, I licked my lips and put the key in the door, opening it wide. When he pulled away, he looked into the room and his eyes went wide before lifting a curious brow my way. He carried in our bags and I followed him through the suite to the king size bed that overlooked to the exquisite fountain below.

"There is no going back, Mason, and I don't want you to show restraint," I murmured heatedly. "You said you wanted to show me how much you love me. Well, here's your second chance. Show me …"

Chapter 8

Claire

"I can't allow myself to do that, Claire. Not when you belong to another man," Mason argued. "I'm an honorable man and I fight fair. Doing this behind Cooper's back was never my intention. I was selfish before with you, and believe me I want to take you right now and feel every ounce of your body around me. I just can't do it this way."

Well, there went my plan.

When he'd asked earlier how Cooper took my leaving, I never gave him an actual answer. I just told him it wasn't any of his business. What really happened was that I made my decision and let Cooper go. It hurt to let my friend go, knowing that this break up might have ruined the friendship we spent years building, but I had to. Even though I hated Mason for leaving me before, I couldn't deny how much I still cared. I loved him.

Turning away from me, Mason gazed out the window and let out a frustrated breath. There was no way around it; I had to tell him the truth. "Cooper and I aren't together anymore, Mason. I ended it before I left. I chose not to tell you when you asked because deep down I wanted you to suffer, but in all reality I guess we both suffered while we were apart."

There, I said it.

He turned around abruptly, furrowing his brows with a smirk on his face. "So what you're saying is that you ended things with Cooper for me?" he asked craftily.

Smiling, I bit my lip and moved closer. "Maybe. Does that mean you're ready to show me what I asked for?"

Without another word, Mason closed the distance between us, fisting my hair in his hands and pulling me tight against his lips in one quick second. Everything burned with his touch like I was on fire; my lips, my skin, and most definitely the spot between my legs rubbing against his thigh. He lifted up my dress and cupped my ass, earning a strangled moan from deep in his throat when all he touched was bare skin. Months of not being together came crashing down on us in one scorching second, with need being the driving force.

"That is so fucking hot," Mason whispered, holding me firmly against the hardness between his legs.

When he met my gaze, he grasped my face in his hands and ran his rough, calloused thumbs across my cheeks. "I know we don't have much time together before you leave, and even then there's still that chance I might not make it back home after this, but—"

"Stop," I cried, putting a finger to his lips. "Let's not talk about that right now. We have today and that's all that matters. Forget about everyone and everything other than me and you right now. Nothing else exists."

He rested his forehead to mine. "Nothing else exists,"

he repeated, whispering across my lips.

He lifted me in his arms and I linked mine around his neck, straddling his waist with my legs as he carried me over to the bed and set me down on the edge. He lifted his T-shirt over his head and unbuttoned his jeans, letting them fall to the floor. I slid further back on the bed and got to my knees, watching him stalk closer. He was hard and ready, and by the dampness on my underwear and the throbbing of my clit I knew I was ready, too. I was past ready.

Mason lifted my dress up slowly, and as he did he kissed my bare flesh as he exposed it, going higher and higher. His tongue traced lightly from my stomach on up to the mounds of my breasts, which were still confined in my bra. However, it didn't stop him from biting my nipple through the fabric, resulting in a strangled moan from my lips. It hurt, but it felt so erotically good in the process. Every single inch of my body felt hyperaware of the man before me. Each little touch or kiss made my insides feel like they would explode. I wanted him inside me; wanted to feel his hands on my body and kissing me with those lips I had craved but thought I would never feel again.

After throwing my dress on the floor, Mason wrapped his arms around my back and unclasped my bra, groaning when my breasts became free. He pushed me back onto the bed and slid my underwear off quickly before doing the same with his boxers. His large hands, the ones he would soon be using to fight with, clasped my thighs and spread my legs apart as he moved closer.

"You are so beautiful, Claire. You have no idea how many times I dreamt of you beneath me, making love to you," he said, his voice deep and husky.

I gazed up into his stormy, sea green eyes. "It probably doesn't nearly compare to the times I dreamt about you."

Settling himself between my legs, he lowered his head to my breasts, first kissing along the mounds before licking one of my sensitive nipples with his warm, wet tongue. Moaning, I arched my back off the bed and squeezed him tight with my legs. He chuckled and decided to tease me with rubbing his cock along my opening and pushing it in just a tiny bit. It was his turn then to grow impatient.

Mason growled low in his throat, "You have no idea of my restraint right now. All I want to do is go hard, to hold you in my arms while tasting and kissing every single inch of you."

"No one's stopping you," I muttered breathlessly. Taking his hand, I placed it on one of my breasts while I reached down and wrapped my fingers around his cock between my legs. He squeezed and massaged my breasts, sucking and biting my nipples, while I pumped his cock up and down with my hand. The harder I stroked, the harder he sucked.

"Please, Mason. I'm so close and I want to come with you inside me," I cried.

His gaze never left mine when he pushed himself completely inside my body as far as he could go. He only had to thrust in and out a couple of times before I exploded around him, raking my nails down his back as I screamed out his name. When the fog cleared, and after the tremors of my orgasm subsided, Mason slowed his pace and smiled down at me.

"Damn, that was fast. I don't count that one so let's

see if I can give you another one," he uttered humorously.

Breathing frantically, I grasped his face and pulled him down to my lips. "I don't think that's going to be a problem."

I licked and sucked his lips, rocking my hips along with his until I could feel him getting closer to his release. Wave after sensual wave rocked through me from his penetrating thrusts, and another orgasm slowly started to build. I could feel his cock throbbing and pulsing inside my body so I clenched as hard as I could, feeling him come inside of me as I gave in to my own release. I had craved this intimacy with him for a long time and that time had finally come. I prayed that my happiness wouldn't be taken away once the reality of the situation finally kicked in.

Mason brushed the hair out of my face, and kissed me softly on the lips, still hard and erect between my legs. "That felt so fucking good, and it's only the beginning of the night for us. I have four months to make up for."

Oh hell, I thought to myself. *I'm not going to be able to walk tomorrow.*

But I sure was looking forward to it.

Chapter 9

Mason

It was eleven o'clock at night, and while the city below was vibrant in colorful lights and people looking for a good time, Claire was passed out on the bed, sound asleep. We ordered in room service and watched the fountain show a couple of times before making love again … and again. I was pretty sure I lived up to my promise to make up for the past four months lost. She fell asleep in my arms, but I was too riled up to relax. The folder in front of me was a stark reminder of why I was in Las Vegas to begin with.

There was a list of places where the dead fighters had been seen last and a list of names of the people they were associated with. The only one who didn't have connections in Vegas was Austin.

Quickly, I dressed in a simple black T-shirt and jeans with a solid pair of black boots. Those boots were known to knock out many teeth on several occasions when I'd use my MMA skills while on duty. In case Claire woke up and found me missing, I scribbled out a letter to let her know I was going out scouting and that I would be back soon. I wasn't sure if she'd be pissed at me for leaving her alone, but she had to realize I had a job to do.

I left the room as quietly as I could, and when I got off the elevator on the first floor, I headed straight outside to hail a cab. The first stop for the night was about two miles away so it wasn't far.

The cab pulled up at the curb and I jumped in. "Where to?" the driver asked, gazing back at me in the mirror. He was a scruffy little man, probably in his late forties, with graying hair and a voice that was gravelly from most likely smoking.

"I need to go to The Labyrinth, please," I said, shutting the door. The Labyrinth was the number one spot on the list so I thought I'd try it first to see if I got lucky.

The driver nodded and started the timer on his dash to calculate the miles. It didn't take long to get there since thankfully the driver avoided the strip traffic. When we pulled up, I groaned looking at the line of people backed around the side of the building. It would take me at least two hours to get inside.

"Is it always this crowded?" I asked the driver.

"Yeah, usually. You need to have connections to get in. It's not a place for just anyone," he informed me.

"What kind of people do you have to know?"

"Not sure, son. All I know is I've had to take many people home after they've been turned down. So if you don't know anyone to get you in then you aren't going in there."

"Fuck," I hissed under my breath. The one place I was sure to find some answers was the one most unattainable. I'd figure out a way … somehow. For now I would just go to my next choice. Surely I'd be able to get into that one.

After three hours of searching through the crowd for the man with the dragon tattoo on his neck, I decided it was time to give up for the night. It was three in the morning and I smelled of cigarette smoke and cheap perfume from all the women trying to rub their shit on me. The night was deemed unproductive for me other than the time I spent with Claire. I planned on going over my notes with her later in the day to see if she knew of the places I needed to go. Hopefully, with her experience in the big city she'd be able to help and direct me in the right directions.

When I got back to the hotel, I took a quick shower and climbed into the bed beside Claire. She was still sleeping peacefully and it wasn't long before I passed out along with her.

Chapter 10

Claire

Mason was still asleep beside me with his arm draped over my stomach when I woke up. My muscles were sore from our many trysts the night before, but at least it was a good sore. Slipping out of bed, I snuck off to the 'her' bathroom since the suite we got had a his and her bathroom. I washed up and did my usual morning routine before walking back into the suite, thinking that since an hour had gone by Mason would be up … but he wasn't. He was still sound asleep.

Hmm … interesting.

It wasn't until I saw the note on the desk that I realized why he was still passed out on the bed; he had gone out last night. Deep down I knew he was itching to get started, and I didn't blame him. He had a job to do, but he was also trying to find out who killed his friend and the other men. I was going to help him whether he liked it or not, even if he wanted me to leave.

Also, on the desk was a file that I didn't remember seeing last night. It had to be the file for the case. *Would it be illegal to look at it since I am a civilian?* I wondered. Mason hadn't talked to me about the specifics yet of where he was supposed to look or who to look out for. *Surely, he wouldn't care if I read through it, would he?*

Opening the file, the first thing I came to was a picture of Mason's deceased friend and his wife who was currently missing. I never thought the bad shit you saw in movies or on the news would ever happen to me, at least until my brother went over the deep end with Melissa and kidnapped her. Anything could happen to anyone; it was all real, and Mason had to deal with it every day. I flipped past the many pictures of the deceased fighters who had been killed, not recognizing any of their names, and moved on to the list of places and acquaintances of the deceased.

None of the acquaintances names sounded familiar, except when I got to the places of interest my eyes went wide in shock and I gasped. I knew them all, some of them I knew really well, and most of them I had been to when I lived in Vegas. One of them, however, I knew very well. It was a place I used to work at, a place where I could live my life and do whatever the hell I wanted. However, that wasn't what had my heart pounding out of control. It was the fact that the place I considered to be a safe haven was the number one suspect place on Mason's list.

Holy shit, what's going on? Why would it be the number one suspect spot?

I didn't realize I had said the question out loud until I heard Mason's gravelly voice call out behind me, making me jump in the seat. "I see you got curious and decided to go snooping."

Quickly, I closed the file and turned to face him. "I

wanted to see if there was anything I could do to help you and to see what you were up against here. Besides, you left the file out anyway so if you didn't want me looking at it then you should have put it back with your stuff."

Mason rubbed his eyes, and then ran his fingers through his hair with a smirk on his face. "I wanted you to look at it. I was going to see if you knew any of the people or places in there. I know it's been years since you've been here and you weren't here that long, but it's a shot at least."

He got out of bed and dug through his bag until he found a pair of blue and white Adidas running shorts and a white tank top. He stretched a few times, flexing those massive muscles of his, and of course I had to watch him before he joined me at the desk. He had seriously put on an amazing amount of muscle mass over the past few months we'd been apart. I handed him the letter he wrote to me last night and lifted an amused brow, wondering if he would tell me where he went. I already knew he couldn't have gotten into the club I worked at, at least not without me.

He rolled his eyes and threw the letter in the trash. "Last night was a clusterfuck," he growled, leaning his elbows on the desk. "I couldn't find anyone's descriptions matching the people on the list, and the one place I really had a hunch to find answers ended up being a place I'm not going to be able to get into without some kind of special connection. It's all a bunch of bullshit."

He reached for the file and slid it to him so he could look at it. "You know, when I caught you looking at the list here, your eyes went wide when you noticed something. What was it? Do you know someone on the list?"

"Not exactly," I confessed sheepishly, "more like the places."

Here I go ...

If telling him about my time in the Sin City was the price to pay for answers then I would certainly do it, but in doing so it would involve cooperation on his part if I were to lead him into the lion's den. Mason lifted a brow, waiting on me to continue, so I took a deep breath and began, "Okay, so you know how you couldn't get into the one club you desperately wanted to get into? Well, what would you say if I could get us in?"

Narrowing his eyes, I could tell he was waiting on me to drop a bomb on him by the way he looked uncomfortable sitting in his chair. Sighing, he said, "I would think that's great, but how do you plan on doing that?"

I paused, hesitating for only a moment before I explained, "Well, it's actually a long story, but what it all boils down to is this ... I used to work at that club. The Labyrinth was like a second home."

Mason's eyes grew wide, burning with a new flame of hope. "Tell me everything," he demanded.

So I did ... almost everything.

Chapter 11

Claire

Twelve hours later, after waiting for the prime time of the night, Mason and I took a cab to the place I hadn't been to in years; six to be exact. The club was like a different world, but also one where not everything was legal. It was easy to carry drugs in there and never get noticed, and there was really nothing you could do to avoid that. You could get lost in there if you weren't careful. It was the size of a large mansion with many different rooms to venture in and out of. There were rooms where the music pounded and all you would see were people drinking and basically dry humping all over the floor. However, there were some hidden alcoves where you could partake in a little nightly fun. I, myself, had snuck off to them before.

If you wanted a mellower scene, there were VIP rooms that were mainly occupied by the social elite like famous actors, singers, athletes, and so forth. It was exciting when I first started working at the club, I got high on it, but after a while I got used to it and actually became friends with several of the regulars.

Mason nudged me in the side as we trudged down the road in the cab. "Are you nervous?" he asked, placing a hand on mine to keep me from fidgeting.

I shrugged. "Not nervous as in going into the club, but kind of nervous with you getting a glimpse into my past. I don't want you to get the wrong impression of me. Also, I haven't really kept in touch with the people I knew from there. After Mom died, I had ignored so many people's calls and just never returned them." I turned away to gaze out the window, but Mason gently took my chin and turned me back to face him.

"Trust me, Claire. I'm sure your friends will understand why you broke away. Anyway, I'm not happy about my past either, and mine is probably much darker than yours. I had a huge head back when I was fighting and I didn't give a fuck about what I was doing. You have nothing to worry about."

He lifted my hand to his lips and kept his heated gaze on mine as he kissed my knuckles softly. His hair was gelled in messy blond spikes, and he looked so unlike himself in a nice white button down shirt and a pair of dark denim jeans. Mason was the typical T-shirt and holey jeans type of man with his favorite New York Yankees baseball cap. I liked that about him, though.

Mason lowered his gaze to my lips, and then slowly down my body, sighing. "If there was a way I could keep you out of this I would, especially with you wearing that sexy ass dress. I'm going to be spending all my time here fighting to keep the dicks away from you tonight."

Bursting out in laughter, I squeezed his hand to reassure him. "No you won't. I'll be by your side all night. I even wore my hair down for you so it would cover my bare shoulders. I couldn't exactly go in there with jeans and a T-shirt on now could I?"

I put on a strapless red dress that hugged every single curve just right and stopped a little above mid-thigh. Not to mention I had five inch red stiletto heels on as well. The heels made me almost the exact same height as Mason.

When we pulled up to the club, Mason handed the driver his money while I stared at the building in front of me. Nothing had changed as far as appearance; it was still a huge, impressive stone building that was made to resemble Roman architecture. The massive white, stone columns in front had to be at least thirty feet tall and were also hand carved. The owner, Jake Montgomery, who I had gotten to know pretty well, was fascinated with Roman culture and had made everything inside the club fit the part as well, including the people who worked there.

"Was it this crowded last night when you came here?" I asked curiously as Mason put his arm around my waist. It was always crowded at The Labyrinth, but it was never *this* crowded. *I guess the business grew since the last time I was here.*

Mason nodded and answered, "Yeah, but it looks like it's more crowded tonight."

"Hmm … interesting. I'm curious to know what's changed since the last time I was here," I muttered as we walked toward the crowd.

From the distance we were at, I couldn't tell who was working the door, so I decided to take a chance and find out. I didn't want to have to wait in that long line if I didn't have to. "All right, Mason. We're about to piss off a bunch of people, but if Wade or Tyler are working the door then we're set. If not, then we'll have to wait in line and do this the hard way."

As Mason and I strutted past the impatient crowd on the way to the door, we heard several disgruntled comments and angry words spewed our way. Mason had a smirk on his face the whole time and it took all I had not to laugh, but those people looked ravenous. I definitely didn't want a fight on my hands just yet.

Up ahead, the door finally came into view along with the two mammoth sized men guarding it. Wade wasn't there, but Tyler was, sporting the usual tight black Labyrinth T-shirt and platinum blond shoulder length hair. The nights when Jake made him work inside wearing a toga were very interesting. The women loved it. Both Wade and Tyler, who were the usual guys who worked the front, were my closest friends when I lived here. They had asked me out when I started working at the club, but it was against Jake's rules and they knew it. However, it didn't stop me and Wade from stealing a few moments here and there for fun. We were the infamous trio at The Labyrinth.

The moment Tyler looked my way he didn't register it was me at first, but then quickly glanced toward me again. He whispered something to the other guy, whom I didn't know, and then came bounding out of the doorway toward me with the biggest grin on his face.

Mason let me go at the same time Tyler scooped me up in his arms and twirled me around in a circle, hollering, "Holy fucking shit, look at what the cat dragged in. You know, I should be pissed at you for not returning my calls for the past year, but being the friend that I am I understood you had a lot going on. We've missed you, kitten! How long has it been ... six years?"

Kitten was my nickname among everyone, since at

the time I was the youngest of The Labyrinth's employees. I was the youngest, but I was the smartest. That was why Jake hired me to begin with.

When I caught my breath from laughing so hard, I swiped the hair out of my face and responded, "Wow, I'm surprised you remembered it's been that long, Ty. I'm sorry I let time slip away. I feel bad for losing touch with you and everyone else from here. Anyway, you know I had to finish college and move back home. My time to run wild had come to a close."

Tyler scoffed and a mischievous smirk tilted up his lips. "Somehow I don't believe that," he teased lightly. "I'm sure you got into plenty of trouble once you went home."

"Whatever, Tyler Rushing," I grumbled playfully. I peered over his shoulder to the door where his partner for the night stood checking ID's. "So where's Wade?" I asked. "I was hoping to see him tonight, too."

I wanted to see Wade, but there were some circumstances there that might not bode too well for Mason. Wade and I were friends, or I guess you could say friends with benefits. Before I left Vegas, he told me he had actual feelings for me, but since I was leaving, we never acted on them. Plus, I was twenty-one years old and I didn't want a long term relationship at that point in my life. Wade was a great guy, though, and I had fun with him while it lasted.

"Oh, he'll probably be around later this week. He's been in the Bahamas for the past week or so. I'm sure he'll come running here once he finds out you're in town. I know he's missed you."

He winked at me, and then his gaze finally landed on Mason who stood by watching our reunion all calm and collected. However, deep down I knew he was anything but calm.

"Who's your friend?" Tyler asked, looking straight at Mason.

Mason extended a hand out to him. "I'm Mason Bradley," he told him.

Tyler narrowed his eyes and took Mason's hand, shaking firmly. "Why does your name sound familiar? For some reason I know I've heard it before."

Mason shrugged. "Don't know, man. I guess it could have been from anywhere."

Tyler pondered for another few seconds and then said, "Yeah, I guess you're right. Well, anyway, any friend of Claire's is a friend of mine. Come on, brother, let's get you a drink. I know Jake is going to be thrilled by this visit."

The moment we stepped inside it was like a maze where each different path would lead you on a journey of ecstasy. There were bars set up in each section of the club where you could order whatever your heart desired, but the section right in the middle of the club was where the magic happened for me. The stage called to me like it did all those years ago when I would dance. It was a time when I could express my feelings not by words, but by the movement of my body. It was like another language for me.

Mason came up behind me, placing his hands on my waist, and whispered in my ear, "Are you okay, baby? You faded away there for a moment."

"I think she misses the stage," Tyler cut in humorously. "I could tell by that dreamy look in her eyes. She had that same look when she worked here, and let me tell you, she was a fucking goddess up on that stage."

At hearing Tyler's words, Mason clenched his fingers into my hip and replied, "I bet."

I could feel the anger pouring off of him, and I was thankful I couldn't see his face. When I explained to him about my time at the club, I left out that I danced at the club also, except little did he know what kind of dancing I did. Judging by his level of intensity he most likely thought I stripped, but it was far from it. I was going to have some explaining to do later.

Tyler led us past everyone to the hidden staircase I knew would be behind a thick, medieval rug hanging from the ceiling. "All right, kitten, you know where to go. I'll let Jake know you're on your way up," Tyler said, winking one of his stormy gray eyes. He smirked at Mason before going back to his post at the front door.

We started up the winding staircase and once we were out of ear shot, that was when Mason exploded, "Please tell me you and Tyler didn't …"

"Oh no," I said quickly, stopping him on the stairs. "Tyler is just my friend. He likes to flirt a lot, but that's just his personality. He flirts with everyone."

I did, however, have something with Wade. Under normal circumstances I wouldn't have a reason to tell Mason about him because it wouldn't matter. However, if we ran into Wade and something was said about our past, I didn't want Mason to think I was keeping something from him. *Should I tell him?* I wondered.

"What's that look for?" he asked. "Is there something you're not telling me? Because most of the time when I see that look it means there's bad news. Just tell me and get it over with. Did you date the bartender or something?"

I shook my head and sighed. "No, he wasn't the bartender. I know you heard me mention his name to Tyler. His name's Wade, and we were really good friends. We weren't exclusive or anything, so it wasn't like that. I know you're probably going to meet him at some point and I know how you guys get when the testosterone starts flowing."

"I'm sure I can handle it, Claire," Mason assured me. "I'm not really worried about the guys you dated. What I am concerned about is the fact you failed to mention to me that you were a goddamned stripper."

We had reached the top of the steps and Jake's office was just a couple of doors down. I didn't want him to hear us so I hissed quietly, "Look, Mason, it's not what you think. I'm sorry I didn't tell you about the dancing part, but I'll explain everything later, okay? So calm down."

Grabbing my hips, he pushed me against the wall and caged me in with his hands beside both sides of my head. He leaned in close, pressing his hard body flush with mine while ravishing my lips in a punishing kiss. It was all tongue, heat, and passion. I could feel the tension melting off of him so I breathed a sigh of relief. *If he keeps this up we might have to visit one of those private alcoves and release the rest of the tension.*

"Oh, I'm calm, *kitten*," he purred seductively. "I'm sure there are plenty of ways you can make up for failing to give me all the information." He backed up, leaving me breathless and alone against the wall.

Once I righted myself, I grinned and smoothed down my dress. "Mason, I would be glad to do whatever you want me to do for not telling you, but just so you know, I wasn't a—"

I didn't get to finish because a door down the hall

flew open, and there with a huge smile on his face was none other than Jake Montgomery. "Well, well, I was beginning to give up hope that you would ever visit. It's been too long, kitten. I never thought this would be possible, but you look more amazing now than you did when you worked here. Come here and give me a hug," he exclaimed.

Jake started down the hall with his arms wide open and gave me a long, hard squeeze. "It's good to see you again, Jake. You don't look a day over thirty," I teased.

Jake Montgomery was in his early fifties, and I wasn't kidding when I said he didn't look a day over thirty. He had short, salt and peppered colored hair that he always kept expertly coifed, and it was no surprise that he was wearing a light blue button down shirt with gray slacks. I don't think he even owned a pair of jeans.

Jake chuckled and let me go. "I may not look a day over thirty, but I sure as hell feel like it." He turned to acknowledge Mason and extended his hand. "I'm Jake Montgomery. If you're with Claire I'm sure she's told you about us."

Mason smirked and shook Jake's hand. "Not everything. I think she forgot to tell me about the dancing part."

Jake's eyes went wide and he gasped, "Really? That's shocking considering that was what she was most known for here … well, other than keeping my ass in line with the books. I tell you what, I'll get Avery down at the bar to send up some drinks and I'll tell you all about our little summer goddess here."

I groaned and waltzed into Jake's office with Mason on my heels behind me. *This was going to be interesting.*

Chapter 12

Mason

Jake ushered us into his office, or better yet, I would consider it a mini suite. He had a large wooden desk in the corner, a small gym set in the other, and a couch with two separate chairs in the middle. Claire and I sat on the couch, and when she sidled closer to me I draped my arm over her shoulders.

Jake sat across from us, and by looking at Claire's expression I could tell she felt at ease with the man, but in my experience, most of the club owners I knew were all a bit shady. Jake might be a good man underneath all that sophistication he wanted to exude, but if there was anything deceitful about him I would find it. Anyone had the capability to deceive, and I learned a long time ago never to trust anyone.

The door to the office opened and in walked a dark haired woman with a blue toga on, carrying a tray of drinks. She smiled warmly at us and set the tray down before walking out of the room without a single word. I passed Claire her glass of wine and gulped my gin and tonic down in one sitting. If I was going to have to sit through a story about Claire's past then I sure as hell needed the liquor floating through my system.

"So how did you two meet?" Jake asked curiously.

Claire took a sip of her wine and set it down, glancing at me quickly before she explained, "Oh, wow, let's see. It's actually a long and complicated story, but all in all he's related to one of my close friends. I actually just ran into him the other day."

"Ah … so new love, huh?" Jake laughed. "I wish I could remember what that felt like. So what brings you back to Las Vegas, kitten? I know it wasn't to visit me."

Claire rolled her eyes and smiled. "Actually, I'm here because of this one," she said, pointing to me. "He likes to gamble and I figured I could show him a thing or two at the blackjack tables. Plus, I thought it would be fun to come by and visit you while I was here. We're staying at the Bellagio."

Grinning, Jake shook his head and then turned to me. "That doesn't surprise me. Mason, did she tell you that's where I met her and offered her a job?"

Claire had told me everything except the dancing part, and she mentioned about him approaching her in the lobby of the Bellagio, but she didn't elaborate on it. "Yeah, she might have mentioned it. She basically only told me about the club and that she worked on the management side of things. So what happened?" I asked.

"Well, let me tell you," Jake began, "I saw Claire sitting in the lobby at the Bellagio looking all studious with her hair in a messy ponytail, biting on a pencil with her books scattered all around her. I just had The Labyrinth built a couple of years beforehand so it was still kind of new, but business was getting stronger every month. I was searching for people to join my team and there was something about Claire's angelic face that caught me."

"Not only was she beautiful, but she had the brains as well. After an hour of listening to her talk about business classes, I offered her a job to assist me in the books and the management side of things at the club. Later on, when she got comfortable working with me, she told me about the injury that hindered her dance career and made her turn down her position at Julliard. So, needless to say, not long after that the summer goddess was born. She was the highlight of those hot summer nights."

"And it wasn't stripping," Claire answered quickly. "I tried to tell you in the hall because I knew that was what you were thinking." Jake burst out laughing and clapped his knee, but I didn't find any of it funny. Sighing, Claire rolled her eyes at him and continued, "There weren't any strippers here when I worked. I'm assuming there still aren't."

"There's not," Jake claimed, regaining his composure. "Believe it or not, I didn't *want* any here. Claire did what she was good at and she looked good doing it ... fully clothed." Pursing his lips, he glanced at Claire and observed her for a moment, pondering. "Perhaps, since you're here," he began slyly, "we could bring in the summer with a performance from the summer goddess?"

Claire's eyes went wide and she stared at him, frozen, the room silent. At least until the loud knock on the door broke her out of the trance, making her jump. "Come in," Jake shouted.

The door opened and Tyler stuck his head in. "Hey,

boss, I needed to ask Claire if I could steal her man for a bit."

Claire glanced at Tyler and then quickly to me. "It's up to you. I'm fine if you want to go. I'll just catch up with Jake and be down there soon okay?" She smiled and nodded toward the door. "Have fun and don't get into any trouble."

I didn't want to leave her, but it was looking like I had no choice. I was interested to see what Tyler wanted anyway, and I was also itching to get into the club to look around. Claire leaned over and kissed me, and in her eyes she was telling me to be careful. To reassure her I'd be fine, I squeezed her hand before meeting Tyler at the door.

Jake called out behind me, "I'll make sure no one puts the moves on her when we come down there. You look like you could put a hurting on someone."

Before shutting the door I turned around, glancing back at Claire then to him. "You have no idea what I can do."

Then I shut the door.

I followed Tyler through the hall, down the winding staircase, and out into the heart of the club. "Do you want a drink?" Tyler asked.

"No thanks," I grumbled, "but I do want to know what the hell you want."

Tyler chuckled and looked at me over his shoulder. "You know, when you told me your name I knew I had heard it somewhere. It just so happens that I figured it out, well, thanks to Google."

"Really, well what might I ask did you find?" I asked.

If someone looked up my name, my history with fighting in the UFC would be the first thing they found. The rest of my life was temporarily hidden, so there was no record of me being in the police force or that my permanent residence was in North Carolina. Replacing my true life was a history of two years in rehab, one year in anger management classes, and the rest gambling my way through life moving here and there.

Tyler grabbed his beer from the bartender and beckoned for me to follow him. Finally, we came to a stop outside of a closed door and he turned around, smiling. "What I found, Mason Bradley, is my opponent for tomorrow afternoon. Once I saw a video of you fighting, I realized I had watched you fight before. I can't believe I didn't know who you were."

Crossing my arms over my chest, I said, "Yeah, well, it's been a long time since I've been in the ring."

Tyler guffawed. "It sure doesn't look like it's been a long time. You obviously still train."

"I do," I commented impatiently. "So what exactly do you want me to do tomorrow? Kick your ass?"

"From what I saw of your moves I'm sure you'll kick my ass, but my father owns a gym and a lot of my friends and I train there. Claire used to go there with me to work out, so I'm pretty sure she'd love to watch us fight. I need a worthy opponent to help me train."

I lifted a questioning brow. "So what makes you think I want to help you train?"

Actually, I was intrigued with the idea because it was

only my second day into the mission and it felt like I was starting to get somewhere. I had to take a chance.

Tyler nodded toward the door behind him. "What would you say if I told you that some of the most hard-core MMA fighters in the world were through this door?"

I snorted, "I would say you were full of shit."

"What if they were?" he countered. "Would you train with me tomorrow?"

He was sure of himself with the confident sneer on his face, and I had to admit I was intrigued. *Could it really be possible?* There was only one way to find out.

"Okay," I gave in. "Open the door, then I'll give you my answer."

Tyler laughed. "Your wish is my command." He opened the door wide, and as soon as I stepped in behind him I stopped dead in my tracks, thinking I had to be in a dream.

Holy shit, I thought to myself. *This couldn't be real.*

Tyler was telling the truth, and I just made it one step closer.

Chapter 13

Claire

Jake had finally worn me down and made me agree to dance on stage the coming Saturday night since Mason and I were still going to be in town. I told him we were staying in town at least for the week, but in my mind I knew that if Mason didn't find anything out in that time then it would be longer. To my surprise, it didn't look like it was going to be much longer. When Jake took me down to the right wing of the club, I was shocked to see that the whole place had completely been renovated.

A portion of the VIP rooms and some of the secluded sex spots had been torn away and opened up to make a small arena, and in the middle of it all was something that made my stomach twist in violent knots … an octagon ring with Mason in the middle of it. He wasn't fighting, but he was standing up there with several other men, comparing moves and techniques. That wasn't the problem … the problem was that everything in front of me was one huge coincidence. There were fighters showing up dead and now Jake has fights in his club. *What if there's a connec-*

tion? Jake wouldn't do that, would he?

Swaying on my feet, I almost lost my balance until Jake caught my arm and helped steady me. "Kitten, are you all right? You look a little pale," he said worriedly, taking my hand and leading me to a seat. He barked out an order for someone to fetch me some water and a couple of seconds later I had a cold bottle in my hands.

Swallowing hard, I lowered my head and whispered, "I'm okay. I got a little dizzy there for a second. I think I drank that wine too fast." It was a lie because growing up with a vineyard and a winery I was accustomed to drinking large amounts of wine and it not affect me.

Mason must have seen what happened because by the time I looked up he was already on his way out of the ring and almost to me. Bending down on his knee, he cupped my face in his hands. In my eyes he must've seen the turmoil because he nodded and slowly helped me to my feet.

"Too much excitement for you, baby," he teased, hoping to lighten the mood. "I guess seeing me in the cage made you feel faint."

He chuckled and so did Jake, but I smacked his arm and rolled my eyes. "You wish, Mason. No, I'm not exactly feeling too good right now. Do you mind if we go back to the hotel?"

Nodding, Mason wrapped his arm around my waist and took the bottle of water in the other. "Of course, it's getting late anyway. We need to get some sleep before tomorrow."

"Why is that?" I asked, furrowing my brows.

"Because you both are coming to the gym tomorrow," Tyler interrupted. He strolled up beside Jake with a huge grin on his face and pointed to Mason. "Your boyfriend here is going to spar with me. Maybe he can teach me some things, or better yet, maybe he'll learn something from me." He bent down closer to me and whispered a little too loud, "I think he underestimates my talents."

Mason snorted and rolled his eyes, but then Jake cut in and asked Mason, "So you're a fighter? Claire never mentioned that to me."

"That's because it was a few years ago," Mason pointed out.

Pursing his lip, Jake glanced at the cage and then back to Mason with a gleam in his eye. "Would you ever consider getting back into it? Even though you don't fight anymore it's obvious that you still work your body for it. I've already gotten Claire to agree to dance for us this coming weekend, so ..."

Turning to me, Mason lifted a brow and grinned. "So I'm finally going to get to see you dance, huh?"

"It appears so," I breathed. "It's been a while so hopefully I won't fall flat on my face."

"Not possible," Jake stated warmly.

Seeing his kind eyes as he gazed at me made me doubt everything. I never felt like I had to watch my back with him, but if he was a part of what's been happening then I was in just as deep as Mason ... if not more because Jake was like family.

"So, Mason, are you in for Friday night? You can fight Ty. He's on the list of fighters for that night," Jake announced. Tyler winked at me before lifting a questioning brow to Mason, waiting on his answer.

Mason groaned and blew out a heavy sigh. "Okay, fine, I'm in. Friday night it is then."

Jake smiled triumphantly. "Great, well then I will put

you down." He kissed me on the cheek and squeezed my arm gently. "You two have a good night. I'll see you again on Friday."

Mason and I said our quick good-byes, but they weren't quick enough for me. I needed air, and I needed it bad.

As soon as we got back into our suite, I couldn't keep silent any longer. "Do you think Jake is the one responsible for all of this?" I blurted out. "When I walked into the room and saw the arena I about lost it."

Sighing, Mason shrugged his shoulders and sat down on the bed to take off his boots. "Claire, I don't know anything yet. Tyler told me that every Friday night they have fights, and they fight by the sanctioned rules. They even have it available to watch on pay per view. Whatever happened to the fighters it didn't happen at the club."

I sat on the bed beside him and kicked off my heels. "What makes you so sure of that?" I asked, laying my head on his shoulder.

"Well, for starters, the bodies weren't found anywhere near the club. In fact, they were found across town. Also, with the time of deaths and when their bodies were discovered they would have been killed late on the Saturday nights. So if the club only has open fights on Fridays and not Saturdays then we're looking at a different location. If Jake is at the club every Saturday night then either he's doing that for an alibi or we're looking at someone completely different. Jake must have been the club owner who the Chief of Police stopped investigating."

Quickly, I lifted my head off his shoulders. "Wait, what? What do you mean? Jake was investigated?"

"Before we came to Vegas, Ryan Griffin, who's the Chief of Police out here, said they investigated a club owner who had ties in the fighting community, but everything about him was legit. I'll give him a call in the morning and get the details. I'm surprised that information wasn't in the file. I guess they ruled him out completely and didn't feel it was necessary to keep it there."

Mason was a smart man with amazing instincts and survival skills. He wouldn't be where he was today without them. "Mason," I murmured hesitantly, "I need your honest in depth opinion on this. When you met Jake, did you get a bad vibe from him? I've always thought I was a good judge of character, and even with my brother I knew he was a bad apple. You could just look at him and tell something was off. I know you hated him, too, especially when he messed things up with Melissa."

He nodded in agreement. "That's true. Your brother was a psychotic prick."

Impatiently, I rolled my eyes and glared at him. "So to answer my question, what was your first impression of Jake? Do you think I need to stay away from him?"

Mason tucked a strand of my hair behind my ear and cupped my cheek. "As much as I want to say yes, at least until this is all over, I know I can't. You are the one who got me in there and you are the one who knows all the people. If you left, I'm afraid I wouldn't have the in I need. From now on you need to stay close to me. I could tell Jake cares for you and he was sincere when he spoke to you, but I've seen people hide their dark sides before. All it takes is one thing to make a person snap and the people they love suffer. We just need to be careful."

"*You* need to be careful, Mason," I pleaded, grabbing onto his shirt. "You are the one who will be fighting. I don't want to see you get hurt."

Watching him fight someone would be both terrifying and exhilarating. If we weren't in the middle of a murder investigation I'd be excited. However, knowing that he could end up in a ditch somewhere like the other men scared the shit out of me … it completely frightened me.

Still cupping my cheek in his rough, warm hands, he leaned down to kiss me gently on the lips. "Claire, I can't promise I'm not going to get hurt because I most likely will. I'm going to figure this all out and then we can go home … *together*."

"Together?" I asked, eyes going wide. "What are you saying?"

He can't be saying what I think he's saying can he?

He trailed his hand down my cheek to my shoulder where he fingered the strap of my dress. The smile on his face was both boyish and handsome even though there was nothing boyish about his rugged exterior. He looked like he hadn't shaved in a week, but surprisingly I actually liked the stubble. It made him look rough … like a fighter. He was my fighter.

"Claire," he whispered, gazing into my eyes, "I don't know what's going to happen with us when we get back, but when this shit is over, I'm going to take some time off and stay in California for a while. My whole life has been in North Carolina, but now there's nothing there for me except my job. My family's in California … *you* are in

California."

Dumbfounded, I stared at him completely speechless. It took him four months and a dangerous mission to come to his senses. I knew he was a male and most of the time men didn't think logically about the simple things, but damn it if he didn't just piss me off a little. Pushing his shoulders back, he fell down onto the bed and I straddled his waist.

Exasperated, I glared down at him and pinned his arms above his head as hard as I could. "So it took you this long to figure out that you're going to stay in California to be with me? I think I'm a little insulted. You may be intelligent when it comes to your job, but I have to say when it comes to relationships you need some practice."

Sadly, his smile faded and he nodded. "I know that, but I'm hoping you can show me how it's done. I know I made a mistake, and I'll always regret the time we lost."

Slowly, I let go of his hands and he settled them on my hips with his fingers grazing my ass. Leaning down, I kissed his lips, his cheek, and then down to his ear where I nipped his lobe with my teeth. Sucking gently, I moaned and murmured in his ear, "If you want me to show you how to love someone you better take notes because this is going to last a while."

I could feel him getting hard beneath me, and since I was straddling his waist I rocked my hips against him and smiled when he groaned and swelled even more. Reaching down, I unbuttoned his jeans and slid the zipper down, freeing him. I massaged him for a few minutes, watching him shudder with my touch before sliding down his body so I was between his legs. Mason groaned deep in his chest when he realized what I was going to do.

I pulled his pants and boxers all the way off and watched his cock jerk with just the slightest touch to his sack beneath. Cupping them gently in my palm, I massaged them for a second before licking the tip of his cock and closing my lips around it. Mason moaned, gripping the sheets beneath him, and rocked his hips along with my movements. The harder I sucked, the more I could feel him losing control.

"Claire," he growled. "You're driving me crazy."

His hooded eyes were dark and glassed over when he gazed down at me. I licked the tip again while he watched me and replied, "I know, but you haven't seen anything yet."

Sliding off the bed, I turned around so my back was to him and reached back to clutch the zipper to my dress. Looking over my shoulder at him, I slowly unzipped my little red dress inch by inch until my bare back was exposed to him. He lifted off his shirt and moved back on the bed so he was propped up on the headboard. Biting my lip, I slid the strap down on my left shoulder and then my right, letting my dress slowly make its way down my body. I hadn't worn a bra since my dress supported my breasts, so when I slipped out of my dress I took my lacy red underwear with it. Once I was completely undressed, I crawled back on the bed and straddled Mason's waist. The tip of his cock glistened with his desire, so I swiped it with my thumb and stuck it into my mouth.

Keeping my gaze on him, I sucked my finger and moaned, earning a strangled cry from Mason's lips in return. "Holy fuck, Claire, if you don't do something now, I'm going to come all over this damn bed."

Smirking seductively, I licked my lips and lifted my

hips so the tip of his cock grazed my opening. I lowered down about an inch and swirled my hips again, coating him with my own desire. I could feel myself clenching, ready to have him inside me fully. The anticipation of it was what excited me. I loved the feeling of almost losing control and being on the brink of orgasm.

Mason dug his fingers into my hips and pleaded, "Please, baby. I need to feel you … to feel how wet you are inside. I want to know what your love feels like."

His face was red and his skin felt warm to the touch. I knew I was tormenting and teasing him, but in doing so I was torturing myself. I lowered myself further onto his cock and immediately my clit throbbed with the need for friction. As soon as I completely wrapped him with my body, I clutched his face in my hands and crushed my lips to his, pushing my tongue in with the force of my thrusts. His grip tightened on my waist, and when I broke away from the kiss, he latched onto my swollen nipple, licking and sucking feverishly.

"Fuck, Claire. I'm going to come if you don't stop riding me so hard," Mason growled.

He couldn't see me with his head at my breasts, but I smiled and rode him harder. I heard him hiss under his breath as he exploded inside of me just as I let go and screamed out my orgasm with him. I rode him softly for a couple more strokes to ride out the last tremors until it ebbed completely. Breathing hard, I collapsed onto his chest and listened to the pounding of his heart.

"I love you," he whispered gruffly. "Damn, do I ever."

I smiled up at him. "I love you, too. In a way I think I always have, even from the very beginning."

"So did I, Claire," he said, placing a gentle kiss to my forehead. "So did I."

Slowly, I lifted my hips and let him slide out of me before cuddling into his side and wrapping my arm across his stomach. As soon as my heart stopped pounding, my eyes began to lose focus and grow heavy. I breathed in Mason's familiar scent, all woodsy and spice with the strong hint of pure male, and let it take me away to a place where we were safe ... to a place we called home.

Chapter 14

Mason

Before Claire got up from bed, I decided to call the Chief of Police, Ryan Griffin, to ask him about the investigation he did on Jake Montgomery. Everything seemed too easy and coincidental for it to be Jake, but I'd seen people like him do very stupid things. Mostly they thought they were invincible, above the law, but eventually they would slip up. It was only a matter of time.

"It's about time I heard from you," Ryan barked into the phone. "What's the update? Where are you staying?"

I moved to the far end of the suite and talked as low as I could so I wouldn't wake up Claire. "I'm staying at the Bellagio. I went to The Labyrinth last night and met a Jake Montgomery. Is he the club owner you spoke about on the phone before I came out here?"

"Yes, he is. Everything checked out with him so we took him off the suspects list. Now, the people who go to his club are a different story. It's not a secret that he has fights at his club every week, but they are all legal and approved. Even some of my guys like to go and watch them. We're pretty certain that the person or persons involved in the case go to that club."

"Okay, I'll keep my eyes open. I'm actually going to be fighting tomorrow night," I informed him.

"That's excellent," Ryan agreed in amazement. "You got in there fast. I'm going to have a package delivered to the hotel for you with some trackers in it. I want you to keep one on you at all times so we can make sure you're in a safe location. Also, if I don't hear from you or if I think something's wrong then we can find you."

The thought brought back memories when I put a tracker in my cousin's watch before she was kidnapped by her husband, Claire's brother. When I tried to find her she had run away into the woods trying to escape and ended up losing her watch. I thought I was going to find her dead in those woods, except instead it was just her broken clasped watch. One good thing about the trackers was that I could put one on Claire. That way I could keep track of her if something was to go wrong and we were separated.

"I'll be on the lookout for it," I remarked.

"Good. I'm also going to send some of my people out to the club to watch the fight. They won't approach you so don't worry about that. Good luck, and be careful. Whoever these people are they don't show mercy."

As soon as we hung up the phone, Claire slid out of bed, her hair a tangled mess and her eyes half open from waking. "Was that the Chief of Police guy you were talking about last night?"

I nodded and scooped her up in my arms. "Yes, it was. He said Jake was clean and they couldn't find anything. He's also going to send me some trackers so he can keep up with me." Claire blew out a relieved sigh, but I still needed her to be wary of Jake until the whole thing came to an end. Lifting her chin with my fingers, I stared into her eyes, wanting her to see the seriousness in my gaze. "You still need to be careful around him, okay? At least until this case gets solved. Can you do that for me for just a little while? Don't go anywhere alone with him or anyone else for that matter, got it?"

She saluted me. "Got it, Detective Bradley. No going anywhere alone with anyone other than you."

Setting her down on the floor, I kissed her quickly and smacked her ass. "All right baby, we need to get busy and get out of here. Your lazy ass slept until lunch time so hurry up and get dressed."

She rushed off and did her thing, and about twenty minutes later we were ready to go. We grabbed ourselves a quick bite at one of the restaurants in the hotel and then made arrangements to rent a car for the rest of the week. It was a four door, silver Chevy Colorado just like the one I had back home, except mine was much better. This one felt like it had been driven hard and not taken care of, which was common in rental vehicles. In my line of work I'd seen more reckless driving in people when they were in rental vehicles than in their own. It just went to show you that most people didn't give a shit about other people's property.

"You need to turn right on the next street," Claire insisted while pointing toward the road. She had her long, blonde hair pulled high into a ponytail with a light green tank top that hugged her breasts and short, black shorts that showed off her smooth, tanned legs. Thoughts of last night and the way her mouth felt on my dick had me growing rock hard almost instantly.

"Are you okay over there?" Claire asked, trying to hide her smile. She glanced down at my lap and bit her lip before tightening up the laces to her sneakers.

"Sorry, but I was just thinking about your mouth on my cock. I think tonight needs to be my night to show you what love is," I stated adamantly.

"Well, I'm sure not going to stop you," she teased, "but you need to calm it down because we're almost there."

We were on our way to the gym so we could meet up with Tyler and I could spar with him. The guy was stout, don't get me wrong, but I had no doubt in my mind that I could take him. It might have been years since I professionally fought with someone, but it sure as hell hadn't stopped me from practicing my moves in my line of work. Sometimes it was necessary when dealing with the kind of scumbags I saw in and out every single day of my life: domestic abusers, drug dealers, pedophiles, murderers, rapists. With all the bad shit I'd see every day it almost made me wonder if there was any good in the world. However, gazing over at Claire and seeing her angelic face I knew there was some left ... there was still some good.

We were venturing closer to the areas where my friend Austin and the other dead fighters were found, but we were still a few miles away. *Maybe Claire and I could drive by when we leave the gym and I could get a look at the surroundings.* Surely, there had to be some connection somewhere.

Luckily, we arrived at Rushing's Gym and Training facility right on time. From the outside it was hard to tell what to expect on the inside, but I was immediately shocked when I walked through the door. The place was much larger than it appeared outside, and everything was up to date and new. The treadmills and weight equipment looked barely used, except that could have been because no one was on them. They were all gathered around the octagon cage off to the left of the gym.

Tyler was in the ring training with a man who was built just like him, but I could tell he was a bit older by the gray hair peeking out of his head gear. "Do you need me to help you wrap your hands up?" Claire asked curiously. "I don't exactly know how, but I thought I'd ask."

I smiled at her and shook my head. "No, that's okay. I've done it a million times on my own."

Claire glanced over at Tyler and then back to me with worried eyes. "Don't hurt him, okay? He's a strong guy and I've seen him take out numerous drunken idiots at the club, but up against you and your fierceness it kind of scares me. He's more of a have a good time goofball, whereas you are the serious and focused type."

"You have nothing to worry about," I promised. "If anything I'm sure you underestimate him." His movements were fluid and full of force, but I could see room for improvement. "Who's that training with him?" I asked.

"Oh, that's his dad," Claire informed me. "He's owned this gym for years. I used to come here with Wade and Ty all the time. There's a room Ty's dad used to let me use to practice my dance routines while the guys all stayed out here."

"I bet they hated that," I groaned, "especially not being able to watch you in those tiny shorts of yours."

She smacked me in the arm. "Oh, stop. If Ty's dad doesn't mind I'll probably leave you out here while I go practice. I have two days to make up a routine. So, see, no one will be watching me in my short shorts."

Reaching behind her, I grabbed her ass and growled, "Good, because you're mine now, and heaven forbid I don't know why. You're too good for me."

Claire leaned up and kissed me gently on the lips. "I know why, Mason," she murmured softly. "It's because you were meant for me; you were meant to be mine as well. I can feel it in here," she said, placing a hand over her heart.

"Oh, isn't that sweet," Tyler teased, coming up behind Claire and putting his arm around her. "Keep softening him up, kitten. The more you do the easier he'll be to beat down."

His dad came up beside him and laughed. "Son, I think you have that all wrong. The more you flirt with Claire, the more I think I'll be scraping your remains off the mat. Now go get the boy some tape and gloves."

Tyler smirked and winked at me before ambling off toward the back of the gym. He had some balls to keep goading me, but I could tell it was in his nature to flirt, just like Claire said. Claire was mine and at the end of the day she would be going home with me.

"It's so good to see you again," Claire squealed, flinging her arms around Tyler's father's neck. "How have you been? The gym looks amazing with all the new equipment."

"It was about time I invested in an improvement with this place. Business has picked up since I did it so I think it was worth it," he answered. "I heard you were going to dance again at the club. Is that true?"

Claire nodded and shifted on her feet nervously.

"Yes, but only for one night. Jake has a way with getting what he wants."

"That he does, child, and just so you know, the back room is all ready for you if you want to go back there and get started. Ty and I will take care of your man for you."

She snorted sarcastically. "Yeah, I'm sure you will. You guys have fun." She smiled at me quickly before rushing off through another door in the back.

Tyler's father extended his hand to me and introduced himself, "Thank you for coming, Mason. My name's Stephen Rushing."

I accepted his hand and shook it firmly. "It's good to meet you, Stephen. I see you've been helping Tyler train. Did you ever compete?"

"Not in the mixed martial arts type of fighting that you and Ty do. That's why I only really help him with his boxing techniques. I competed for the heavyweight boxing championship in my day, but I never made it. I came close, though."

Tyler sauntered back into the room and threw a roll of black tape and gloves in my direction, interrupting us. "Here you go, man. Tape up and let's get started." He jumped into the cage and grabbed his gloves while I taped up my hands.

"How long are you and Claire going to be in Vegas?" Stephen asked.

I finished taping up my hands and reached for the gloves. Nonchalantly, I shrugged my shoulders and replied, "Probably another week or so. I guess it all depends on how my money supply holds up. My luck with gambling hasn't been going too well." It was all a lie, but it was the story I had to stick with.

Stephen chuckled. "Oh, I know how that goes. When my wife and I moved here thirty years ago I was addicted to the casinos. She almost left me because I lost our vacation money one year."

"I'm waiting," Ty yelled, waving his arms impatiently in the air. "Get your pansy ass up here."

Stephen rolled his eyes at his son and sighed. "Yes, get up there and teach my son a lesson. He's getting on my nerves."

"I would be glad to," I remarked happily. *It'll be my pleasure.*

Chapter 15

Claire

Secretly, I watched Mason and Tyler spar for a few minutes while I was hidden behind the door. I wanted to observe Mason, to see what kind of fighter he was. It was amazing to see him move, and the way the muscles worked in his body. He had just lifted off his shirt, showing all of his muscles, including the eagle tattoo on his shoulder and bicep. Back when my brother was married to Melissa they always had a huge annual pool party once every summer. It was the first summer I took notice of Mason, and I suspect the first time he ever paid attention to me.

After everyone had left, he was still sitting by the pool with his shirt off, drinking a beer. I was curious as to why he chose to get an eagle tattoo, and when he explained the reason to me I knew there was a much deeper side to him then what he let on. He may have been drunk, but what came out of his mouth came from his heart.

He told me the eagle stood for honor, strength, and courage. When his mother was diagnosed with terminal cancer he said for the first time he felt alone and scared. He told me the one thing she loved most was her music, and each time she would be sad or in pain he would play her favorite song, "Wind Beneath my Wings" by Bette Midler.

He needed strength to get through her death, and the courage to let her go. She was all he had left other than Melissa. After joining the police force he knew what it felt like to honor the badge and to fight for what was right. The eagle stood for all of that as well. I wasn't too sure if he remembered telling me the story, but every time I saw his eagle it reminded me of the pain he felt. After we talked that night, I watched him from the guest room in my brother and Melissa's house; he was just sitting by the pool, staring at the water. I cried for him, knowing very well he wouldn't give in to it. I cried for us both.

Remembering all of that emotion, it gave me an idea. My ability to dance came from inside me and in the way I felt. Mason's story was inside my heart, and I was going to dance it.

The back room where Stephen let me dance was a quarter of the size of the main room that the guys were in. The flooring was like one huge mat that flexed underneath my feet when I walked on it. It was similar to the flooring a gymnast would use, and it definitely helped when I needed air for my jumps. The wall in front of me was nothing but a huge set of mirrors just like a dance studio. *I guess Stephen never found another use for the room.*

In thinking up a routine, I always put together the steps and then picked out the music last. I liked the room to be silent when I came up with my dances. I never knew of another dancer who did it that way. Most of them listened to the music and then came up with the steps … I danced to the music in my heart. However, this dance came from Mason's.

Time must have slipped by because one minute I was dancing my heart out and the next Mason appeared in the doorway, his gaze alit in wonder. I didn't realize how tired my muscles were until I stopped to catch my breath.

"How long have you been standing there?" I asked breathlessly, resting my hands on my knees.

"Long enough to see how beautiful you are when you dance. The look on your face was something I've never seen before."

He handed me the hand towel that was in his hand and I used it to wipe the sweat away from my forehead. "Thank you. Dancing was the only way I could express myself other than words."

Mason cupped my face and gently kissed my lips. He tasted a little salty, but I was sure I did too from all the sweat. Taking a nice hot soak in the tub would do my muscles good.

"Come on, baby, let's go. You've been in here for two and a half hours."

He put his arm around me and led me out through the gym where Tyler and Stephen were putting up equipment. "So how'd the dancing go?" Tyler asked. "Did you come up with something good? You know Jake is going to have a full house of people paying to come watch you."

Exasperated, I threw my hands in the air. "Not help-ing, Ty. Thanks for the loaded pressure."

Tyler grinned mischievously. "Any time, kitten."

Rolling my eyes, I smiled sweetly up at Mason and said very loudly, "Make sure you kick his ass hard tomorrow night in the fight… in front of everyone!"

Mason guffawed and so did Tyler.

"Will do, baby," Mason promised. "You have my word."

We said our good-byes and headed on our way. It was seven o'clock at night and I was starving, but I knew Mason wanted to drive by the sites where the dead bodies were found. It didn't take long to get there considering the areas were only a few miles north from the gym.

"Are we just driving by, or are we getting out to look?" I asked warily. The area we were in was kind of run down and I didn't have a good feeling about it. Soon, it would be getting dark and it definitely wasn't the place I wanted to be in at night.

Thankfully, Mason shook his head and said, "No, we're not getting out. This is the last place I'd want you walking the streets. I just want to drive around and get a look at the surroundings. I don't plan on stopping the car."

There wasn't much to see except dilapidated housing, warehouses, and run down stores that looked like they hadn't had business in a very long time. Most of the larger places were restricted with barbwire fences and no trespassing signs. *I wonder if the police had investigated those places.*

Mason was on full alert, scanning everything as we drove by with his brows furrowed. I didn't want to break his concentration, but I had to inquire, "Have the police looked through all these warehouses around here for clues? There has to be something they missed."

Mason sighed, and kept his eyes on the road. "According to the information Ryan gave me, they did a walkthrough of all these places, but couldn't find anything.

Someone has to slip up somewhere and leave some kind of trail. This shit can't happen and there not be some kind of evidence."

After another thirty minutes, the sky started to darken and Mason knew we needed to get away from there. I could see the turmoil and sadness in his gaze and I could feel it pouring out of him. He reached over and grabbed my hand, intertwining his fingers with mine as we rode the rest of the way back to the Bellagio.

"I tell you what," I started softly, "since we're both sweaty and nasty, how about we order in room service, take a shower, and then relax for the rest of the night? You have a busy night tomorrow."

He lifted our linked hands and kissed my knuckles before smiling over at me. "All of that sounds good, baby. We'll do whatever you want to do. I just need to stop by the front desk and see if Ryan left me the trackers before we head up to the room."

"Okay."

Mason stopped by the front desk as soon as we got in and was handed a small, brown envelope. By the time we got up to the room and ordered our food, Mason busied himself with reading over the file and putting one of the trackers in his watch. He had probably read over those papers a million times, but knowing how determined he was, he most likely felt he hadn't done enough. There was one thing about Mason I had noticed over the years; he put too much pressure on himself.

My stomach was crampy and screaming at me by the time our food finally came, and the smell only made it worse; it smelled heavenly. Mason was still concentrating on putting the tracker in his watch when I set our food down on the table. I took the plate of his filet mignon, baked potato, and steamed broccoli and set it beside him, kissing him on the cheek, before I got my plate and sat in front of the crescent shaped window to watch the fountain show.

I had ordered my favorite on the menu: parmesan crusted chicken, asparagus with lemon butter, and the truffle mashed potatoes. Back when I stayed here a long time ago, if I wasn't eating dinner with Jake at his house or with the guys, I would always order the chicken and follow it up with a chocolate pastry from the café. I don't know how long I sat there watching the fountain when Mason came up behind me and wrapped his arms around my shoulders.

"You've been staring at that fountain for an hour, baby. Let's go take a shower and go to bed. I know we're both exhausted," he murmured in my ear.

It was true; I was tired and I could barely keep my eyes open. "What happened to showing me how much you love me?" I teased. "Since I showed you last night how much I loved you it's your turn now."

He picked me up in his arms and carried me to the bathroom, smiling. "And I still plan on it," he claimed wholeheartedly. "I plan on showing you every day for as long as you let me."

When he set me down in the bathroom, the whole room was dimmed with candles around a tub full of bubbles. "You did this for me?" I cried. I had no clue he'd even got up from the desk, much less run me a bath.

Slowly, he lifted my shirt and unhooked my bra before lowering my shorts and underwear to the floor. He then took off his shirt and shorts and carried me over to the tub, setting me down into the hot, bubbly water.

"I did it for us, baby. Tonight I'm going to take care of you in another way."

He climbed in the tub so he could face me and massaged my feet, legs, arms, and then my back when he sidled in behind me. After he washed my hair and my body I did the same for him, letting my hands gently caress his skin as I cleaned him with the soap. The night wasn't about sex or anything like that, it was sensual and caring. It was a side to Mason I hadn't seen yet, but it was one I thoroughly enjoyed. I loved that he could touch me in more ways than one. On one hand he could be passionate and aggressive with his love making, and on the other he could be sweet and gentle.

Once we were finished cleaning up, Mason dried me off and slipped one of my T-shirts over my head before grabbing a pair of boxers. Sleep came easily for us both and I welcomed it with open arms. However, my dreams didn't embrace me ... they frightened me.

Chapter 16

Mason

It was three o'clock in the morning and the sound of Claire's scream jerked me awake. She thrashed and kicked her legs hard, letting out tiny whimpers as she fought to get out of the sheets that tangled around her body. I flipped on the switch to the lamp beside the bed, and as soon as I did that Claire finally woke from her nightmare. Sweaty and breathing hard, the moment she saw me she jumped in my arms.

"I had the worst nightmare," she cried, digging her nails in my back to hold me tighter.

Wiping the hair away from her face, I rubbed her back and murmured soothingly, "Shh … it's okay, Claire. I'm here. Nothing's going to happen to you."

She laid her head against my chest and I could feel her warm tears falling down my bare skin. "It was terrible," she whispered. "I watched them dump you out on the street. You were beaten and bloody, but still alive … barely. They took me away from you."

"I promise that's not going to happen, baby. No one is ever going to take you away from me," I uttered gently. *I wasn't going to let them.* First thing in the morning I was going to put one of the trackers in one of her bras so I would always know where she was at. I held her until her eyes grew heavy with sleep, and eventually I gave in to it as well. The rest of the night went by in a flash until morning came, signaling it was the beginning to Friday, and also the day of my first return fight as Mason "The Eagle" Bradley.

In the morning, I slipped one of the tracker devices inside the padding of one of Claire's bras. Even though she had other ones with her, I needed to make sure she wore the one I chose more. It was also my favorite one of hers. *Surely, she wouldn't notice I deliberately put the tracker in the sexy, black Victoria's Secret one, now would she?* She would get a kick out of that.

When Claire woke up, she didn't talk about her nightmare. In fact, I was beginning to think she didn't remember having the dream. "What are you doing with my bra?" she asked quizzically.

Peering over at her, I grinned and said, "I put the tracker in it so if anything happens you'll be located. I just want to make sure I know where to find you."

Yawning, she stretched her arms wide and muttered, "I understand. It's perfectly fine. I hate to think what would have happened if you didn't have one on Melissa when my brother took her."

I didn't want to think what could've happened to her either if I didn't know where she was headed. I was going to ask Claire about her nightmare, but then my phone rang, interrupting me. It was Melissa.

"Hey," I answered.

"Hey, yourself," she remarked, sounding a little agitated. "Did you forget to call me or something? I've been worried about you and Claire. How are you doing? Did you two work things out?"

Claire walked over to me and smiled, so I put the phone on speaker so she could talk to Melissa, too. "Yes, we're doing fine, aren't we Claire?"

Claire snickered and said into the phone, "We didn't at first, but I think he's grown on me just a bit."

Melissa chuckled. "Well, that's good news at least. I just wanted to make sure you both were safe. Do you know when you're coming home, Claire?"

Claire furrowed her brows and glanced at me for an answer, but I had no clue either on how long we were going to stay away. "I'm not sure," Claire replied. "Mason kind of needs me right now. Is everything okay with the vineyards?"

"Of course everything's all right. Brett and Cooper have been helping a lot with making sure your house is secure and that everything is running smoothly at the winery."

Rolling my eyes, I scoffed at the phone and Melissa snapped at me, "Hey, don't be like that, Mase. Cooper wanted to help out and I think it's sweet of him to do that after Claire let him go. He's also a friend of Brett's as well. Don't worry, though, I'm sure you'll never see him again since you never visit us out in California anyway."

Claire's eyes crinkled in the corners when she smiled. "So are you going to tell her or should I?"

"Tell me what?" Melissa squealed excitedly.

"I'm going to be staying out in California for a while," I confessed, "with Claire."

Melissa screamed into the phone, "Oh my goodness, that's amazing news! How long will you be staying?"

I winked over at Claire, making her cheeks blush crimson. "For as long as she'll have me," I muttered wholeheartedly.

Melissa shrieked a little more, going on and on about how I'd love California and whatnot. I grew up in North Carolina and lived there all my life so it would be a significant change living on one coast and then moving all the way across the states to another. That was if I made it out of my mission alive.

Night had come and the club was packed; the line wrapping around the building like before. Claire dressed herself in a skin tight black dress that plunged low in the front and also low in the back, revealing the whole expanse of her skin to the top of her ass. She shuddered when I put my arm around her waist and placed my hand on the small of her bare back. Tyler wasn't at the door, but we were recognized immediately and allowed to pass right on by.

"They're all waiting for you in the arena," the guy at

the door called out.

I nodded to him once and took Claire's hand, leading her to the right wing of the club. "I wonder how many people will be here to watch the fights," I murmured.

Claire shrugged. "I'm not sure, but I guess we're about to find out."

The door to the arena room was open, and the moment we stepped in she gasped and I stared, wide-eyed at all the people. "Holy shit," I breathed in awe. "It's packed."

Every single chair around the cage was occupied and there were people standing around everywhere. There were two guys already in the cage battling it out, except they looked to be part of the Lightweight division. When I fought several years ago, I was competing for the Heavyweight title. If they did fights in order of division then I would be going up there last.

"Hey, guys," Tyler exclaimed, carrying a beer in his hands.

Disapprovingly, I glared at the beer and then back up to him. "You should know better than to get drunk before a fight. It makes you sloppy," I scolded him. I really didn't care either way what he did, but I knew better than to drink when I had to compete.

Tyler chugged his beer and threw his cup in the trash a little too roughly. "I do know better than to drink when I have to fight, but unfortunately, I'm not fighting tonight," he announced.

"Wait, what?" Claire cut in. "What do you mean you're not fighting? If you're not the one fighting Mason then who is?"

Tyler glanced around the room with narrowed eyes

until he found the person Mason was to fight and pointed to him. "That's the guy over there with the blue mohawk. I think you might know him. He said he owed you for something you did a long time ago. Care to explain," Tyler inquired curiously.

Following the direction of Ty's pointed finger, I groaned when I saw the guy with the blue mohawk. *Fuck, I knew who he was, or better yet, I knew his wife … very well.*

"What is it Mason?" Claire asked worriedly. "Who is he?"

His name was Chase Benfield and I did the unthinkable by fucking his wife. Blowing out a frustrated breath, I lowered my head and began to explain, "Do you remember when I mentioned I had a dark past?"

"Yeah," she said, drawling out the word. "Let me guess, you fought him back in the day?"

I nodded. "Yes, but that wasn't just it." I didn't want to tell her what I did because I was ashamed of the way I acted and the way I did things. I was sure she would understand, hopefully, but I didn't want her thinking less of me.

Claire let go of my hand and crossed her arms over her chest defiantly. "Dammit, just tell me already. You did this same shit to me when I was keeping something from you."

"Fine," I gave in, "but I need you to know it was a long time ago and it was before I even met you. I was stupid and did lots of stupid things that I shouldn't have."

She rolled her eyes. "Let me guess, you slept with his girlfriend," she guessed blandly.

Sighing, I regretfully nodded my head and waited for

the angry words to come spewing out of her mouth. Instead, she said, "So, what's the big deal? You slept with her. That shit happens all the time. Why would he be angry about that still?"

"Well," I began, "it was actually his wife and I hooked up with her in my prepping room during his fight for a spot at the Heavyweight title. His trainer had come looking for her and found us. Needless to say, word got back to Chase awfully fast."

Claire groaned and hung her head. "Oh, hell, this isn't going to be good."

Chase finally spotted me from across the room and snarled his lip. *No,* I thought to myself, *this definitely wasn't going to be good.*

Chapter 17

Claire

Tyler led me to the front row where three seats were left vacant. "Are these for us?" I asked.

"Yep, and the other's for Jake. He'll be down here in a minute. My dad was up in his office talking to him about something," he said.

The moment Mason got into the cage it was like something switched in him. His eyes took on a new glow of excitement and he strutted around the cage with perfect confidence. He was shirtless, showing off every single curve and dip of his muscles, but the shorts were something I had never seen before; he must have put them on under his jeans before we left. They were black with spatters of red on them, like blood, and white line designs on the thighs as well, but on the very bottom hem of his shorts was the outline of an eagle. It was almost the exact replica of the eagle he had on his arm.

The arena Jake had built had at least three hundred seats around it which were all occupied with none to spare. The women all hooted and hollered for Mason, especially when he jumped up on the fence and flexed his muscles. No wonder he screwed another fighter's girl. They probably lined up outside his room after the fights hoping for a chance. I bet he even had his own groupies. I had been to many concerts where I'd see the band's groupies all waiting for a chance to be noticed.

Ugh, I'm so glad I didn't know him back then. If I did I probably wouldn't have given him the time of day. Chase glowered at Mason and looked like he was about to explode. His veins protruded from his forehead and biceps like they would burst any moment. Mason smirked over at him and that only fueled Chase's anger more. His coach had to hold him back from charging after him.

By the time the announcer stepped into the cage, Jake made it into the arena and took his seat beside me. He nodded at Tyler before saying to me, "Sorry I'm late, kitten. There's been a lot of stress I've had to deal with lately." The weary look on his face was definitely evidence of that. He was impeccably dressed in a gray suit sans the tie and that sophisticated air about him that always exuded power. I never thought there would be a day I'd see him look defeated, but he did; he looked tired.

"Like what?" I asked curiously.

He sighed and put his arm around my shoulder, leaning in close. "I'm sure you've seen on the news about the fighters showing up dead, right?"

I nodded. "Yes, I have. It's craziness."

"Yeah, well, ever since that's been happening I've been getting a lot of hate mail and threats from people who swear I have something to do with it," he confessed warily. "They want me to shut down the fights. My name had been cleared from all involvement, but it still hasn't stopped people from trying to bring me down."

"Jake, I told you," Tyler cut in, "those people are probably the jealous fuckers who can't get in here. You need to think about that and not let this get to you. What about all the guys who are depending on you, especially me?"

Lifting a questioning brow, I glanced at Tyler and then back to Jake. "What's he talking about?"

Jake gazed proudly around the room and smiled. "When I started this part of the club it was actually Tyler who I thought of. I knew he was training with his old man and learning how to fight. I love the sport of MMA fighting. It takes great talent, strength, and most importantly dedication to do what those guys do. With the people we have coming into the club I thought it would be a good idea to help the guys who wanted to get noticed. Some of the guys who fought in here have earned sponsorships and are on their way up to becoming well known UFC fighters."

"That's great, Jake," I uttered honestly. "If you don't have anything to do with the dead fighters then why are you going to tuck tail and run? It would make you look guilty."

Sadly, he said, "I know, but until the case gets solved with the police I might not have a choice."

I could understand where he was coming from, but if he shut down the fighting then Mason might never get the 'in' he needed to figure out who was behind the deaths. I squeezed Jake's hand to reassure him. "I agree with Ty," I expressed firmly, "if you are doing this to help people find their breaks in life then keep doing it. You might be helping the future champion of the world and not even know it yet."

Jake grinned and pinched my cheek. "You always knew how to cheer me up, didn't you?"

"It's just part of my charm," I bragged. "So what are you going to do?"

"I guess I'll keep the fights open for now. However, if the shit starts getting really heavy for me I'll have no choice but to shut it all down."

All I could say was, "I understand."

"Ladies and gentlemen, thank you for joining us tonight for this epic battle that's about to take place. Tonight's fight will be between Chase "The Charger" Benfield and Mason "The Eagle" Bradley!" The crowd roared and clapped ferociously as Chase and Mason took their places beside the announcer. With his black suit and slicked back brown hair, the announcer turned to Chase and said, "So tell me, Mr. Benfield, from what I heard before the fight you made quite an ordeal about getting in this cage with Mason. What's up with that?"

"Oh no," I groaned.

Chase leaned into the microphone and glared straight over at Mason. "Let's just say it's for payback that's long overdue."

The crowd was intrigued, staring mesmerizingly at the stage when the announcer turned to Mason. "I see we have a grudge match tonight."

Mason rolled his eyes and shrugged his shoulders dismissively. "Yeah, I guess so."

"Now what made you take up the name, 'The Eagle?' I see you have one tattooed on your arm there," he said while nodding toward his arm.

Mason's gaze was on the floor of the cage, but I saw

the ghost of a smile spread across his face before he lifted his head and answered, "Eagles are strong ... warriors of the sky. They seek out their prey without being detected, and when they strike, they strike hard and fast."

The way he said it so seriously made shivers race across my skin. I knew the meaning of his words, but I knew no one else did. Seeking out his prey meant seeking out the ones responsible for the deaths, and once he found them he would strike hard and fast. I had no doubt.

Before the bell sounded, beginning the fight, Mason took one quick glance my way and winked. The sound of the bell echoed loudly throughout the room and the moment it struck, Mason got into stance and attacked. I thought Chase would have been the one to strike first, but he didn't; Mason beat him to it.

The sound of flesh hitting flesh made me cringe, except at least it was Mason getting all of the good hits in. "He's really good," Jake announced in awe. "Why did he quit fighting?"

As much as I hated lying to him, I went with what Mason's record would show. "He got involved with drugs and such and had to go to rehab. I didn't know him then so I really don't know all the details."

Jake didn't push for more information and I was thankful for that. After three rounds of brutal kicks, punches, and wrestling around on the mat, Chase finally started to wear down. I could tell Mason was getting tired, too, but he hid it well. With one last burst of energy, Chase took Mason to the mat, trying to capture him in a submission hold. He failed miserably, giving Mason the opportunity to lock him in an armbar hold.

"This is it," Tyler yelled. My heart pounded anxiously

as I waited for Chase to submit. The second I saw Chase's hand beat against the mat signaling his submission, I screamed for joy and bounced out of my seat along with everyone else in the arena. Mason immediately let Chase go and ran around the cage with his arms lifted victoriously.

"Everyone, I'm happy to announce that our winner who delivered a spectacular armbar submission hold is Mason 'The Eagle' Bradley!" the announcer roared into the microphone.

"Mason, you did it!" I screamed excitedly.

The second he heard my voice he ran to the fence and jumped over it, landing in front of me on the floor. "You're damn right I did," he boasted, scooping me into his arms and crushing his lips to mine. He was all sweaty and hot from the fight, but I didn't care. If he wanted everyone to see him kissing me I was all for it.

"Let's get out of here," he growled low in my ear. When he let me go, the way he gazed at me with those heat-filled green eyes made my insides clench in anticipation. It was a raw and primal look that promised a night of hard, rough sex. I had never seen him so pumped with adrenaline or so full of life like he was now. It was like he was high on it.

Tyler congratulated Mason on winning, along with many other people walking by to show their congratulations. "I didn't realize how much I missed it until I got up there," he admitted truthfully.

Jake patted him on the arm. "Well, you did great, son. You should consider getting back into it … professionally."

Mason's eyes lit up with hope for only one second before he sighed and shook his head. "I don't know if that's possible since I've been away from it for so long, but I'll keep it in mind."

"Either way, I think you missed your calling. Would you want to fight next Friday night if you're still in town?" Jake extended his hand and lifted a brow, waiting on an answer.

Mason put his arm around my shoulders and squeezed while shaking Jake's hand with the other. "I would love to, but I want the best fighter you have on your list," he requested.

Jake's eyes went wide. "Are you sure about that? You know you'll most likely go up against one of the pros. They often agree to fight for fun when someone gets a wild hair up their ass to test their worth."

"It doesn't matter," Mason replied. "Set it up and I'll be here."

"All right, I'll get it scheduled," he said to Mason, and then to me he said, "You get your rest, kitten. Make sure you get here early so you can warm up. You can change into your outfit when you get here."

"Is it the one I used to wear when I danced before?" I inquired eagerly.

Jake nodded. "Of course it is. What else would the summer goddess wear? However, it's not exactly the same one you wore. I had another one made for you since the other one is over five years old." He grinned at us both and motioned toward the door. "Now go and get out of here. I'll see you tomorrow night."

We strolled past him and out of the arena to the inside of the club. "Yes, let's get out of here," Mason insisted impatiently. "I'm dying to get your legs wrapped around me."

Bursting out in laughter, I smiled up at him and joked teasingly, "Is that all you want?"

When we got out to the parking lot, instead of opening the door for me he caged me against the truck with his arms on both sides of me. We were hidden from prying eyes and I was thankful for that. He kissed me on the lips then down my neck to my bare collarbone while gripping my hips and pulling me in tighter against his hard cock. Moving his hips, he rubbed his body against my already sensitive clit.

"You know that's not all that I want. I'm going to have you screaming and begging for me to take you tonight. I want to taste you … touch you until your body only craves what I can give you." He trailed his tongue down my chest to the top mounds of my breasts, still moving his hardness between my legs. I was soaked and on the verge of orgasm, and his next words sent me over the edge.

"I want to see your face when I make you come over and over again as I fuck you. I want to feel how wet you get when I release everything I have deep inside your body."

I gripped his shoulders hard as my body exploded, sending a warm rush of liquid coating the inside of my underwear. Mason moaned in my ear and bit down. "I could tell that felt good," he teased huskily. Breathing hard, my knees grew weak as the last tremors of my orgasm had me shaking against him. Quickly, I glanced around the parking lot, making sure no one was around, and I took his hand and placed it on my bare thigh. Slowly, I lifted his hand under my dress to the wetness that saturated my black, lacy thongs. He pushed a finger inside of me and groaned, leaning his forehead to mine.

"Fuck, you're so wet. We need to get back to the hotel ... now."

He slid his finger out and slowly brought it to his mouth, moaning as he sucked off every drop of my desire. "You better be ready for tonight because I'm going to enjoy every single minute of it."

He opened my door and shut it behind me, quickly coming around to his. We didn't have too far to go until we got to the Bellagio, but even five minutes was excruciating. I wanted him desperately and he wanted me just as much. I had never felt that level of passion before and it was intoxicating. He said he was going to enjoy every single minute of what he was going to do to me, and there was one thing I knew for certain ...

I was going to enjoy it more.

Chapter 18

Mason

I was high …

I was high from the fight, from the adrenaline that pumped through my veins with being in the cage and being noticed again for the first time in years, not to mention I kicked Chase's ass. The fighter I used to be was still in me, but this time I fought for a different reason. I fought for the chance to be better, to be better than what I once was. I fought for the blue eyed girl whose naked flesh was wrapped around my body.

The moment we got back to the hotel room I ripped the little black dress off her body and all of my clothes as well. I kissed her, tasting the sweetness of her tongue as it mingled with mine. She always smelled like raspberries and I knew it came from the Bath and Body Works lotion she loved to wear. It smelled so fucking good on her.

She giggled as the stubble on my chin grazed across her neck. "Maybe you should fight more often," she teased. "I think I like this side of you." *I liked this side of me, too.*

Eyes closed, Claire moaned and arched her back, making her perfectly plump nipples perk up higher, inviting me to them. I flicked my tongue across one of them and smiled when I saw her bite her lip. My dick was so hard it hurt, but I loved watching her squirm. I circled my tongue around her nipple before closing my lips and sucking as hard as I could. She gasped and clenched her legs tighter around me, trying to thrust her hips up. Her tits were perfect and just the right size to fit under my hand as I massaged them ... so soft.

"Does it feel good when I suck hard like that?" I asked as I kissed my way down her stomach.

"Yes," she breathed. "It feels so good it almost hurts."

As I moved down her body, tasting every inch, as I promised her I would do, she ran her fingers through my hair and held on tight. I loved it when she touched me and even more so when I could feel her shaking with the need to have me inside her. I kissed the insides of her thighs until I got to the delicious spot between her legs that was already swollen and ready to be touched. Spreading her legs wider, I teased her clit with my tongue and watched her tremble as chill bumps fanned out across her skin.

"Please," she begged.

Her voice came out a strangled whisper, but it was all the motivation I needed. No more teasing ... no more playing around. As deep as I could go, I tasted her and watched her face as I brought her to climax. She was so fucking perfect and she was mine ... always going to be mine. I don't know how I ever let her slip away.

Slowly, I crawled up her body so I could gaze down at her clear blue eyes when I made love to her. "Did you like that?" I asked with a smirk on my face.

She chuckled and wrapped her legs around my waist. "You have no idea how much," she murmured in that seductive voice of hers. "Now I want to feel you inside me."

Pushing in just a little bit, I circled my hips to get her ready for me. "Like this?" I asked, thrusting in a little deeper.

She shook her head and whispered, "No, I need more."

She was so tight and clenching so hard I felt like I was going to lose my fucking mind. When I entered her fully, she gripped her legs tighter around my waist and moved her hips along with mine as I thrust inside of her. I licked and sucked her nipples one after the other as I pounded my hips against hers. Her cries and moans were about to send me over the edge, especially when she groaned out my name.

"Mason …"

"I love you, Claire," I murmured in her ear.

"And I love you," she breathed.

The second her nails dug into my back and her muscles clenched tighter around my cock, I knew it was game over. She started to scream as her orgasm started to hit its peak, but I covered my mouth over hers and muffled her cries with my own as I came inside of her. Gazing down at her and that beautiful smile on her face, I realized there was nothing in the world I wouldn't do for her. She was smart, funny, adventurous, and extremely tough for a female. The only thing about loving hard is falling hard when you lose it.

"Why are you looking at me like that?" she asked quietly.

I brushed the hair off her forehead and smiled down at her. "Because you're everything I've always wanted, and now that I have you I'm so afraid of losing you."

Her eyes welled up and a tear fell down the side of her face. "I feel the same way, Mason," she admitted. "I'm ready for all of this to be over so we can go home."

I knew exactly how she felt. I had no clue where to go or what to do. I was no closer to figuring out the case than when I first started. Lying down beside her, I pulled her to my chest and ran my fingers through her soft blonde hair.

"It'll all be over soon, baby. I promise," I told her.

She nodded and wrapped her arm around my waist. After she fell asleep I laid there for a while contemplating ways to find the opening I needed. *What did the fighters who died have in common?*

Quietly, I slipped out of bed, trying hard not to wake her, and started up my laptop. They all died on a Saturday night, which had me on edge because in the next twenty-four hours it would be Saturday night, and I had no clue if there was going to be someone showing up dead.

There had to be something that linked them all together somehow. I went down the list and searched every single thing I could find out about each fighter. It only took me getting through half the list to see a trend. The only thing that didn't make sense was that Austin wasn't like any of them, or maybe he was and I just didn't know it. People changed all the time.

Hell, I did. *I'm not the same man I was before.* However, I had a feeling my honor was going to keep me from getting where I needed to go. To get noticed I had to bring someone back from the past.

The old Mason needed to return.

"You want to do what?" Claire asked incredulously.

She glared at me from the bathroom doorway, hands on her hips and wearing a silky blue robe that hit mid-thigh. We had to be at the club early so she could warm up and change and while she was getting ready in the bathroom I went into detail with what my plan was. Obviously, she didn't like it.

"It's only when we're out in public," I assured her. "Trust me, I don't want to do this, but I've only been in the cage once, and if someone out there is scouting for fighters they're not going to want someone straight-edged like me. They would want someone cocky, someone greedy enough to accept their challenge. That's what the other fighters were like. From what I found on the internet they were arrogant assholes."

Claire blew out a frustrated breath and sat beside me on the bed. "What exactly are you going to do other than be a complete dick? You're not going to be all over other women and stuff in this act are you?"

I couldn't help it, but I burst out laughing and pushed her back on the bed, hovering over her. "Would you be jealous?" I teased, hoping to lighten the mood.

She pursed her lips and glared. "No, I wouldn't be jealous, but the last thing I would ever put up with is a guy I'm dating flirting with other women in front of me. Jake would probably kick you out of the club if he thought you treated me bad."

I wouldn't consider ever doing that to her anyway.

Being around other women never even crossed my mind. Gently kissing her lips, I pulled back and smiled. "Oh, Claire, you never cease to amaze me. I hadn't planned on flirting with any other women. I'm not stupid, and furthermore, it never crossed my mind. I don't plan on doing anything to jeopardize me and you. The only thing I need to do is be my old hotheaded and conceited self."

Staring at me with a mischievous gleam in her eyes, she relaxed underneath me and said, "Okay, I think I can handle that … especially if you make love to me like you did last night."

Shit, why did she have to say that now when we needed to get ready to leave? Groaning, I laid my forehead down on hers as my dick jumped to attention. She laughed under her breath and shook her head. "You're insatiable, aren't you?"

Reluctantly, I rolled off of her and helped her off the bed. "Only for you, baby. Now go finish getting ready before we're late. I'm ready to see you work your magic tonight."

The excitement in her face mirrored mine from last night. It was surreal how we finally ended together, and also got the chance to relive our dreams from the past. Last night was my night … now tonight was hers.

We got to the club on time, and since it was still early there wasn't a line at the front to get in. The door opened before we got to it and Jake appeared around the side with a huge grin on his face when he saw Claire.

"Oh, kitten, you look beautiful," he uttered whole-heartedly, opening his arms. He hugged her and kissed her on the forehead before motioning toward the staircase I knew was hidden behind the giant rug hanging down from the wall. "If you want you can go on up to my office and change while Mason and I grab a drink."

"What about me? I think I need one too to calm my nerves," she scolded.

Jake grinned wickedly at her. "Don't worry, kitten. I already took your nerves into consideration. Your favorite bottle of wine is up there and perfectly chilled."

Pursing her lips and with her hands on her waist, Claire lifted a brow and asked, "Are you trying to butter me up, old man? Because if you are it's not going to work. I'm only dancing one night and that's it. Bribing me and giving me everything I want isn't going to get me back here."

Jake burst out laughing and shrugged his shoulders. "Hey, you can't fault me for trying. I had to at least give it a shot."

Claire shook her head and smiled. "Thank you anyway, though. I appreciate it." Before she disappeared to go up to Jake's office, she turned around and demanded one last thing, "You two better be in the front row, got it?"

"I wouldn't want to be anywhere else," I told her.

As soon as she was gone, I followed Jake to the bar. "Fix whatever drink you want, Mason. It's on the house," he offered, motioning to the bottles behind the counter.

"Don't mind if I do," I accepted.

The liquor looked mighty appealing, so I grabbed the bottle of whiskey and poured myself a double shot of it. I sucked it back in one huge gulp and poured another. "Rough night?" Jake asked.

I stared into the amber liquid in my glass and chuckled halfheartedly. It was Saturday night and I had no clue if someone was going to die in a fight somewhere. So, yeah, I guess I could consider that a rough night.

Tossing back the whiskey, I took a deep breath before answering, "There's just a lot going on in my life right now."

"Well, cheer up, son. I have some good news." He grabbed the bottle of whiskey and poured me another shot. "You will not believe who agreed to fight you next Friday."

With wide eyes, I turned to him quickly and asked, "Who? Who is it?"

"Does the name Matt Reynolds ring a bell?"

The moment he said the name the whole world froze on its axis. *Did I hear him right?* Surely, he didn't say the name I thought he did. Matt Reynolds was one of the best UFC fighters in the Heavyweight division. He came along and made a name for himself shortly after I left the sport. I knew who he was and he wasn't going to be easy to take down, but I sure as hell wasn't going to pass up the chance to fight him.

"You do still want to fight, don't you?" Jake asked, looking concerned with his brows furrowed.

"Of course," I exclaimed, "I'm not an idiot. How in the hell did you get him to agree to this?"

Jake grabbed a glass and poured himself a shot of whiskey. He offered another one to me, but I shook my head and waved him off. The last thing I needed to be was drunk in a club with Claire. "That's the funny thing," Jake began, "Matt Reynolds comes in here a lot and he'll watch the fights and network along with others while he's here, but he's never offered to fight. I guess he saw a challenge in you. This could be a good thing, Mason. This could be your opening to get back in the sport and do things right this time."

Sighing, I turned away and decided one last shot of whiskey wouldn't hurt me. After I poured it, I glanced at Jake over my shoulder and said, "I don't think so. I lost that chance a long time ago."

The thought was tempting, and I'd love nothing more than to do things right, especially with Claire by my side, but it just didn't seem possible.

Or was it?

The club was packed, and if I had to estimate the number of people I would have to say at least five hundred or more were in the room. It was a good thing I had my place in the front row with Jake and Tyler beside me. Tilting my head to Tyler, I asked quietly, "So does Claire like to do this for free or does Jake pay her?"

Tyler chuckled under his breath. "Oh, she would do it for free, but Jake always paid her eighty percent of the ticket sales. She used to bitch about it all the time, but Jake didn't care. He put it in her check each week anyway."

Wow.

Eighty percent was a large chunk of change. She probably made thousands each week. A few nights ago when she first told me she worked at the club she said she was ashamed to tell her family what she had done. She dabbled with drugs and made some stupid choices, which thankfully she didn't go into detail about. However, I knew firsthand what those choices were because I made plenty of them with women I didn't even know. I would rather forget those times, too.

Jake leaned forward, addressing me and Tyler, "All right you two, it's time for me to begin the announcement. Be prepared to be amazed, Mason. I have never seen a dancer with as much heart as Claire."

He got up and left, shaking hands with several of the people in their seats before making his way behind the curtain. The overheard lights began to dim, and were replaced with shimmering blue lights that glowed from the stage.

The curtain pulled back and Jake appeared, smiling at the crowd with a microphone in his hand. "Good evening, everyone. As some of you know we haven't had a show like this in a really long time. It just so happens that someone special has come in for a visit and has offered to bring in our summer season with a little bit of magic."

He paused for a moment, and then began moving toward the edge of the stage. "Ladies and gentlemen, I give you Claire O'Briene, our summer goddess of The Labyrinth."

Jake quickly took his seat, and as soon as he did the lights shut off completely … everything silent. The sound of music slowly began to echo through the room while the blue lights grew steadily brighter. The misty fog in the room swirled around Claire when she took the stage, and it was so thick I could barely see her. However, when the smoke cleared nothing could prepare me for what I saw on that stage.

Claire beamed down at me with the most serene smile I'd ever seen on her face. She looked exactly like a summer goddess in what appeared to be a short, pale yellow toga with crystals that glowed a brilliant shade of red in the light. She looked liked the sun, but moved gracefully like the wind. I could care less about any kind of dancing, but watching Claire do what she loved made it special. It was a part of who she was, just like fighting was a part of me.

I was entranced by her movements, except all too quickly it was over and I was broken out of the trance when the music stopped, the booming voices of the crowd cheering in my ear. Getting to my feet, both Tyler and I whistled and clapped as loud as we could for her. Laughing, she shook her head as she made her way to the microphone.

"Good evening, everyone. I just wanted to say thank you for taking the time to watch me tonight. Some of you may already know that I used to dance here a few years ago when I worked here. I'm honored that I was given the chance to do so again, and I'm glad that you all made it a special night for me. Thank you."

She waved at everyone and then ran down the side steps straight for me, Jake, and Tyler. "That was so amazing," she breathed, wrapping her arms around my neck. I lifted her in my arms and kissed her quickly on the lips.

"You were beautiful up there," I murmured in her ear. "I can't believe I've never seen you dance before."

"I'll try to do it more," she promised as I set her down on her feet. She turned to acknowledge Jake and he hugged her, whispering something in her ear, before walking off to mingle with his guests.

Tyler gave her a sideways hug and squeezed. "You looked awesome, kitten, like always. However, now I have to work the door. Jake let me off so I could watch you." He kissed her on the head and reached out to shake my hand. "You two have fun tonight. I'll catch you both later."

As soon as he left, there were several women who started coming up to Claire, hugging her and wanting to talk to her. I understood there would be people who wanted to mingle with her so when she looked over at me I mouthed the words 'going to the bar' to her so she would know where I was going. I ordered a beer and stood there for a moment watching the people come and go. For about fifteen minutes I stayed at the bar hoping to give Claire some time with her people before going back to her.

However, when I got a clear view at her from across the room I wasn't expecting her to be in the arms of another man. I could tell Claire was excited to see him by the joy in her wide-eyed gaze.

Who the hell is he? I wondered. *Better yet, why was he all over her?*

The closer I got, the more the guy came into view. He was about my age and same build with short, black hair. He happened to catch my eye and glared at me for a second before smiling back down at Claire who had the biggest grin on her face and was talking nonstop. Before I could march the rest of the way down to the stage, I felt the vibration of my phone buzzing in my pocket. The moment I saw the name pop up on the screen I knew something was going to be wrong. Ryan wouldn't bother me this late at night if it wasn't important.

As soon as I walked out of the room to answer the phone my gaze caught something I wasn't expecting to see … the telltale signs of a dragon tattoo snaking its way down a guy's neck. He was most likely in his early forties, judging by the lines in his face and the light graying mixed in with his shortly cropped brown hair. The tattoo didn't exactly fit in with the whole businesslike and arrogant persona he exuded, and if I wasn't consciously looking for it on people's necks I probably wouldn't have seen it behind the collar of his crisp, white button down shirt. His pace slowed as he approached, his gaze narrowing as if he recognized me. A mischievous smirk splayed across his face as he walked past, heading into the stage room.

Holy shit! I can't believe I finally found the bastard.

The only thing that made the situation completely screwed up was that not only did he go into the room I just left, but I watched him go straight down to where Claire and the other guy were standing by the stage. My phone stopped buzzing in my pocket and then immediately started back up again.

"Dammit," I hissed under my breath. Keeping my gaze on Claire and the guys around her, I clicked on my phone and answered it by saying, "Yeah, what's going on?"

Ryan cleared his throat. "I need to tell you something," he replied.

"I need to tell you something, too," I cut in. "It looks like I found the man we've been looking for. He's at The Labyrinth right now."

"Good, keep your eye on him. The sooner we figure out who he is and what connection he has to the deaths the sooner we can end this mess. However, the reason why I called is …" He paused, hesitating for a second, which only made me more irritable. *Just tell me!* I wanted to scream.

"What is it?" I demanded impatiently.

The last thing I expected to hear come through the phone was the words that came out of his mouth. "We found Austin's missing wife," Ryan said. "We found her in an alley off the main strip."

The moment he said those words I had images of a blonde haired beauty beaten and broken on the side of the road. Taking a seat, I kept the phone to my ear and closed my eyes. I didn't want to ask where he found her at. I had seen death numerous times over the years and I didn't want to see it with someone I knew.

Hanging my head, I sighed and kept my voice low when I asked, "She's dead isn't she? You called to tell me she's dead."

"No, Mason, she's not dead. I called to tell you that she's alive … Summer Moore is alive."

Chapter 19

Claire

Mason looked pissed about me being with Wade, and I was sure he'd be even more angry when he found out who he was, considering our history. I glanced past Wade to Mason who was on the phone with a distraught expression on his face. *I wonder what's going on.*

"So are you coming back to us or just passing through?" Wade asked, grabbing my attention. He noticed me sneaking glances toward Mason, but he didn't mention anything about it. Instead, he gazed at me with his mysterious hazel eyes and gave me his famous devilish smile that I was sure won him many hearts since I left. His once shoulder length dark brown hair was now cut shorter and gelled in messy spikes, and I had to admit it suited him better.

"You looked sexy as hell up there on that stage. I'm sure Jake would love to have you back."

I laughed. "I'm sure he would love to have me back, but it's not going to happen. Hey, Ty told me you went to the Bahamas. Did you have fun?"

"I did," he agreed, but then quickly changed the subject, moving closer. With a confident grin on his face, he put his arm around my shoulders and slowly brought his lips down to my ear so he could speak quietly. "So how long are you in town for? I thought maybe we could spend some time together. I can show you what you've been missing all these years."

Rolling my eyes, I pulled away and smacked him playfully on the arm, making him chuckle. "You never give up do you?"

A man came up behind him, placing a hand on his shoulder, and stated, "No, he doesn't, which is why I like him. However, he's going to have to show you what you've been missing at another time. We have somewhere else to be right now." The man whispered something in his ear and then walked off, waiting for him by the door.

"Before I go," Wade began, "I'm having a party tomorrow night at my house. I want you to be there. Will you come?"

"Yeah, that would be great. I have a question though … who's the guy who was just here?" I asked. There was one thing I knew for certain, I didn't like him. He seemed like he would be a complete dirt bag … arrogant. Arrogant men were a complete turn off for me. Mason was confident, smart, and strong, but never full of himself. If he ever did get like that I would kick his ass myself.

"He's my agent," Wade said with a grin on his face. "I take it you didn't care too much for him."

"Not really," I admitted honestly. "Since when do you need an agent?"

Wade sighed, his eyes going wide once he looked down and noticed the time on his watch. "Shit, Claire, I really need to go. I'll talk to you more about it tomorrow, okay? I'll text you the address to my house sometime in the afternoon."

He kissed me on the cheek and hurried off to his agent who had a scowl on his face, looking perturbed and impatient. By the time they were out the side door Mason stalked toward me, his eyes blazing … searching. I could actually feel the heat of his anger, and it wasn't good.

"Where did they go?" he demanded, examining the room.

"Are you talking about the two men that were with me?" I asked nervously. By the wild look in his eyes I was afraid to tell him anything.

"Yes," he hissed through clenched teeth. "Which way did they go?"

I hesitated for a moment before pointing to the side door that led out to the right side of the club where the arena was. "They went out that way. Why? What are you going to do?"

Taking me by the arm—it didn't hurt, but I could tell he was ready to get out of the club—he pulled me to the door. "Mason, don't do anything," I pleaded. "Wade is just my friend now. You don't have to go kick his ass because he got a little too close to me."

Huffing, he let go of my arm and reached down to take my hand, keeping his gaze on the people around us. "So that was Wade, huh?" he growled.

"Yes."

Mason pulled me to the side and glared down at me. "Claire, that's not what I'm angry about. I mean, yeah, at first I wanted to break his fucking face for being all over you, but it's not exactly him I'm interested in at the moment. Who was the other man who talked to you?"

I scoffed. "Oh, you mean the one who acted like an arrogant prick? I didn't exactly like him."

"So you don't know him?" Mason asked, narrowing his gaze.

Shaking my head, I said, "No, I don't. Tonight was the first time I met him. Wade said he was his agent."

"What kind of agent? What's his name?"

"I don't know," I answered, shrugging my shoulders. "They were in a hurry to get out of here and he didn't have time to tell me."

"Fuck," Mason hissed under his breath. "Do you think Tyler would know who he is?"

"Probably since Wade is one of his good friends. He should be at the front entrance so we can ask him." His grip on my hand was tight, but it was probably because there were so many people in the club that if he wasn't holding onto me he would easily lose me in the crowd if we got separated. *Why does he want to know who the other guy is?*

Once we got to the door where Tyler stood flirting with a group of girls, I stopped Mason and mumbled quietly, "Let me handle this, okay? I'll ask Tyler the questions."

Mason nodded and blew out a frustrated sigh. "That's fine. Just ask him who the guy is and who he agents for. That way I can run a search on him and figure out how to find him."

"Why do you want to know who this guy is so badly?" I asked.

Leaning closer, Mason pierced me with his emerald green gaze and answered in a low, menacing voice, "Because he's the guy I've been looking for. He's the one who has been seen with each of the deceased fighters around the days before their deaths. I have to find out who he is."

No wonder he was acting the way he was. I had no idea about it or I would've made sure to talk to the guy myself. However, it wasn't just the guy that had Mason torn up. I saw his face when he took the phone call and I knew a look of worry when I saw one. It was the same look he had on his face when Melissa had been taken by my brother on his attempt to flee the country. As soon as we got to the car I was going to ask him.

Up ahead, Tyler was by the front door flirting with a couple of women, but when he saw us approaching he left them to come to us. "Don't tell me you two are leaving already? It's only," he drawled, glancing down at his phone, "one o'clock in the morning. It's early."

Rolling my eyes, I shook my head and chuckled, "Maybe for you, Ty, but for me I'm used to getting my sleep. Anyway, did you happen to see Wade leave by any chance?"

"Oh, yeah," he responded, "I saw him leave with his agent. I think he had some kind of promotional party he had to go to or something. I never know anymore these days. Wade's kind of gone off doing his own thing now. Once he landed his agent he's been spending more time away and working out at one of the high end gyms. It's all good, though. Someone in our circle needs to make a name for themselves."

"Like what? What do you mean doing his own thing and making a name for himself?" I asked. Mason stood by my side, listening intently, but I could already tell he knew what Tyler was going to say. I didn't like the feeling I had gnawing away at my stomach at all.

Tyler gazed at me incredulously. "Didn't Wade tell you when you spoke to him? Surely, he wasn't trying to be modest."

"No, he didn't have time since he had to leave shortly after the show. Tell me," I demanded.

"All right, let's see," Tyler began, "It all started when Jake brought up the idea of having in house fights. We all wanted to train so we could be in them. Wade was one of the best ones in the cage and eventually he got noticed." He glanced over at Mason. "I'm sure you'll know who the sponsor is since you were a part of it before. They're one of the top UFC sponsorships any fighter would die to be a part of. You were one of the lucky ones."

I held in my gasp and glanced nervously over at Mason who stood frozen, his eyes growing wide in shock. I couldn't begin to fathom what he must've felt, learning that something he used to be a part of could actually be a part of what was happening now. Mason swallowed hard before speaking. "So you're saying—"

Mason couldn't even finish the sentence before Tyler cut in, "Yep, your old sponsor, MMA Pride, picked up Wade 'The Destroyer' Mitchell, or at least it's in the works. I don't think it's officially finalized. What a lucky bastard, huh? I wasn't good enough for them."

Tyler's smile faded when he noticed Mason clenching his hands into tight fists. "Dude, are you okay?" He glanced over at me, lifting a hesitant brow.

I waved him off and smiled, putting a reassuring arm around Mason's waist. "Oh, he's fine," I explained. "He's just mad that Wade kissed me on the cheek, but I told him that was just how Wade was. He liked to flirt with anyone and everything, right?"

"You got that right," he agreed a little hesitantly. "Well, anyway, I'm going to get back to work. You two have a good rest of the night." He went back to his spot at the door while Mason and I headed for the truck. I could tell he was worried about me by the strange reaction he got from Mason. Glancing back at him, I nodded so he'd know I was okay and that everything was fine. Actually, everything was far from fine. I was even still in my costume.

When we got in the truck, he started it up and finally spoke, "I can't believe this shit. MMA Pride is one of the best and sought out sponsors. Surely, they wouldn't be involved in something like this."

"Do you still have your old agent's contact information? Maybe you could call him and just catch up."

I didn't know if that was a long shot, but if he left on good terms I didn't see where there would be an issue for that. Mason closed his eyes and lowered his head. "I can't do that, Claire. My agent died two years ago from a heart attack. His wife called to tell me. You know, when that guy stared at me in the theater, he looked at me like he knew me. Now I know why. I just hope I run into him again."

I wonder if he'll be at Wade's party. The only way to find out was to go. I just feared of what Mason would do to Wade when we got there. He looked really pissed at us when he was on the phone. Taking a deep breath, I turned to face him, biting my lip. "I know of a way you might be able to see him again … tomorrow," I told him.

Mason's eyes narrowed. "And how is that might I ask?"

"Well … before Wade had to leave he told me about a party he's having tomorrow night at his house. I don't know if that guy is going to be there, but it's worth a shot. We could always go and find out." I paused to weigh in his reaction, but all he did was turn and stare out into the parking lot.

Mason's hands were gripped so tight on the steering wheel that I was afraid he'd rip it off. Reaching over, I placed my hand on top of his and squeezed. "Mason, talk to me. I need to know what you're thinking," I pleaded.

Closing his eyes, he sighed and leaned his forehead down on my hand. "Claire, there's something I need to say and you're not going to like it." He lifted his head and gazed at me with his sorrowful green eyes.

"What is it?" I asked. *Why is he looking at me like that?*

Taking my hand, he rubbed his thumb soothingly across my skin before explaining, "Okay, first off, I'm not saying this is the case, but if Wade is hanging out with a man we suspect to have involvement in these recent deaths then there might be a good chance Wade knows about it or is involved himself."

I had no clue what he was going to say to me, but I definitely wasn't expecting that. There was no way in hell Wade would ever be involved in that mess. "No," I argued, shaking my head briskly. "There's no way Wade would have anything to do with this. I know him, Mason. I may not have seen him in a while, but I've kept in touch with him over the years. Well, maybe not so much this past year since I've been busy, but that's not the point. People aren't always like the company they keep. That would be like saying I'm going to turn into a greedy psychopath like my brother and start kidnapping people."

Lifting my brows, I crossed my arms over my chest,

daring him to contradict me. I wasn't going to back down from sticking up for him. Wade was my friend and I knew he was a good person. *People can change,* a nagging voice in my head said. Whatever was going on, I had to believe Wade was still the same person I knew all those years ago.

Still glaring at Mason, I watched him clench his teeth and mumble something under his breath before lifting his hands in the air … giving in. "Okay," he grumbled. "We will go to the party tomorrow night and I'll play nice with your friend. I just don't want to see you get hurt by people you think you can trust. This isn't a game, Claire, and you've seen firsthand what desperation and greed can make a person do."

I nodded. "I know, but I always try to see the good in people."

Mason scoffed and put the truck in gear, pulling out of The Labyrinth parking lot. "See that's what makes us different," he uttered, glancing over at me before looking back at the road. "I only get to see the bad."

When we were almost to the hotel, Mason drove past it and kept going. "Where are we going?" I asked. It was closing in on two in the morning and I was exhausted.

Mason ran a hand through his hair and pointed to the hospital that slowly came into view. "We're going to the hospital," he remarked warily.

"Umm … why?"

"You know that phone call I got while at the club? Well, it happened to be the Chief of Police. He told me they found Summer."

Gasping, I cupped a hand over my mouth and cried, "Oh my God, is she okay? What did he tell you?"

Mason found us a parking place and shut off the

truck. "They found her in an alley off the main strip. She's not talking and Ryan was hoping that if she saw someone she knows then she'd snap out of it. I guess we will see."

Mason opened the door and got out so I followed suit and did the same. I was still in my costume from the club, but I didn't care. Summer was alive. That was all that mattered.

Chapter 20

Mason

By the time we got off the elevator, a man I could only assume was Ryan Griffin charged toward us with a scowl on his face. He was around six foot tall, average build, with red hair and gray, beady eyes that looked too close together.

"It's about time you got here," Ryan snapped, looking down at his watch. "I called you over two hours ago." When he spotted Claire following behind me, dressed in her little toga, he turned those too close eyes to me and glared.

"Well, I see now what the hell you've been doing," he hissed, instantly making my hackles rise. He pulled out his wallet and took out a wad of money, thrusting it at Claire. "Look, I'm sorry he brought you here, but you need to leave. The money I gave you should get you a cab ride home or to wherever you need to go."

The way he looked at me and her with disdain pissed me the fuck off. Before I could say or do something that would probably land me in jail myself, Claire beat me to it. The look in her furious gaze along with the firm set of her lips, I could definitely say I'd felt the wrath of that look before. She was enraged, but nothing would ever take away the priceless vision of the surprised look on his face when she threw the money back at him.

"Excuse me, Mr. Griffin, but I'm not going anywhere. If it wasn't for me you wouldn't know half the shit Mason has been telling you. You need to show a little respect, especially when you're speaking to a woman. I'm trying to help *you*," she warned. I had to give it to her, she had balls.

"What is she talking about?" Ryan hissed, glaring at us both.

"Claire used to work at The Labyrinth and got us in there. She's been introducing me to people and while we were there I found the guy with the dragon tattoo," I informed him through clenched teeth.

Ryan sighed and shook his head. "Mason, you should know better than to get someone else involved with this. It's not a good idea no matter how good her connections are." He turned to Claire and asked, "What's your full name? Who are you and what do you do?"

Claire crossed her arms over her chest with a smug expression on her face. "My name is Claire O'Briene and I'm from Sonoma County, California. I own the O'Briene Vineyards and Winery. I'm here to help Mason and I think I've done a pretty damn good job of it, too."

"All right, enough questions to Claire," I cut in, glaring at Ryan. "She's not some hooker I picked off the street as you can see now. Let's get on to more important things."

Ryan blew out a frustrated breath and closed his eyes.

"Fine, tell me about the man with the tattoo. Do you have his name ... anything?"

"No, I didn't get his name, but I did get a tidbit of other information." Ryan lifted an impatient brow and beckoned for me to continue with a wave of his hand. I was going to break that hand if he waved it in my face one more time. "It looks like the guy we're looking for is an agent for a well-known company who sponsors MMA fighters."

"Interesting," Ryan responded curiously. "Well, I guess we need to start looking into that. You probably know of—"

"There's no need," I cut in dryly. "I already know who he's with ... because it happens to be the same sponsor I had when I fought."

Ryan's eyes grew wide. "Are you serious? Do you have any connections with them still?"

Warily, I shook my head and explained, "I don't. My agent died a couple of years ago. He was the last tie I had to them. I'll look on their website and see if there are any pictures of the listed agents. Anyway, Claire and I are going to a party tomorrow night and there's a pretty good chance our man will be there. I'll figure it all out when the time comes, but right now I came here to see Summer. We can discuss things in detail later when I know more."

Ryan nodded and pointed to the room across the hall. "I understand. Her room is right there. We'll talk about everything later."

Turning away from Ryan, I faced the closed door to Summer's room. Taking a deep breath, I reached for the handle and opened it slowly, quietly. Claire came up beside and whispered, "Do you want me to go in there with you?"

Not knowing what happened to Summer or what she looked like, I didn't want Claire to have to see it. Instead, I gazed down at her and said softly, "As much as I want you with me, I don't think it's a good idea."

"Okay," she murmured gently. Squeezing my hand, she nodded sadly and took a seat out in the hallway.

The room was dim, the only light coming from a small lamp in the corner of the room, and silent other than the light beeping sounds of the machines Summer was hooked up to. The second she came into view I could barely recognize her. Her skin was ghostly pale and there were tubes going in and out of her body everywhere. She was sound asleep, so I lifted her chart out of the bin and took a seat in the chair beside her bed. She didn't appear to have been physically beaten or abused which was definitely a good thing. However, it looked like she hadn't eaten anything in the past two weeks she'd been missing. Her once full face, which was always so glowing and bright, was now sunken in and skeletal.

What the hell happened to her?

Opening up her chart, I glanced through all the different findings and according to her condition when she came in she was dehydrated, malnourished, and suffering from severe emotional distress. No one had been able to get her to talk and even though she hadn't seen me in a while I hoped she would at least recognize me. I needed to know what happened.

Lightly, I laid my hand on top of hers; it was cold and dry. Her fingers jerked and slowly she pulled her hand out from under mine and placed hers on top, weakly trying to squeeze.

Leaning over the bed, I watched her eyes flutter a few times before she slowly opened them. "Summer," I murmured, "it's me, Mason."

Confused, she blinked and narrowed her gaze at me, scared. She let go of my hand and pulled it away, staring at me like I was a complete stranger. "Summer, can you talk to me? Do you recognize me at all?" I asked her. "I was one of your friends, remember?"

Tears fell down her cheeks, but she kept her gaze on me and never once opened her mouth to speak. Ryan caught my eye in the doorway, but I shook my head so he'd know I hadn't made any progress. I had no clue what to do to get her to talk to me. Whatever she went through when Austin died completely messed her up. Her once bright blue eyes even looked dull and devoid of life.

"Please snap out of this soon, Summer. I hate seeing you like this," I whispered. *Austin would hate to see you like this*, I wanted to say. "I'm going to be here until you get better, you hear me? I know you remember me, Summer, and I can promise you this … whatever happened to you I'm going to make sure the people who did it are found. You can count on that."

I waited for a couple of extra minutes, hoping she would speak, but when it was obvious she wasn't going to I put her chart back and walked out the door. I had a promise to keep.

Chapter 21

Claire

When the sun came up the next morning, Mason and I had only been in bed for about three hours. As soon as we got back from the hospital we both laid on the bed and immediately fell asleep. I was still wearing my costume, which wasn't exactly comfortable to sleep in, but I did it anyway. Mason was still asleep when I got out of the shower so I decided to get dressed and grab some breakfast from one of the restaurants downstairs.

After putting my hair up in a messy ponytail, I threw on a pair of yoga pants and a teal tank top with my sneakers so I could work out in the gym after I ate. Mason needed his rest and the last thing I wanted to do was make noise and wake him up. I wrote him a quick letter to tell him where I was going, placed it on the pillow beside him, and walked quietly out the door.

When I stayed at the Bellagio years ago, I always ate breakfast by myself so it didn't bother me to sit alone in the restaurants. After being seated at a table, the waitress took my order, which was a gourmet egg and cheese omelet with freshly squeezed orange juice … my favorite. While I waited on my food to come out, I flipped through the pictures on my phone to pass the time. There were many of them with me and Melissa goofing off, and then several of me and Cooper over the past few months. I hadn't spoken to him since I left, but I hoped we could find a way to still be friends. We had too much of a history just to let it go.

I kept scrolling until I got to the one picture I secretly stored in my phone. It was of me and Mason at Brett and Melissa's wedding, with him in his tux and me in my bridesmaid's dress. After he left me, and even though I hated him, I didn't have the heart to delete the picture. We were both a little tipsy, and I could still remember the way my heart pounded in my chest when he pulled me close, putting his arm around my shoulders. It was the night that changed everything.

Too busy looking at my phone, I didn't notice that someone had taken a seat across from me until I heard them speak, "You know, I've always appreciated the way a female looks in the mornings. You have a natural beauty to you, Claire."

Fumbling with my phone, I glanced up quickly to find none other than Wade's agent and the man Mason desperately wanted to see again leering at me. Instead of wearing the expensive clothes he wore at the club, he now wore a Cincinnati Reds baseball cap, a simple black T-shirt and running shorts as if he just got through working out along. *Was he staying in the same hotel?*

"Um … thanks, I guess," I answered dryly.

With a wolfish grin on his face, he extended his hand and introduced himself, "I just wanted to say I'm sorry for being in such a rush last night and taking Wade away from you. I know I must've seemed rude. I'm Erick Young by the way."

Snorting, I shook his hand quickly and let go. "Yeah, you were a little rude," I blurted out honestly, "but it's okay. I'm used to being around assholes."

Tilting his head back, he bellowed out a laugh. "Wow, I can see why Wade likes you so much. I have to say it's refreshing to hear a woman speak her mind. You know, Wade talked about you almost the entire night. Claire this and Claire that."

What the hell was he up to? I wondered, narrowing my gaze.

Being around the guy made my skin crawl, and my instincts screamed at me to run as far away as possible. The one day I decided to go out on my own, away from Mason, was the one day I had to run into this man alone.

"Wade is a good friend," I said matter-of-factly. "I've known him a long time."

"Hmm … well, what I heard was a different story. I heard you two were a lot more than just good friends."

"That was a long time ago. Things have changed in the years I've been gone," I stated adamantly.

"I see. So are you coming to the party tonight?" he asked, leaning over on his elbows with a gleam in his eyes.

The waitress finally came and set down my omelet and orange juice. Was it bad that I'd already lost my appetite? "Thank you," I said, smiling up at her.

She glanced over at Erick, setting down a menu, and politely asked, "Is there anything I can get for you this morning while you look over the menu?"

Please say no, please say no, I repeated over and over

in my mind. While he looked over the menu, I quickly texted Mason, hoping he was awake, or at least hoping my text would wake him up.

Me: Please get down here to the restaurant now! Erick, the guy with the dragon tattoo, is down here and sitting across from me. HURRY!

Even though I wanted to fly my fingers over the letters, I did it calmly so Erick wouldn't think I was panicking. He handed the menu back to the waitress and said, "Actually, I think I'll just have a cup of coffee. I'm not going to be here long."

When she left to get his coffee, he glanced back at me and repeated his earlier question, "So you never answered … are you going to the party tonight?"

Taking a bite of my omelet, I drank a sip of my orange juice, forcing it down. "Yes, I'm going. Wade is supposed to text me later to give me his address."

The waitress came back with Erick's coffee and set it down along with some cream and sugar. Picking up his cup, he blew off the steam and lifted a curious brow. "So, will your friend be joining you to the party? I know Wade will be sorely disappointed."

Clearing my throat, I took another sip of my juice and studied him. "Who exactly are you talking about? I do have more than one friend."

He guffawed and set his cup down. "There's no need to play coy, Ms. O'Briene. I saw you come in last night with Mason Bradley. When I saw him at the club I knew I recognized him from somewhere."

"Well, not that it's any of your business, but yes, Mason will be coming with me. How did you know his name?"

Erick drank the rest of his coffee and pushed his cup to the side. "He used to be one of MMA Pride's best fighters," he pointed out. "You do know he used to fight professionally, right?"

"Yes, I know," I remarked coolly. "He's a good fighter. I watched him for the first time the other night."

Erick's eyes went wide in delight. "Is he fighting again? When did he start that?"

As much as I hated that Mason needed to get involved with him, I knew that the only way was to get him on the inside, and to get on the inside he needed to fight. Nodding my head, I replied, "He just started back as a matter of fact. I think he wants to get back into it, though. He has a fight against some guy named Matt Reynolds next Friday night."

Erick cleared his throat, surprise clearly written on his face. "Holy shit, that's going to be an interesting fight, there's no way I'm going to miss that." His phone started to buzz, so he glanced down at it and got to his feet. "Claire, it's been a pleasure, but I must be on my way. I'll see you and Mason at the party tonight."

After laying down a couple of twenties on the table, he answered his phone and strolled away. As soon as he walked out the doors to the restaurant, I left my half eaten omelet and stalked after him. Once I made sure he was out of the hotel, I ran straight to the elevators to rush back up to Mason. He was probably going to be so pissed that he wasn't down here with me.

Impatiently, I pounded on the button, waiting on the doors to open. "Hurry up," I hissed under my breath. As soon as I heard the elevator settle into place and the ding-ing sound of the door, I rushed in and ran straight into Mason. He caught me in his arms, his chest heaving up and down in anger. "Where is he?" he growled, moving us back out of the elevator. He examined the room, raking his gaze here and there, and when he couldn't spot Erick he blew out a frustrated breath.

"He's not here, Mason. I watched him walk out of the front doors just a couple of minutes ago," I told him.

"From now on don't ever come down here without me. Is he staying here in the hotel?"

I shrugged. "I would think so. He told me he saw me and you come in last night together."

"What else did he say?" he asked. Taking my hand, he led us back to the elevator. Since we were the only ones in there, I went ahead and filled him in.

"He knows who you are, Mason. He said he recog-nized you at the club and that you used to be one of MMA Pride's best fighters. He's also going to be at the party to-night and asked if I was going to bring you. His name is Erick Young."

"What did you tell him?"

The doors to the elevator opened, and as we walked down the hall to our room I kept my voice quiet when I spoke, "I told him yes that I was bringing you to the party. I also told him about your fight next Friday. He seemed very interested about it and said he wasn't going to miss it."

Mason froze as he was about to put the key in the door, and looked over at me with a look of contemplation on his face. "Hmm ... I wonder if he's going to say some-thing to me tonight," he murmured. "I wish I knew what the hell he was up to."

"I don't know, Mason. All I know is that I didn't get a good feeling from him. Whatever happens tonight at the party, or if he talks to you, just please be careful. I didn't want to tell him a thing about you, but I know I needed to."

Sighing, he bent down to kiss me on the lips. "It's okay, baby. I'm just glad you're all right. The whole time I was racing to get down to you, thoughts of Summer came to mind and I didn't want to imagine anything happening to you. By the time I woke up alone and saw the text I almost went out of my fucking mind. I need to call Ryan and give him Erick's name and see what he can dig up."

He opened the door, and when I walked in, the room was a complete disaster. There were clothes strewn all over the bed and the floor. "See, I told you ... out of my fucking mind. I threw my bag on the bed and ripped it apart just to get to my clothes. Don't worry, I'll clean it all up, but I was just in a hurry to get to you," he uttered sheepishly.

"Mason, I'll straighten up the clothes while you call Ryan and give him Erick's name. That's more important right now. So go," I commanded, shooing him off.

He dialed Ryan's number and opened up his laptop, pounding away as he waited for Ryan to pick up. Once he got on the phone, Mason gave him the name and that was about it. He typed away on the computer a little more, and by the time I finished straightening his clothes he was done.

"So what did you find out? Anything?" I asked, coming up behind him. He was looking at the MMA Pride website, but then he closed his laptop and sighed.

"Ryan's going to search for information on all the Erick Young's in the system. I looked on the website, but I couldn't find anything on him there. I don't know when they updated the website last, but from their current agent list there wasn't an Erick Young on there."

"What if Erick isn't even his real name," I remarked incredulously. "How are you going to find out who he really is?"

Mason shrugged. "A lot of searching, I guess. I'm sure Ryan will figure it out. They reopened a case of this same thing happening a few years ago in Ohio. Maybe they will find a link."

Oh, wow. I had no clue this sort of thing had happened before.

With Mason's clothes all folded on the bed, I stacked them neatly into piles. We still had a while before the party and I wanted to spend some time with him … just him. I didn't want to have to worry about anything else. Being in Vegas had brought our pasts back, but I wanted Mason to spend time with who I was at the moment and vice versa. We played our roles and I hated not knowing who to trust or what to believe. All I knew was that Mason was real, he was mine, and I wanted to know all of him, right down to his deepest and darkest fears.

Mason was stuffing his clothes back in his bag, and when I cleared my throat he lifted his green gaze to mine, lifting his brows. "Something you need to say?" he asked.

Biting my lip, I nodded with a huge grin on my face. "Actually, there is. Let's go do something together today, something that doesn't pertain to dancing or fighting. We've been here for a week now, trying to figure out our relationship on top of trying to solve a case. All I want is a few hours to ourselves, just me and you."

Mason set his bag on the floor and smiled, his eyes gleaming in anticipation. "What did you have in mind?" he inquired, sneaking a glance toward the bed and then back to me.

Playfully, I scoffed, putting my hands on my hips. "Is that seriously all you think about?"

"Only when I'm with you," he confessed. "Besides, I need to get my mind off of everything going on."

"Do you want to visit Summer again today?"

Sighing, he shook his head and objected, "No, I don't think it's a good idea to go today. If I see her again I'm just going to get angry and that's not how I need to go to the party tonight. I can go first thing in the morning to see her."

Averting his gaze, he was on the other side of the bed, gripping his hands into tight fists. Mason was a strong man, and in his line of work he was used to seeing people who had been killed in accidents, murdered, raped, molested, and so forth. It was easy to keep your emotions in check when you didn't know the people, except now it was all hitting close to home … close to his heart, and he didn't know how to handle it.

Slowly, I walked over to him and wrapped my arms around his waist. His hands gradually unclenched and he brought them up to hold onto my arms. Placing my head on his back, I could hear the erratic beat of his heart thumping deep inside his chest; *thump-thump, thump-thump*.

"It's okay to be upset, Mason. You don't have to hide how you truly feel. I know you think you have to be strong all the time, but with me you don't have to be." I squeezed him tighter. "I want to be there for you … always."

Grabbing my hands, Mason pulled me around so I could face him, draping my arms around his neck so he could hold me close. "You know, when I first met you I didn't think there was a serious bone in your body."

"It's because there wasn't," I teased. "I was only twenty-two years old. You forget I'm four years younger than you. Although, I will admit that I thought you had *too* many serious bones in your body."

With a devilish smirk, he lowered his hands to my ass and held me tight as he pushed his hips against mine. "I can show you one of those serious bones if you want me to," he murmured, swaying us back and forth.

Biting my lip, I groaned as he rubbed his hardening cock against my stomach, taunting me. I wanted to make love to him and I could see it in his hungered gaze that he was about to lose control. I loved that look. I craved it just as much as I craved his touch. In that one gaze alone I could see everything he wanted to do to me. I wanted him to rip my clothes off. I wanted to feel him thrust so deep and hard that it hurt, but in a good way. My insides ached as if a fire burned through every nerve ending of my body … and Mason was the only one who could put out that fire.

Licking my lips, I let my hands trail down his chest to the waist of his shorts. "You know, we have several hours before the party. What on earth are we going to do with all that time?"

In one quick move, Mason swept me up in his arms and we both went down on the bed. Lifting my tank top over my head, he pushed my bra out of the way and palmed my breast. Moaning low in his throat, he revealed,

"I'm sure we can think of plenty of things to do … starting with this."

He quickly rolled my nipple with his tongue before closing down and sucking as hard as he could. Arching my back, I cried out with the pleasure and pain of it. It only intensified more when he spread my legs open and reached inside my pants, groaning as he pushed his fingers inside my damp opening. I was ready for him, especially when my first orgasm exploded, making my body clench around his fingers.

Mason chuckled and grazed his wet fingers over my throbbing clit. "That's one down, baby. Be prepared for a lot more because I plan on making love to you and fucking you in every way I know how."

Just the thought made my body tremble. It was going to be one hell of an afternoon.

Chapter 22

Claire

My whole body was sore by the time Mason and I finished for the afternoon. He had to carry me into the bathroom and place me in the bathtub because I was completely spent. "You better liven up, baby. We have a party to go to tonight."

"Can't we just stay here," I groaned halfheartedly. I knew we *had* to go to the party, but the hot water and soothing aroma of the bath salts fizzing around my body felt amazing. The whole room smelled like lavender.

Mason chuckled and splashed water in my face to wake me up. Before I could protest, my phone started to ring in the other room. "Do you want me to get that for you?" he asked.

I wiped the water away from my eyes and nodded. "Yeah, you can bring it here. It's probably Wade. He needs to give me directions to his house."

With a glum expression, Mason brought me my phone; when he handed it to me it wasn't Wade on the caller ID … it was Cooper. *Just my luck.* I held my phone, staring at it like an idiot, not knowing if I should answer it or not.

"Just take the call, Claire," Mason said. "I'm a big boy. I can handle it if some other guy calls you. It was *me* who fucked you senseless today so I'm not too worried."

He left me alone in the bathroom and shut the door behind him as he walked out. The last time I talked to Cooper was when I left him angry and alone at my house, so needless to say I was kind of nervous. Taking a deep breath, I finally answered the phone, "Hey, Cooper, is everything okay out there?"

He didn't answer right away, but when he did, my heart broke for him all over again. I could hear the hurt in his voice. He tried to mask it, but I knew he was still angry at me.

"Yeah, everything's going fine. Brett told me Melissa was worried about you and Mason since you hadn't called in a while so I thought I would check up on you."

Shit! Melissa was going to be furious with me and Mason for not calling. It had only been a couple of days, but given the situation it probably felt like years to her. Also, with her raging pregnancy hormones I bet she was driving Brett crazy.

Groaning, I sat up in the tub and switched the phone to my other ear. "Oh, no, I bet she's furious with us right now. I'll make sure to call her as soon as I can."

"Sounds good," he replied awkwardly.

We sat in silence for a few seconds and it killed me that it had come to that. Cooper was my best friend for so long and now nothing was ever going to be the same. "Is that the only reason why you called?" I asked softly.

Blowing out a heavy sigh, he said, "No, it's not the

only reason. I wanted to tell you that I've been helping Brett look over your house and the vineyards while you're gone. I've stacked your mail up on the counter and watered the flowers in your garden. I know you spent a lot of time taking care of them." Of course he knew I spent a lot of time on them; he was there helping me for the gazillion hours it took to plant them.

"Oh, Cooper," I cried, choking back my tears. "You didn't have to do all of that."

"I know I didn't, but I wanted to. I'll give you back your house key when you get home. It's strange being there knowing you're gone and that you're with someone else."

My heart ached, and I couldn't stop the tears from flowing even if I tried. "Coop, you know I didn't want to hurt you, right? You are the last person in the world I ever wanted to hurt."

"I know," he murmured sadly, "but I still love you, Claire. I think deep down I knew it wouldn't work. We had our fun messing around and having our nights together when I was in town, but I wanted you so bad that I tried too hard to keep you when you finally opened up to me. I should've known it was a losing battle."

"No, it wasn't, Cooper. You helped me when I needed someone and you picked me back up. I don't regret anything about our time together," I wailed.

"Neither do I, Claire," he claimed wholeheartedly, and before hanging up he repeated those words again, only softer, "Neither do I."

As soon as I set down my phone on the counter beside the tub, Mason opened the door and leaned against the frame with his arms crossed. "Were you listening?" I asked, splashing water in my face to wipe away the tears. The water was beginning to lose its heat, so I took my washcloth and bottle of raspberry shower gel, lathering it up good.

Mason came up to the tub and took the soapy washcloth from my hands so he could wash my back. He cleared his throat, and sounded almost guilty when he spoke, "I didn't mean to listen in, but it was kind of hard not to when I heard you start crying. Is everything okay?"

Nodding, I moaned when he massaged the soap into my neck and back. "He called to tell me that Melissa was worried about us. You need to make sure you call her to tell her you're all right."

Groaning, Mason moved to the front of the tub so he could look into my eyes. "I'll call her in just a minute. Is that all he had to say?"

"Yeah, pretty much. He wasn't angry like he was when I left him to come after you. I'm glad he called, Mason. I didn't like the way I ended things with him, but at the time I didn't have a choice. I needed to get to you as fast as I could. At least now I have closure with him and I don't feel as if things are completely on bad terms."

Shamefully, Mason turned his head and nodded. "I understand completely. I know he was there for you when I wasn't. That's the one regret I will always have to live with."

"Hey," I called out gently to get his attention, hoping he'd turn back to me … which he did. "We all have regrets. We just have to move on from them."

His smile was sad, but he leaned over the tub, tilted my chin up with his finger, and kissed me on the lips. "I'm going to call Melissa while you finish up in here. How about we actually go out to dinner tonight instead of ordering in?" he asked, sounding hopeful.

"I think that would be a great idea," I told him excitedly. "It can be our first official date."

It just so happened that two of the best five star restaurants in Las Vegas were in our hotel. We didn't have to go far, and it was a welcome change of pace to get out of the hotel room and enjoy a pleasant dinner out. It was also great seeing Mason cleaned up and dressed in something other than jeans and a T-shirt. While I finished getting ready, he went out and bought a nice pair of khaki dress pants and a navy blue polo shirt. When he packed to come out to Las Vegas he didn't expect to need any nice dressy clothes. I was prepared considering the places I knew I would need to take him.

However, tonight I went for a different look. Instead of wearing one of my tight, fitted dresses that I would wear to the club, I opted to go with something a little more sensual and fun. It was a black, sleeveless dress with a sequined bodice and a flared skirt that hit about mid-thigh. When I stepped out of the bathroom, Mason and I both froze as we took each other in. The aching and burning feeling I got in my stomach when I looked at him was something I'd never felt before. It was enthralling yet terrifying all at the same time.

Mason had called a little earlier and made us a reservation at the Prime Steakhouse restaurant. We arrived on time and were seated on time as well. The food was amazing, as always. I had the peppercorn New York steak with creamed spinach and truffle mashed potatoes; it was heaven. Mason stuck to his usual with a filet mignon and decided to try the mashed potatoes since I loved them so much. I needed to work on getting him to try new things.

While we waited for the check, Mason stared at me over the rim of his glass as he sipped on his gin and tonic. I had come to learn that it was his favorite mixed drink even though I thought it tasted like pine trees. I grew up on wine and I had yet to find anything else that I preferred more.

Mason finished the last of his drink and set the glass down before taking my hand in his. When he spoke, he kept his gaze on my hand as he caressed my skin with the pad of his thumb. "When all of this is over, where do you want it to lead us?" he asked, finally lifting his green gaze to mine.

Smiling, I moved my wine glass out of the way so I could reach for his other hand. "That all depends … were you serious about staying in California for a while or was that just something you said on a whim?"

"I was serious, Claire. I meant everything I said. I told you before I would fight for you and if I have to move myself across the states to be with you then I will. It's what I want, but the question here is if it's what you want. I need you to be certain."

Moving closer, I squeezed his hands and leaned toward him over the table. Mason and I were from two different worlds, and I wanted to know his just as much as I wanted him to know mine. *Could I really ask that of him? To move away from the place he's lived in for thirty years?*

I felt guilty about it, but there was no way I could move away from my family's land. It was my life, it was where I belonged. Furrowing his brows, Mason shifted in his chair, waiting on me to answer.

"Mason, I want that more than anything, but I also don't want to be selfish. I've been thinking about everything lately and I have an idea," I suggested.

Lifting a curious brow, he grinned and asked, "What kind of idea?"

"Well, for starters I thought I could show you around Vegas and take you to all my favorite places once this case ends. There's more to Sin City than just gambling and pretty lights."

"I'm sure we can do that," he agreed. "Was there anything else?"

"Yeah, actually there is," I began, but then I paused and took a deep breath before continuing, "I also thought that maybe once this was all over I could go to North Carolina with you and you show me around *your* home. I know I've visited there plenty of times, but I never saw much except for Charlotte. I heard both the mountains and the beaches are gorgeous. I'd like to see how it compares to the west coast."

Mason chuckled. "You might want to reconsider that because once you see our mountains you might not want to go back. Every year my father would take me to one of the campground sites off the Blue Ridge Parkway and we'd stay there for the whole weekend, fishing and hiking. He died when I was in high school and after that I still went up there every year and did the exact same things we would do. It's kind of a tradition now."

The burn of unshed tears prickled behind my eyes. I

couldn't imagine him going up to the mountains by himself every year and facing those long lost memories alone. Mason was a loner, except I knew he wasn't always so. It was time to get him out of that.

"When do you go there and reminisce?" I asked.

His smile was sad, but I could see the happiness in his gaze when he answered, "I go every second weekend in October. The weather is perfect at that time and my dad always wanted to go when the leaves would begin to change. He was a photographer, among many of his other talents."

"He sounds like an awesome man," I murmured, "except this year you're breaking tradition because I'm going with you."

Mason gazed at me in disbelief. "You would actually do that for me? Have you ever been camping before?"

"Umm … no, but I'll be with you. You can teach me everything your father taught you, just like I'll show you everything you want to know about my vineyards. We're in this together, Mason, you and I. You've been doing things alone, not depending on anyone to be there for you, but that's not how it works when you want to be with someone. I want to know who you were then so I can see how you became who you are now."

Our moment got interrupted when my phone started to vibrate in my purse. I reached in and pulled it out to see Wade's name pop up. "Is that him?" Mason asked with a slight hint of annoyance in his tone.

I nodded and read the text.

Wade: Are you still coming tonight?

"Yeah, he asked if I'm still coming. I don't think he

knows you're going to be with me. I know Erick knows, but I don't think Wade does," I said.

Mason narrowed his eyes. "Is that going to be a problem?"

If Wade behaved it wouldn't be an issue, but it was a gamble we had to take. I just hoped Mason could keep his calm around him. "I sure hope there's not any trouble," I replied, "but this whole night is going to be a dilemma since Erick's going to be there. I don't think we can get bigger problems than that." I texted Wade back.

Me: Yes, I'm still coming. I need your address.

He texted me his address and my jaw about hit the floor when I recognized the name of the neighborhood. It was one of the richest neighborhoods in Las Vegas. How the hell could he afford that? The waitress brought us our check, and while Mason looked it over I texted back.

Me: Moving up in the world, huh?
Wade: You know it! It's about time luck was on my side. Now get your ass here! It's a housewarming party!

Wade didn't come from a wealthy family, and before I left Vegas he lived in an average sized apartment with one of his friends. To live in the neighborhood he was in it would cost hundreds of thousands of dollars while some houses could be pushing toward the million mark. Surely, he didn't make that much money working at the club.

"Why do you have that look on your face?" Mason asked. "What's he saying?"

Biting my lip, I glanced at Mason and then back

down to my phone. "Well, he just gave me his address and I'm a little confused. The houses in that neighborhood are really expensive. I don't see how he's affording it. I know he's not making it at the club. When you were fighting did you make hundreds of thousands of dollars?"

"No, not at the beginning, and since I've never heard of your friend, Wade, I'm assuming he's just getting started. He wouldn't be making near that amount until he got a name for himself, and even then it's not guaranteed," he informed me warily.

"That's what I thought. I don't think I like the sound of this, Mason."

Mason stood from the table and helped me up by taking my hand. "Neither do I, and that's why you need to be careful around him. Don't put your trust in anyone until I get this handled, okay?"

Sadly, I nodded and said, "Okay."

The last thing I wanted to believe was that Wade was fighting for the wrong side. He was a good person, or at least he used to be. I had to believe he still was. I had a habit of believing in the wrong people even when deep down I knew there was something dark and tainted inside their very soul. My brother was proof of that. He let greed and money take over his life, always wanting more and never being satisfied even though he had plenty to support him comfortably for the rest of his life.

Once out of the hotel, we got in the truck and Mason placed a small piece of paper in my hand. "What's this?" I asked, glancing down at the phone number scribbled on the paper.

"It's Ryan's cell number. I need you to have it in case something happens to me. If you feel like something's wrong or if you can't get a hold of me all you have to do is call him and he'll find me. It's very important that you know how to get help, so program it in your phone and memorize it."

Taking out my phone, I programmed it into my contacts and hoped that I would never have to use it.

Chapter 23

Claire

From the hotel, it only took us fifteen minutes to get to Wade's luxurious neighborhood. I came from a wealthy family, but even I couldn't afford a house in that area. A GPS didn't come in the rental truck, so we drove around the neighborhood streets until we spotted the house with a bunch of cars parked along the road. Saying it was a huge house didn't do it justice … it was a damn mansion.

"Wow," I breathed in awe. The whole house looked like it was made of stone, very modern with its blocked style architecture. The massive water fountain in front with a long, circular driveway just added to the opulence.

"I'm assuming this is it," Mason guessed.

"It appears so," I breathed in awe.

He parked us as close to the house as possible and we walked the quarter of a mile it took to get to the front door. There were people everywhere, and I recognized a couple of them from the club, but other than that I had no idea who the rest were. When we got inside the house, the floor and the imperial staircase was all Saharan gold marble while the railings added to the shimmering decadence with its airbrushed golden finish. He had paintings lining the walls in the foyer, and if there was one thing I loved almost as much as dancing it would be art. It was magnificent.

However, I was brought back to reality when a drunken idiot bumped into me and almost spilled his beer down the front of my dress. "Sor-rrry about that," he slurred, staggering toward the front door.

Mason put his arm around my waist and held me close to him as several of the other occupants stumbled their way in and out of the house.

"Do you know any of these people?" Mason asked, whispering in my ear.

I shook my head. "No, not really … do you?"

Peering around the room, I watched as Mason's gaze hardened as soon as he locked eyes on someone. "Hey," I muttered, squeezing the hand he had on my waist, "who do you see?"

"It's Chase Benfield," he growled.

"You mean the same Chase you just beat in the fight the other night?"

"Yep, that's him. This isn't going to be good," he warned. "Do you see Erick anywhere?"

I didn't see him or Wade for that matter. Given the size of the house there was a good chance we wouldn't see either one of them. "Well, since we're here we might as well walk around and see if we find him," I suggested.

I also wanted to get him as far away from Chase as I could. Chase seemed like a cocky bastard, and if alcohol was anywhere in his system I was sure it would magnify that cockiness even more. There were a lot of people going in and out of the kitchen so Mason and I headed in that direction. There were bottles of liquor and beers everywhere, not to mention Wade had actual bartenders tending to the guests and mixing their drinks.

I glanced up at Mason who had his ever watchful eyes circulating the room. "Do you want to get a drink?"

"I don't think that's a good idea for me, but have at it, baby. I need to be coherent right now," he uttered in all seriousness.

He hung back, leaning against the counters while I strolled up to the bartender's station. "What'll it be, sweetheart?" the bartender asked. She was a petite, red-headed female who appeared to be in her mid-twenties with a strong southern belle accent. It kind of reminded me of how Mason's southern accent sounded, but his was only slight. I could definitely tell he was from the south, though.

I looked at the selections, narrowing my eyes wondering what I would want. "Do you have any wine?" I asked her.

She smiled and pulled out a bottle from underneath the counter. "Will this do?"

Immediately, my eyes went wide at the sight of my family crest on the label. "Oh, my God," I exclaimed, reaching for the bottle. She looked at me like I was crazy, but she let go of the bottle so I could hold it. It was then that Wade came around the corner, his gaze instantly locking onto mine. He grinned mischievously when he noticed I had the bottle of wine in my hands … my wine.

"What's wrong, kitten, trying to steal the bottle of wine?" Wade chuckled and bent down to wrap his arms around my waist. When he let me go, I rolled my eyes at him and handed the bottle back to the bartender.

"Trust me, I have plenty of it at home. I don't think I need to steal any away from you." Laughing, I turned to acknowledge the girl behind the bar and said, "I'd like a glass of the wine, please." She nodded and went to work on pulling out the cork.

Wade moved closer and leaned against the bar, keeping his gaze on mine. "Thank you for coming tonight. I was hoping we'd get a chance to catch up."

"Yeah, we need to," I remarked incredulously, "like take for instance this house. How in the world did you get the money for it? Please tell me you're not doing anything illegal. You're not selling drugs, are you?"

I said it jokingly, but I wanted to gauge his reaction. Laughing, he rolled his eyes and put his arm around my shoulders. "Now why would I have to do something illegal to get a house like this? Is it hard to believe that I actually earned it? You should be happy for me considering what my life was like before you left."

I wanted to be happy for him, but only if he was doing things right. He never had much, only living paycheck to paycheck, but I knew all too well what happened to people when they grew desperate to be something more. I wanted to ask him *how* he earned it, but I didn't want to pry just yet. Maybe I was in denial thinking he was still the same guy I knew even though I could see it in his eyes that things had changed.

"Of course I'm happy for you, Wade, and I'm glad you're getting the things you've always wanted."

At that moment, the bartender set my glass of wine on the counter. Wade picked it up, but before handing it to me he bent down low and whispered softly in my ear, "I haven't gotten everything I've wanted. There's still one thing I want, but she left me and never looked back."

No, not this again, I screamed in my mind.

I didn't even want to imagine what Mason was thinking right now with Wade whispering in my ear. When I first met Wade I thought he was the most gorgeous guy I'd ever seen, other than Cooper. He liked to joke a lot, kind of like Tyler, but the one thing he wasn't very good at was being responsible. Wade liked to do his own thing on his own time; basically, he was a little self-centered. He wouldn't be someone you could have a long, lasting relationship with. That was why when we had our trysts every now and again I didn't let it get too serious as far as the emotional side of things.

"Please," I scolded incredulously, wriggling out from under his arm. "That was a long time ago, Wade. I was twenty-one years old and you knew I had to leave at some point. You know very well you couldn't have handled a long distance relationship and remained faithful. You had plenty of women falling all over you back in the day. I'm sure nothing's changed since then."

He shrugged, tilting his lips up in a playful leer. "Yeah, well, we always want the ones we can't have, don't we?"

"True, but those ones end up being the people you weren't meant to be with anyway," I uttered wholeheartedly. "You just have to find the right one."

The last thing I wanted was to hurt his feelings. I seemed to have a habit of hurting the men in my life over the past week. Tilting up my glass, I drank the rest of my wine in one huge gulp and set it down on the bar. "Can I have another glass please?"

Or maybe thirty of them ...

I think Wade was slowly getting the hint of my disinterest because he put some distance between us and pointed down to my now filled glass. "I think I made a good choice on the wine selection tonight, don't you?"

Breathing a sigh of relief, and thankful that he changed the subject, I took a sip and smiled. "Well, of course. Nothing beats the taste of my family's grapes. When did you have it brought in?"

"I had it rush ordered," he explained. "I talked to a woman named Melissa, I think, and she handled everything. How is business going at the winery?"

"It's going good, but my brother tried to take it all away from me. It was a huge clusterfuck." Not only did my brother go mentally crazy when he got in trouble for stealing his client's money and kidnapping Melissa, he also tried to steal our family's land out from under me. After our mother died, he sent me on a trip to England, saying he wanted me to relax while he handled all of the things at home. What I didn't know was that he took a copy of our mother's will and destroyed it just to forge another one stating that she left the land to him instead of me. He failed to realize that I had several copies of the will that were hidden.

Wade's eyes went wide. "Wait ... what? What happened with your brother?" He seemed really interested at first, keeping his attention on me when I started to explain, but then something caught his eye over my shoulder and I completely lost him after that.

"Um ... It's a really long story, I guess since you're not even listening," I began slowly, trying to get his attention. I waved my hand in front of his face before turning around to see what he was looking at. He was staring at Mason, except that wasn't the only thing; Erick was with him as well.

"What the hell is he doing here?" Wade growled.

Quickly, I glanced from him to Mason and back, trying to play it coolly. "Who are you talking about? Your agent? I thought you would want him here," I questioned curiously.

His whole demeanor swiftly changed from playful to downright angry in a single second. "No," he snapped. "I'm talking about Mason Bradley. I saw him at the club and now he's here. I know I didn't invite him."

"How do you know him anyway?"

He scoffed. "I don't *know* him, but I heard a lot about him through some friends. Erick told me he used to be one of the best fighters a few years ago, and now that he's back everybody's been talking about the big fight next Friday night between him and Matt Reynolds."

If I didn't know any better I'd say he was jealous, but there was something more to it. "So … what are you so pissed about? He's fighting Matt Reynolds, big deal. Can't your agent talk to him? It's not like Erick's going to replace you, right?"

Fuming, Wade hissed under his breath as Mason and Erick started to walk off toward another room. *Where were they going?* I wondered.

"Fuck, this isn't good," Wade growled, running his hands nervously through his dark, mussed hair. "Claire, I have to go. I'll be back."

He stalked off through the room and out the back door, but not before Mason had a chance to see our interaction with a concerned look on his face. Erick had just disappeared through the doorway so Mason took a quick second to glance at me to make sure I was all right. I nodded and gave him a small smile before he, too, disappeared through the door.

What the hell was going on?

I didn't know where Mason or Wade went, so I settled on sitting at the kitchen table. The room was filled with people, but I appeared to be the only one not having a good time. I knew better than to go traipsing off by myself with a bunch of drunken people I didn't know. Especially, in a house the size of Wade's with a gazillion rooms to get lost in. I had a friend in high school who had been raped at a party by a guy at our school and no one heard her screams because the music was up too damn loud. It was then that I vowed I would never be a victim. I wasn't the type of female to cry over every sad thing in movies or to beg a guy to take her back. I also wasn't the type to be afraid.

I wasn't afraid to jump out of an airplane because I'd already done it … twice. I'm not afraid to try new things and be adventurous. I tried to impress Mason and all of his police buddies by jumping off of my brother's roof into the pool one year when I first met him. I liked feeling fearless, but there was one thing that had me terrified. Mason was my weakness and with him off with Erick somewhere I had that unsettling and panicky feeling eating away at my gut.

Or maybe that panicky feeling came from the voice that spoke in my ear, making the sickening stench of beer, bad breath, and liquor waft across my nose. Cringing, I tried to move away, but his arms came around my chair and locked me into place.

"Well, aren't you a pretty thing," he sputtered, slurring his words. "I can tell you aren't from around here." I immediately recognized his voice along with the tattoos decorating his whole left arm. It was Chase Benfield … Mason's number one rival.

Holy shit, this isn't going to be good. What the hell am I going to do?

He leaned in closer, putting his nose in my hair and taking a deep breath. "Damn, you smell so fucking good, too … so sweet. Mason always got the good ones. I think it's about time he shares, don't you? After all, he did fuck my wife behind my back."

"Get away from me, Chase," I hissed through clenched teeth. "It's not his fault your wife chose to screw around behind your back. Just get over yourself already and leave me alone."

There was one girl in the room who actually noticed my uneasiness and ran out of the kitchen. I could only hope she was getting someone to help.

"Or what?" Chase retorted. "What are you going to do, get Mason to kick my ass? He's probably off somewhere in this house fucking another bitch while you sit here alone. Let's say we go find him, huh?"

He grabbed my wrist and pulled me out of the chair. That was his first and last mistake.

Chapter 24

Mason

Watching Claire with Wade was fucking torture. It took every ounce of strength to keep to myself and let her get as much information out of him as possible without me hindering her. I wanted to rip his fingers off one by one each time he touched her and put his arms around her. There was no way a guy and girl could be friends with each other, especially after they've already had a past of hooking up. It just wasn't humanly possible, and anyone who said otherwise were fooling themselves.

During my session of trying to rein in my self-control, I was approached by Erick who pushed my buttons even more. I didn't want to leave Claire, but he insisted that we talk in private. However, seeing the look on Wade's face as I talked to Erick was priceless. He was about to shit his pants and I knew why.

I followed Erick out of the kitchen, through the foyer, and up one side of the double staircase. There was an office off to the right with its doors wide open so he motioned for me to go in and sit. Shutting the door behind him, he strolled over and took a seat at the leather topped mahogany desk that probably cost at least a couple grand.

"So what's so important you had to talk to me in private?" I inquired, taking in the room. It was almost completely bare except for the desk, which would make sense since Wade just recently moved in.

Erick steepled his fingers beneath his chin and grinned. "I heard you're fighting Matt Reynolds this Friday night. You know he's one of the best UFC fighters in the circuit, don't you?"

I nodded. "Yes, I do. I've watched him fight many times."

"And you're not nervous?" he wondered.

"Not really," I admitted honestly with a shrug of my shoulders. "He's just a guy, right?"

I wasn't exactly nervous per se, but fighting against someone who could seriously kick my ass was a little daunting. Any time you fight, you face the chance of getting beat, but it's the risk you take. I never got the chance to fight against the best for a title so this fight was going to be my one chance of closure, to feel as if I actually made it to the top.

Erick guffawed and shook his head. "Either you are seriously fearless or severely delusional. I like that about you. Have you thought about fighting professionally again?"

I thought about it every day since the time I left it all behind, but I didn't want him knowing that. In a noncommittal way, I said, "Yeah, I've thought about it, I guess, but I've been away from it for so long that I thought it would be nearly impossible to get started again."

Erick scoffed. "You've got to be shitting me. You've been here all of one week and look how far you've come. I didn't get to watch you fight Chase Benfield, but I sure saw the damage to his face tonight when he showed up. You stuck it to him hard."

Yes, I did, and it felt fucking amazing.

He leaned forward in his chair and rested his arms across the desk, a sly smile spreading across his face. "So with that being said what would you say if I told you I could get you a sponsorship with MMA Pride? Would you be interested?"

"What about Wade? I thought you took him on," I inquired, narrowing my gaze.

"Oh, I did, but it's not set in stone just yet," he noted. "I thought I had made my decision until you came strolling in. Where are you living at now? What do you do?"

I had a strange feeling he had already tried to find out that information, and since my life had been temporarily erased he wouldn't find much. Theoretically, I was actually living in Las Vegas at the moment until the case was solved, and then after that I was going to move to California. I'd stayed in one place for so long—leading the same life—that it seemed almost surreal to be doing something else ... something I loved doing and finally finding someone to share it with. I never thought it would be possible.

"I'm kind of floating around at the moment. I plan on moving to California as soon as my time here is up," I told him.

"Ah, isn't Claire from California?" Erick asked, grinning mischievously. "Are you two moving in together?"

"I don't think that's any of your business. How about we stick to the topic at hand," I suggested dryly. The last thing I wanted was for Claire to end up on his radar. I feared it was already too late, but he had no business knowing anything about our personal lives, especially hers.

Erick lifted his hands in surrender and chuckled. "Okay, sorry. I won't talk anymore about Claire. I don't think she likes me too much anyway from the way she acted toward me this morning. So, again, back to the topic. I'm looking for the best and you are one of the best. I just need to know how much you want it."

Here we go, we're finally getting somewhere. It was time to play the game.

"What exactly do you mean by that? Of course, I would want to fight again. I'd give my left nut to get back in the cage professionally. What do I have to do?"

Lowering his voice, he leaned closer and smiled. "First off, do you think you stand a chance at winning against Matt Reynolds?"

Shrugging a shoulder, I said, "I think it's a fifty-fifty chance. The guy's solid, but as far as strength I would say we handle about the same. Why?"

"Well, like I said, I want the best. If you can beat Matt Reynolds like you did Chase Benfield then I think you deserve the chance to *try* for the sponsorship," he replied with a leer.

Try for the sponsorship?

I scoffed incredulously, "So you're not going to give me the sponsorship if I beat Matt? What else would I have to do to prove that I want it? I think that's proving a shit ton if I can beat him."

"Oh it does, but this decision isn't completely up to just me. There are others that play a part in the decision as well. I'm just the main one who scouts out the talent. Okay, so this is what I'm going to do. On Friday night, I'm going to come to the fight and watch you. If you win I'll find you afterwards and tell you what your next step is. If you don't, then I wish you luck in your endeavors."

Standing from his chair, he extended his hand as he came around the desk. "Do we have a deal?"

Without hesitation, I took his hand and shook it, sealing my fate. His grasp was hard and firm, but mine was harder. "I don't remember there being a next step when I was a part of the Pride. Is that something new?"

Releasing my hand, he chuckled and waved me off. "Trust me, you'll be able to handle it. Besides, just think of all we could do for you. You never got the chance to make it to the top and I can get you there. If you desire fame, it's yours … money, it's yours. All you have to do is show me that you're worth it. Can you do that?"

"You're damn right I can," I promised. "I accept the challenge."

I had to give it to the man, he was a smooth talker. Any rookie fighter would fall hard for it, but not me. I grinned, even though what I really wanted to do was punch the motherfucker in the face, but restraint was necessary.

"Good, I'm glad …" he started to say, but then stopped when his phone rang. He answered the call and I could hear a frantic voice shouting on the other end. Erick's smile immediately faded, and as soon as he ended the call he rushed past me toward the door.

What the hell is going on?

"We have a problem downstairs," he exclaimed.

"What kind of problem?" I asked, following him out of the office toward the staircase.

"It's Claire ... something's happened."

The moment her name slipped out of his mouth I almost lost every single ounce of sanity I had left in my body. Deep down I knew I shouldn't have left her alone. Even to get closer to figuring out the case I knew it was a mistake. I ran down the steps as fast as I could, following behind Erick who headed through the kitchen to the back door.

I didn't like the feeling that crept over my skin, nor did I like the fact that everyone was crowded around in a circle out on the back lawn. There were angry shouts coming from everywhere, but I couldn't concentrate on what they were saying. All I wanted was to find Claire before the panic that crept up my spine turned into full mode panic.

Not caring who I trampled over to get to her, I pushed through the people and shouted, "Get out of the fucking way!" When I finally got through and saw what had transpired, I knew one thing and one thing only ... someone was going to die.

Chapter 25

Claire

Everything moved so fast and it was kind of like I was in a dream. I never expected Chase to grab my arm like he did, nor try to pull me out the back door into the dark. He was drunk and obviously high on something, and thankfully, I didn't give him the chance to do whatever he was going to do. Hence, the reason he was being held back by two of his friends with tiny shards of glass stuck in his head. The broken bottle neck in my hand was evidence as to what I did.

One thing that really pissed me off was when Chase pulled me out the door, I was clearly struggling, but *no one* tried to stop him. It was like they were too afraid to mess with him. *Well, I wasn't.* Mason was nowhere to be seen and neither was Wade. Chase was a scary looking guy, and for a moment the fear clouded my judgment and I couldn't think of anything else other than what was about to happen to me. The farther he led me away from everyone, my survival instincts kicked into overdrive and I reacted, not caring about the consequences.

"Claire!"

Out of all the roaring and screaming, I heard his voice … Mason's voice. When he pushed his way through the crowd and saw me with the bloody bottle in my hand, his face turned into a mask of confusion. However, when he saw Chase being held back by a couple of other men his confusion turned into rage.

Fuming, he stalked toward me, took the broken bottle away, and flung it across the yard. His warm hands grasped my face, holding tight, to keep my gaze on his. "What the hell happened?" he demanded, shaking in anger.

The girl standing behind me had been in the kitchen and saw everything. She was the one who got someone to help me, eventually. Hesitantly, she came up to me and Mason, and when he acknowledged her, she muttered nervously, "Um … Chase had gotten a little rough with her, and I watched him pull her out of the house to out here. I don't know where he was planning on taking her. Anyway, she hit him over the head with a bottle that was sitting on one of the patio tables. He completely deserved it, especially since everyone was too scared of him to help her. My boyfriend was somewhere in the house so I texted him and he came to help."

The moment she said that I knew it was over. Slowly, he turned his head to me, his green gaze turning as black as night. "Claire, is that true? Did he try to hurt you?"

Knowing I had no other option, and regretting what was about to happen, I closed my eyes and nodded once. That nod was all it took before his hands left my face and I felt the rush of air from his immediate absence. I didn't want to open my eyes, but I did. Mason charged toward

Chase and as he did everyone backed out of his way, even Chase's friends who were holding him back from me. His fists flew once, twice, over and over with the sickening sound of flesh hitting flesh. Bones were broken because I could hear the crunching sound echo in the night air as Mason pounded against Chase's face.

Wanting him to stop, I yelled out his name, but nothing came out. I was frozen in time while everyone else moved in slow motion. It wasn't until Wade finally made his appearance and put an end to the brutal beating. He grabbed Mason around the waist and jerked him away, off of Chase. Breathing hard, Mason pushed him off and backed away toward me, keeping his gaze on Wade as he approached. Slowly, Chase got his feet with an evil sneer, which showed off his bloody teeth.

"What the fuck do you think you're doing?" Wade shouted, glaring at Mason. "Get out! *Now!*"

"Oh, I plan on it," Mason hissed, spitting on the ground toward Chase. "I was teaching your friend a lesson. He better be glad I didn't rip out his goddamned arms. If my knowledge is correct, he could be charged with assault and attempted rape from what I hear."

Wade's eyes grew wide, panicked. "You have got to be kidding me! Where's the girl? Is she all right?"

Mason stepped out of the way and glanced at me over his shoulder before replying back to Wade, "Why don't you ask her yourself since she happens to be one of your closest friends."

Wade's confusion only lasted for a second before his gaze landed on me. Shaking his head back and forth, he fisted his hands in his hair and rushed over to me. "No, no, no … Claire, please tell me you're okay," he pleaded, placing his hands on my arms.

Wriggling out of his grasp, I said, "I'll be fine. It's just a couple of bruises. Besides, I shattered a really large bottle of beer over his head."

Angrily, Wade growled and immediately stalked over to Chase, grabbing him by the shirt and hitting him straight in the nose. Chase's head snapped back and a new wave of blood started flowing out of his nose. Keeping a firm hold on Chase's shirt, and even though the two were almost the same size, Wade threw him around as if he were nothing.

Chase landed on the ground, gasping for air, except that didn't stop Wade from delivering a swift kick to his ribs. Bending down, Wade lifted Chase by his shirt and hissed in his face, "That girl over there that you tried to mess with happens to be one of my closest friends, asshole. What's worse is that you brought her out here, alone, to do who knows what with her and I can only imagine what that could've been. If anything would've happened to her you'd be dead right now."

Letting him go, Wade turned away from him and started to come toward me, but stopped when Chase's words froze him in place. "I was only doing what you told me to do," he hissed. "You told me to fuck with Mason any way I knew how, and I did. I went after his bitch. I wasn't going to do anything to her."

I gasped while Mason tensed beside me, ready to fight again if need be. How could Wade do something like that? What was the point?

Glaring back and forth from me to Chase, Wade settled on Chase and snapped, "Wait … what? She's not with him, dumb ass."

Chase spat a mouth full of blood onto the ground and

coughed. "Why don't you ask her then?"

The whole crowd around us watched like vultures, their eyes wide in amusement and anticipation waiting on the next part of the show. That clearly made Wade angrier and you could not only hear it, but feel it when he shouted, "I want everyone to back up, *now*! The show's over, so either go inside or leave before I make you look like him." He pointed to Chase to emphasize his request.

The people in the crowd slowly dispersed, except a couple of guys Wade must've known and of course, Erick. Whatever he and Mason talked about in private it had better be something good to at least make up for the night being a complete disaster. Once everyone was gone, Wade settled his gaze on me, and lifted an angry finger toward Mason. "You're actually *with* this guy, Claire? Are you serious? Why didn't you tell me?" he asked venomously.

Was he actually getting angry with me after everything that just happened? His friend attacked me and his only concern was why I didn't tell him I was dating Mason? Whatever it was, either the sound of my teeth clenching together or the blood rushing to my face, Mason could see that I was about to explode and grabbed my hand to keep me in place by his side. I really wanted to break another bottle over someone's head and this time it was going to be Wade's.

Mason spoke softly in my ear, "Claire, let's just go. You've already been through enough, and if I stay here any longer I'm liable to beat the shit out of your friend and I'd rather not hurt you that way."

"No, not yet," I argued, shaking my head, "I need to say this first."

Mason nodded, letting go of my hand, and stepped

back a pace to give me room.

Taking a deep breath, I glared at Wade and went off, "Let's get something clear, who I'm with or who I'm seeing is none of your damn business. Second, I don't know why you have a problem with Mason when I know he hasn't done anything to you, maybe its jealousy, I don't know, but getting your little crony to do your bidding is just sad. It's wrong and completely immoral. I never thought you would stoop so low."

Desperately, he tried to reach for me, but I jerked away. He let his hand fall, and for a moment I could see the trepidation in his eyes, but then they hardened just as quickly. "It's not like that, Claire. You don't understand," he argued.

"It doesn't matter," I spat. "I'm done here, and I'm done with you. Good-bye, Wade."

I turned to Mason, who kept his complete attention on me, not even acknowledging Wade, and put his arm around my shoulders. "Let's go," he murmured.

I didn't want Mason to have to go into our hotel with bloody hands, so before leaving the house he quickly washed up and we left it all behind. By the time we got to the truck, I was a nervous wreck. Everything came crashing down and I let myself go, bursting into tears. Mason reached over and held my hand as we began the fifteen minute drive back to the hotel in complete silence; the silence was deafening.

It wasn't until we pulled into the parking lot at the hotel that he finally spoke, "I can't believe I wasn't there to protect you. I wanted to kill him, Claire. Just the thought of what he could've done to you set my blood on fire. I don't think I could handle it if anything were to happen to you, not when this is my fight. You shouldn't have to suffer because of me. Which is why …"

He stopped mid-sentence and turned to stare at me with his somber gaze. I knew what he was going to say because his eyes said it all. Little did he know that I still had some fight in me. I wasn't going to let him win and I wasn't going to let him send me home, but it didn't stop me from asking, "You want to send me home, don't you?"

He sighed and nodded his head, his voice rough with conflicting emotions. "I'm sorry, Claire, but it's for the best. It's too dangerous for you to be involved. I need to know that you're safe and away from here … away from me, and the best place for that is back in California."

Defeated, I leaned my head against the seat and stared at him, a lone tear escaping the corner of my eye. "I don't think I can do that," I cried. "Not when everything is coming together and you're so close. From what I understand, Friday night is going to be an important fight for you and I don't want to miss it. You may not need me there, but I need to be. I can't miss it, Mason." He still hadn't even told me what Erick said in their little talk.

Groaning, Mason reached over and twirled a lock of my hair through his fingers. "I had a feeling you would say something like that. There's only one other option."

"What would that be?" I wondered.

"It's simple," he explained. "We need to compromise and I need you to be reasonable. Can you do that?"

Narrowing my gaze, I crossed my arms over my chest and breathed out a heavy sigh. "I think I'm a very reasonable person," I noted halfheartedly.

Mason scoffed, his facial expression claiming otherwise. "Okay, fine, I'm a little hard to reason with, but I do know how to compromise. However, before I do that I need you to tell me something first."

"Anything," he replied. "What do you want to know?"

"I want you to tell me what you and Erick talked about, and if you think Wade is a part of it." Almost hesitantly, he stared at me for a moment as if contemplating his next words. "I want the truth, Mason. I need to know if you're going to be okay."

Please tell me you're going to be okay.

Chapter 26

Mason

Claire wanted the truth.

I gave her the truth, but not all of it. I left out the part about Erick offering me a spot at MMA Pride if I won the upcoming fight against Matt Reynolds. When she found out I kept the truth from her, I could only hope she would understand my reasoning. She needed to leave, that was for certain. If Chase could get to her to hurt me, then there's no telling who else would do the same thing. I made it very clear last night that I would fight for her, and whatever happened with Erick and his sick plans I didn't want her anywhere near it; hence, the reason she was leaving on a plane back to California the Saturday morning after the fight.

The terms of the compromise were simple and thankfully she agreed to them all. For the rest of the week we were both going to stay away from the club until Friday night for the fight, and once we were there she promised to stay with Tyler and Jake in plain sight. In return, I promised to make it up to her in any way she wanted, and of course, her first request was for me to fuck her. Those were her exact words.

Needless to say, my dick got rock hard the second she said that. However, to torture me she decided to take an excruciatingly long shower first. "Claire, if you don't hurry up I'm going to come in there and fuck you in the shower. You have one minute," I shouted impatiently.

She giggled and that was all it took. I marched toward the bathroom only to be stopped by the sound of my phone. "Dammit," I hissed. "I can never catch a break."

Snatching my phone off the bedside dresser, I saw that the incoming call was from Tyler. "This better be good," I barked into the phone. "I'm kind of busy here."

Tyler bellowed, and by the sound of the fumble I'd say he dropped the phone. "Oh shit, man, sorry about that. Give my regards to Claire. I didn't mean to interrupt your play time," he said jokingly.

"Get to it, Tyler. What do you want?"

"Dude, calm down, I'm trying to help you here. The fight is Friday night, right?" he asked, but it sounded more like a statement.

"Yeah, and your point," I remarked. I had other things on my mind at the moment like the naked woman I was about to wrap around my cock.

He chuckled again. "My point is this … you need to be prepared and my father and I want to help you."

"Help me how exactly?"

"You need to train as hard as you can and you're not going to be able to do that in the hotel gym by yourself. My father's going to coach you and I'm going to be your sparring partner. Come on, what do you say?"

"Why are you doing this for me?" I asked skeptically.

Don't get me wrong, Tyler was a good guy, but he didn't know me for shit other than the short amount of time I'd spent with him. He had no reason to want to see me succeed.

"It was my father's idea, Mason. He saw something in you. He said it reminded him of himself when he won his boxing championships back in the day. Not to mention it's a perk for me because I can beat your ass every day to help you get prepared."

I scoffed. "Yeah, keep telling yourself that."

"Anyway," he started again, ignoring my comment, "Claire deserves a winner and we can make you one again. Who knows, maybe this could be your big break going against Matt Reynolds … that's sure to get some eyes looking your way."

Yeah, the wrong ones, I thought. Dripping wet, Claire stepped into the bathroom doorway with her hands on her hips, pursing her lips.

"Should I just tend to myself since the call is more important?" she teased. She licked her lips, gazing down at my growing cock, and then turned on her heel to head back for the shower. I almost lost it the second she started to moan. *Holy shit, she's fucking killing me.*

"Okay, Tyler, I'm in. What time do you want me there?" I asked hurriedly.

"Every day at three o'clock starting today."

"I'll be there," I said and immediately hung up.

Throwing my phone on the bed, I rushed straight into the bathroom. The shower doors were fogged up, but I could still see the outline of Claire giving me a show by rubbing her breasts. "It's about time you got in here," she said, opening the doors.

"You can blame it all on Tyler. He was the one who called," I informed her.

"What did he want with you?"

"He and his dad are going to help me train this week to get ready for the fight. So you and I will be going to the gym every afternoon."

"Fun," she mumbled, smirking devilishly. With hooded eyes, she took her soap and started rubbing it over her breasts and then down to in between her legs.

"Shit," I groaned, not being able to take my eyes away. "I think I might need to stay out here and stare at you a little longer. I could sit here and watch you touch yourself all day," I said, stepping into the shower.

Giggling, she took the soapy washcloth and rubbed it on my arms and my stomach before moving around me to get my back. It felt so damn good, especially when she reached around and cupped my balls with one hand and wrapped her fingers around my cock with the other.

"Well, I'll definitely have to remember you like that. At least it got you to come into the shower quicker." She pressed her tits to my back and worked her hands up and down, over and over. She was relentless and she wasn't stopping.

Placing my hands on the shower wall, I leaned forward and groaned. "Claire, I'm going to come if you don't stop."

"I don't want to stop," she muttered, moving faster. "I want you to come."

I could feel it coming, and it was coming fast. Her hands were like magic, squeezing so tight it could almost pass for the tightness between her legs. "Ah, fuck!" I shouted. Closing my eyes, my body jerked when her relentless pace made me explode. She slowed her rhythm as the last of my release spurt out and washed away.

"How did that feel?" she asked, bending underneath my arm so she could face me. I had her caged in my arms with water dripping all over her body, down her breasts to the slit between her legs.

Pushing her against the wall, I opened her mouth with my lips and licked the water off with my tongue. She wrapped her arms around my neck and held on tight as I grabbed her thighs and lifted her above my waist, spreading her wide.

She gasped as I pushed her against the wall again, gazing down at me with heat-filled eyes. "You said you wanted to get fucked. Are you ready?" I growled huskily.

She moaned breathlessly, "Oh yes, Mason, please."

I sucked on her nipple and bit down at the same time I pushed into her hard. She screamed out and dug her nails in my back, holding on tight as I thrust inside of her hard and fast. The harder I licked and sucked her nipples, the tighter she clenched around my cock. Her breasts were her weakness and I loved that I could get her off by tasting and teasing them.

Wrapping her legs tighter around my waist, I took my hands off her ass and leaned against the wall so I could push harder. "Is … this … what you wanted?" I asked in between kisses to her lips on down to her neck.

Moaning, she nodded her head quickly. "Yes. It feels so good."

Rocking my hips more vigorously, she countered my motions, moving her body along with mine. Her flesh clenched and tightened around my cock, and I knew she was close … so was I. "I'm going to come so hard in you, Claire, and you're going to feel every single drop explode inside of you."

Claire lowered her lips to my neck and bit down, screaming out her orgasm, as I pounded harder, coming inside of her. I held her against the shower wall, breathing hard, letting the aftershocks of our orgasms ebb off before lowering her feet to the floor.

She swayed when I set her down and gazed dreamily into my eyes. "I needed that," she uttered, smiling lazily up at me.

"So did I," I admitted honestly. "I think shower sex might be one of my favorites."

Claire laughed and kissed me again. "I think it's one of mine, too. Now let's go get something to eat."

By the time we got dressed and ate our room service breakfast, my phone rang with another call. This time it was Ryan Griffin. "Hey," I said, answering the phone. "What's going on?"

"Well, for starters, Summer is starting to come around. She asked for you," he said.

My eyes went wide. "Are you serious? Has she said anything?" Claire perked up and turned to face me.

He sighed. "No, she won't talk to anyone else or tell us what happened. I just got here and tried to talk to her, but she refuses. She only wants to talk to you. She's pretty shaken up. Also, I wanted to talk to you about Erick Young."

"What did you find?"

"That's the thing, Mason. I found nothing. I can't find a single thing on a guy named Erick Young. It's like he's a ghost."

Grabbing the keys to the truck, and with Claire on my heels, we rushed out of the room. "I'll be right there," I told him, and hung up the phone.

Ryan was pacing back and forth when Claire and I showed up at the hospital. "When did you get the call she was awake and asking for me?" I asked, rushing up to him.

"It was about an hour ago. As soon as I got the call I came straight here and called you. Hopefully, she'll give us something to go on. Her sister is flying over from Virginia to stay with her until she can be released."

"That's good. At least she won't be alone," I agreed.

Hopefully, with her sister coming it would help her cope and heal with the loss of Austin. I really needed to tell him about Erick and everything that happened, except I didn't want Claire around when I told him. Feeling guilty as hell, I turned to her and smiled apologetically. "Baby, do you mind getting me a cup of coffee, please? I could really use it right now."

Her eyes went wide, skeptical. "Oh, I didn't think you drank it. I hadn't seen you drink any the whole time we've been here," she noted diligently.

I should've known I couldn't get anything by her. She was a very perceptive person, seeing things that no one would expect, so I answered as best as I could, "Actually, I hardly ever drink it these days, but today I'm going to need it if I'm going to get through the day."

Appeased by my answer, she nodded and turned to

Ryan. "Would you like a cup, too, Mr. Griffin?" she asked politely.

"I would, thank you."

"Okay, I'll be right back." She smiled at us both and turned on her heel, heading straight for the elevator. As soon as she disappeared behind the door, Ryan chuckled and slapped me on the shoulder.

"All right, she's gone. I knew exactly what you were doing. What do you need to tell me that you didn't want to say around her?"

Sighing, I averted my gaze away from the elevator to him and replied, "I finally talked one on one with our guy. He wanted to offer me a spot at MMA Pride, but only if I win the fight this Friday night."

"So, is that it? You win, you get the contract?" he questioned.

I glanced at the elevator quickly to make sure Claire hadn't returned before speaking again. "No, that's not all. He told me that winning is the first step and that after the fight he would tell me what the next step is. I don't know what it is just yet, but I think we can assume it's another fight."

"Shit," he grumbled. "Make sure you keep your tracker on at all times. Keep in touch with me as much as possible, and if I don't hear from you I'll find you."

I nodded. "If I win the fight on Friday, I'll call you Saturday morning once I drop Claire off at the airport. I'll let you know what Erick says and what I'll be doing."

"Is there a reason you're not telling Claire all of this?" he asked curiously. "She seems to be able to handle anything that comes her way."

I scoffed. "You don't even know the half of it. At the

party last night I had an old rival try to attack her. While I was talking to Erick he had grabbed her and dragged her outside. I don't know what he planned on doing to her, but she stopped him by hitting him over the head with a beer bottle."

Ryan scowled, but then glanced down at my hands, which were a little torn up from beating them against Chase's face. With a sly grin turning up the corner of his lips, he pointed to my hands and said, "I see you handled it as well. Give me this guy's name and we'll run it through the system. Me and you both know what could've happened if she didn't fight back."

"Yeah, I know, which is why I want her away from here. I didn't tell her about what Erick said because if I did it would be harder to get her to leave. If she thinks I'm in trouble she's going to want to stay. I need her gone so I know she's safe," I told him. I hated that I even brought Claire into all this mess, but I wouldn't have gotten anywhere without her.

Ryan placed a hand on my shoulder. "I understand, and just so you know she just got off the elevator."

"All right, guys, here you go," she said, handing us the coffees. "I didn't know if you wanted sugar so I made sure to bring a couple of packs."

"Thank you, Claire," Ryan responded, taking two packs of sugar.

She offered some to me, but I shook my head. I didn't like coffee at all so adding sugar wasn't going to help anyway. "Thank you for getting this for us," I mentioned gratefully.

"You're welcome. Have you talked to Summer yet?" She took the seat next to Ryan and gazed up at me.

"No, I was telling him about last night and what happened to you," I informed her. "If you don't mind I'd like you to tell him what all happened while I talk to Summer. Can you do that for me?"

"Yeah," she replied sadly. "I'll tell him."

Taking my coffee, I turned toward Summer's door and knocked on it gently before going inside. When I turned the corner she was wide awake and watching the news. "Summer?" I called gently.

She turned her head slowly and spotted me, her voice gravelly and weak. "Mason? Is that really you?"

Her skin was still sickly pale, but I could see somewhat of an improvement with the knowledge in her eyes. She didn't look as lost. Approaching the side of the bed, I reached out and took her hand before sitting down in the chair. "Yeah, it's me ... Mason Bradley. Do you remember me?"

"I do," she whispered. "I'm sorry for not speaking to you yesterday. You remind me so much of Austin." Chin trembling, she closed her eyes and squeezed my hand.

"It's okay, Summer, I need you to talk to me. I know you probably don't want to have to do this, but I need to know where you've been the last two weeks and what happened. I need to know what happened to Austin," I finished cautiously.

Tears poured down her cheeks and she shook her head. "I can't remember it all, Mason. I try to think, but it's all a blur. The past two weeks have been nothing but a giant hole in my brain. I heard the doctor say I have post traumatic stress and that's why I'm having trouble remembering everything, and that all my memories will most likely come back to me at some point. I may not remember where I've been, but I sure as hell can remember the pain. My heart aches, Mason, and in any moment I feel like I'm going to lose my mind and go insane."

She broke out in sobs and curled into a ball, hiding her face behind her arms. "Shh ... Summer you're going to be okay, I promise. Just please bear with me for another minute." Leaning over the bed, I scooped her upper body into my arms and put her head on my chest, rocking her. I was never good at offering comfort, it always made me uncomfortable, but I knew Summer needed it.

Her breathing started to slow and she wiped the tears away with the palms of her hands. "I got a text from him," she muttered softly. "That night I got a text from Austin telling me he needed me to pick him up, but when I got there it wasn't him waiting for me."

"Who was it and what did they look like? Where did Austin text you to meet him?" I didn't want to overwhelm her, but I had to know.

"I don't know what he looked like; I couldn't see his face. He wore a hat and dark glasses, but he looked young, maybe mid-twenties. The text from Austin told me to meet him in the parking lot of the MGM. When I didn't see him I got out of the car and looked around. I didn't realize the mistake I made until I was grabbed and put in the back of another car."

"How many were with you?"

"There were two of them. I didn't see much after that because they blindfolded me. I tried to talk to them, to fig- ure out what was going on, but they ignored me."

Taking a deep breath, I paused before asking the next question. "Did they hurt you?" I asked through clenched teeth, waiting on the answer.

It was the question I hated asking any female after they'd been in a hostage type situation. Her medical report indicated that she wasn't raped, so knowing that gave me a little bit of peace, but she still went through an ordeal that put her in a complete catatonic state. It was scary seeing people when they were like that. It was almost like they were dead, but with a beating heart.

"No, they didn't hurt me physically, other than pulling me this way and that. I think the damage came from hearing and not seeing. I never got to see Austin alive again, but I heard him as he struggled to breathe, begging them to let me go. I couldn't go to him as he called my name. I felt so helpless."

"There was nothing you could do, Summer," I murmured soothingly, "but I'm here to do something about it. I'm close to figuring out who was responsible for this. Do you remember seeing Austin with a man that had a dragon tattoo on his neck at the UFC fight?"

Slowly lifting her gaze to me, she shook her head, furrowing her brows. "I don't know. I didn't go to the big fight that night. I wasn't feeling good so I stayed in the hotel."

"So Austin never mentioned anything about a man maybe wanting to offer him a sponsorship or anything?" I inquired curiously.

"He did mention something about it, but he didn't give me specifics. He was afraid of getting his hopes up, but I could see the excitement in his eyes. He said if he could get the sponsorship he could open up the restaurant he's always wanted. The day it all happened was the day he was supposed to meet somebody to talk about it. He told me I didn't need to go so I stayed behind. If I would've gone none of this would have happened."

"You don't know that and you need to stop analyzing all of this with the 'ifs.' None of this is your fault, and if Austin talked to the guy I've been dealing with then I know how easy it would have been to give in. This guy is a manipulator and he's damn well good at it. I'm going to take him down, Summer. You have my promise on that."

She nodded quickly and the tears started to fall again. "Thank you, Mason. Austin missed you so much. He used to watch you fight and he would always point out what moves he taught you. I used to laugh at him every time. I honestly don't know how I'm going to go back home without him. How am I going to get past this?"

Standing up, I squeezed her hand one more time before letting go. "You *will* get past it, Summer. Austin was a fighter and so are you. That's what made you two perfect for each other. When you get back to Virginia, if you don't think you can handle it there, then you are more than welcome to rent my house while you get on your feet. It's still the same house I lived in when you and Austin were in North Carolina."

Sighing, she looked away, fiddling with the blankets, and asked meekly, "Where will you be staying if I'm in your house?"

"I'm moving to California as soon as I'm done here in Vegas. My family is there," I told her. I didn't exactly want to tell her that I was moving there to be with the girl I loved, especially after she just lost the man she loved.

Time was moving swiftly away and by the clock on the wall I had one hour left until I needed to be at Tyler's gym. Also, Summer's eyes started to look heavy and I knew she needed her rest.

"Take care of yourself, okay? The offer to my house is still open if you change your mind," I assured her.

Sadly, she smiled. "Thank you, Mason. I appreciate that, and if I decide to go that route I'll call you." I turned to walk out of the room, but the desperation in her voice stopped me cold. "Mason," she cried.

I glanced back at her quickly, at her wide panicked eyes. Her chest heaved up and down with her short, anxious breaths. "Please be careful," she sobbed. "I don't want anything to happen to you, too."

"Don't you worry about me. All you need to worry about is getting yourself better. I'll talk to you soon. Your sister should be here sometime today." With that, I said my good-bye and left the room.

Claire was staring at her phone, but when she saw me, her eyes went wide and she jumped out of her seat. Ryan also got out of his and came over to find out the verdict.

"Is everything okay? How did it go in there?" she asked.

I glanced at Ryan and then back to her. "She told me what happened, but there was still a lot she wasn't able to help me with. However, there was one thing she told me that confirmed one of my decisions."

Claire narrowed her gaze in confusion and responded, "And what exactly would that be?"

Taking her face in my hands, I gazed down into her majestic blue eyes. "As much as I hate to see you go, from what Summer told me if I ever needed you as far away from here as possible now would be the time. They took her, Claire, and made her listen to Austin fight. She heard him die and there was nothing she could do about it. I'm not going to let them get to you to get to me."

Her eyes misted over and she nodded. "Holy shit, I can't believe someone would do that. For you, I'll make sure to leave just as planned."

She must have seen the pain in my face because she didn't fight me on it like she normally would. I just wanted her safe, and being around me only made her more of a target.

Chapter 27

Claire

On the way to the gym, Mason explained everything about the conversation he had with Summer. I couldn't imagine what she went through; however, it still didn't deter me from wanting to stay with Mason during this whole thing. We compromised and I was going to honor that. If I stayed he wouldn't be able to concentrate on his tasks without worrying about me.

"Did you tell Ryan about what happened last night?" Mason asked.

"Yeah, he asked if I wanted to press charges, but I told him no. Maybe next time he'll think twice about messing with a female. I regret not kicking him in the balls with my stilettos when I had the chance."

Mason cringed. "Ouch, that would've hurt, but he deserved it."

We arrived at the gym right on time, and when we got inside Tyler and his dad were already prepared. Stephen shook Mason's hand and Tyler did the same before coming to my side. "Are you going to watch us or are you go-

209

ing to go do your thing in the other room?" he asked.

Mason lifted a brow and smirked, taking the tape from Stephen so he could wrap his hands. "Actually, I think I'm going to watch you guys today. Maybe I can learn a thing or two," I teased.

Mason took off his T-shirt, which happened to be a Duke basketball shirt, his favorite college basketball team, and handed it to me. It smelled just like him and it took all I had not to bury my nose in it and breathe him in. His muscles rippled and flexed as he warmed up and every time he caught me staring he would grin at me and wink. I watched him train for about an hour when a text came through on my phone. I groaned when I saw it was from Wade.

Wade: Please call me, Claire. I need to tell you I'm sorry.

Me: You just did. Now leave me alone.

Wade: That's not good enough. I'll see you Friday at the club.

Rolling my eyes, I didn't even bother to respond because there was nothing more I wanted to say to him. Mason surely wouldn't like it if he saw me talking to Wade at the club, especially after what happened at the party.

"Hey, Claire!" Mason shouted from the cage.

I glanced up to see him and Tyler motioning me forward. "What do you want?" I hollered back. After putting my phone in my gym bag along with Mason's shirt, I approached the ring with my arms crossed at the chest, waiting on a reply.

Mason jumped down and landed in front of me, dripping sweat and sexy as hell. Taking my hand, he pulled me up to the cage and helped me inside. "We're going to show you some defense moves," he explained. "After last night you need to know more than just how to smash a bottle over someone's head."

Tyler scowled and shook his head. "You know, I can't believe I didn't go last night. I would've kicked Chase's ass."

I scoffed. "Trust me, he got his ass kicked last night. Mason did a really good job at that."

Mason smirked and grabbed my shoulders. "Okay, first things first, I'm going to teach you how to get out of someone's grasp if they grab you from behind." He glanced at Tyler and pointed to me. "All right, Tyler, put your arms around her, but if I see you trying to cop a feel I'm going to beat your ass, got it?"

Tyler chuckled and put one arm around my waist and the other just under my throat to around my shoulders. Mason circled around us, explaining what I had to do to get out of Tyler's arms. After several failed attempts, I finally started to get an idea on how to maneuver my body. It was empowering learning how to protect myself. Mason taught me several defense moves before moving to offensive techniques. It was actually fun learning the different ways to strike and all of the different submission holds. When it came time for the groundwork, Mason made Tyler step back so he could grapple with me himself.

Tyler scoffed and glared halfheartedly at Mason, but his voice came out teasingly. "I see how you want to be. You let her hit and punch me, but you won't let me roll around the floor with her. That's just wrong, dude."

Mason and I both laughed while Tyler jumped out of

the cage and went to work out on one of the weight machines. "Where do you want me?" I asked.

He stalked behind me, putting his hands on my hips,
and whispered in my ear, "I want you down on the mat and
I'm going to straddle your waist."

I did as he said and he took me by the wrists and held
them above my head. "Okay, now try to get loose," he
commanded.

I tried with all the strength I had, but I couldn't get
out of his hold. He smiled down at me, and the more I
fought the bigger his smile got. Relaxing my body, I let
my arms and legs go limp. Biting my lip, I gazed up at his
green gaze and begged in a soft, husky voice, "Kiss me,
Mason."

Letting my arms go, he took my face in his hands and
lowered his lips to mine. Deepening the kiss, I could feel
his guard slipping with each second that passed by. Only a
few more and I'd have him. Once I slid one of my legs
free, I pushed up with my body and kicked my leg over
him as he toppled off to the side, ending with me straddling his waist.

"I got free, sucker," I shouted triumphantly.

Mason put his hands on my hips and held me down
on his cock, which I could feel getting harder by the second. "I think we might've just found another form of
foreplay, don't you think? That was fucking hot."

Nodding excitedly, I lowered my head and whispered
in his ear, "Oh yeah, and you are more than welcome to
show me your moves anytime you want. Better yet, why
don't we use both your talents? You can pin me down *and*
handcuff me with your cuffs. I can get the best of both
worlds."

Mason groaned, biting my earlobe. "You better be careful what you ask for, baby, because right now that sounds like a great idea. I'd love nothing more than to see you at my mercy."

"Well, then what are you waiting for?"

I was ready to go ...

Chapter 28

Claire

THREE DAYS LATER

The week went by too quickly and I regretfully counted down the days until I would be on a plane back to California. During the daytime, I showed Mason my favorite spots and even took him to the Hoover Dam. I tried to convince him to go on a helicopter ride through the Grand Canyon, but he said if we died then no one would be able to solve the case. *Honestly, I think he's just afraid of heights and didn't want to tell me.*

With that being said, we stayed on the ground. The afternoons were all tied up with his training at the gym with Tyler and his dad. He tried to get me up there with him in the ring, but I enjoyed just watching him move. Tyler was a great opponent, working well with Mason, and one of these days I knew deep down he would get noticed by the right people. His father had faith in him and wasn't so bad himself being a retired boxer. The three made the perfect team.

Tonight was the last night I would completely have

with Mason before the big fight against Matt Reynolds. I had a feeling he was keeping something from me, but I didn't know how to get it out of him. Every time I would mention Erick's name he would stiffen and try to change the subject. Eventually, I just gave up, because no matter what I did or what I said he still wouldn't tell me. I had to trust he was doing the right thing.

While Mason was in the shower, I changed into the last set of lingerie he hadn't seen on me since being in the Sin City. The red, mesh and lace babydoll was mostly see through with a set of matching red thongs. It was definitely sinful. Climbing into bed, I pulled out my phone and scrolled to that same picture of me and Mason all those months ago at Melissa's wedding. We really needed to get some new pictures taken; ones with happy memories. Lost in my thoughts, I didn't even know Mason was there watching me until he spoke.

"Claire, are you okay? What's on your mind?"

I looked up just in time to see him release the towel from around his waist and use it to dry off his back and run it through his hair. It was hard to think or answer him with him standing there dripping wet and completely naked. He knew what he was doing, especially, when I looked up to see the smirk on his face.

"Are you going to answer me? What's on your mind?" he repeated.

Leaning my head against the headboard, I smiled and turned my phone to him so he could see the picture. Melissa had snatched mine and Mason's phones so she could take them, to show proof that he and I had a connection. Mason moved closer and sat down on the bed beside me, taking my phone.

"Oh wow," he breathed in disbelief, eyes going wide. "I can't believe you kept this picture of us after all this time. I figured you would've deleted it after I left."

I snorted. "Trust me, I wanted to, but I couldn't let it go."

He placed my phone on the bedside table and reached over to grab his. "You know, it's funny because I couldn't let mine go either," he admitted, showing me the same picture on his phone. Sighing, he looked at it again. "It was a reminder of what I lost."

Gently, I took his phone and set it aside. "I'm not lost anymore, Mason. You found me, and even though that picture brings back bad memories it still had its good ones, too. I remember that night being one of the best nights of sex I'd ever had."

"Really?" he asked incredulously. "How about we make tonight another one as well?"

Slowly, I pulled away the sheets that covered my body, and exposed the lacy red lingerie underneath before replying to him, "Aren't you supposed to refrain from all kinds of sexual activity before a big fight? I could've sworn I'd heard that somewhere."

Mason threw the sheets back further and climbed on top of me, separating my legs with his knee. "Yes, we're supposed to, but not everyone goes by that. There's no way in hell I'm going to let something like that keep me from making love to you tonight, especially now that I've seen you in that," he said, gazing passionately up and down my body.

Inch by inch, he lowered his lips to my thigh and kissed his way up to my stomach, lifting my lingerie as he went. "The only thing that's going to get me through all of this when you leave is the thought that no matter what happens I'll be able to come home to you every day once I make it back. I'll be able to touch you like this," he murmured, caressing his thumbs across my peaked nipples, "and like this," he continued, slowly trailing his fingers down my stomach. He pushed my thongs aside and slipped a finger inside the heat between my legs.

"Mason," I breathed, gripping onto his arm as he moved it back and forth with his thrusts.

Arching my back, I gave into his touch, moaning in delight as he explored me with his fingers. All too soon, he pulled them out, leaving me breathless. Slowly, he slid my underwear down my legs. Using his tongue, he licked a path all the way up my leg to the inside of my thigh before sucking on the spot that ached to feel his touch. Nuzzling my clit with his nose, he kept his gaze on mine as he fucked me with his tongue. I was getting close to losing control and before I could hit that peak, Mason chuckled and left me hanging while continuing his torturous path up my body to my breasts.

"That's not funny," I growled. Mason smiled and bit one of my nipples teasingly through my top.

"Your orgasms tonight will all be with me inside you, Claire. Just like mine will all be with me inside you."

He lifted my lingerie, exposing my bare flesh, and tossed it on the floor before wrapping his warm lips around my breast, making everything tighten and throb with need. Mason lifted his head and gazed down at me with his sensual green eyes. Pressing his hips against mine, he positioned himself between my legs, grazing his cock along my opening as he swiveled his hips in a slow circle.

"Claire," he whispered.

Taking my face in his hands, he lowered his lips to mine and stayed there, breathing me in with just the gentlest of touches. When he pulled back, he caressed my cheeks with his thumbs and tenderly pushed inside me until he was all the way in.

"Other than touching you and seeing your beautiful face every day when I come back to you, do you want to know the main thing I look forward to the most?" he asked, groaning as he slid in and out of my body.

Panting, I bit my bottom lip and nodded. "Tell me," I replied breathlessly.

Even though the room was dim with the lights of the city below giving us a semblance of light, I could see the sheen of tears misting in his eyes. "The thing I look forward to the most is coming home to you every day and being able to look into your eyes and tell you that I love you. I'm going to tell you that every single day for the rest of my life."

Tears began to stream down my face, but I chuckled through them. "I look forward to that, too, Mason. I love you so much."

There was no rushing, no going fast as Mason and I made love. It wasn't the usual heated and wild sex we'd been having; it was something different ... something I felt all the way down to my soul. This was what love felt like and it was beautiful, it was what I'd been waiting for. Mason pressed his lips to mine and slowly caressed my tongue with his while thrusting deep and slow. His torturous pace only heightened my desire, so I locked my legs around his waist and held on while moving my hips against his.

Picking up his pace, Mason moaned and murmured in

my ear, "Let it go, baby, so I can come inside you."

His words were all it took to send me over the edge. Gripping his shoulders, my skin tingled and my toes curled as the longest and strongest orgasm I had ever felt exploded across my entire body. Mason's body jerked as he filled me with his release, his cock pulsating. I loved the feel of him coming inside of me, and knowing that he felt the same level of ecstasy while still being connected to my body.

Mason smiled down at me without a single drop of sweat or heaving for air. Biting his lip, he leaned down and kissed me more firmly, lifting my back off the bed so my breasts were brought up straight to his lips.

"Are you ready for the real fun to begin?" he asked, licking a taut nipple. My body trembled and I could already feel myself tightening around his growing cock. "That's right, baby. I see that you *are* ready. Going slow was my way of showing you how much I love you and that I will treat that love with tender hands. However, now … I will show you what my determination and loyalty to you feels like."

Oh, wow, here we go. I could see it in his eyes it was going to be an interesting night.

He grinned as he pushed harder and faster between my legs. "Damn, you're getting so wet for me. I take it you like me showing my emotions this way."

"You have no idea," I breathed, moaning with each thrust. "How many emotions are you going to show me?"

"There are too many to count, baby. Just bear with me because it's going to be a long, emotional ride tonight. I want you to feel what I feel," he murmured.

I do, and I always will.

Chapter 29

Claire

FIGHT NIGHT

The whole morning and afternoon Mason pretty much kept to himself and didn't say a whole lot. I figured it was because tonight was the big fight and he needed to stay focused. However, I couldn't shake the feeling that something was going on that he wasn't telling me about. I left him alone, though, and let him do his thing. He didn't go to the gym, but as I sat on the bed I watched him practice and warm up in the hotel room before it was time to leave. He loaded up on a plate of pasta and drank an energy drink to get him started while I ate my favorite dish of parmesan crusted chicken. We stayed up almost all night, but at least he slept in until late morning. I was worried it would affect his fighting, but he seemed to be going strong.

Before arriving at the club, Mason's phone rang with an incoming call, and when I handed him his phone, I recognized the number as one from the hospital. For the past couple of days, Summer had been doing better and was showing signs of improvement. I could only hope she was being discharged so she could go home to be with her family. Mason answered the call and I could hear the happiness in his voice as he spoke to her.

As soon as Mason hung up, he turned to me with a sad, but peaceful smile. "Summer's being discharged right now, and since it's late, her and her sister are going to stay the night before getting a flight back to the east coast. Austin's body will be flown over as well so his family can have his funeral."

"When are they doing that? Will you be able to go to it?" I asked sadly.

Mason shrugged. "I don't know. Summer didn't have the details, but I'm assuming it'll be in the next three to four days. I'd like to go, but she said she understood if I wouldn't be able to make it."

"Well, at least she gets to go home and start the healing process. I can't imagine the scars she'll have over all of this," I mentioned sadly.

Mason nodded, but stayed silent as we rode the rest of the way to the club. We pulled into the parking lot and the crowd was already backed up around the building. "Wow," I breathed. "These people must really want to see you and Matt fight tonight."

Mason snorted. "Matt's one of the best fighters out there. I'm sure most of them are here for him." It was the longest set of words he'd spoken to me all day, and I could hear the doubt in his voice. The last thing I wanted was for him to get psyched out. He was an amazing fighter and even though I didn't know who Matt Reynolds was, I knew Mason would be able to take him down.

Reaching over, I squeezed the hand he had fisted in

his lap. "Either way, Mason, you're going to do great. I have complete and utter faith in you," I assured him. "You can do this."

We bypassed all of the people in line; a lot of the women waiting hooted and hollered at Mason, wishing him good luck, while some screamed for him to fuck them. As soon as we got inside we went straight to the hidden staircase to go up to Jake's office.

"All for Matt, huh?" I teased sarcastically. "Did you always have women calling after you like that?"

Sighing, he said, "Sometimes, but that was a long time ago. You have nothing to worry about." Taking my hand, I followed him the rest of the way up the steps. I know I had nothing to worry about, but it would take some getting used to if I had to be around women fawning over him all the time.

Mason wanted me with him while he changed into his fighter shorts and taped his hands; he didn't want me alone. He also wanted to ask Jake if he wouldn't mind sitting with me and making sure I wasn't by myself while he fought.

Once we reached the top of the steps, the door to Jake's office was open so we went right in to find him at his desk. Lifting his head, he smiled and motioned for us to sit on the plush, leather couch in front of him.

"Hey, kitten," he said to me, then to Mason he asked, "Are you ready for the fight? We're going to have a full house tonight."

"Yes, I saw that already," he responded. "I'm ready, though."

Jake got to his feet and came around the desk. "All right, you two, I'm going to go downstairs and get me a drink before the fight. You have twenty minutes until you need to be down there, Mason."

Mason nodded. "I understand. We'll be down there soon. However, I do have a simple request."

Jake leaned against his desk, furrowing his brows. "What do you need from me, son?"

Mason glanced over at me quickly before looking up at Jake. "Would you mind staying with Claire during the fight? It's not safe for her to be alone right now."

Crossing his arms over his chest, his eyes went wide, panicked. "What do you mean it's not safe? Why would Claire not be safe here?"

This time it was me who answered, "Jake, it's a long story, and I'll tell you once we get seated for the fight. The main thing right now is that I not be alone. I was attacked by Chase Benfield the other day and Mason's afraid that something else might happen to me."

Jake's face turned bright red, the muscles in his jaw clenching as he reached behind him to grab the phone on his desk. He dialed a couple of numbers, and as soon as a voice spoke out on the other end, Jake snapped into the phone, "If you see Chase Benfield anywhere near my premises I want him gone immediately! Do you under-stand? I don't care what you have to do, but I don't want that fucker anywhere near my front doors."

He slammed the phone down and rubbed his temples before eyeing me. "Why am I the last one to find out any-thing? I want you to tell me everything. I should've known he would be trouble."

"That's not even the half of it, Jake," I informed him warily. "So do you mind sitting with me? I'm sure Tyler wouldn't mind either."

"Kitten, you don't even have to ask. I'll wait for you both down there." He patted me on the shoulder as he walked by and closed the door on his way out.

Mason got to his feet and changed out of his jeans and shirt into his fighter shorts with the eagle on the side. He started to tape up his hands, but stopped when I approached him and ran my fingers over the eagle tattoo on his arm.

"Mason, I can tell when something's eating away at someone. I know you're keeping something from me and I trust that you're making the right decision by doing so. Whatever it is, just know that I stand behind you no matter what. I don't want to see you lose this fight because you're worried about something. Clear your mind and focus only on doing your best and being the best fighter you can be. There's nothing else you need to worry about. That all will still be there after you fight."

Finally looking up at him, he abruptly pulled me into his arms and held me tight. I laid my head on his bare chest and breathed him in while he laid his soft, warm lips on my forehead. "How did you get so wise?" he asked teasingly.

I laughed. "I don't know. I just felt like you needed those words of encouragement. You haven't spoken to me much today and it had me worried."

Grabbing my shoulders, he pulled me away from him and took my face in his hands. "I've had a lot on my mind today and I'll admit I've been worried sick about your safety. If I had my way you would already be back in California right now. I'm only letting you be here because you wanted to be. I'm not going to make your choices for you."

He kissed me on the lips and lingered there, placing his forehead to mine. "Thank you, though. I needed those words of encouragement, by the way. It definitely helped," he murmured sweetly.

"You're welcome, but now you need to finish taping your hands. I'm ready to watch you kick ass."

Mason chuckled and resumed to tape his hands while I watched. *Please let him win.*

Jake was by the bar drinking a tumbler of whiskey when we got downstairs. When he spotted me and Mason he held out a glass of wine. I graciously took it, gulping it down. I needed it to get through the fight.

"Are we ready to go in there?" Jake asked, lifting a brow at Mason.

Mason nodded, keeping his face blank and devoid of any emotion. It was different seeing him like that, but I knew he was getting his mind right for the fight. It was actually kind of sexy seeing the tough, alpha male side of him.

I must've been smiling like an idiot because Jake chuckled under his breath and snapped his fingers in front of my face. "Are you done staring at him now? We have to go," he announced with a wink of his eye.

Grabbing his glass of whiskey and a bottle of wine for me, Jake set off toward the arena while Mason and I followed. Mason put his arm around my waist, and leaned down to whisper in my ear, "While I'm in the cage, stay where I can see you. Don't go wandering off by yourself, okay?"

"Don't worry about me, Mason, I'll be fine. I'm not going to go anywhere by myself. Anyway, you need to keep your mind on the fight ... not me. This is about you and showing people what you can do and what you're made of. I know you can do this."

When we got into the arena, Mason pulled me aside and crushed his lips to mine, claiming me with his tongue. The people around us whistled and made some inappropriate comments, but Mason didn't care. Lifting me in his arms, he held me tight and before putting me down, he whispered gruffly in my ear, "Thank you for having faith in me. I love you."

"And I love you. Now go!"

Setting me on my feet, he walked me over to Jake and ran off to the back of the arena where the announcer was getting primped for the camera, along with Tyler and his dad. Jake nudged my arm with his elbow and pointed toward the ring.

"All right, kitten, let's go get our seats. I'm assuming Tyler and Stephen are going to be Mason's entourage tonight?"

With a smile on my face, I watched as Tyler and his dad gave Mason a pep talk and helped him warm up. "It looks like it," I said. "The three make a great team."

"Tyler and Stephen are good people. They've worked hard for what they have. Mason should consider hiring them if he wants to keep fighting," he pointed out.

"You know, he hasn't really talked about his fighting much. I don't even know what he's going to do."

It made me wonder what Mason's plan was going to

be after everything finally came to an end. He said he was going to take time off from the force, except now that he had a chance to pursue his fighting again, would he? *I don't think he even knows what he wants to do.* Either way, I supported him no matter what he wanted to do in life. If it was his dream then I wanted him to live it. Twenty-seven was too old to try and get into dancing professionally. I missed my chance years ago, but if one of us could live out their dream then he needed to go for it.

"We have one minute, kitten. This is going to be one hell of a fight," Jake exclaimed.

People kept pouring in through the doors and the seats were already packed with none to spare except the one beside me. The front row seats around the cage were only for people Jake approved such as the professional UFC fighters and all the people associated with them. There were camera crews all around getting the cameras ready to host the fight live since Matt Reynolds was the highlight.

Leaning over toward Jake, I made sure to lower my voice so no one else could hear. "How much do you make doing the whole pay per view thing?"

Jake shrugged. "It all depends on who's fighting. Tonight with Matt being here I'd estimate it being several hundreds of thousands of dollars."

"Wow," I breathed. "That's amazing. Not to mention the money you get from the people that are actually here. So I guess with paying the film crew there would be a lot of leftover money. Who gets the rest of that … you?" I took a sip of my wine and almost choked on it with his next words.

Rolling his eyes, Jake scoffed incredulously. "Hardly,

my dear. I do take a small percentage, but I'm not a greedy man. I think you know that. The rest gets divided between the fighters."

"Are you serious?" I sputtered. "You mean Mason is going to get some of the money? He never told me that."

"It's because he doesn't know," Jake remarked slyly. "Not many fighters around here will fight just because they like the sport. They fight to get the benefits of it, the money … the fame. Mason never asked about any of that. I thought it would be a nice surprise for him."

I couldn't begin to imagine what Mason was going to say when he's given thousands of dollars for just one night of fighting. Mason lived comfortably in North Carolina, but he wasn't brought up in all the finer things in life like my family had. He worked hard for everything he had and it was time he got his break. I couldn't wait for Jake to tell him.

"Thank you for everything, Jake," I murmured, hugging him tight. "It'll be one hell of a surprise."

"What kind of surprise you talking about?" someone spoke out beside me. The seat beside me was empty just a second ago, but now it was occupied by a guy I didn't want to speak to ever again.

Jake looked over my shoulder and grinned. "Wade, you made it! Tonight's going to be a good one, isn't it?"

Shit! This isn't good. The last thing Mason needs to see is Wade right now. Not to mention, I hadn't had the chance to tell Jake that it was basically Wade's fault about Chase.

Leaning back in my seat, I gave Wade a glowering side-long glance, but then turned my face straight ahead toward the cage. He was dressed in a pair of expensive dark blue jeans and a thin gray sweater which had to cost over two hundred dollars according to the brand label. He never dressed like that or even cared about wearing designer clothes when I was here. He leaned forward and rested his elbows on his knees so he could get a better view of Jake on my other side.

"Yeah, it's going to be a good one. I just wish you could land me something like this," he grumbled half-heartedly. He tried not to sound bitter, but I could hear the resentment in his voice. He was mad because Mason was the one picked to fight.

"Isn't that what Erick's for?" I stated smugly, not looking at him. "He's your agent, is he not?"

Before Wade could reply, Jake cut in, "You've been asked to fight here, Wade. That's how you got noticed in the first place. Anyway, Matt was the one who requested Mason. If you have a problem with that you might want to ask him. Although, I don't think that would be a good idea."

Arrogantly, Wade huffed and added, "I could beat him. I'm sure I could beat Mason, too."

Rolling my eyes, I turned to him and glared. "What is your problem? You were never like this before. If you want to apologize to me then this isn't the way to go."

"Well, it's not like you're going to forgive me anyway, Claire. You've ignored me all week when I tried to tell you I was sorry," he snapped. "I don't know what else to do."

"What's with you two?" Jake asked, narrowing his eyes at us both.

"It's just a misunderstanding," Wade said. "Something happened at my party and it got a little out of hand."

"Seriously, Wade? A little out of hand?" I hissed, scowling at him. "You don't even know what Chase was going to do to me. I doubt you would think it was a mis-understanding if that bastard had raped me out in the woods. You were the one who started it all in the first place."

"What!" Jake growled, about to get to his feet. I placed a hand on his shoulder to keep him in his seat while I finished with Wade.

"Hell, Wade, what if it wasn't me? What if Mason was with another girl and something like that happened to her? Would you even care? Something tells me that you wouldn't. It makes me sick, and I don't want to have any-thing to do with you or the piece of shit people you hang out with. You've changed, Wade, and honestly I don't like what I see. So I'm going to say this one last time … stay away from me, and if you know what's good for you you'll stay away from Mason."

Sighing, Wade got to his feet and stared down at me, clenching his hands into tight fists at his side. Through gritted teeth, he spat, "I'm sorry, Claire, but unfortunately that's not going to happen."

Wide-eyed, I watched him stalk off through the throngs of people and disappear into the crowd. He wasn't going to leave Mason alone and he just confirmed it. *Why did I agree to leave tomorrow?* When I turned my head, my eyes caught a familiar set of green eyes staring angrily my way.

"Shit! Has he been watching the whole time?" I asked, turning to Jake.

"Yeah, for the most part, but it'll be good for him to feel the anger. He'll take that frustration out on Matt and hopefully kick his ass." Jake paused, releasing a heavy sigh, and peered back toward the door where Wade disappeared out of. "I don't know what's going on with Wade, but he's changed over the past year or so. I barely recognize him anymore."

"I know what you mean," I mumbled. "So much has changed since I've been here last, and with everything that's happened I think I'm going to head back home. My flight leaves tomorrow late morning."

"Is Mason going with you?" Jake asked.

I shook my head. "No, he's not. He said he wanted to stay here a little while longer."

"And you're okay with that?"

Mason finally met my gaze again and my heart ached just thinking about him going through all of this alone. With Wade gone I think it helped relieve some of his tension because he winked at me and tilted his lips in the same devilish way he did on the first day I met him.

"I trust him, Jake," I uttered wholeheartedly. "He may have a wild past, but he's changed. I love him."

With sorrow filled eyes, Jake smiled sadly and glanced toward Mason. "Well, I'm happy for you, kitten. I can see it in his eyes that he loves you, too. It reminds me so much of the way I used to look at my wife before she passed."

Jake's wife died of breast cancer a year before he opened the club. He engrossed himself with work to help deal with the grief of her loss. Over time he thrived and made a new family with all of us. I never saw him date anyone when I was living in Vegas, but I never asked either. Even when Mason and I weren't together I knew I wouldn't be completely happy with anyone else, and now that we're together the thought of him being gone forever was terrifying. I didn't want to ever experience that pain.

"Good evening, ladies and gentleman, we have a special treat for you tonight." The announcer finally entered the cage with his microphone in hand, waving out to the crowd. I clapped my hands along with the audience; the sound was almost deafening as it echoed in the arena.

Stephen had Mason's face in his hands and was talking quickly to him, trying to get him pumped up and ready, almost like you would see a coach do with his fighter. Smiling from ear to ear, Tyler slapped him on the back and waved over at me when he saw me looking at them.

As the music began to play, the lights around the cage beamed in all sorts of colors, almost like a concert. It wasn't like that when Mason fought last time, but then again, it wasn't being shown live either. The announcer, with his slicked back dark hair, wore a white dress shirt under his black tux with a black bow tie at his neck.

His voice was amazingly loud, and even without the microphone I was sure he would be heard across the room. "As you all know, Jake Montgomery hasn't disappointed us tonight. In all of The Labyrinth's history there has never been a fight as epic as this one's going to be. Last week we saw Mason 'The Eagle' Bradley manhandle Chase Benfield in his first match back in almost seven years of being away from the sport. Looking at him you wouldn't think so, though. If anything I'd say he improved since the last time he competed. So, ladies and gentlemen, let's give a warm round of applause to Mason 'The Eaaaggggglllle' Bradley!"

The crowd cheered, hollering out Mason's name as he made his way into the ring. He circled around the mat, waving at everyone, and flexing his muscles to a set of women who held up signs for him saying they wanted to have his babies. A light shone in Mason's eyes after that and I couldn't help but smile and be proud. Grinning over at me, he did something I hadn't ever seen him do. He kissed his fingers then touched his heart before pointing toward me. I did the same thing to him, not caring about the bitchy looks thrown my way.

Lifting his arm, the announcer waited for the crowd's cheers to die down before he continued, "Okay, so now that I've mentioned Mason let's get down to introducing his opponent for the evening. This guy is no stranger to the UFC scene and by his own personal request he recommended he be here tonight. I'd like to hear the story behind that. Anyway, you all know him as this year's UFC Heavyweight Champion, Matt 'The Destroyer' Reynolds! Come on out!"

Music began to blare through the speakers and the lights all focused on a door out toward the back of the arena. There were three men who walked through and there was no mistaking who Matt was. His shorts were red with different sponsor logos on them and on his left arm he had a tattoo of an ankh to go along with his golden tanned skin. There sure were a lot of tattooed fighters. I thought Mason's eagle on his arm was sexy as hell.

When Matt got into the cage it was easier to see what he looked like. His hair was so dark it had to be black, and along with his sun kissed tanned skin it made his bright green eyes stand out even more. He and Mason were very similar in build and height so it was hard to see where an advantage would come in. Their stats displayed across the billboard screen, but the only thing I understood were their weight and height. Mason was an inch shorter and there was a five pound difference between them with Matt being the heavier one. I couldn't even see the difference.

Matt walked straight over to Mason, and instead of talking shit, he smiled at him and extended his hand. Mason smiled back, returning the shake, and they both seemed to be engrossed in an interesting conversation.

Turning to Jake, I asked, "What do you think they're talking about?"

Keeping his eyes on the cage, he shrugged his shoulders and replied, "I'm not sure, but Matt was the one who suggested he fight Mason. Maybe there's a story there or something."

The announcer handed Matt the microphone and stepped back while he spoke to the crowd, "Everyone, I just wanted to say that tonight's fight was my decision. Before I started competing there was one fighter I watched diligently, his moves, everything, and I knew that when the time came I would compete with him for the Heavyweight championship. It just so happens that he pulled out of the sport before I even had a chance at him … until tonight. That guy was Mason Bradley."

The crowd went crazy and cheered, stomping their feet and clapping their hands. "Oh my God," I breathed. "This is insane."

Jake chuckled and agreed, "Yes, it is, but it's amazing. This is definitely going to be the best fight we've ever had here."

Mason and Matt got into place, facing each other, while the announcer stood in between them. Mason glanced quickly over at me and smiled before turning back to Matt with a renewed determination.

"All right, gentleman, you know the drill. When the bell rings, begin." The announcer exited the cage and the whole room immediately went silent. I couldn't look at anything else other than Mason and it was as if the whole world moved in slow motion. It felt like hours went by with no sound of the bell and all that while I held my breath, waiting. As soon as the bell echoed through the arena, I gasped and gripped onto the arms of the chair.

The fight was on.

Chapter 30

Claire

My knuckles were white and my hands were numb by the time the first two rounds were done. Breathing hard and bodies glistening with sweat, Mason and Matt were both bleeding, Mason from above his left eye and Matt from his right cheek. I'd watched Mason fight Chase with no problems, but this one was way more intense.

"Kitten, you can let go of the chair now," Jake teased, "Relax, they still have thirty seconds before round three."

Relax? Yeah, right.

Each round lasted five minutes a piece with a one minute break in between. The fight was scheduled to be only three rounds long, but if they kept fighting the way they were it was probably going to extend to another round or two. Tyler wiped the blood off of Mason's face and used a water bottle to squirt some water in his mouth. Before the bell rang, signaling it was time to get back in, Mason looked over at me and beamed, the red and black mouth guard being all I could see when he smiled. He was bruised and beaten, but he was happy.

236

He isn't going to be happy when the adrenaline wears off.

Round three started off a little slow, both guys circling around the cage, but then Mason psyched Matt out, pretending he was going to land a punch and ended up doing something completely different by bending low and tackling him to the mat. Rolling around on the mat, they grappled and had each other in different holds at times, but never anything solid to put them in submission. However, just when I thought Mason had Matt in his clutches, Matt reared back and landed a hard blow to his ribs before getting to his feet.

Mason grimaced, but he swiftly got up, and out of nowhere, head kicked Matt so hard that a stream of blood flew out of his mouth when his face snapped to the side and he fell to his knees. *Please go down, please go down,* I chanted over and over in my mind. *It's over,* I thought excitedly to myself, but my disappointment came when Matt got right back on his feet. *Holy hell, these guys were relentless.*

When the bell rang, ending the fight, Mason and Matt bumped fists and then went to their corners to replenish and get semi-cleaned up. Tyler and Stephen both worked on Mason's hands to get his gloves off while he sat back in the chair, breathing hard with his eyes closed. Since neither of them were knocked out and they both fought like champs, I was curious to see who the judges picked as the winner.

"Who do you think won?" I asked Jake, hoping he would say Mason.

Jake furrowed his brows and sighed. "I honestly don't know. They were both amazing and if I had to guess I'd say their scores were really very close. It could be any-one's match really."

After about three minutes or so, Mason and Matt joined the announcer in the center of the ring and both shook hands. Once the announcer was given the slip of paper by the judges, all sound ceased to exist as he opened it up, the sound of the paper crinkling in the microphone. *This is it!* Jumping to my feet, I watched as the announcer's eyes grew wide in delight as he held up the paper in his hands.

"Ladies and gentleman," he announced excitedly, "this is the first time I've witnessed this, but all three judges have agreed to a unanimous draw. According to the scorecards, both fighters earned a total of forty-eight points each per judge. It looks like we have ourselves a tie!"

The announcer took each of the fighter's wrists and held their arms high in the air. As soon as he did that the crowd erupted in cheers and got to their feet. Jumping up and down, I squeezed Jake around the neck and whistled and hollered out in joy for Mason. Even if he didn't knock Matt out, he was a winner in my eyes; he was unbelievable. Matt was one of the best fighters in the UFC and Mason came out on equal ground. That was a huge accomplishment.

Before Mason and Matt could leave the ring, the people in the crowd started to chant a set of three words, over and over, "We want more! We want more! We want more!"

They were bloody and beaten and they wanted more? The fight was absolutely brutal, how could they want more?

The announcer walked back to the middle of the ring and turned around in a circle, acknowledging the crowd. "Are you all saying you want more? Is that what I'm hearing?"

"*Yes!*" the crowd roared, clapping and stomping their feet. It was so loud it felt like the whole place was vibrating.

Mason and Matt both smirked at each other as they met in the middle of the ring, facing off. They shared a few words and then fist bumped before going to their corners. *What were they doing?* Tyler and Stephen quickly fetched Mason's gloves and started getting his hands ready.

With eyes wide, I gasped and turned to Jake. "Are they going to fight again?"

"It sure looks like it," he replied with a grin. "I've never had this happen before. Maybe Mason can redeem himself in another round and come out on top."

The announcer's booming voice came through loud and clear when he announced, "All right, ladies and gentlemen, you said you all wanted more well it looks like you got your wish. Both fighters have agreed to give you one more round. So stay in your seats and enjoy what we're going to call the sudden victory round. Good luck, fighters."

He nodded to both men and exited the ring. My nerves were shot, and I honestly didn't know if the chair was going to handle another five minute round of my incessant gripping. Once the bell rang, it all started again.

They fought harder this time because they knew it was their chance to make up for the tie. Mason wanted to prove he could do it, and even though this fight was unofficial I was sure Matt still didn't want to mess up his unde-feated statistics. My heart pounded with each second that passed and with each punch and kick my stomach would twist, especially when I could hear the force of it project-ing from their skin.

Blood dripped from their faces, coating the mat in ti-ny droplets of red and I prayed that it would be over soon. Five minutes of it was like an eternity. Mason was great at both strikes and kicks, but watching him on his ground game was absolutely fascinating. It was almost like he was a spider, able to wrap his arms and legs around his prey, trapping them. He took Matt down to the mat just like I'd seen him do with Tyler during practice. If he could just get his arm in the right position he would have Matt where he wanted him.

"Come on, Mason, you can do this!" I shouted, jump-ing to my feet. There was one minute left and he had to move fast. His eyes caught mine for one quick second be-fore he struck.

Lying on his back, Mason grabbed Matt's forearm and pulled him closer, trapping his arm between his legs. Once he had him in his hold, I could see the strain on Matt's face as Mason held his elbow perfectly straight and started applying pressure to his wrist by pulling it up. The arm bar technique was one of Mason's favorite moves, except if he put too much pressure on Matt's arm it could cause some major damage. He didn't want to do that be-cause I could tell he was going slowly at it.

He had twenty more seconds to get Matt to tap out. More pressure was applied … nothing. Matt was being a stubborn bastard, definitely testing his limits, but he didn't become a Heavyweight champion by giving in. With the veins bulging on his blood red face, Matt's expression contorted into one of extreme pain.

Ten seconds left and Mason upped the game by applying even more pressure. When the clock hit three seconds, Matt growled in agony and did the one thing I wasn't expecting to see ... he tapped out with only one second left of the fight.

The bell rang ... the crowd roared. Tyler and Stephen both were grinning from ear to ear when I ran up to them, screaming excitedly as Tyler scooped me up and swung me around. "Can you believe this shit?" he asked incredulously. "He was fucking amazing out there!"

Mason helped Matt up off the mat and what surprised me most was that even though they just got through beating the shit out of each other, they both had smiles on their faces and slapped each other on the back in one of those typical guy hugs. After waving to everyone, he jumped out of the cage and lifted me in his arms. His skin was hot and sweaty with blood dripping down his face, but I didn't care. He was mine.

"I did it!" he shouted.

The sound of his laugh as he swung me around brought tears to my eyes. I had never heard him sound like that, nor had I ever seen the light in his eyes like I did in that moment. Once he set me down, I gently kissed his lips and gazed into his sparkling green eyes. "Yes, you did and you were amazing. I had faith that you could do it," I murmured, a tear escaping the corner of my eye.

Glowing, Mason clutched my face and leaned down so he could whisper across my lips, "And that faith and determination of yours is what helped me win, Claire. Without you I would be nothing."

Smiling through my tears, I laid my head down on his chest and sighed. "I feel the exact same way about you, Mason."

Chapter 31

Mason

The fight was over and I won. I couldn't fucking believe it. For a moment, I thought, *Maybe I can do this ... maybe I can pursue a dream I thought was lost so long ago.* It was all in my grasp if I wanted to take it, but the question was, did I want to? Erick never approached me nor did I see him in the crowd during the fight. I had no idea if our deal was still open or if he decided I wasn't good enough. In a way, I didn't care because I knew I *was* good enough.

Jake had invited Matt and his people along with ours to a private room for drinks. With Claire by my side, I walked on air for the rest of the night. She watched on in amusement as Matt and I bantered back and forth, both claiming we kicked the other's ass. He reminded me so much of Austin and how we would do the same thing.

Matt clapped me on the shoulder and extended his hand. "Well, Mason, I can't exactly say it was fun getting my ass kicked in the fourth round, but it was definitely a fight I'll never forget. Maybe next time we should settle on the draw," he joked.

Guffawing, I shook his hand and responded, "I doubt there will be a next time. However, I am honored that you wanted to fight me."

Matt scoffed, furrowing his brows. "What? Why wouldn't there be a next time? After tonight people will be lining up at your doorstep to represent you. What's holding you back?"

My eyes wandered over to Claire who was smiling and laughing at Tyler. *Would she honestly like this life?* Following me around from fight to fight just to watch me get beaten and bruised for a title. It wasn't just my life I had to consider … it was hers. *She* was my life.

Chuckling, Matt glanced from Claire then back to me, a knowing smirk on his face. "Ah, I see. I think I get it now. If I had someone like that beauty of yours I'd probably want a different life too. Anyway, if you change your mind and you're ever out in California give me a call." He pulled out his wallet and handed me one of his cards.

When I glanced down at it, I couldn't believe the coincidence staring at me in the face. "Actually, I'm moving out to California in a couple of weeks," I told him. The card said he was in Santa Rosa which was only a short distance away from Claire's home.

"Really? Where are you moving to?" he asked.

"Claire's vineyards are out in Sonoma. I also have family out there as well. I guess being alone in North Carolina kind of lost its appeal."

"Dude," Matt scoffed, thumping the card in my hand, "then you have every reason to hit me up. I'm right down the road from you basically. If you don't, I'm going to hunt you down and kick your ass." He clapped me on the shoulder and looked down at the time on his watch. "Speaking of California, I leave tomorrow morning to go back. Take care of yourself, Mason, and stay out of trouble. Sometimes I hate coming out this way. It seems like there's always trouble around every corner."

"Yeah, I know," I remarked in all seriousness. I was the one who always went after it.

Matt said his good-byes to everyone and even said something to Claire that made her smile and shake her head. Once he left, I joined her, Tyler, and Jake.

"What did Matt say to you?" I asked, sidling up to Claire.

She chuckled and wrapped her arm around my waist. "He told me to wear you down and get you to join the UFC again when you move out to California. He also asked if he could have permission to kick your ass if you don't."

"And what did you say?"

Poking me in the side, she smirked up at me and said, "I guess you'll just have to wait and see, won't you?"

Knowing her, she probably gave him the address and told him to come just to mess with me. With Claire, there was no telling what she would do. It was one of the things I loved about her. She was spontaneous, which was something I had never been. I needed spontaneity in my life.

"Mason, I want you to have this," Jake insisted, holding out a thick, hefty envelope. Taking it from him, I lifted a brow and asked, "What is it?"

Smiling mischievously, he winked at Claire and pointed to the envelope. "Just open it and stop asking questions. I figured since Claire's leaving tomorrow this might be the last night I see you. I'll send the other half when I get everything sorted out."

Other half of what? I wondered. Sliding my finger under the seal, I pulled it open and almost lost my shit when I saw what was inside. I didn't even have to count it to know there was at least twenty grand in there.

"What's all of this?" I asked incredulously.

"It's your down payment for the night. I wanted it to be a surprise," Jake beamed. "I'll have to send you the other amount when I get all of the funds situated from the pay per view. It'll be about a week from now."

"I can't accept all of this. It's too much." I tried to hand him back the envelope, but he wouldn't take it.

Claire gently pushed it back toward me and said, "You deserve it for everything you went through tonight. You earned it, Mason. Just take it."

The glare she gave me was all it took. I would have another fight on my hands if I didn't take it. I hadn't held that much money in my hands in a long time, not since I fought before. Yeah, I was bad with money then, but over the years I became responsible enough with taking care of my mother to where I knew I couldn't blow money on stupid shit anymore. In my hands, I held half a year's salary for me.

Sighing, I nodded at Jake and said, "Thank you, Jake. I really appreciate it."

"No problem. Just make sure you two don't stay strangers, okay? Maybe next time you come down to visit you could stay with me instead of at a hotel. I have a cook that can make food better than any of the five star restaurants around here."

"We will definitely keep that in mind," I replied.

Jake said his good-bye to Claire, hugging her tight, and I gave them their space so she could say her farewell to him. It was getting late and I knew she needed to get back to the hotel to pack for her flight tomorrow morning. Stephen came up behind me, patting me on the back with a firm hand. "I want to thank you for letting me coach you, son. You made me proud up there. One of these days I hope to see Tyler make it to the big time."

"He will," I insisted confidently. "Just have faith in him like you did with me. I also want to thank *you* for helping me. Your guidance helped me out a lot."

Stephen nodded and walked away, leaving me with Tyler who put his arm around my shoulder. "You know you wouldn't have won tonight without me, right? I was, indeed, the person you sparred with over the past week, not to mention who made you better, and probably suffered a concussion in the process."

Coming into this mission and meeting Tyler that first night in the club, I never expected him to be as down to earth and genuine as he was. I thought he would be a complete douche bag just like all the other club bouncers I'd met in my time, but he took me by surprise.

"I'm sure you'll live," I teased, slapping him on the arm. "Anyway, good luck with the fighting. I wish you all the best."

He winked slyly. "Thank you, I'm going to need the luck. Although, I do have a strange feeling I'll be seeing you on TV soon. Maybe we'll get to see another encore of you and Matt, only this time fighting for the championship."

Yeah, in my dreams.

I couldn't even think about that at the moment. The

only thing going through my mind was trying to find another plan of action. What was I going to do about finding Erick and getting where I needed to be?

Chapter 32

Mason

When we got back to the hotel, I took a shower, bandaged up my wounds, and took a bunch of Ibuprofen. The adrenaline coursing through my veins dulled the pain of my swollen cheek and the nasty gash above my left eye, but come morning it would throb like hell along with the rest of my body. Sitting on the bed, I watched Claire move back and forth from the wardrobe as she packed up her things. I didn't want to see her go, and now that Erick never found me after the fight, I had a strange feeling I was going to be here a lot longer than I expected.

"What are you going to do when I leave?" Claire asked as she folded up her clothes.

The whole car ride back to the hotel she was bouncing on air, excited that I'd won, and wouldn't stop talking about the fight. However, once we got in the room and I recommended she pack her things before morning, everything changed. I knew she didn't want to leave, but I *needed* her to go.

Sighing, I scooted across the bed and put a hand over hers; stopping her from refolding the same shirt she'd been trying to fold for the past five minutes.

"Claire, stop," I demanded gently.

She dropped the shirt and turned a tear-streaked face my way. *Oh hell, why did she have to cry? She hardly ever cries.* Taking her hand, I pulled her down beside me and held her in my arms, breathing in the raspberry scent of her skin. For so long I never thought I'd touch her silky, golden skin or make love to her again, and now I had to let it go when I'd just gotten it all back.

With her back to me, I couldn't see her face, but I could hear the soft sound of her cries as she tried to hide it. "I know you want me to tell you to stay, but I can't," I murmured sadly. "I'm only looking out for you, baby."

"I know," she whispered. "I'm just worried about you. With me not being here with you I won't know if you're okay or not. The agony of not knowing what's happening to you will be torture."

Holding her tighter, I kissed the back of her neck to comfort her. "I'm going to be fine, Claire. You have to trust me."

As soon as I said that, my phone on the desk buzzed with an incoming text. "Who do you think that is?" Claire asked suspiciously. "You never get texts this late."

Sliding off the bed, I walked over to the desk and picked up my phone; the name on the screen read 'unknown.' Claire stared at me curiously as I read the text.

Unknown: Meet me in the lobby downstairs ~E

Knowing I couldn't tell her who it was, I chuckled

and pretended it was a wrong number. "I think they have the wrong number. This person asked if I wanted to order a pizza and chicken wings."

Claire smiled and licked her lips. "Mmm … actually, that does sound pretty good about now. I can't remember the last time I've had a good pizza."

Quickly, I texted the number back.

Me: I'll be there in 5.

Deleting the messages, I ambled back over to Claire who started folding the same shirt again. "Do you want me to go get us one from downstairs?" I insisted, tilting up her chin with my finger so she'd look at me.

She shook her head and grinned. "No, it's kind of late for all of that. However, you know what would be good? They used to be my favorite dessert when I was here before."

If it required me to go downstairs then I'd get her anything she wanted. "What do you want, baby?" I asked.

"Do you remember walking by the café downstairs and seeing all of those pastries? Well, let me tell you, the chocolate ones are absolutely amazing. If I didn't want to watch my weight I could've eaten about a dozen of them in a day."

Why women cared so much about being super skinny was beyond me. I personally loved it when a girl had more than a handful to grab onto. I'd seen pictures of Claire when she was doing the whole ballet thing and I had to say she was much hotter now with the curves. If she wanted to eat pastries every day I would still love her no matter what.

Tilting my head, I kissed her on the lips and reached around her back to grab her ass, making her squeal. "You stay here and finish packing and I'll go get some of those pastries. I might have to try one myself. Maybe I'll get you a dozen of them so it'll make your ass a little bit bigger," I teased.

Playfully, she scoffed and hit me on the arm. "Hey, what is it with guys and big butts?"

Chuckling, I grabbed my wallet off the nightstand and headed for the door. Before turning the knob, I winked back at her and replied, "It's nice having something to grab on to when you're riding my cock, and not to mention, it makes walking behind you a lot more enjoyable."

Exasperated, Claire rolled her eyes and shook her head. "Fine, get me two of them then. I'll eat them both for you."

With the biggest grin on my face, I nodded and opened the door. "You got it. I'll be right back."

As soon as the door shut, the grin vanished and I headed for the elevator. It was time to find out my next move.

As soon as I got off the elevator I saw him. Dressed in an expensive gray suit and a watch that had to cost more than my truck, he sat there in sheer confidence or most likely it was arrogance. *Smug bastard.*

When he spotted me walking toward him, he got to his feet and grinned. "Well, well, look at you. How does it feel to know you beat a Heavyweight champion?"

"It feels pretty damn good other than the pain I know I'm going to feel in the morning," I replied. "Were you there? I didn't see you."

He motioned toward the seat opposite him. "Of course, I was there. You left with the others before I had a chance to get to you. Please, have a seat," he offered politely. "Does Claire know you're down here?"

I sat down and said, "Yes, she knows I'm down here, but she doesn't know I'm with you. Which means I don't have too long before she starts getting curious."

"Why didn't you tell her?" he asked, gazing curiously at me.

Nonchalantly, I shrugged and lounged back in the chair, playing it coolly. "There are some things I want her knowing and some I don't. I didn't think this was one of those things I'd want her involved in."

"Good call," Erick agreed. "So I'm assuming you're still interested in what I have to offer?"

"You're damn right I am. Just tell me what to do."

Erick leaned forward in his chair and lowered his voice. "I'm going to warn you this isn't for the faint of heart. From what I've seen of your fights in the past and of your reputation I don't think that's the issue here."

"What's the issue then?" I remarked impatiently. *I wish he would get to the fucking point already.*

"My issue is this," Erick began, "I need to know how far you would go to win. How far would you go to earn say … five million dollars?"

"Five million dollars?" I exclaimed, eyes going wide. Leaning forward in my chair, I glanced around the room quickly and lowered my voice. "You're shitting me, right?"

That was a lot of money just for a fight.

"No, I'm not shitting you, Mason. So again, the question is … how far would you go to earn it? Would you steal for it?"

Now we were getting somewhere. "Yes," I answered, settling back in the chair.

Erick moved closer. "Would you lie for it?"

"Yes."

"Would you break your opponent's arm for it?"

I smiled. "Gladly."

"What if the price upped to ten million? What would you do then? If you knew you could get away with murder, would you kill for it? Let's say, take for instance, Chase Benfield. After he basically attacked Claire and was about to do who knew what with her, would you have had the guts to follow through?"

My smile vanished and the thought of Chase with his hands on Claire made my blood boil. I *wanted* to kill him that night; I wanted to rip his head off with my bare hands so I'd never have to see that smirk on his face ever again. Not only would I have done it for her, but for every other female he'd probably terrorized and most likely raped over the years. I knew what Erick's game was, but even I couldn't deny the truth in my answer. I would kill anyone that ever tried to hurt Claire in that way.

"I would do more than kill him," I answered through clenched teeth. "I would make him suffer ungodly amounts of pain before I did him and everyone around a huge favor of wiping his miserable fucking existence off this planet."

Erick was stunned speechless for a second, his mouth

wide open, before bursting out in laughter. "Whoa, that was intense. I guess it's a shame you're not going to be fighting him then. I have a lot of people betting on you so bring all that you have to the table. The rougher you play, the more you get paid, understand?"

He held out his hand, and not thinking twice, I shook it. "I understand completely. I'll be ready."

Pleased, Erick smiled and nodded his head. "That's good to hear. I'll have someone pick you up here tomorrow afternoon at four. Be ready for a tough competition because it's not going to be easy. If you win you'll get the sponsorship and the money. All your dreams will come true. Oh yeah, and make sure you come alone. I don't think you'll want Claire there."

Getting to my feet, I checked the clock on the lobby wall and groaned. I'd been gone way longer than expected. "You don't have to worry about that," I told him quickly. "Claire's leaving tomorrow."

"Oh," he muttered, pursing his lips. "I figured she would be with you while you were here. I'm sure Wade will be disappointed about that. The whole time Claire's been in town she's all he's been able to talk about. He was really torn up about her not forgiving him for what happened."

"He'll get over it," I snapped. "He doesn't deserve her forgiveness for what almost happened to her. He can rot in hell for all I care. It was his fault to begin with."

Erick sneered, his eyes gleaming mischievously. "That's true, but before I leave I have one more question." Grinning, he came up to me slowly and lowered his gaze to his hands, pretending to be interested with his fingernails. "So you said you would steal, lie, and even kill for ten million dollars, with one of those being an ultimate sin. However, I'm curious to know if you'd give up something else as well." He finally looked up at me, lifting a brow with that evil smirk on his face.

I didn't like the way the conversation had turned, and I certainly didn't like the excitement in his eyes when he faced me. The more time I spent around the man, the more it felt like he wasn't even human. He was a complete sociopath with psychopathic tendencies. There were so many people in the world like him it was ridiculous, and they were always the ones to watch out for.

"I don't think there's much else I could give up other than my soul," I replied blandly.

"Oh, I beg to differ. You'd be surprised what one would give up for the taste of money. I've known of some who even gave up their own kids for it. So the question is … would you give up the one thing you love the most? The one thing you cherish above all else?"

"How would you even know the answer to that?" I asked.

Erick smirked, lifting a condescending brow. "True, but I have a pretty good guess. I would say it'd have to be that beautiful blonde headed goddess you have waiting for you up in your room, am I right?"

Crossing my arms over my chest, I glared at him and remained silent. I was not going to bring Claire into any of it. When I didn't answer, his eyes went wide in wonder. "I guess that means your answer would be a no. You would seriously choose a woman over money? This girl must be something really special because Wade said he wouldn't give her up either."

Oh fuck no, this couldn't be happening. If it wasn't so

late I would put Claire on a plane that very minute and get her as far away as possible. They lured in Summer when Austin fought and I knew without a doubt that was going to be the plan for Claire. What was worse was that I knew who I'd be fighting, and if Claire found out …

Erick started to turn and walk away, and I counted down the seconds he would be out that door and away from me before I exploded. He stopped and turned around, his brows furrowed. "You know, I never thought I'd ever see the day where a woman would be worth that much to a man. It baffles me."

With that last note, he turned on his heel and saun-tered away. Before my time was up, I *was* going to find out who Erick really was, and I *was* going to put him away, even if it killed me.

By the time I rushed to get the pastries and made it to the elevator, I wasn't surprised one bit when Claire stormed out, almost bumping into me. "Whoa, what are you doing?" I asked, catching her in my arms.

"I came to find you," she snapped with her arms crossed over her chest. "You've been gone for a really long time, Mason. I know it doesn't take that long in the café."

I hated to lie, but I had no choice. Pulling her back in-to the elevator, I hit the button for our floor and passed her the bag of chocolate pastries. "I'm sorry it took so long, baby. When I was walking to the café a couple of people from the club stopped me while on their way to one of the bars here. I didn't want to be rude so I talked to them for a bit. Time slipped by me and when I realized how late it was I told them I had to go. I know it's our last night together and I feel terrible. Do you forgive me?"

Sighing, she glared at me for another minute before looking into the bag. A smile finally splayed across her face when she noticed I got not only two pastries, but four. "Okay, I think I can forgive you now. You better be glad chocolate can heal all wounds."

"Oh, does it?" I asked, reaching into the bag. "I have plenty of them so let's see if it helps." I grabbed one of the pastries and took a huge bite. Claire laughed and grabbed one as well, taking a bite and getting chocolate all over her lips.

Leaning down, I licked the chocolate off her lips and pushed her against the wall of the elevator, pressing my hips against hers. My dick was hard as a rock just imagining how fun it would be to suck chocolate off her nipples and possibly other places if she'd let me. She gazed at me wide-eyed and gasped, "I didn't think you'd be up for anything tonight after the fight. I was sure you'd be in too much pain."

Chuckling, I took her finger and dipped it inside the pastry before putting it in my mouth. After I sucked it off, I shook my head and whispered gruffly, "Oh no, baby. I may have gotten my face a little beat up, but there certainly wasn't any damage to the goods. I'll be more than happy to show you."

Once we got into the room, it wasn't me who showed her … it was the complete opposite. It was an eventful night and I owed it all to the chocolate pastry.

Chapter 33

Claire

"What are you smiling at?" Mason asked.

"Oh, I'm just wondering what the maids are going to say when they find the bed sheets all covered in chocolate when they clean the room today. I wish I could be a fly on the wall when they find them."

Mason chuckled, and reached over to hold my hand. We were in the truck and headed for the airport so I could make my ten o'clock flight back to California. I had called Melissa first thing and asked her if her or Brett could come pick me up when I landed. It would be good to get back home, but I didn't want to go back without Mason. Secretly, I was hoping the truck would break down so I couldn't make my flight. To get my mind off of leaving, I decided to concentrate on our chocolate rendezvous. Thankfully, it helped … if only for a short while.

Mason bellowed out a laugh and kissed my hand. "I have to admit, last night was very interesting. I think we need to experiment with chocolate a little more when I get back to California. I never thought watching you eat a pastry off my dick would be so fucking hot."

"It was a first for me, too," I added, "but I thought it would be interesting. I'm glad you liked it though."

We had ten minutes left before we reached the airport and the weight of that knowledge hung heavy in the air. "I want you to call me when you land in California, okay?" Mason insisted in all seriousness. "I'll feel much better when I know you're home and that you're safe."

Nodding, I tried to plaster on a fake smile and complied, "I will. It says my flight should land around two o'clock."

The airport loomed closer and closer and with each inch of progression I could feel the dread settling like a weight in my stomach. My instincts told me that something wasn't right, but I couldn't decipher what it meant or what I should do. Mason slowly crept down the road because up ahead we would have a choice to make. Either park and go in with me or drop me off at the terminal.

"Do you want me to park and walk you to your gate?" he asked softly.

Closing my eyes, I tried to keep the burn behind my lids at bay. I wanted him to walk me in, except it would only add to the agony of saying good-bye. Instead, I released a heavy sigh and shook my head. "Mason, if you don't mind I want you to drop me off at the terminal. Prolonging all of this is just going to make it harder," I muttered warily.

Taking a deep breath, he blew it out slowly and murmured, "Okay. If that's what you want that's what I'll do."

Pulling up to the drop off terminal it was almost like déjà vu staring at me in the face. It reminded me of the time when I was the one who dropped him off at the airport on that fateful day all those months ago. Mason squeezed my hand, and tilted my chin in his direction.

"Come on. I'll get your bags out of the trunk."

Once he got them out, he walked me to the door and set them down. Scooping me in his arms, he held me tight and buried his face in my neck. "I love you so fucking much, Claire. I promise I'll come home to you soon," he vowed wholeheartedly.

"You better ... and I love you, too," I whispered back.

Breathing him in one last time, I prayed the woodsy smell of his Burberry cologne and the natural male scent of his skin would stay ingrained in my mind while he was gone. I didn't want to let go, but I only had an hour to get through the gate, check in, and make it to my terminal. Reluctantly, I loosened my hold on him and leaned up to kiss him on the lips. It started off gentle, but then Mason clasped his strong fingers around my neck and held me to him as he deepened the kiss.

"I have to go," I cried, pulling away.

Nodding quickly, he bent down to pick up my bag, and placed it on my shoulder. With my rolling suitcase in hand, I was ready to go. I smiled at him one more time and kissed him hastily on the cheek before turning to walk away.

"Be careful, Mason," I called out, keeping my gaze on the approaching door.

"I always am, baby ... I always am."

I didn't look back, either out of necessity or the fear that I would break down and refuse to leave. I had to keep going. When I made it to the ticket counter there wasn't that long of a line so I got through it pretty quickly. By the time I sat down to gather my thoughts I had thirty minutes left before departure. They would most likely let us board soon so I checked my emails from my phone and scrolled through Facebook to kill the time. Most of my friends were married or were about to get married while some posted pictures of their newborn children. I didn't think anyone would want to know my true status update. It would read something like this: *I'm sitting in the Las Vegas airport, just being dropped off by the man who dumped me over four months ago who now happens to be the man I'm in love with. He's an undercover cop on a dangerous mission to figure out why there's been a string of deaths in the MMA community. Not to mention, he used to be a fighter himself who was undefeated and screwed countless women in celebration to his undefeated wins. I don't know if he will make it home safe or if he will make it out alive. Please keep me in your prayers.*

If I were to post something like that my friends would probably laugh and think it was all a joke. Nothing bad ever happened to them or at least that was what it seemed. I couldn't be the only one out there with a psychotic family member and a boyfriend who ran to danger instead of away from it.

"First class passengers for Flight 2578 to Sonoma can now proceed to board at this time. I repeat, first class passengers for Flight 2578 to Sonoma can now proceed to board at this time."

Groaning, I put my phone in my bag and zipped it up as soon as I heard the announcement. People lined up to get on the plane and as I waited for the line to clear, I laid my bag down on the seat beside me and stood up to stretch. I didn't see the point in rushing to the plane when I was going to have to do more waiting once inside.

After stretching my legs, I turned to reach for my bag that I had placed in the seat and noticed it wasn't there. "What the hell," I hissed.

Frantically, I searched around, looking under the chairs and at the people walking around nearby. It would be hard to miss since it was bright pink with white stripes on it. *How the hell could I lose it?* My bag had my phone in it and everything. I couldn't leave without it.

Out of the corner of my eye, a flash of pink caught my attention. It was my bag, except it wasn't just lying on the floor; it was in someone's hands. The guy holding it let it swing back and forth, no doubt to get my attention and it surely did. I couldn't tell who he was because of his lowered head and the baseball cap hiding his eyes. *What do I do?*

The decision was made for me when the guy with my bag started to saunter off still carrying my things. He looked over his shoulder and I could see the telltale sign of a smile when he noticed me following. The last thing I wanted was to follow him outside alone; however, I didn't get the chance to do that because out of nowhere an arm draped over my shoulder and I yelped in surprise. "Quiet," a voice hissed in my ear.

Gasping, my breaths came out in rapid pants as I was pulled to a corner and backed into a wall with the hulking frame of none of other than Chase Benfield in front of me, blocking me from view. *You have got to be kidding me! Can I not catch a break!* He wore a black T-shirt and jeans, and instead of a blue mohawk like he had the last time I saw him it was now raven black to go with his black as coal eyes.

Before I could open my mouth to call for help, he slammed his hand over my lips, growling low, "I'm going to warn you now; if you scream I'll make sure Mason suffers for every ounce of attention you draw to yourself. I need you quiet and I need you to come with me."

"What are you talking about? Where's Mason?" I snapped.

He moved forward so quickly that I hit my head against the wall to get as far away from him as possible. I didn't get very far.

"Oh, you'll see him later, sweets. Did he not tell you what's going on?" Chase asked smugly.

Closing my eyes, I clenched my teeth and sucked in a sharp, angry breath. *No, he didn't tell me.* I knew something was going on, that Mason was keeping something from me, but I didn't expect it to involve me. Thoughts of Summer came to mind, and in that moment it all made sense. *That's why he wanted me to leave, but I didn't get away fast enough.*

"Oh, I can tell by the look on your face that he didn't," Chase sneered. "Well this is going to be fun. Are you sure he didn't tell you about the fight?"

Glaring at him, I pushed my hands against his chest to get some space, but being a wall of muscle he didn't move. "No," I hissed through clenched teeth. "He didn't tell me about the fight."

Chase guffawed. "You know I bet that's why he wanted to send you home packing. He's a smart guy, but I guess not smart enough when he told Erick you were leaving this morning. That just wasn't going to do because we had plans for you."

Turning my head, I crossed my arms over my chest,

hoping it would get him to back off. He moved back slightly and finally I could breathe again.

"So you followed us here?"

"Yep, and here we are. I'd say everything worked out perfectly," he chided. "However, now we need to leave and I need you to come quietly. Can you do that? I don't want anything bad to happen to Mason before we have our fun."

I didn't know what other choice I had other than to go. "Fine," I said darkly. "Just back up and give me some space. I'll come quietly if you stop touching me."

Lifting his hands in the air, he smiled wide and backed up, letting me out of the corner. "As you wish," he chimed.

Walking side by side, we made it out the doors to the airport and there waiting by the curb was the guy who took my bag, standing by a black Mercedes G500 with dark tinted windows and the backseat door wide open.

"Mason's going to get the surprise of his life when he sees you tonight. I'm sure he's going to love seeing you with me," Chase whispered in my ear, coming around behind me. His fingers grazed across my arm and over my breast right before he grabbed my waist and pushed me forward. Sliding into the backseat, Chase came in behind me and reached around to pull the seatbelt over my chest.

"We have to keep you safe," he chided tauntingly.

He put his hand on my bare thigh, and I wanted to kick myself in the ass for wearing a pair of shorts. Thank God, it wasn't a skirt. Either way, I could feel my blood pressure rising by the minute. Inch by inch, he moved his hand up higher on my thigh and being in the position I was in, I reacted out of pure anger. As fast and as hard as I could do it, I elbow struck him in the neck since my reach could only go so far. Immediately, he removed his hand and grabbed his throat, sputtering and gasping for air. Snickering, the driver pulled away from the curb and led us away from the airport.

"So help me God, Chase, if you touch me one more time I'm going to do a lot worse to you than just hitting you over the head with a bottle or a simple elbow strike. Next time you won't be getting up," I growled. I tried to put as much force behind my hit as I could muster, but given the fact that he righted himself quickly it must not have been too effective. At least I tried to make a point.

Chase coughed and then burst out laughing while pulling out his phone. "You are too much, Claire. I love a woman with fire." Rolling my eyes, I turned away from him and stared out the tinted window of the Mercedes.

Chase dialed a number on his phone and when the person answered on the other end he responded, "Yeah, I have her, and no, she didn't put up a fight," he paused, and rubbed his neck, "well not much of one anyway. Once I mentioned harming Mason she complied immediately." He listened to the other person speak a little longer and then hung up the phone.

"All right, everything is set to go for four o'clock," he said.

"Four o'clock?" I gasped, turning to face him. "That's six hours away. What are you going to do with me until then?"

Chase moved closer and moved the hair away from my neck so he could speak into my ear, "Don't worry, sweetheart, you're going to spend a little quality time with me. You might enjoy it."

So help me, God, please don't let him try anything with me. There was only so much fight one has in their body, and I was getting close to my limit. A tear escaped the corner of my eye, but I knew I mustn't show fear. I was beginning to think I should've ran when I had the chance.

Chapter 34

Claire

Blindfolded and with my hands tied in my lap, I sat quietly in the backseat while Chase talked heatedly on the phone outside the car. I couldn't understand what he was saying, but I heard my name come up a couple of times. The only thing that kept me sane was that at four o'clock I would see Mason again.

"You're awfully quiet considering the circumstances," the driver said, sounding curious. "Most people in this situation would be frantic, but not you. I find that rather interesting." It was the first time he'd spoken since being in the car, except I wasn't exactly in a talking mood.

Clenching my teeth, I sat up straighter and pursed my lips, refusing to acknowledge him. He must've been watching me in the mirror because he chuckled and turned around in the seat, making the leather creak as he moved. "You're angry. That's a good thing," he admitted. "Don't worry, though; Chase isn't going to do anything to you. Our boss specifically said for him not to and if he goes against that he'll find himself in a ditch with a bullet inside his brain. Anyway, I heard what you did to him at the party. I wish I could've seen it. I never understood why he wanted revenge on Mason when he constantly fucked other women behind his wife's back. The ladies love him though."

Disgusted, I spat angrily, "He's a worthless piece of shit. I should've hit him harder on the head with that bottle and put him out permanently."

"Would you have really killed him?" he asked in wonder. Taking someone's life wasn't something I would do lightly, but if it came down to my life or my attacker's … I would gladly pick the former.

"If he tries to do me harm I will in a heartbeat. I'm not anyone's victim, especially his."

Just about the time I finished saying that, Chase opened the car door and huffed as he scooted in beside me. "It looks like we're going to Erick's," he suggested indignantly. "It appears he has a soft spot for Mason's bitch here and wants her in good hands before the fight. His exact words were that I wasn't capable of achieving that."

That's for damn sure, I wanted to say, but taunting him wasn't a smart move.

"You know, it's a shame Erick didn't give me the chance to fight for you," Chase added, "but who knows, I might get lucky. I don't know why Erick even wanted to give Mason the opportunity to get ahead anyway. He doesn't deserve to win."

"Wait," I shouted. "Are you saying the fight is going to be over me?"

Chase tapped me on the chin with a finger, saying, "That's right, love."

"Well, what happens if Mason and the other guy

don't want to fight for me?" I stormed impatiently.

I could feel his breath on my face as he moved closer, whispering in my ear, "Then you, my lovely goddess, will belong to me for the night if they don't comply. I'm pretty sure they'll both fight to the death to keep you from me."

My blood boiled.

"Who gives Erick the right to determine who I belong to? That's not his choice to make. I would rather rip out my own hair and choke on it than spend a night with you. I do know how to fight and I will kill you if you so much as touch me in that way," I argued vehemently.

"Ooh, I like it rough, baby, but given who's fighting for you I hate to admit that I'm probably not going to get the chance. I haven't had any complaints from the women as of yet so I honestly think you'd enjoy it."

"Ugh …" I scoffed. "What about your wife? Aren't you married? How could you do something like this to her?"

"Easy," he remarked flippantly. "I find a girl and I fuck her. Have you seen the amount of women that flock to us after the fights? I'm curious to see how you handle it after watching Mason get chased by countless women day in and day out. You won't stand a chance against a fresh piece of ass every week."

"You're disgusting," I sneered.

Chase and the driver both laughed. "I aim to please," he joked.

For ten minutes, I listened to Chase and the driver talk about the fight, who they thought would win, and what they hoped would happen to Mason. They still never told me who the other fighter was. Blowing out an annoyed breath, I interrupted their joking and demanded to know, "I want to know who the other fighter is. Tell me who he is."

I had a feeling I already knew, but I wanted to hold out hope that I was wrong. My suspicions were confirmed almost immediately when Chase scoffed and answered, "Oh, come on Claire, I know you're not stupid. You know who Mason will be fighting, and one thing's for sure, Wade's determined to see it through to the end. That boy is completely hard up for you. It'll definitely be interesting to watch him go against Mason, not to mention the amount of money riding on this fight."

"How much are we talking?" I asked, my voice a harsh whisper.

Chase chuckled and patted my knee. "Five million dollars, baby. However, that's only for a submission. The bloodier the fight, the more money you get paid. Who would've thought that a piece of pussy would be worth so much."

Scooting as far away from him as I could, I leaned my head against the window, trying to keep the bile from rising in my throat. *Did Summer go through this same shit when her husband was killed?*

"You know this is considered kidnapping, right?"

"No, it's not," Chase countered matter-of-factly, "you came with me willingly."

"You threatened me," I shouted. "How is that willingly?"

"I didn't force you to come. I just suggested that it might be in your best interest. There's a big difference there. You are more than welcome to back out of this, except I wouldn't recommend you do that. Erick has a lot riding on this fight. He gets pretty angry when things don't go his way and bad things tend to happen when he gets like that, but when things do go his way he's very rewarding."

Rewarding for whom? I wondered. It sure as hell wasn't going to be me. From every angle of looking at this, it appeared I was the one who suffered the most. The fate of my life for one night hung in the balance between two men ... my lover and a friend who used to be more.

Either way, I was going to lose.

Chapter 35

Claire

I had to stay blindfolded until I was escorted into Erick's house and put in a room. Chase took off my blindfold and thankfully he left immediately along with the guy who drove us. "Thank God," I whispered to myself.

The room I was brought to happened to be a large suite with a bedroom and separate sitting room. Everything was done in all golden hues from the walls to the pale yellow bedspread on the king size bed. It was really bright and sensual ... not what I would imagine one of Erick's rooms to look like. The sitting room doors were open so I walked toward it and gasped, not expecting to see Erick sitting on the couch, waiting for me.

"Now don't you think this is better than spending your time with Chase?" he asked smugly.

Glaring, I crossed my arms across my chest, pursing my lips. "That all depends on what you have planned for me. From what I hear, you're threatening to hand me over to Chase for a night if Mason and Wade don't fight for me. I don't think that inspires me to want to be anywhere near you."

He patted the seat beside him and motioned for me to sit, but instead, I walked right past him and sat in the chair on the opposite side. "I'm not going to give you to Chase," he explained incredulously. "I may be an arrogant son of a bitch, but I would never give someone like you over to him. He doesn't exactly know that at the moment, and the only reason why I'm doing it is so I can get a good fight out of your guys. They both hate him and they're not going to want to see you with him."

Leaning forward, he rested his elbows on his knees and said, "Now whoever the winner is, that's who you will leave with. What you do after that is your own business. I may like you, but I'm going to give you a fair warning. If I so much as hear a peep out of your mouth about what went on tonight after it's all over I'm going to make sure you stay silent for a really long time. Do you understand?"

Closing my eyes, I nodded, lowering my head. "I understand, but what about Mason and Wade? One of them could get hurt or even killed."

"Oh, I truly hope so," he uttered honestly. "It makes for good entertainment, and the guys know the risks. However, what you fail to realize is that this whole thing wasn't completely my idea. It was brought to my attention by someone else."

"What? Who?" I demanded. By the gleam in Erick's eyes I already had my answer.

"No, it couldn't be possible," I cried, shaking my head. "He wouldn't do that."

"Believe me, sweetheart, Wade would."

"What if I don't cooperate and agree to the terms," I countered stubbornly. "What if I don't want to be fought over, huh? Are you going to kill me?"

Chuckling, Erick quickly got to his feet and slammed his hands down on the arms of my chair. Gasping, I moved as far back in the seat as I could, but he kept getting closer. His eyes looked almost black and the smile he had on his face had turned into an evil sneer. "That is all up to you, Claire, on if I kill you or not. Frankly, I think that's a bit extreme considering all you have to endure is just one fight. All you have to do is suck it up and keep your mouth shut. However, if you want to be stubborn, I have my ways of making you change your mind."

"How?" I breathed, swallowing hard.

"Oh, Claire," he murmured, closing the space even more. "I researched a lot of things about you, sweetheart. How would you like to have your vineyards and your winery taken away from you? I'm pretty sure I have the means to come up with something, or better yet, how about Cooper Davis?"

Eyes going wide in panic, I clenched my teeth and hissed, "What about him? He has nothing to do with this." I couldn't allow Cooper to be brought into this.

"You didn't think I'd find out about him, did you?" Erick boasted. "Well, it wasn't hard to do a search on you and see pictures of you with him. There are plenty of them out there. So would you change your mind if I told you I could get him kicked off the football team and have his career ruined for the rest of his life? I don't think he'd appreciate that at all now would he, especially, if he finds out it was all your fault?"

He looked down at his watch and then back to me with a smug grin on his face. "Tick-tock, Claire. I don't have all day." If he was bluffing, I would have no way to prove it, but if he was telling the truth, I could lose every-thing. There was no thinking … I had to do it.

"Fine," I snapped. "I'll agree to the terms of the fight."

He patted me on the cheek. "I knew you'd see it my way, and now that we've come to an agreement I'll leave you to your thoughts. Mira, my housekeeper, will bring you lunch here shortly and anything else you desire. You're not a prisoner, but I strongly suggest you stay put and not cause trouble. I have cameras in all my rooms so if you do something stupid I'll see it."

Slowly, he moved away from my chair and ambled toward the door. Before he walked out, he turned to me one last time and grinned. "I hope you enjoy the rest of your day."

My reply to that was a certain middle finger and a scowl, and I heard his laugh the whole way down the hall.

When Erick walked out of the room, he left the door standing wide open. He said I wasn't a prisoner, but he also said he had cameras in all the rooms. That alone basi-cally said I was being watched. My safest bet was to stay put, so I did. Mira, Erick's housekeeper, came in with a tray of food and set it on the table in front of the couch while I was looking at the books on the bookshelf. Mira was a middle-aged Asian woman, with short, black hair to her shoulders and wearing a blue uniformed smock that reminded me of what hotel maids would wear. She smiled kindly at me when I turned to acknowledge her.

"Your lunch, Miss Claire. If there is anything else you would like don't hesitate to let me know. You can reach me through the messaging system by the bedroom door. You'll see my name on the keypad and all you have to do is press it and I'll come."

"Thank you, Mira. I appreciate that," I said whole-heartedly. I had no clue if she knew why I was actually there, but again, I didn't want to reach out to her and have everything come crashing down on me.

Mira left the room, and as soon as I lifted the cover on the tray, my stomach growled and began to cramp. I was hungry, but there was that gnawing fear of being poisoned plaguing the back of my mind. Groaning, I turned back to the books and scanned the shelves. There were mainly books on art, architecture, medieval castles, and Old English literature. I was pretty sure Erick didn't have any romance novels, but it didn't hurt to look.

Frustrated, I lay down on the couch and stared at the ceiling. "Would it have hurt to have a TV in here if I'm going to be stuck here for five hours?" I mumbled to myself.

"There's one in my room," a tiny voice replied.

Bolting upright and grabbing my chest, I sucked in a shocked breath as my gaze found a little girl in the doorway, smiling shyly. She stared at me for a moment before tiptoeing in the room. "Geez, you scared me, little one. What's your name?" I asked delicately.

Looking down at the floor, she whispered, "Madison."

Is she Erick's daughter? I wondered. She was the most adorable little girl with blonde ringlets and bright blue eyes. What made her even cuter was that she wore a pink tutu and purple leotard. She almost looked exactly like me when I was her age.

Smiling back at her, I said, "You have a very pretty name, Madison. My name is Claire." Slowly, she made her way to the table and inched closer to me, looking down at the food.

"Are you going to eat your lunch? Mira always tells me not to waste my food," she scolded with her hands on her hips. Biting my lip, I tried to hide my smile because it looked like the little girl was being serious.

To appease her, I sat on the floor in front of the little table and slid the tray closer to me. There was a triple decker club sandwich with a mound of French fries. Picking up my sandwich, I took a huge bite and lifted a brow at her. "Are you happy now?" I asked her, talking with a mouth full of food.

She giggled and sat beside me on the floor. "Can I have a French fry, please?"

I pushed the plate over a little so she could reach it. "Of course, help yourself to as many as you want, Maddie."

She dug in and we both ate them all up before finishing the sandwich together. "Are you my mommy?" she asked, gazing up at me with her innocent blue eyes.

"Oh, honey, no I'm not. I'm just a visitor here today. Does your mommy not live here with you?" I wasn't about to tell her the truth of why I was there, but it wouldn't hurt to get more information on who she was. A little girl like her didn't need a father like Erick who manipulated and hurt people.

Madison shook her head. "No, my mommy's in heaven. I don't remember her, but I saw a picture of her in my daddy's room. He told me it was my mommy in the picture. You look just like her." My throat closed up, and all I wanted to do was wrap my arms around her and take her away. It was strange to think that Madison thought I looked like her mother. Even stranger was how could a sweet thing like her come from someone like Erick?

Turning to her, I ruffled her little curls and lifted her chin. "My mother's in heaven, too, Maddie. I miss her every single day."

"Will you be back after today?" she asked.

Sadly, I shook my head. "I don't think so, sweetheart. I'll be leaving here in just a couple of hours. I have to go back home soon."

"Where is your home?"

"It's in California. I came down here to visit some friends," I explained.

"Is my daddy your friend? I don't like his friends. Mira makes me stay away from them and always sends me to my room when they come over. I don't ever see my daddy much."

Not knowing how to answer, I switched the subject. If I was being watched I didn't want to get on the subject of her father or his people. "So, Maddie," I announced, pointing to her frilly pink tutu. "Do you dance? I used to take ballet when I was little."

She beamed and jumped to her feet. "I do ballet, too. Mira takes me every Tuesday and Thursday. Do you want to see? No one ever comes to watch me other than Mira."

This little girl was breaking my heart. I never grew up in a house where the housekeeper watched after me instead of my own parents. I couldn't imagine how lonely it had to be.

Smiling brightly, I nodded my head and motioned for her to start. "I would love to watch you dance. Show me what you've learned."

I watched her dance around the room and clapped every time she finished a move. I even got up and taught her a couple of things as well. "You are a terrific dancer, Madison. I bet one day you'll get into Julliard and be a famous dancer when you get older."

She giggled and cuddled up next to me on the couch when she was done dancing. "Can I come home with you to California? I want you to be my mommy."

Putting my arm around her, I squeezed her tight and sighed. "It doesn't work that way, sweetheart. You live here with your dad. I can't just take you away." She gazed up at me, frowning. "But if I could I would be honored to have a little girl as beautiful and as smart as you. One day I hope I will."

We sat there on the couch for a while, and we both must've fallen asleep because one minute it was peaceful and the next we heard Mira calling out for Madison. "Madison, where are you? Hit a button so I'll know where you're at."

"Uh oh," Madison cried. "I think daddy's friends are here." Taking my hand, she tried to pull me to the door. "You can hide in my room with me."

We made it to the door and I peered around the edge. Mira looked frantic, gazing up and down the hallway until her eyes landed on Madison. "There you are, Madison. I was worried about you. You disappeared and I didn't know where you went. I need you to go to your room for just a few minutes okay?"

Bending down on my knees, I wrapped my arms around Madison's little body and squeezed her tight. "Thank you for trying to hide me, but I have to stay here. I had a wonderful time with you, but you need to get to your room, okay? I'm going to miss you."

"I don't want you to go," she cried.

Mira gasped and bent down on her knees beside me, turning Madison's face toward her. "Oh sweet heavens, Madison, you spoke. I can't believe I finally got to hear your voice." She gazed over at me with wide, tearful yet joyful eyes. "She's never spoken before, or at least not to anyone here. Whatever you did, thank you."

Downstairs, we could hear the sound of male voices and footsteps pounding across the floor. I hugged Madison one more time and put her in Mira's arms. A tear fell down her cheek and before Mira ran off with her down the hall, I whispered in her ear, "You take care of yourself, Madison, and whatever you do, keep dancing and be strong. I wish more than anything that I could take you with me."

"Good-bye, Miss Claire," Mira uttered. She bolted down the hallway and disappeared around the corner just as Chase turned the other corner and noticed me standing in the doorway.

"It's time to go have some fun, sweetheart. Are you ready?"

No, but I didn't exactly have a choice.

Chapter 36

Mason

"So, you think today is the day?" Ryan asked. He knew everything Erick had told me from the night before because I spent the last hour discussing it with him.

"I know it is," I responded confidently. "Erick's people will be here at four o'clock to take me somewhere for the fight. I don't know where it is, but I'll have my trackers on so you can find me."

"All right, I'll have my people ready. I have a file being sent over to me today with information from the Ohio killings. There's an outstanding warrant for a man named Michael Turner. I'll have his picture in a little while and I'll send it to you so you can let me know if it's him. But in the meantime, do what you have to do until we get there. I don't want you getting yourself killed. Do you think you'll be able to carry your gun with you?"

They were probably going to check me for weapons and take my phone in the process. I didn't know if I should risk it. "I don't know if that's a good idea," I uttered in all honesty. "If they find it there'll be questions. That's the last thing I want when I'm so close."

Ryan sighed. "Fine, but be careful. This all ends today."

"Yes, it will, and I'm going to be there to end it."

It was a little past three o'clock and I had less than an hour until I met the unknown. Claire should've landed in California about an hour ago, except I hadn't heard a word from her yet. I tried calling her phone, but it went straight to voicemail all ten times I called.

I hated to do what I was about to do, but I knew she still had the tracker inside her bra. Picking up the phone, I dialed Ryan again and he answered immediately, "Mason, what's going on?"

"Can you do me a favor? When you gave me the trackers I made sure to put one in one of Claire's bras. She left to go back to California and she should've called me by now. I have to know she got there safely before I go into this fight tonight."

"Yeah, sure, give me one minute to pull it up. I was about to do that so I could keep tabs on where you go once four o'clock hit." I heard the tapping of his fingers hitting the keyboard keys, and after about thirty seconds he had it. "Okay, it looks like she's at the Charles M. Schulz Sonoma County airport. Is that where she's supposed to be?"

"Yes," I breathed, releasing a relieved sigh. "Thank you for checking."

"No problem, Mason. Now get your head in the game, okay?"

"I will. Have you gotten the file yet?" I asked. "Because I'm running out of time."

"No, not yet. I don't know what's taking so long, but it should be soon," he grunted impatiently.

After he hung up, I dialed Melissa since she was the one who was supposed to pick Claire up from the airport. If Claire didn't call before I left, I knew there would be no way to talk to her once I did.

Melissa picked up on the second ring and squealed, "Hey, Mason, how are you? Are things going okay there?"

"Hey Mel," I said quickly. "Yeah, things are fine for now. Have you picked Claire up yet?"

"Well, I'm here to pick her up, but her flight was delayed about an hour. The plane just pulled up so I should see her here in the next little bit."

Groaning, I ran my hands impatiently through my hair. "Okay, I was hoping to talk to her before I had to leave. Will you do me a favor then, please?"

"Of course, what do you need?"

I wanted to hear Claire's voice, but it didn't look like I was going to get the chance. Sighing, I spoke softly into the phone, "Tell her that I love her and that I'll be coming home soon."

"Oh, isn't that sweet," Melissa cooed. "I'll be sure to tell her as soon as I see her. So I guess this means things are wrapping up if you're coming home, right?" She paused for a moment before everything snapped into place and her tone changed. "Oh hell, Mason, what's going on? You're doing something dangerous today aren't you? That's why you're getting all weird on me right now."

Warily, I collapsed onto the bed and closed my eyes, taking in deep, calming breaths. "If I tell you what's going on I know you'll tell Claire so it's best to keep it to myself. All you need to know is that it's all coming to an end."

Melissa sighed. "Just be careful, Mason. You're all the family I have left other than Brett."

"I know, Mel. I'll be safe. Just tell Claire what I said for me." Looking over at the clock, I noticed I had fifteen minutes left. "Okay, I have to go now, but I'll see you soon."

As soon as she said her good-bye's and hung up, I grabbed my bag and made my way out the door. When I got into the lobby, I sat down and glanced up at Claire's favorite part of the Bellagio hotel, the massive collection of glass flowers on the ceiling. She had a passion for art.

I couldn't recall how long I stared at them before the sound of someone clearing their throat caught my attention.

"I hate to drag you away from your flower gazing, but it's time to go."

My head snapped forward, and there in front of me was a guy about the same build as me, with a black hat hung low on his face, shadowing his eyes. However, it didn't disguise the mischievous leer turning up the corner of his lips. I also didn't miss the slight bulge on the waist of his jeans signaling that he was sporting a firearm underneath.

Standing, I grabbed my bag and smiled. "Let's go then. Lead the way," I said. As we walked out of the hotel, my phone buzzed and I hastily looked down at it. It was Ryan, but the image he was sending me was taking forever to load.

Once out to the parking lot, I followed the guy to a black, Mercedes G500 with illegal, dark tinted windows. I checked my phone again and the picture still hadn't loaded. *Dammit!* I exited out of the file he was sending so the douche bag in front of me wouldn't see it. Looking down at the duffle bag in my hands, he shook his head and held out his hand. "Before you get in I'm going to need to look through your bag and take your phone," he requested.

Lifting a brow, I handed him my bag and chuckled. "Are you afraid I'm going to call someone or something?"

The guy shrugged his shoulders and looked through my bag. "We just like to play it safe, you know? I'm sure you understand."

There wasn't much in there except a pair of my fighting shorts, tape, and a pair of my black gloves. He pocketed my phone and handed me back my bag. "Okay, everything looks good. Hop in the back and put the blindfold over your eyes. I'll give you back your phone later."

"What happens if I don't win the fight? Are you going to keep my phone?" I inquired sarcastically.

The guy smirked. "No, it's just you won't need it if you lose. It's kind of hard to call someone if you can't use your hands, right? I'll leave you to your imagination on that one. Now get in so we can go."

The second I opened the door and slid in the backseat, my whole body froze when I saw the blindfold lying on the seat and a certain, familiar scent engaging my nose. My blood ran cold and I couldn't decipher if it was my mind playing tricks on me or if I actually smelled the hint of raspberries; the same raspberry scent I always associated with Claire.

There was no fucking way. If her scent still lingered

that would mean she was in the car just recently. The situation only got worse when I picked up the blindfold and there, hanging off of it, was a strand of bright, blonde hair; the same color as Claire's.

"Dude, come on. Put the blindfold on and let's go. You're not scared, are you?" the guy teased.

No, I was pissed! If anything happened to Claire someone was going to die.

Putting the blindfold on, I sat back in the seat and clenched my teeth together to keep my anger in check. "No, I'm not scared," I snapped. "I'm ready to get this started." *Or better yet, ended.*

With the blindfold on I couldn't see where we were going, but of course, that didn't matter. As soon as Ryan followed the trackers he'd get everyone in motion. We were about two minutes down the road when my phone began to ring.

"Let's see what we have here," the guy crooned. "Ah, it looks like you have a Melissa calling. Who is this Melissa by the way? Is she a friend, lover, a girl you like to fuck?"

Trying to sound as disinterested as possible, I replied, "Not that it's any of your business, but she happens to be my cousin."

"Well, shit, I thought there'd be a story there … unless you fuck your cousin," he teased.

I snorted, disgust curling my lip. "Sorry to disappoint you, but no, I don't swing that way."

"It was just a joke, dude, lighten up. Anyway, we have about thirty minutes before we get where we need to go." My phone stopped ringing, but then started right back up again. "Wow, this Melissa must either be annoying or really wants to talk to you."

The feeling in the pit of my stomach grew heavier and heavier. Melissa wouldn't call me like that unless something was wrong, and it only added to the confirmation that Claire wasn't on that plane. The only time they could've gotten her would have been after I dropped her off at the airport. I had to imagine she would scream and fight if someone tried to take her. Unless …

"Are you going to let me answer it or let it keep on ringing?" I asked impatiently. I really wanted to answer the phone. I had to know for sure if Claire was on that plane or not.

"Neither," he responded, "I'm going to shut it off so I don't have to listen to its incessant ringing."

"What if it's important?"

He scoffed. "Dude, nothing is as important as tonight. You're getting the chance to win a shit load of money. Do you know how many people would kill to be in your place right now? In just one night you could pursue all your dreams and do anything you want."

"Have you done it before? Battled for money?"

"I did once a few months ago, but I only got two million dollars for my reward. It doesn't matter though because what I do now pays pretty damn well. Erick saw potential in me and offered me a job with him. I get everything I want so it's hard to complain."

"What kinds of things do you have to do to get what you want?" I inquired curiously. "Do you have to kill people for it?"

He chuckled, but there was nothing humorous about it. "I don't think you want to know the answer to that. The less you know the better. So take my word of advice … do as Erick says tonight and you'll be fine. There's a lot riding on this fight and if you fuck that up there'll be consequences. My bets are actually on you to win so if you lose I'm going to lose five-hundred thousand dollars."

Gasping, I almost choked on my words when I hollered, "You have got to be shitting me! How much will you get if I win?"

"That depends," he said. "It's all based on your opponent. The bloodier and more violent the fight, the more money you get. The same goes for the people gambling on you. Some people are simply just betting that you lose while some will bet for you to win. Others are getting more technical, take for instance, there is one person who thinks you'll break your opponents arm and such. It's a win-win for everyone involved if you gamble on the right fighter."

"Are you supposed to be telling me all of this?" I wondered out loud. I still didn't know the guy's name and here I was talking to him like everything was normal when obviously the situation was all shades of fucked up.

"That's part of my job, Mason. I'm the one who picks up the fighters and explains everything to them so that when I drop you off you'll know exactly what's expected of you. He doesn't want to waste time on the semantics once you get there. I'm very perceptive and that's what Erick likes about me. I can tell who's going to flake once they're in the ring and the ones who are going to be the moneymakers."

It was all more in depth than I thought it would be. This didn't just involve me and another fighter; it was with a whole goddamned lot of gamblers voting on the enjoyment of watching two people beat each other to death. Instead of it being dogs people were gambling on, it was actual people. Austin's situation finally began to fall into place. He was one of the ones they thought would flake and that was why they brought in Summer; to ensure he didn't. I was the one who told Erick that Claire was leaving town, and in doing so I condemned her to this fate. If she was gone, they knew they wouldn't have anything for me to fight for. *She's going to be so angry at me for keeping this from her.*

The time went by quickly and I spent the majority of the ride thinking about all the vile things that could be happening to Claire. If anything happened to her I'd never forgive myself.

"All right, we're here," the guy announced, "but I do have to make sure you leave on the blindfold until we get inside. For security reasons, I can't let you see where we're at."

He got out of the car and opened my door, and once I stepped outside I could tell we were inside a building from the musty smell of dust and mold. It felt open almost, and not an enclosed space. I remembered there being several abandoned warehouses out where Austin's body had been found and by the way the air smelled it reminded me of something an old warehouse would smell like.

"Okay, just a little bit further and then I'll let you take off the blindfold before we go down the stairs. The last thing we need is you falling down them and breaking your neck."

"Thanks for your concern," I mumbled sarcastically. "You know, I don't even know your name."

"You can call me Brody for now. It'll suffice for the time being." We took a few more steps and then stopped while Brody punched in a few numbers on a keypad, or at least that was what it sounded like. When he was done, I heard a lock unhinge and the sound of a heavy metal door creaking as it opened.

"Okay, you can take the blindfold off now," he told me.

When I slid it off my head, I had to blink a few times to get my eyes adjusted to the surroundings. It was kind of dark, but once I got used to it I was able to see what was in front of me. I was right about the heavy metal door, but with it having a security code it'd take Ryan and his people at least a couple of minutes to crack it. Those valuable minutes could be the difference between life and death.

Please, God, all I ask is that you let me get Claire out of this, I prayed.

I followed Brody down the steps and the closer we got to the bottom, the more light that filtered in. When I turned the corner, the hallway was fairly narrow and reminded me of a stoned passageway leading to the dungeon below a medieval castle. It even had the sconces blazing with fire lining up and down the hallway.

"What the hell is this place?"

Brody laughed and started down the hall. "Yeah, I know, it's a little over the top, but it's what Erick wanted. He's the one who pays the bills so I guess he can have his place however he wants it."

Trailing him down the hall, the deeper we went the more unsettled I became. I had no clue if the trackers would hold up being that far underground so I had to have faith that they would or at least have faith that Ryan pin pointed my location before the signal was lost.

Brody turned to me and pointed to a large set of

doors. "All right, I'm going to show you where you'll be fighting and then I'll take you to a room so you can change and warm up if you'd like."

Replying with a simple nod and silence, I followed him through the large wooden doors. The moment I stepped through, my eyes went wide in wonder. "Holy shit," I mumbled under my breath.

The room reminded me of a dungeon with more lit sconces on the outer walls. There were throne like seats placed in a circle around the ring, and to my surprise the ring was the same as the modern ones we used today. Given the style of the room one would assume everything would be medieval style. Above, there were stage lights that added a little bit more light to the room, but they only shone down on the ring, giving it an ominous glow.

There was one other thing I noticed while I looked up at the ceiling; there were video cameras everywhere. I counted at least five of them with their red blinking lights.

"What are the cameras for?" I asked, nodding toward the ceiling.

Brody glanced up and answered, "Those are for the people who don't come to the fights. They just watch it on a live feed when it starts. Most of them can't risk being exposed or recognized. Any more questions?"

Yeah, if you have Claire here, where the hell is she?

Instead, I told him, "No, I think I'm good. Let's get this going."

While Brody led me through another hallway with various doors on either side, I couldn't help but wonder if Claire was in one of them. I thought maybe I would get a chance to explore once I changed clothes, but that hope was squashed when Brody put me in a room and locked the door behind him. There was no way out.

Chapter 37

Claire

"All right, my dear, it's time. The cameras are live and connected to the respected parties. So here's how it's going to go. First, I'm going to have the guys come out, talk to them for a few minutes and then it'll be your turn. You'll walk in with Chase, got it?" Erick explained hurriedly.

"Yeah," I mumbled in reply.

Erick dashed off quickly, but I watched his every move on the cameras in front of me. There had to be about fifteen of them in the control room I was in. I was brought early to the underground dungeon, or at least that was how I referred to it as, but while I was waiting around Erick directed me to the control room. I watched as both Mason and Wade arrived and went to their separate rooms.

Wade wasn't locked in his room like Mason was. After Mason changed into his shorts with the eagle on the side, he taped up his hands and put on his gloves. His movements were strong and precise when he warmed up, but the expression on his face was as cold as ice. He was angry, ready to kill, and what scared me most was that I knew he would kill just to save me.

Wade, on the other hand, had a smug expression on his face as he warmed up. It made me want to smack it off his face. He wore a pair of royal blue fighting shorts with a red dragon emblem on the left leg. His dark hair wasn't gelled like it was the past couple of times I'd seen him and it was the first time I'd seen his bare skin since being in town. His perfectly tanned skin had been marred by a large dragon tattoo that covered the whole expanse of his back. I didn't like it because it was the same dragon tattoo Erick had on his neck.

What got me the most was that judging by his appearance he didn't appear to be unhinged by the whole fighting to the death thing. It made me wonder how many of the deceased fighters he was responsible for killing. I understood the concept of accidents in the sport since it was a very dangerous game, but what Erick was doing were not accidents. It was straight up murder.

Erick went to Wade's room and fetched him before going to Mason's. Once Wade got into the main room with the ring, he jumped up in the cage and arrogantly strolled around it. It just confirmed that he had done this before. No wonder he had the money to pay for his expensive house. It was blood money.

On another camera, Erick escorted Mason down the long, stone hallway until the double wooden doors came into view. Once he pushed through them, I had to look at another camera to watch him go in. Wade was all smiles, and honestly, I couldn't wait to see that smile disappear. Mason was ready for this; I could see it in his gaze. He was always ready for a fight. Confidently, he climbed up the steps and entered into the ring, followed by Erick.

Words were said, but I couldn't hear them so I searched around the control board for a volume button and slowly turned it up so I could listen.

"It was so nice of you to come, Mason," Wade sneered. "I figured you'd be one of the flakes."

Mason's lip tilted up slightly. "Sorry to disappoint you, but I don't ever run away from a fight if it's for something I want."

Wade's gaze hardened when he replied, "Neither do I."

Erick stepped between them and held up his hands for them to be quiet. He then strutted to the middle of the ring and turned in a full circle so he could acknowledge every single camera.

"Good evening, ladies and gentlemen. As you all know, tonight is going to be a fight of wills, to see who can outlast the other and survive. For five rounds they must fight until the allotted time is through, which means no matter what condition they are in, they have to fight."

He turned to Wade and Mason and said, "What I mean by that is if you're knocked out on the mat the fight doesn't end. You keep hitting until that buzzer stops. Do you understand?"

Wade nodded with an evil leer on his face while Mason stood there, perfectly still, with a murderous look on his face. "I understand," he growled low.

Erick turned back around and walked back and forth on the mat while he finished his speech with the biggest grin on his face, "Tonight, however, is going to be a little different. Not only are these fighters competing for the extravagant amount of money you brought to the table, but they will also be competing for something else."

Holding my breath, I couldn't take my eyes away from the video, especially from Mason when Erick revealed the final prize. "That something else is something both of these men treasure. I'd like to show what I'm talking about."

That was my cue.

Chase was there, excitement written all over his face, as soon as I walked out the door. Wrapping his hand around my arm he pulled me the rest of the way and stopped just outside of the large, wooden doors. "It's showtime, baby. I can't wait to see the looks on Wade and Mason's faces."

Yeah, me too.

Chase pushed open the doors, and immediately Mason's head snapped in my direction. Clenching his jaw, he closed his eyes and lowered his head, his voice going darkly low. "Why is she here, Erick?" Mason demanded furiously.

Erick chuckled. "I would ask your opponent. He's the one who came up with the idea, but don't be too sore on him, Claire was the one who agreed to the terms. The terms are as follows: whoever wins this fight will leave with the young woman. She will belong to you for the night and you two can do as you wish."

Erick focused back on the cameras and extended a hand out toward Wade's side of the ring and then to Mason's. "Ladies and gentlemen, on one side we have the past and on the other we have the present. Both have loved her and both still do. Which one will be her future? I guess we will see."

I thought I'd be able to stay strong and defiant standing there, but my resolve slowly depleted. My eyes burned, chin trembling, as I watched Mason try to keep it together by a mere thread. With his gaze focused solely on me, he ignored everything else, including Chase, and marched to the edge of the ring so he could peer down at me.

"Are you okay?" he asked in a low voice.

"Of course she is," Chase sneered. "She's been with me all day."

Closing his eyes, Mason took a deep breath, his hands trembling with rage, and let it out slowly before glancing back down at me. "I'm fine, Mason," I told him. "I think you know I can take care of myself."

He didn't seem convinced with my answer, especially when he turned his lethal glare to Chase and pointed at him. "When this is all over … you're dead. This is the last time you fuck with me."

Turning on his heel, he stalked back to his side of the ring, fuming. Erick watched on in amusement and roared in laughter. "Whoa, I think we might need to up the game here after witnessing that. There's obviously some bad blood between these two fighters. Okay, so here's the new terms …"

"New terms?" Wade hissed. "There are no new terms."

With the tension rising in the room, I wasn't surprised that a group of four large men sauntered through the doors, and took up posts around the cage. I would assume they were Erick's protection if Mason and Wade decided to attack him.

"Oh yes there is, son," Erick challenged, grinning devilishly. "I have to make it a little more interesting, don't I? So, with that being said, if you *both* don't hold up your end of the bargain and fight as hard as you can then your lovely little Claire will go to someone else for the night."

"Who?" Mason and Wade yelled at the same time.

Erick looked down at Chase and he was the one who spoke up. "Me," Chase said. "If you two pussy out, your girl belongs to me."

"Like hell she will," Wade spat. "I'll kill you myself before—"

"Enough!" Erick shouted. "It's time to get this party started. After each round, the people watching will be our stand in judges. They will decide which fighter won the round or if neither of you did. If the vote is neither, that point goes to Chase. It's all up to you, gentlemen, on how you want to decide her future."

Erick pointed to me and then down to the mat of the ring. "Claire, if you wouldn't mind coming up here and saying what could be your last words to your men. I'm sure they'd both enjoy one last kiss."

His last request wasn't a suggestion, it was a demand, and I could hear it in the tone of his voice. Surprisingly, Chase let me go and I walked slowly over to the steps that led up to the gate. Hesitantly, I glanced at all the cameras, swallowing hard as I entered into the cage and pondered on who I wanted to talk to first. I chose Wade.

Wade averted his gaze from me as I approached him. With the cameras being all around, I didn't want the people seeing the anger on my face nor did I want them to hear me. Sidling up closer to Wade, I grabbed his arms and put them over my shoulders so my face would be hidden by his muscles.

"Can you not look at me after what you did?" I hissed quietly.

He bent his head toward my neck to conceal his face in my hair. "I'm so sorry, Claire. It wasn't supposed to be like this. I thought once you saw me achieving something in life that you would think I was good enough for you. You loved me then, and I know you can again. That's why tonight you're coming home with me."

"Not like this, Wade. I only accepted the terms because Erick threatened me. Besides, you can't fight for a heart that's already been won."

Holding me tighter, he nuzzled his nose in my hair and kissed my neck. "Watch me," he growled low. Cupping the back of my head, he tilted my face toward him and closed his lips over mine. I let him kiss me, but I didn't give anything back … I couldn't. When he pulled away, he sighed and whispered across my lips, "When this is over, you will kiss me back."

Looking into his corrupted hazel eyes, I couldn't even see a tiny fraction of the old Wade inside them; he was gone. Slowly moving out of his arms, I wiped the lone tear away from my cheek, whispering, "Good-bye, Wade."

Mason wasn't even looking at me or Wade when I turned around to make my way over to him. I had so much to say and I knew I only had a small amount of time. As soon as I got within reach, he pulled me to him, squeezing me to the point it actually hurt.

"Mason," I gasped, choking for air.

Immediately, he loosened his hold and grumbled in my ear, "Sorry, I'm just a little pissed off right now. We need to do this quickly. How did they get you?"

"At the airport. They threatened to hurt you if I didn't

come."

He sighed. "Fuck, I knew I should've walked you inside. Okay, listen baby, Ryan and his team should be here soon. I don't know when, but whatever you see and whatever happens I want you to know that everything will be all right. We'll get through this."

I nodded and finally let the tears fall down my cheeks. "I believe you. Now kick some ass for me so we can go home."

"It'll be my pleasure, baby."

He wiped away my tears with his thumbs before slowly lowering his lips to mine. I opened myself up to him and kissed him as if it would be my last one. All too quickly, Erick was by my side, with a warning glare on his face.

"Gentlemen, when the bell rings, begin."

Erick ushered me out of the cage and down the steps to our seats. Mason and Wade got into position, ready to strike, and both were almost unrecognizable with murderous scowls on their faces. *You can do this, Mason,* I chanted in my mind. All I could hear was the sound of my breathing and the beating of my heart in my ears; it was deafening. It was so loud I was afraid I wouldn't hear the bell; I didn't want to hear the bell. I didn't want it to ring at all.

Unfortunately, that didn't happen. The bell rang and the guys went on the attack.

Ryan, please hurry and get here.

The first round was sickeningly brutal. There was so much anger ... so much hate. Mason fought by the rules of the sport, except I noticed Wade sneaking elbows in where he shouldn't have. Even after the fact, Mason still didn't sway from his honor. I wanted to scream at him, to tell him this wasn't the time to play by the rules, except I knew he wouldn't do it.

Both guys were on their side of the ring, drinking their water and wiping down their skin. Mason's lip was busted, thanks to one of Wade's elbows, and the gash he had above his left eye from the fight with Matt Reynolds reopened and bled down his face. Wade didn't look any better, either. He had a busted nose that wouldn't stop bleeding and an eye that started to swell shut. I had no clue how they were going to last all five rounds.

"How do your people vote on who did the best? Where do you get the results?" I asked Erick. He had his tablet open on his lap, typing away, but I couldn't tell what he was doing. When he finished typing, he handed me the tablet and showed me the answer.

"I have a special program that I use that tallies all of the results within a minute of the votes. The minute is almost up, and their decision should come through right about ... now," he claimed excitedly.

Round 1 winner: Mason Bradley

"You see," he said, taking the tablet back and setting it to the side. "The winner will be the one who had the most votes in their favor. In this case, it was Mason." Standing up, he clapped his hands and approached the ring. "Good job, guys. The votes are in and Mason was the winner for the first round. Round two is about to begin."

Wade threw his water bottle angrily out of the cage in

frustration while Mason kept it calm and cool, not even acknowledging Erick. I couldn't tell if he even heard what Erick said. Chase grumbled beside me, but I ignored him as best as I could and tried to get the murderous thoughts of smashing Erick's tablet over his head as hard as I could; the bell helped with that. Round two had come and Wade and Mason started at it again. Mason landed a hard punch to Wade's midsection and I couldn't tell if it was my imagination or if I actually heard a rib crack. It was different watching it as a sport, but watching it as a matter of life or death was too much to bear. I wanted to scream, yell, kick, fight … anything to let the pressure go. Now I knew why Summer went crazy, she was terrified, but I was … fiercely enraged.

"How can anyone find this entertaining?" I spat vehemently. "You're all nothing but a bunch of sick fucks. How many people have you watched die because of this sadistic crap?"

Chase scooted over to me and put his arm around my shoulder with an evil grin on his face. "Oh, Claire, you disappoint me. If you can't handle it maybe I should take you to another room so you don't have to watch. I can take your mind off of it."

"Chase," Erick growled, "I would appreciate it if you kept your hands to yourself and scampered off. I have half a mind to tie you up and throw you in the cage with Mason and Wade so they can finish *you* off."

Chase snorted and glowered at us both before leaving to take a seat on the other side of the ring. Round two was almost over and when I noticed Mason trying to get Wade into an armbar, I jumped to my feet, but then reality hit; there was no tapping out in this fight. Mason would end up breaking Wade's arm or worse, except it didn't matter because Wade wriggled out of it.

One thing I noticed about Wade was that his movements were quick and choppy. He was faster than Mason, except not as efficient. I did regret, however, my decision to get to my feet. When I looked down at the mat there was blood smeared everywhere and if I breathed in deep enough I was sure I'd be able to smell the metallic scent of it. Putting my head in my hands, I sank to my chair, closed my eyes, and breathed in and out through my mouth. I had faith in Mason, that he could do this, except it didn't make this any less easy.

On the verge of hyperventilating, my reprieve came when the bell rang, signaling the end of round two. "Thank God," I breathed.

Erick went back to his tablet and fiddled around on it. Keeping his gaze on the screen, he said, "You know, at first I thought I liked Chase. He's strong, ruthless, and an arrogant ass. I'm starting to think I should've put him up against Mason instead of Wade. That way I wouldn't have to kill the bastard myself, not unless you want to take the honor and do it. Surely, you'd want to, because you and I both know what his intentions were when he tried to drag you off into the dark."

As much as the thought was appealing, I couldn't kill someone in cold blood … I wasn't like him. "Let me guess," I began, facing off with him, "you'd televise it just like this and get your millions. Am I right?"

Erick winked, an evil leer spreading across his face. "You're damn right. Just think about the money we could make off of it. We could tie him up a bit to give you an advantage and put razors in the tip of your gloves while you fought him. It would be epic."

At the look of horror on my face, Erick bellowed and nonchalantly turned back to his tablet as if he didn't just mention something so sadistically sick that it made my stomach turn. *Was he actually being serious?* The way he said it was all joking, but in his eyes I saw the glint of seriousness. Chills swept through my body and I trembled. I had never been more freaked out being around Erick than I was in that moment. Jumping out of my seat, I had to get some distance and I didn't care if I was allowed to get up or not. Quickly, I went to Mason's side of the ring and gasped when I saw the towel at his feet was drenched in blood and heard the sound of his hoarse breaths as he inhaled.

"Oh my God, Mason, are you okay?" I cried. "You don't sound good at all."

Grimacing, he turned so he could face me and clasped his fingers through the fence. They were bloody, but I still put mine over them and held on. "I'll be okay, baby," he promised. "I have a broken rib. I felt it crack and the pain's just making it a little hard to breathe. I don't know what's taking Ryan so long."

As quietly as I could, I whispered softly, "Listen, Erick's not going to hand me over to Chase. It was all a ruse to get you and Wade to fight harder for me."

Mason leaned his head against the cage and closed his eyes. "Knowing Erick, I'm sure he has another plan for you then if we lose. Wade's getting tired and if he wasn't such a dumbass with using all of his energy in the first round trying to take me down we'd both have more energy. He's a good fighter, but he's not going to last. If I have to keep hitting when he goes down it's not going to be good, and if I refuse to follow through, I'm outnumbered here until help comes," he murmured regretfully.

Reaching through the openings in the cage, I tried to run my fingers soothingly through his sweat drenched hair. If it came down to him or Wade I'd choose Mason in a heartbeat. "You listen to me, Mason. You're not in a professional UFC ring right now. I want you to do whatever you have to do to get this over and done with even if it means putting your honor aside. Sometimes you have to break the rules to survive. You're fighting for your life here, not a title."

Erick cleared his throat loudly, looking down at the tablet in his hands, and we both turned. "Okay, so for round two, the voters have chosen Wade as the winner. Round three will begin shortly. Take your places, gentlemen, and make it good."

Wade gloated in his corner while Chase hollered triumphantly behind him, flipping Mason off with both hands. "I'm going to stay right here, Mason. I'm not going anywhere. You can do this," I told him. Putting his mouthpiece back in, he took a deep breath and nodded before getting into place on the mat.

The bell rang and round three began.

Chapter 38

Mason

Claire.
Fight.
Win.

Those were the three words running rampant through my mind. Nothing else mattered except those three things. My body was on fire, burning and ripping away at my flesh, yet I was numb at the same time. In my mind, I made myself believe that every hit that fucker landed on my body just rolled off and didn't connect. I tasted sweat and blood on my tongue, and I could smell it as it dripped down my face. Unfortunately, a drop of it fell into my eyes, obscuring my vision, and that was all it took for Wade to get an advantage.

The pain exploded from my face all the way down to my feet and my legs gave out. I couldn't see from all the blood, but I'd fought blind before. Austin was the one who taught me how to fight blindfolded. Wade pounced as soon as I hit the ground and dug his knee into my side, the same side with the broken rib. Growling, I elbowed him in the cheek, making his head snap back, and it was his turn to fall over.

"Come on, man, fuck him up like you did that pussy a few weeks ago!" Chase shouted.

Instantly, I froze, hearing Claire's gasp behind me …

I knew someone had been the one to kill Austin, but I never expected the possibility that I could be fighting the same fucker who took him out. Pinning Wade with my weight, I grabbed his neck and squeezed until his face turned as red as the blood dripping down onto the mat from my wounds.

"Who the hell is he talking about?" I shouted in his ear.

Wade clawed at my hands and gasped for air when I finally gave him a reprieve so he could answer my question. He choked and coughed, and instead of answering he tried to get out of my hold. Switching positions, I wrapped my forearm around his neck, tucking him into my side so I could squeeze and apply pressure. It was called a neck crank submission hold, and if I applied more pressure I could do some serious damage. Wade kept his lips firmly shut even though his face was turning blue. *Stubborn prick.*

"Answer me!" I demanded, applying more pressure to his neck. "If you don't answer me I'm going to snap your neck and be done with this shit. I knew a fighter who died here a couple of weeks ago and I want to know who killed him. His name was Austin."

Wade opened his mouth and wheezed so I loosened

my grip, bending low so I could hear him. If he said he did it, I was going to snap his neck and not think twice about it. In that one selfish moment, I wanted revenge more than justice. I wanted to tell Summer that the man who killed her husband paid for what he did, and that everyone involved were going to rot in hell. I wanted revenge for all they put Claire through. With my heart pounding against my chest and the adrenaline coursing through my veins, my body shook as I waited for him to reply. I was so close to snapping his neck.

"I … didn't … fight … Austin," Wade choked.

"Don't you dare fucking lie to me. If you didn't fight him, who did?" I yelled.

Never had I been so consumed with hate or rage to where I thought I'd actually *enjoy* killing someone. There would be no remorse, no sadness … just the knowledge that I made them suffer by my hands. That thought only intensified when I heard Chase's tauntingly arrogant voice holler out the answer my question, "I did it, shithead! I was the one who fought that pussy ass bitch."

Chase's smiling face was all I could see as he came around the cage to face me. Out of everything Chase had done to Austin, Summer, and Claire, he deserved to die a slow and agonizing death. He only made it worse by deepening the wound and confirming his fate.

"Yeah, that fight was pretty interesting," Chase sneered. "When Austin didn't agree to the terms we had his wife brought in, just like we had to snag Claire before she left, in case you flaked. His wife was a hot little number, too, but the bitch went crazy. She's probably dead in an alley somewhere right now."

"You worthless son of a bitch," I snarled, my voice

thundering through the room. "You're the one who's about to be found dead in an alley somewhere."

Keeping my eyes on Chase, I got to my feet and let Wade's limp body fall to the mat with a hard thud. I honestly didn't know if I killed him or if he passed out from my hold. I didn't fucking care. The whole room grew dark and all I could see was the color red with Chase's face right in the middle of it. Either Chase was stupid or the adrenaline in my body had me flying, but one minute I was in the ring and the next I had Chase on the ground, pounding my fists over his bloody face until the sound of Claire's scream brought me back to reality.

"Mason!"

Claire.

Chase was a beaten and bloody mess beneath me, and now there were two men who lied unmoving and helpless because of what I'd done. My mind was in a fog, but then Claire's scream echoed throughout the room again, bringing me back, "Mason!"

Frantically, I searched trying to find her in the room, but no one was there; they were all gone. *Fuck!* I was too busy in my violent rage to keep my eye on the one person I needed to the most. Claire and Erick were gone as well as his other men who were standing guard around the ring during the fight. Claire's voice echoed through a hallway on the other side of the room and I immediately took off toward the sound; however, when I got there, someone was blocking my way to her with a Glock 22 pointed straight at my chest. It was Brody, the guy who picked me up from the hotel and brought me there.

All I heard was the sound of my blood pumping wildly in my ears until the booming resonance of the gun ripped through every part of my soul.

It was over ...

Chapter 39

Claire

"Mason!" I shouted his name over and over, hoping he'd look up, but he never did. I had no clue what was going on, at least not until Erick pulled out his phone and barked out a command that would forever change my life.

"When Mason gets done with Chase, I want you to kill him, got it?"

"No!" I screamed, fighting against his hold. I screamed his name again until one of the guys came up behind me and grabbed me around the waist, putting his hand over my mouth. My screams were muffled, but it didn't stop me from kicking and fighting with all the strength I had.

Satisfied with the response Erick received on the phone, he hung up and grinned smugly at me. "Now, since that's taken care of, we can keep going. I don't like being played, Claire, and you'll come to realize that very shortly."

The guy, who had me in his arms, handed me back off to Erick who gripped my arm with punishing force and continued his rapid pace down the hallway. It was hard to believe that within a span of five minutes I was watching Mason pummel Wade into the mat, and the next, Erick grabbed me by the arm while jamming a gun into my back. From the frantic conversation Erick had with his guys, it all started when the video cameras all lost their signals; they came up blank. Erick and his people were blind to what was going on outside his underground compound, but someone from the outside had informed him of the heavy armed police storming through the outside gates.

Erick fled with me in tow, and the one thing I couldn't get out of my head was the murderous way Mason looked when he flew over the ring and went after Chase. It was the scariest look I'd ever seen on his face, and one I hoped to never see again. However, the fear of never seeing him again became real when the sound of the gunshot echoing off the tunnel walls rang loud and clear.

"No!" I screamed over and over, tears streaming angrily down my face. "Mason!"

He can't be dead! This can't be happening! Jerking my arm away from Erick's grasp, I rushed past his guys and ran as fast as I could up the tunnel. I had to get to Mason.

"Get her!" Erick commanded.

Through my tears I couldn't see where I was going, but I kept running until a large hand clamped down on my shoulder and tackled me to the hard concrete floor. Pain exploded in my wrist when I landed and I could feel the skin scrape away from my knees and elbows as I slid across the cement. However, no amount of pain to my body could outweigh the pain in my heart. Lifting me over his shoulders, the guy who tackled me trudged back to Erick, who glared at me as if I was a petulant child.

"What do you want with me?" I cried breathlessly. Erick rolled his eyes, not acknowledging the question, and turned on his heel, leading us farther and farther away from Mason. I didn't know if he was dead or alive, or if he was writhing in pain waiting on someone to help him. For the first time since all of this started, I was empty, alone, and honestly and truly terrified.

The hallway felt like it went on for miles, and after a while it ended up turning into a tunnel that separated into three different ones. It was then that Erick came to a stop and addressed the others.

"All right, you all know what to do. We'll meet in our usual spot and figure out what's going on. If we have to we'll leave Vegas immediately. We've done this before so you all know the drill."

The guy who held me set me down, and disappeared off into one of the tunnels along with the others. My knees were so weak that I collapsed onto the wet, cement floor and sobbed, "If you leave, you're not taking me with you. They'll find me," I warned.

Erick chuckled and squatted down in front of me. "On the contrary, Miss O'Briene. I've been on the run now for almost five years and haven't been caught yet, and I don't plan on being caught now. What gets me, though, is that someone led the police here. I was completely oblivious until now. I should've known there was something wrong when I couldn't get all of Mason's information. It was like his life completely went nowhere after he left the UFC."

"What are you talking about?" I cried.

Grabbing my chin with his firm hand, he jerked my face up and hissed, "That's right, Claire, play dumb. I bet

Mason's a cop, isn't he? Well, at least I don't have to worry about him anymore. You know, this whole time you've been stubborn and completely fearless. Under normal circumstances that's unheard of, not unless you knew help would be on the way or you're seriously a person who isn't afraid of anything. No one is going to find you, sweetheart. Your hope of getting out of this diminishes with each passing second."

Closing my eyes, I shivered and shook my head. "There is still hope," I whispered.

"Not for you, my dear. Everything you knew of life before is now over. Now get your ass up and let's go. Brody will be waiting for us at the meeting point to pick us up."

"Why don't you just kill me now if that's your plan? Why prolong it by making me go with you?"

Jerking me up by the arm, he glared at me and thundered impatiently, "Because that's not my plan, Claire. I have another use for you and you can't do that being dead. Now come on!"

My legs moved, but my body was still back with Mason wherever he was. If he was gone, I'd rather be dead than live my life with Erick doing God knows what on what borrowed time I had. That wasn't life; it was an empty existence that I wanted no part of. Up ahead, the tunnel came to a dead end, but there was a ladder that led up to what looked to be a metal pothole you would see in the roads.

"You go first, Claire," Erick ordered, pushing me toward the ladder.

Looking up, I took a deep breath and slowly started to climb, one step at a time. When I got to the top, Erick climbed up beside me and pushed the metal cover open with ease. It was dark and quiet outside from what I could see, and I had no clue where we were at until I stepped out of the hole. We were just around the corner from Tyler and Stephen's gym. *If I could get away, I could run to them,* I thought desperately to myself. I didn't know if they would be there, but I had to try.

I had one quick second to make a move, except before I could get my legs running, Erick grabbed my ankle, making me fall face first onto the road. The road was deserted, but I screamed as loud as I could anyway. Struggling against Erick's hold, he tried to keep a firm grip on my leg while pulling himself up the rest of the way.

"Goddammit, Claire, you must seriously have a death wish. Stay still or I'm going to break both of your fucking legs," he growled.

My survival instincts were in full force and the one thing that came to mind were my training sessions with Mason and Tyler. They taught me some defense moves and I never thought I would need them … until now.

Since Erick's face was unprotected, I twisted my body as fast as I could and thrust my palm up toward his nose as hard as possible. I heard and felt something crack when I made the hit and almost instantly his nose gushed with blood. Shouting, his eyes watered and he immediately grabbed his nose, letting go of one of my legs.

When his other hand disappeared behind his back, I knew he was reaching for the gun. *He was going to kill me.* With my legs finally being free, I wasn't going to give him that chance so I kicked him in the face, not only once, but as many times as I could, screaming desperately out of fear. When I stopped kicking, Erick's head hit the edge of the road, rendering him unconscious, before he fell what had to be twenty-five feet to the cement bottom. The sickening sound of the thud his body made as he hit the ground made me completely and utterly sick. Clutching my stomach, I crawled to the edge of the road, dry heaving and choking on my tears. There was no way he could survive that kind of fall and if he did it would be a miracle.

Oh, my God. I just killed someone.

I had to get help, but all I wanted to do was wrap myself in a ball and cry. I might have lost Mason and possibly killed someone all in the same day. *How am I going to recover from that?*

Even though I was exhausted and scared, I wiped away my tears and pushed my legs as fast as they could go to Tyler and his father. Their gym was only about a half mile from where the pothole was and I knew I could get there within three minutes. It felt like I was going in slow motion, especially when the gym came into view and the lights were still on inside. *They were there!* I could even see Tyler in there lifting weights.

In three seconds I would be at the door ... one ... two ... three!

Smashing the door open, I shut it and locked it behind me, clutching my chest and hoping my heart would stop hurting. It was broken. Sagging to the floor, I curled into a ball and finally gave in to the overwhelming grief and fear I didn't allow myself to feel before. *I didn't have to be strong now.*

"Claire!" Tyler shouted. I could hear his steps, fast and hard on the floor as he ran up to me. I knew he was touching me, but I couldn't feel him even when he lifted me in his arms and carried me to the back.

"Dad, call the police, now!" he yelled.

Tyler rocked me in his arms and held my face to his chest. I was spattered in blood and my legs and arms were skinned up from the falls I took before sending Erick down his twenty-five foot fall.

"He's dead," I cried, burying my face in his shirt. "I think they killed him, Tyler. They killed Mason."

"Oh my God, Claire," he breathed sadly. "What are you talking about? Were you robbed? I thought you went back to California this morning."

"No, I never made it back," I whispered. "They took me and now it's over. It's all over and he's gone."

Everything after that happened in a blur and I couldn't remember if I spoke to the police or not. The ambulance came and took me away, and Tyler stayed with me the whole time. Every time I opened my eyes he was there, holding my hand. I kept imagining it was Mason with me the whole time, and in my dreams it *was* him so I tried to stay in my dream world for as long as I could. It was better there.

"Claire, can you hear me? Wiggle your toes if you can hear me."

The voice sounded so familiar, but that voice didn't belong in the hell I was in. She needed to leave before my hell consumed her, too. Knowing I would see the same pain in her eyes, I didn't want to open mine to witness it. Mason was gone … her cousin was gone, and I was alone.

"Melissa?" I whispered sadly.

"Oh my God, Claire, yes it's me. We've been so worried about you. We got the call last night and came first thing this morning," she cried.

Feeling around for her hand, I grabbed it and squeezed tightly, hesitantly opening my eyes in the process. Melissa was right beside me, eyes puffy and red from crying.

"I'm so sorry, Mel. I didn't want any of this to happen," I sobbed.

"I know you didn't, Claire, but you and Mason both knew there would be risks. You can't blame yourself for what happened."

Shaking my head, I gazed at her incredulously. "You don't understand. How am I going to get through all of this by myself?"

She snorted and ran her fingers soothingly down the side of my face. "You're not by yourself, Claire. You will always have me by your side. I've always been there for you, haven't I?"

Turning my head away, I closed my eyes and blew out a shaky breath. "It's not the same, Mel. I can't get through all of this without Mason. He's the one I need."

"And I'm right here, Claire," his voice spoke out.

Gasping, my throat closed up and I froze. *Did I really just hear his voice? Is he really here?* I didn't want to get my hopes up in fear that I had truly lost my mind and was imagining it. I ached for him, my heart ached for him. My body jerked when a hand reached out and brushed the hair off my face. It wasn't Melissa's soft hands, but large and strong, warm.

Gasping, I grabbed the hand that touched me and held

on tight, feeling the calluses and the broken skin. My eyes burned behind my closed eyelids and my lips trembled. "Mason?" I wailed, "Is it really you?"

"It's me, baby. I'm here," he murmured. As he leaned over me, I could finally breathe in the intoxicating scent of his skin. *It was him!*

Opening my eyes, I gasped when his face came into focus. He was beaten and bruised with nasty cuts and gashes everywhere, but he was still my Mason. "You're alive," I cried, throwing my arms around his neck. "I thought you were dead. When Erick made the call and told whoever to kill you I thought you were gone when I heard the gunshot. Oh my God, I was so scared." Squeezing my eyes shut, I held him tighter and whispered in his ear, "I thought I lost you forever."

Mason shook his head and pulled back, putting a finger to my lips. "What you heard was Ryan's shot. Before Brody could pull the trigger, Ryan and his people barged in and got him before he could get me. That was the shot you heard, baby. I'm so sorry you thought it was me."

With tears in his eyes, he took my face in his hands and placed his lips gently across mine. "I thought I lost you, too. After we found Erick and you were nowhere in sight, I thought I was going to lose my mind. Then I heard about the call saying that you were at the gym so I rushed over as soon as I could, but you had already been taken to the hospital. I had no idea what had happened to you."

The mention of Erick brought back all of the horrid memories. I wish I could go through the rest of my life not knowing what happened, but I needed to know for my own sanity.

"What happened to everyone, Mason? To Wade,

Chase … Erick? I need to know."

Sighing, Mason gazed down at me warily while Melissa got quickly to her feet and retreated toward the door. "You know, I think I'm going to leave you two alone for a while," she said. "I know there's a lot you need to talk about. Do you need anything, both of you?"

I shook my head and smiled and Mason did the same thing before taking the seat she just vacated. Grasping my hand, Mason closed his eyes and took a deep breath. "Claire, I didn't want to have to tell you all of this so soon. There's a lot you don't know about. Are you sure you want to know?" he asked hesitantly.

With my heart thumping wildly, I licked my dry lips and nodded quickly. "Yes," I answered desperately. "Just tell me and get it over with."

"Okay," he agreed sadly, moving closer to the bed. "Here we go."

After clearing his throat, he soothingly ran his thumb over my knuckles and began, "All right, I'll start with Chase first. If I didn't hear your scream I'm sure I would've killed him. I let anger and revenge cloud my judgment from what was truly important. He has a few broken bones, but he'll live. He's been charged with second degree murder for the deaths of Austin and one of the other fighter's named Patrick Ross."

"Does Summer know that you found the guy who killed Austin?" I asked. "Have you talked to her?"

Mason nodded. "Yeah, she knows. She wants to leave Virginia and move back to North Carolina to get away for a while. I offered her my house to rent and possibly to own in the future if she wants it. Once I move my stuff out, she's going to move in. It actually saves me from having

321

to sell it once I come to California."

Mason lifted my hand to his cheek and closed his eyes, breathing in deeply. It was hard to believe that just a few hours ago I was devastated and alone thinking he was dead, but now he was in front of me, breathing … alive. I wasn't going to ever let him go. "That was really sweet of you, Mason, to let Summer stay at your house. I know Austin would be proud of you for finding justice and taking care of her for him. I'm just glad it's over."

"Me too," he agreed, opening his eyes.

"Now continue with what you were saying and tell me about Wade. I have a strange feeling you're leaving the really bad news for last," I grumbled.

Mason settled his gaze on our clasped hands and blew out a shaky breath. When he lifted his gaze to me there was sadness there, but there was also something else staring back at me … regret. "Wade's condition wasn't looking so good when he was brought in," he explained, "When I had him in submission he wasn't getting the adequate amounts of oxygen to his brain. He had what you call brain hypoxia. Last I heard, he was awake and actually talking again, but once he leaves here he's not going back to that nice, beautiful house he just bought."

Yeah, I figured that. I was almost afraid to ask, but I did it anyway. "What is being put away for?"

"He was responsible for one of the other fighter's deaths. His name was Grayson Hubbard. He'll be charged with second degree murder," he told me.

My eyes burned with unshed tears, but I refused to cry any for what Wade had become. I wanted to cry for the fun, caring, and passionate Wade that must've died somewhere along the way. He made his bed and now he had to lie in it. It was disturbing how someone could be good one minute, and then turn into someone who would kill and sell his soul for money and fame. Deep down I guess he always had that dark side … he just kept it hidden.

"All right, Mason, enough about Wade. It's just a reminder of how I try to see the good in people and then turn up disappointed. I need to know about Erick now," I demanded, "and don't beat around the bush. I want the truth even if it's not something I want to hear."

I already knew it was going to be something I didn't want to hear.

Mason licked his lips and sighed. "Erick's dead, Claire. Actually his name wasn't even Erick. Apparently, the information Ryan had been waiting on came just in time. He had tried to send me a picture of this Michael Turner before I got picked up to go to the fight, but it never loaded in time before they took my phone. Erick's real identity is Michael Turner. He had a warrant out on his arrest for killing his wife and kidnapping his newborn daughter. We traced him back to a house out near Wade's and found his daughter and a housekeeper there. The housekeeper was taken in for questioning and I think social services took the little girl away."

"Oh my God," I cried. *Madison.*

So that's what happened to Madison's mother, she was killed … murdered. Madison had been through so much and now this; taken away by the system. She didn't deserve to be transferred from home to home, and neither did any of the other children in the world who got tossed around.

Mason was oblivious to my inner turmoil and continued, "So basically the case of the Ohio deaths has been solved now. Erick was the one who did it."

Taking my hands out of Mason's, I covered my face and sobbed. I wasn't crying about Erick's death, no, I could care less that he was gone from the world. He needed to be taken out of it, except it was a little unnerving knowing that I played a part in it even though I was defending myself. Actually, my heart went out to one person, to a tiny little girl who deserved so much more than a murderous father who killed her mother and took her away, only to put her in a dangerous world she didn't belong in.

Mason pried my hands away and tilted my chin up. "Look, I don't know what happened, and I was hoping you would feel comfortable enough to talk to me about it. Right now, Erick's death has been ruled an accident. Other than the broken nose he sustained which I'm assuming is from you, the other injuries he acquired came from the fall alone. If you're worried about getting in trouble you don't need to be. If anything it was self-defense and there's no reason to feel guilty about that. If I had caught him before he fell he'd be dead anyway. It was inevitable."

Mason wiped away my tears and pressed his lips softly against mine. The cut in his lip had to hurt, but he still offered me his comfort. Pressing his forehead to mine, he breathed me in and nuzzled my nose with his with a smile on his face.

"After you give your statement to Ryan, I'm taking you home and never letting you out of my sight again. I'm taking a very long vacation to figure out what I want to do with my life, but there is one thing I know for certain."

"What would that be?"

Taking a seat on the bed, he placed his arms on both

sides of me and leaned close so he could gaze into my eyes. "I want to be with you every single day, Claire. I want to make love to you and wake up to your smiling face for as long as I live. One day when we're ready, I don't care when it is, hell, it could be tomorrow for all I care, but I want you to be my wife. I love you so damn much it hurts. Before, all I've ever done is live for the job. I never even thought I would want a family of my own until you came and showed me what love could be like and how it felt. You've had me addicted ever since and now I want it all."

A tear escaped the corner of his eye, but this time he let it fall without any shame. Hearing those words come from Mason's mouth was both shocking and beautiful. He wasn't a man of voicing feelings so I knew if he ever did propose it wouldn't be anything elaborate, but hearing the words alone come from his lips made it more special than if he proposed on top of the Eiffel Tower. If he wasn't in visible pain I would jump out of the bed and into his arms. I wanted to be his wife more than anything and I wanted it all too … including a family.

"So, with that being said," I began with a sly smile, "was that your idea of a proposal?"

Mason chuckled and I laughed along with him. He nodded sheepishly and rubbed the back of his neck when he replied, "Yeah, I guess it was. My whole point was to let you know that I'm serious about this and that's where I want it to lead. I want a family, Claire. I have no one other than you and Melissa. I want a son so I can do the things with him like my father did with me and teach him things." He grinned at me and winked. "I'll even let you tag along if you want."

Smiling, I could just imagine what it would be like to have a smaller version of Mason running around. It would happen one day. However, there was something else I had on my mind that didn't involve a son, but a daughter.

"Mason," I murmured nervously. "I need to talk to you about something, or better yet something to ask you." What I wanted to do was a big decision and I needed his support since we planned on staying together. The only problem would be the circumstances. I couldn't stop my hands from shaking I was so nervous.

Mason furrowed his brows, growing concerned by the wariness in his eyes. "Claire, you're shaking, what is it? You know you can talk to me about anything."

"What would you say if we had a little girl first instead of a boy? Would you still love her just as much?"

Incredulously, Mason guffawed and shook his head. "Seriously, Claire, that's what you're all nervous about? Of course, I would love a girl just as much as a boy. She could be a little dancer just like you and hopefully get her looks from you too." He paused for a moment and then his eyes went wide. "Wait, are you pregnant? Is that what you're telling me?"

Smiling, I shook my head and laughed. "No, I'm not pregnant. As soon as you want to have kids of our own I'll be ready. However, what would you say if I knew of a little girl who looked just like me, was a dancer, and also needed a home?"

"If she's just like you I'd say she sounds amazing, but what are you getting at?" he asked skeptically.

Taking a deep breath, I sat up in bed and let the tears fall down my cheeks. With all my heart and soul, I began the story of the little girl who stole my heart.

"It all begins with a little, curly blonde headed girl in a purple leotard and pink tutu. Her name is Madison and in the short amount of time I spent with her she wrapped me around her little finger. She's going to need a home, Mason, and I want to give it to her," I cried.

It didn't take long for Mason to know who I was talking about. At first he seemed hesitant, but then he smiled and cupped my face in his hands. "Well then, let's go get her."

Chapter 40

Claire

SIX MONTHS LATER

The ending of The Little Mermaid played on the screen, and Madison was sound asleep, snoring softly, with her head on my lap. I loved playing with her little blonde curls and wrapping them around my fingers. It took three months to get the adoption process finalized and usually it took longer than that, but given the circumstances we were able to get it rushed. Madison lived with Mira during those three months, but Mason and I visited with her almost every weekend so we could spend time with her. It took her a couple of visits to open up to Mason, but when she did, he fell in love with her and her with him. To this day, they were inseparable.

"Do you want me to carry her to her room?" Mason whispered.

I nodded. "Yes, please."

Smiling, he picked her up gently and she squirmed in his arms, but her little eyes stayed shut. Every night after

I'd give her a bath, we would cuddle on the bed and watch a Disney movie. We'd been doing it now for the past three months, including Mason. It was actually fun because I liked watching them and always had when I was growing up. Mason, on the other hand, endured them solely for Madison. It was sweet that he did it and only made me fall in love with him more.

When Mason came back into the room, he shut the door quietly behind him and took his shirt off, throwing it to the floor. I cuddled up next to him when he got back under the sheets and traced my fingers along the lines of his well defined stomach muscles. For the past month he'd been training with Matt Reynolds, who tried every single day to coax him back into fighting for the UFC. Mason was torn between not knowing what to do or if he'd make the right decision. I told him to follow his heart and if he did that then he couldn't go wrong. He was still undecided.

"Do you know what time it is?" he asked, twirling my wedding band around on my finger with a mischievous gleam in his eye. We finally said our vows about two months ago on a crisp, autumn day in our backyard with our close friends gathered around and little Madison as our flower girl. It was the perfect day.

"I don't know," I answered. "Why don't you tell me what time it is? I think I forgot." I knew very well what time he was referring to, but I loved playing the game.

Mason growled low in his throat and spread my legs with his knee. He slid his hand under my shorts and pushed a finger inside, but only slightly, teasingly. "I would say you know what time it is," he murmured gruffly in my ear. "You're soaking wet."

He nipped my ear before moving down the bed so he

could grasp my shorts and yank them off my body. He then ripped off my shirt and did the same with his boxers. Climbing on top of me, he licked a trail around my nipple, making me gasp in pleasure, and then slid his tongue all the way up to my neck. When we got married, he told me not to tell him when I decided to stop my birth control and little did he know I stopped it two weeks ago. I wanted to tell him, but he was adamant on it being a surprise when I got pregnant.

Mason pushed inside of me gently while rubbing his thumbs up and down my cheeks as he held my face in his hands. He slowly made love to me and never took his gaze off my eyes the entire time. One day soon, I was hoping I'd be able to tell him that our family was about to grow.

Breathing hard, Mason leaned down to kiss me and smiled. "Do you want to know why I don't like to take my eyes off of you when I make love to you?" he asked.

"Yes, tell me," I breathed, running my hands soothingly down his back.

"I do it because even to this day I sometimes think this is all a dream and I'm going to wake up and you'll be gone. I didn't deserve a second chance, but you gave me one. I told you I would fight for your heart and I will continue to do so for the rest of my life to keep it. Even if I were to die, I would never stop fighting because what you have in here," he said, placing a hand over my heart, "is mine ... and I'm never letting it go."

"Ever ..."

Epilogue

Claire

FIVE MONTHS LATER

The roar of the crowd going wild and cheering for the fighters in the ring echoed down the hall to the room where Mason was warming up for his fight. His hands were taped and ready to go, and on the other side of his fighting shorts was the logo for MMA Pride. Instead of going back to the force, he decided to follow his dreams and do it right this time, even though it took him months to make the decision. When he was offered a sponsorship, I could see it in his eyes that he didn't want to turn it down. I was glad he took it.

It just so happened that we were back in Vegas where everything began in the first place. However, this time we were at the MGM Grand Garden Arena, and instead of the audience being around five hundred people, it was about fifteen thousand.

A knock came at the door and Matt Reynolds stuck his head out to the side, his boyish grin spreading from ear to ear when he spoke, "Hey, man, I'm sorry but I'm about to steal your woman so we can take our seats. You're almost up and I don't think you want your hot, pregnant wife walking out there by herself."

Mason rolled his eyes and made sure to flex his muscles. "You know if I win this fight my next one will be with you for the title. You do know that, right?"

Matt chuckled and shrugged a shoulder. "Oh I know. I guess it's a good thing I know how to kick your ass, isn't it?" Quickly, he acknowledged me and said, "I'll be right out here when you're ready."

I nodded. "Give me one second and I'm yours."

He shut the door and I couldn't help but laugh. Even little Mason thought it was funny because I could feel him dancing around in my belly. I was nineteen weeks pregnant and Mason and I had just found out it was a boy a few days ago when I went for my ultrasound. Madison came with us as well and I had never seen her so happy. She couldn't wait for her little brother to come.

"I can't believe Matt's still single," I said, glancing at the door he just left out of. "You would think he'd have women fawning all over him."

Mason snorted, rolling his eyes. "Oh, he does, but he says he's waiting for someone like you to come around. He said that if I can score a woman like you then he could. I seriously need to kick his ass, don't I?"

We both laughed, but then were interrupted when the phone rang.

"Hello," I answered.

"Mommy, it's me," Madison squealed. While Mason and I were gone for the night, Melissa had volunteered to keep Madison while we were away. Madison loved spending time over there because of the twins so I didn't feel too bad with leaving her.

"Hey, Maddie, are you okay?"

"Oh yes! Aidan threw up all over Uncle Brett and I laughed. It was really nasty," she said, giggling. "Has daddy fought yet?"

Mason was listening in and spoke into the phone, "No, baby, I haven't yet. I'm about to though. Do you want to send me a good luck kiss?"

She squealed. "Yes! Here I go!"

Putting her lips to the phone, she made the loudest kissing noise I'd ever heard. "Did you get it?" she asked.

Mason smiled. "Yes, baby, I got it. We'll see you tomorrow, okay?"

"Okay," she said. "I love you."

"We love you, too, honey," I murmured back. "Now get to bed it's getting late."

We hung up the phone and it was time to let Mason have his moments of peace before the fight. Leaning down, Mason kissed my slightly swollen belly and whispered to our son while rubbing him gently, "Take care of your mother, little man. One of these days you'll be a fighter just like me."

"You'll do great tonight," I uttered wholeheartedly. "Fight hard, and know that whether you win or lose, you will always be a winner in my eyes. You won my heart a long time ago."

Mason smiled and kissed me gently on the lips. "And you've won mine. That's all that matters."

Matt waited for me outside the door just like he said and walked me through the arena where we had front row seats. The music began to play and the lights went wild.

Mason's opponent walked down the aisle and entered the octagon ring with his fists pumping to get the crowd riled up. They cheered and hollered for him, but then the music changed. It was Mason's turn. When he walked out, the cheers got even louder and the whole floor felt like it rumbled. The second he got in the ring, he came over to the side I was at and kissed his fingers before placing them over his heart. It was his salute to me, and my stomach always fluttered each time I'd watch him do it.

Once the announcer made the introductions and the bell rang, Mason was on fire. Over the past few months he'd gotten even better, unstoppable. Matt groaned beside me so I looked over at him, furrowing my brows.

"Are you okay?" I asked.

Slumping in the seat, he chewed on his thumbnail and sighed. "He's going to kick my ass next month, isn't he?"

Gazing back up at Mason, I couldn't stop the grin from spreading on my face. "Yes, he will," I murmured to myself. "He's a fighter."

He's my *fighter*.

The End

Fighting for Love - Second Chances, #4
(Matt's Story)
Coming Feb/March 2014

About the Author

L.P. Dover is the bestselling author of the Forever Fae series, as well as the Second Chances standalone series, and her NA romantic suspense standalone called Love, Lies, and Deception. She lives in the beautiful state of North Carolina with her husband, her two wild girls, and her rambunctious kitten called Katrina.

Before she began her career in the literary world, L.P. Dover spent her years going to college and then graduated to cleaning teeth, which she loved doing. At least until the characters in her head called her away. She has never been the same since.

You can find L.P. Dover at:

Her website: www.authorlpdoverbooks.com

Email: lpdover@authorlpdoverbooks.com

Follow her on Twitter: @LPDover

"Like" her on Facebook:
https://www.facebook.com/pages/LP-
Dover/318455714919114

Pinterest:
http://www.pinterest.com/smiley317537/boards/

OTHER BOOKS BY L.P. DOVER

Forever Fae Series

Second Chances Standalones

Standalone (Romantic Suspense)

ALSO CHECK OUT THESE
EXTRAORDINARY AUTHORS & BOOKS:

Alivia Anders ~ *Illumine*
Cambria Hebert ~ *Recalled*
Angela Orlowski Peart ~ *Forged by Greed*
Julia Crane ~ *Freak of Nature*
J.A. Huss ~ *Tragic*
Cameo Renae ~ *Hidden Wings*
Tabatha Vargo ~ *Playing Patience*
Alexia Purdy ~ *Breathe M*e
Beth Balmanno ~ *Set in Stone*
Lizzy Ford ~ *Zoey Rogue*
Ella James ~ *Selling Scarlett*
Tara West ~ *Visions of the Witch*
Heidi McLaughlin ~ *Forever Your Girl*
Melissa Andrea ~ *Flutter*
Komal Kant ~ *Falling for Hadie*
Melissa Pearl ~ *Golden Blood*
Sarah M. Ross ~ *Inhale, Exhale*
Brina Courtney ~ *Reveal*
Amber Garza ~ *Falling to Pieces*
Anna Cruise ~ *Maverick*

Read on for some really great sneak previews!

Here's a sneak peek of
Pretty Little Dreams by Jennifer Miller
Scheduled to be released on Jan. 13, 2014

Chapter One

Olivia

I'M LYING IN bed with the man I hate. I wake up, and for a brief moment I am at peace. Then, as fast as fashion lovers rush to a sale at Bloomingdales, I remember. I'm painfully and vividly aware that the peace I momentarily feel is not real and that the man I'm lying next to is not the one my heart longs for.

Another day in hell. I have no idea how many days it has now been. I don't know how long I was out before I woke up and found myself bound and gagged lying on a bed. Deacon injected something in my body to knock me out initially, but I don't know what. When I would arouse during our journey here, he would force me to drink a liquid – water, I think, laced with some kind of sedating drug. The drug would immediately impose a haze and then a deep fog would engulf me, until once again, I was oblivious to everything. Just as today, there was no rest or peace during that sleep, but rather a repeated, tormented struggle:

at times a longing to find consciousness and formulate a plan for securing my freedom and, at other times, as fear suffocates me, a desire to sleep into eternity.

I feel myself start to panic again, recalling those moments of pure hysteria when I finally woke up. I can't go there. I can't let myself feel what I really want to feel right now. Instead, I lock the fear in a box. If I don't, it will consume me. I can't let myself think of the unknown, of the what-ifs. When the fear starts to drag me into its dark abyss, I defy its grip and force my thoughts to focus on the people I love. Pyper. My parents. And then, with my heart twisting painfully in my chest, Luke. I roll onto my side in a slow, deliberate and cautious manner, as close to the bed's edge as possible, careful not to wake the living, breathing, nightmare lying beside me. Putting my back to him provides me the illusion of placing even more distance between us than I actually can. I hate being in bed with him.

My pulse starts racing as I give that too much thought, so I quickly lock my feelings and thoughts up in that box again, putting them away to pursue later. Effortlessly, Pyper again comes to my mind, and I could swear it's like she's standing before me waving her arms to get my attention. I smile at her image. I hope she's okay. The last thing I remember before Deacon took me is my best friend tied up, helpless, echoing the wide-eyed fear I also felt. As our eyes met, I tried to convey to her how much I loved her. We both knew what was going to happen. I begged Deacon to leave her, to not hurt her. Whether he listened to me or not, I have no idea. I only know from asking him over and over again about Pyper that he left her tied up on the couch, but in what condition, I do not know, and he refuses to say. He only states that his major objective was to take me. And he was willing to do so at any cost. I can only hope he did not hurt her, that he merely left her as he said. But honesty is not one of his strengths. Regardless, I pray to God that someone found her quickly. I hope she's alive and well and not worrying too much. I hope she was able to tell Luke what happened.

Luke. During my darkest times when I'm most afraid, thoughts of him are constant. He's my happy place. I daydream frequently about him holding me, whispering to me, kissing me. Sometimes, I even let my thoughts venture to the life I wish to have with him some day. My favorite is when I picture us in a home. Our home. Not an apartment or townhouse, but a house. I know without a doubt that it will have to be a house, because Luke will want something that is ours. In my daydream, our house looks like one of those old plantation estates in Georgia. It has a wraparound porch, with his and hers rocking chairs in front; our favorite spot. Luke and I sit in the chairs, sipping iced tea on a warm summer day. Our chairs face each other and my feet are in his lap. I smile, listening to him tell me about the new night club he is excited about opening, while he rubs my feet, his enthusiasm evident. His voice, combined with the breeze blowing through the trees brings me contentment. A dog, a golden retriever named Dakota, is lying next to our chairs. While we talk, I drop my hand down to scratch the top of his head. I think even the dog smiles with contentment. I don't know if dogs actually smile or why we have one, I just know there is one in my perfect day dream; the daydream and the life I hope and wish to have with Luke. I miss him so much that the ache in my heart nearly crushes me, takes my breath away and I find myself gasping for air. The pain is incredible. It's worse than a punch in the gut, the unfairness of it all. After seven long years, we have finally reconciled, and then Deacon comes and ruins our plans. Ruins our dreams.

I still thank God that we found each other again. After hearing him tell his mom I meant nothing, when I took off and married Deacon, I really never thought I would see him again. Thoughts of Luke would venture into my mind often, but I always stubbornly pushed them away. While painful, the best thing that could have happened for me and Luke was the time I caught Deacon cheating and finally took a stand against him and his abusive ways by divorcing him. Moving back to Chicago was the right choice because eventually, surprisingly, and unexpectedly, it brought me back to Luke. And I was finally happy again.

I confess that at some level, I am still in denial. I had no idea that Deacon would do something like this. I knew he was angry and has been obsessive and borderline crazy over my leaving him, but I never thought he would go this far. I never thought he would take me - kidnap me - from my own home. I've tried to reason with him, to ask him what he's thinking, to make him feel guilty, and to try to scare him. I've begged him to just let me go. I've promised him that I won't tell anyone, that it will be our secret. I've told him to just leave me here and save himself before it's too late. He refuses. He shakes his head, laughs. Instead, he makes me do things I don't want to do, and makes it clear that I am far from being in charge here.

My thoughts are suddenly interrupted as I feel Deacon moving next to me, his fingers touch my back, and I stiffen, acutely aware that he's awake. He asks me the same thing each morning, "Have you come to your senses yet? I'm tired of your refusal, no more games."

Jaw clenched so tight my teeth grind together, I roll over and bravely stare into his eyes, "Let me go, Deacon. Each day you keep me here, you're only digging yourself deeper and deeper. There's still time for you to do the right thing." I respond the same each time too.

"I have plans for us tonight." Ignoring my comment, Deacon rises from the bed, completely naked. I avert my eyes from his body.

"Plans? What kind of plans?"

"We are going to have a nice dinner together, for starters."

I scoff, "I don't want to have dinner with you."

"Too bad, you don't have a choice."

The room I'm being kept in isn't bad. We are in some house in the middle of nowhere, as far as I can tell. I'm in a room that has the bare necessities. A large bed and a dresser, there is also an attached bathroom, but it too has the bare minimum. There isn't even a mirror. I can, however, see where the wall paint changes color, indicating that at one time, a large one had hung above the sink. I wonder if Deacon removed it, and if so, when that was. How long had he been planning this? Each time Deacon leaves me alone, which isn't often, he locks me inside the bedroom. Sometimes I hear him talking to someone through the door. There was a time when I wasn't sure if he had someone helping him or if he was talking on the phone. I think back to the time when I found out the answer to that question.

Rolling out of bed, Deacon pulls on a pair of pants. "I will be back. Don't do anything stupid while I'm gone."

"Be back? What do you mean? Where are you go-

ing?"

"Aw, isn't that sweet? Are you concerned about me? Are you going to miss me, princess?" he asks, walking over to my side of the bed.

"No. I don't care where you go. I'm just surprised you would leave me alone."

An angry look flashes across his face and he leans over me, grasping my wrists hard, holding them up near my shoulders. I turn my face to the side trying to avoid him. "You better start caring, princess, or you aren't going to like what happens." Then he moves his hands to the side of my face, forcing me to face him again. He kisses me hard on the lips.

As soon as he lets go of me, I wipe my face with the back of my hand. He laughs as he walks out of the room, slamming the door behind him.

Throwing the covers back, I run to the door and press my ear against it – all I hear is murmuring on the other side. He must be on the phone again. It isn't long before I hear a hard slam which I assume is a door closing. I think I'm alone; this could be my only chance for a while.

I run to the sliding balcony doors and creep out onto the balcony. This is the first chance I've had to come out and take in my surroundings. Deacon told me when he locked me in this room that we are in the middle of nowhere and I could yell and scream as much as I want – no one will hear.

Looking around, I see he was telling the truth. There doesn't appear to be anything for miles. I'm too high up to jump down and tying my sheets together would be useless; I couldn't even reasonably reach the ground.

Frantically, I start running around the room, looking

for something, anything, to use as a weapon. I search the dresser, the top of the closet, under the bed, the bathroom cabinets. "Dammit." I can't find anything.

Running back to the bed, I rip the sheet from it and wrap it around my hand. Heading to the balcony doors, I brace myself. If I can manage to shatter the door, I can use the glass as a weapon. Please let this work. I take my fist and slam it against the door as hard as I can. I scream. Not even a scratch and all I managed to do was hurt my hand. In anger, I beat against the door over and over until I'm a heap on the floor. I pull my hand out of the sheet and glance at it. It's beginning to swell, but I hardly feel it.

There's nothing here. Nothing. Feeling defeated, I walk back out onto the balcony and decide it's worth a try, no matter what Deacon said.

"HELP! PLEASE SOMEONE! HELP ME!" What do I have to lose? Maybe I will luck out and someone is around.

I wait a moment and then try again.

"HELP! I'VE BEEN KIDNAPPED. SOMEONE HEL..."

Suddenly, I am grabbed from behind and dragged into the bedroom and thrown on the bed like a rag doll. I try to roll onto my back but instead a weight settles on my back, and my face gets shoved into the mattress.

"Shut the fuck up, bitch."

The voice is not Deacon's. I freeze as shock runs through my body from head to toe, paralyzing me in fear.

"Lover boy isn't here to save you. It might be worth facing his anger to shut you up permanently."

I don't speak. I'm afraid to move. Who is this man? He moves off me so he can roughly flip me over. I stare up into his hard eyes. He's not an attractive man. Light hair, pointy nose, and lips so thin they're hardly there at all. He has a scar that runs from the tip of his eyebrow to the middle of his cheek. "Leave me alone."

"I don't think I will... what does he call you? Princess? I don't think I will, princess." He says mockingly. Then, to my horror he runs his hand down the front of my body, squeezing my breasts painfully and then gripping my hip. His breathing starts quickening.

"No, please don't touch me."

"That's right, beg, you bitch. Next time you will think twice about breaking the rules and trying to yell for help."

Oh God. He's going to hurt me, or worse. I do the only thing I can. I start struggling. I kick my legs like a three-year-old having a tantrum. I throw my head back and forth and get one of my hands loose and scrape my nails down the front of his face. "Let go of me!" I scream.

He roars in pain and touches the side of his face where I scratched him. The next thing I know I feel a hard smack on the top of my head. I see stars and I panic, afraid of what he will do to me when I can't defend myself. Just as I start to lose consciousness, I hear Deacon yell, "WHAT THE FUCK?!" Against my will, I succumb to the darkness enveloping me.

My eyes well up from that awful memory. I remember when I came to, Deacon was angry. "You don't have to worry about Ronnie, princess, I took care of him. He will think twice about ever touching you again," he said while stroking my face. My head hurt too much for me to react to his touch, until I realized I'm completely naked. I ran to the bathroom heaving into the toilet, not sure if I was sick due to the ache in my head – did I have a concus-

sion? - or the fear coursing through me as I had no clue
how I had ended up naked or what, if anything, had happened in addition to what I could recall.

Deacon distracts me from my thoughts when he yanks
open the closet door and grabs a box I've never seen before from the top of the closet. He turns towards me, and
throws the box on the bed. "You will wear this to dinner
tonight."

Opening the box, I pull out a slinky black dress that I
can already tell will barely cover my body. "I'm not wearing that."

"Oh, yes you are, princess. We are going to have a
nice, romantic meal, and you are going to wear that dress."

"I'm not dressing up for you, Deacon."

Faster than I can blink, Deacon is on me. I shrink
back as much as I can, trying to avoid his nakedness from
touching mine. Grasping me by the top of my arms, Deacon's face is mere inches from mine, "You will wear the
fucking dress, Olivia. This is not up for discussion." As he
speaks each word, he shakes me and squeezes me tighter,
making me cry out in pain.

"Deacon! You're hurting me."

"Stop making me hurt you. Do you think I like this?
Do you think I want to hurt you? Why do you keep making me hurt you? Just do what I tell you to do and we will
be fine. I've told you over and over again that this is our
future. You and me, princess. Once you accept that, the
happier you'll be."

"Okay. Okay, Deacon." I force the words out of my
mouth because it is the exact opposite of what I want. I've
learned the hard way what happens when I don't keep my
mouth shut or if I don't say or do what he wants.

"Good. I will be back later. Make sure you are dressed and ready." And with that, he grabs some clothes off the floor and leaves the room.

WHAT MUST BE a few hours later, I'm running a brush through my hair. It's one of the few personal items Deacon allows me. I have no idea what I look like. I have the hideous dress on and I keep pulling it down. The scrap of fabric barely covers my ass and my boobs are barely contained. I look like one of the very girls I tell all my readers on *Pink Sugar Couture* not to emulate. My inner fashion diva has officially curled up and died.

Entering the room, Deacon whistles low, "You look hot, princess."

I feel revulsion internally and just stare at him. He's dressed for dinner in what I can't help but notice is a well-cut, charcoal-colored, European suit and tie. Where he gets the clothes, I have no idea. Not for the first time I wonder where we are exactly, and how this house is associated with him. The things that I don't know about this man continue to shock me. How I was ever married to him, I don't know.

He walks toward me and places his mouth on mine. I refuse to open for him and I know it will only make him mad, but dammit, I hate feeling helpless in all of this.

Pulling away from me Deacon looks into my eyes, "I'll let that one slide, for now. Come with me."

Grabbing hold of my arm, already covered in bruises, I slightly wince at the discomfort, as he hauls me out of the room and down the hall. Bringing me into a large sitting room that includes a dining table, I see that he has set up a candlelight dinner. Dread fills me. What is he up to?

Steering me towards a chair, I take a seat - or more accurately, am seated. The table is set and there are even silver domes over what I presume are our meals. Deacon takes a lighter from his trouser pocket and lights the tall candles set perfectly in a silver candelabra at the center of the table. As he leans over, his suit jacket opens slightly and I see a gun tucked into the front of his pants. It certainly isn't the first time I've seen it while I've been here, but it is just as disconcerting this time as the first. I secretly hope when he sits, the gun will go off and shoot his dick off. He certainly deserves far worse. I smile at the thought.

Deacon, seeing the smile on my face, returns it with one of his own. "I knew you would like this, princess. I wanted you to see that we can have wonderful, romantic dinners like this. You don't have to spend so much time locked up in your room. Once you finally realize this is where you should be, we can have dinner like this every night."

"I don't want to have dinner with you every night. When are you going to get a clue, you fucking douche?"

The smile that was just present on his lips quickly vanishes and anger seizes his entire countenance. I know I should just shut up and play along with what he says, but I can't; I will never stop fighting. Not ever. I will not let him strip away who I am.

After taking a few deep breaths, Deacon's eyes once again meet mine, "Tonight, things are going to change. The time for you to start accepting that we are together again is right now. I've apologized to you over and over for sleeping with Tracey. I'm so sorry you walked in on that, but I'm done apologizing for it. I've forgiven the fact that you betrayed me with that man, so you will forgive me about Tracey. I know once you forgive me, we will be fine. Everything will be fine, princess, and we will be happy."

"Not for the first time, you are out of your fucking mind. Tracey was merely the straw that broke the camel's back. I quit loving you long before that."

"ENOUGH! I am done being easy on you."

I laugh at that comment. Easy? He calls this easy? My laughter only angers him.

He rips me out of my chair and yanks me against the front of his body. "You are my WIFE and you will do what I say. You *will* provide your wifely duties. You are no longer allowed to talk back to me."

"Fuck you, Deacon. I am no longer married to you. I don't love you. I love Luke. I will ALWAYS love Luke."

He pulls me just far enough away from him to give him room to backhand me across the face. I feel pain, blinding pain, and taste blood in my mouth.

"DO NOT SPEAK HIS NAME TO ME!" He screams. Then, while seething with fury, he continues, "I will not allow you to talk about the man you whored yourself out to. Do you hear me?"

Before I can respond, his mouth is on mine. I want to throw up. He pulls me tight to him and I can feel that he is obviously turned on from the violence. His erection presses against my hip and his hands are all over my body. I'm stiff and don't move, refusing to participate in his complete violation.

Then suddenly, an idea enters my mind. It's crazy,

but it may just work.

Hesitantly, I reach my hands out and run them up Deacon's arms. He stiffens, surprised at my touch. I never return his touch. Leaving one hand on his arm, I cup the side of his neck with the other hand and start returning his kiss. When his tongue enters my mouth, I shudder and Deacon mistakes it for pleasure, pulling me closer and moaning deep in his throat. I grab the hair at his neck, and squeeze it into a fist, deepening the kiss while my other hand starts unbuttoning his shirt, one button at a time.

Deacon pulls away from me and looks into my eyes questioningly. It kills me to do it, but I whisper, "I want you, Deacon. You're right, we belong together. Kiss me."

He wastes no time pulling me back to him and kisses me hard once again. His tongue is brutal in its exploration of my mouth. He starts sliding my dress off of one shoulder and just as I reach the bottom button of his shirt, I quickly pull the gun from his pants and back up, pointing it at him.

"Back the hell up right the FUCK NOW." I feel like a bad ass. Finally, I have the upper hand and I feel euphoric.

Shock is displayed all over his face. He's breathing hard and his eyes are glassy. I can tell it's taking him a minute to completely comprehend what has just happened. He takes a step towards me.

"I SAID TO BACK UP, DEACON."

"You aren't going to shoot me. You don't even know how to use a gun."

Calling his bluff I click the safety off the gun and see his eyes widen.

"That's right, motherfucker. I guess you don't know everything about me, do you?"

"You won't shoot me, Olivia. You don't have it in you."

Deacon starts walking towards me again and I take a step back for every step he takes forward. Before I know it, my back is at the doors leading out onto a balcony. I'm trapped, but I refuse to give up. I reach behind me and open the doors, happy they aren't sliding glass like the bedroom. The cold air takes my breath away.

"Just give me the gun, Olivia. You don't want to do this. Give it to me, and we will go back to dinner. I made your favorite, cheese ravioli. Come on, I will show you." He takes another step towards me.

I keep backing up, "I said stay away from me, Deacon. I am not afraid to use this. I *will* shoot you."

I feel the railing at my back. I don't know what to do. I can shoot him and then try to find a phone and call 9-1-1. That's what I will do. It's all I can do.

I grasp the gun with both hands, and before I can get off a shot, I see the intent in Deacon's eyes right before he lunges for me.

I overcompensate for his lunge and throw myself backwards, right over the side of the balcony. I see his eyes widen in horror as the gun goes off and he reaches for me, but it's too late. I'm falling.

The fall feels like an eternity, and my life flashes before my eyes as expected, but another thought occurs to me as well… *where are parachute pants when a girl needs them*?

Here's a sneak peek of
SKYLER TOWER by the bestselling author,
Khelsey Jackson.
Scheduled to release on April 17, 2014

CHAPTER ONE

EVANGELINE SKYLER ALWAYS got what she wanted, and since she was the CEO of Sky Tech – a computer company she built from scratch – it had made her a very wealthy woman. She took pride in her work because she was the only woman to do what she had done.

Her driver, Axel Roberts, parked her BMW at the curb and she grabbed her sunglasses to place on her eyes. She had her long brown hair pulled back in a tight bun and she reached for her black Hermes purse, waiting for Axel to open her door for her. When he did she smiled at him as he helped her out. He had been with her for the past five years and had become a close friend.

"Have a great day, Ms. Skyler," he said and smiled at her. She never noticed how attractive he was until now. His ash-blonde hair was cut short and aquamarine blue eyes that were surrounded by thick, dark black eyelashes. His chiseled cheekbones and square face made her swoon. He caught her by the arm and his worried eyes stared down at her.

She pulled herself up and away from him. Feeling

embarrassed, she had no clue what in the world was wrong with her; she had never acted that way before. "I should have eaten this morning," she muttered halfheartedly, hoping he'd believe the lie. She did eat, but he didn't know that. "Thank you," Skyler offered with a nod, and turned right around to her building.

Skyler Tower was her baby; she was the one that built the little company from the ground up and now she had over one-thousand employees working for her. After strolling into the front door, she was greeted by the security guard, Mike, who had been working for her since she opened the doors five years ago.

"Hey, Mike. How is your family?" He had two teenage girls and a wife who passed away almost a year ago.

Mike grinned. "They are hanging in there. I wanted to thank you for my bonus."

Skyler blushed, but gave him her best innocent look. "If you got a bonus it was because you earned it."

She winked at him as she made her way to the elevator. A hand appeared in the closing doors and a man in a gray suit walked into the small space. She glanced at him and his dark, beautiful angular face was strikingly handsome. His raven black hair was slicked back to show off his handsome face and his deep chocolate eyes were on her. She felt her body heat up because he was taking her in too.

"Can you press thirty for me?" he said in a thick Italian accent. She bit her lip, forcing her eyes away from him, and to the numbers in front of her. She had to slide her card and was so distracted by him she forgot to press her own floor which was the same as he requested.

Skyler was never the one to be shy and bashful, but

the dominance rolling off of him caused her to lose her train of thought. "You didn't press your floor number," he murmured.

Trying to pull herself together, Skyler glanced at him over her shoulder and said, "I am on the top floor."

He stared at her as if he was figuring something out, and then his deep chocolate eyes went wide. "You're Evangeline Skyler." She loved the way her name sounded with his accent.

She was used to people being surprised by her, she wasn't what you thought of when you heard CEO of a computer company. She had long, dark brown hair and light blue eyes. Normally, she would get mistaken for a model or an actress, but never that she was a CEO.

"I am," she replied with pride in her voice.

"Well, Ms. Skyler I am here to interview you for The Times." That was right, she remembered someone calling her office for months asking for an interview with her. She ignored all the calls and the emails. She liked her privacy, and being in a newspaper wouldn't keep her life so private.

Skyler stood a little straighter and slowly turned around. "I wasn't aware that I had agreed to an interview."

His alluring lips lifted into a seductive smile. "You haven't … yet."

Arching her eyebrows, she studied him and watched him lick his lips. She couldn't comprehend why she didn't want to turn him down. There was something about him that was calling to her. "You have ten minutes before I have to go to a meeting," she stated as he grinned at her.

She was so happy when the doors opened revealing her floor. The once carpeted office now gleamed with white marble and all the wood was black walnut. A well-known artist had also painted the walls with beautiful scenery.

"This office is beautiful just like the woman who runs it," his Italian accent said from behind her; she smiled. She was used to taking complements, except there was something about the way he said it that made her turn around to face him. She wasn't the only one that was beautiful; he was breath taking.

"Thank you. I put a lot of my heart and soul in my building and business." He took a step towards her and she had to remind herself to step back. She didn't like to show any weakness when she was at work, and he was hers. "What's your name?"

He smiled down at her, revealing dimples in his cheeks when he answered, "Angelo Giovanni."

When he talked it made her think of things, and she didn't like where her mind was taking her. She didn't do relationships, she had sex. The last relationship she was in was when she was nineteen, and when it left her heart broken she vowed to never fall in love again. So far that was working for her, but there was something about Angelo that made her want to break that vow. Another thing she made sure of, was to be the one in charge and he radiated control.

She placed her hand in front of him and his smile widened. "Mr. Giovanni," she said and when he put his hand in hers she sucked in her breath. Instantly, her pulse raced and her panties dampened.

"Ms. Skyler, I am honored." He took her hand and slowly brought it to his luscious lips, keeping his chocolate eyes on hers.

She mentally had to shake herself because they were

standing in the lobby of her office where many people were working. "Follow me," she commanded as she tore her hand from his grip, heading toward her corner office.

Her office was different than the rest of floor with dark marble covering the floor along with the large desk that sat in the middle of the room. The walls had wallpaper with a silver elegant design. She waited for him to enter and closed the door behind him. She had a well-known painting from Vincent van Gogh hanging behind her desk. It was her pride and joy.

"I was wrong before, this is what suites you." He slowly turned to face her and grinned. This man was dangerous, but she wanted him.

"Thank you I pay a lot of money to get what I want," she said as she made her way to sit behind her desk, needing distance between them.

"You seem to often get what you want."

She kept her face blank of emotions because her personal life was just that ... personal. "I thought you were interviewing me, Mr. Giovanni."

Smiling, he reached in his pocket to pull out a small notepad and a pen. "If that is what you want," he remarked, opening up the little black note book so he could write something down. "You are only thirty years old, how did you become so successful?"

Skyler was used to people asking her that. "I knew what I wanted and went for it with everything I had."

He stared at her for a second before writing her answer down. "If you could do one thing differently what would it be?"

Skyler lifted her eyebrows because that wasn't your typical interview question. "I wouldn't do anything differently; everything I have done was for a reason." She did miss one thing, but fulfilled it with sex, not love.

Angelo narrowed his eyes. "There is nothing you would change in your life? An old lover you would want back in your life or maybe a different career path?"

"What I have is what I always wanted. I knew when I was younger I wanted to be my own woman and that I didn't need a man to make me successful." She had read articles on her being called heartless, but she wasn't ... she was cautious.

"Why are you still single?" he asked.

Skyler licked her lips and lifted an eyebrow. "That is personal, Mr. Giovanni." His face showed his amusement, except he quickly covered it up with his hand, rubbing the jaw line thoughtfully.

Closing his notebook, Angelo sat it on her desk and leaned forward. "I want to kiss you," he said in a thicker accent than before. It made her tremor thinking about what that voice could do to her.

He stood up and walked towards her. She didn't know if she was going to stop him or rip off her clothes. When he moved around her desk, she allowed her gaze to follow his every step toward her. Angelo stopped beside her and she had to tilt her head to match his deep chocolate eyes.

"Stand up," he ordered. Skyler narrowed her at his show of dominance.

"Kneel," she said with a challenge in her voice. She thought he would laugh at her or demand her to do as he said. She knew when she was staring at another dominant. Sitting a little taller, she kept her eyes on his, never wavering.

Slowly, he dropped to one knee in front of her and she licked her lips knowing what was coming. She didn't move. Skyler waited for his lips to capture hers; steadily, he leaned forward and kissed her neck. His scorching mouth hovered above hers and his eyes seemed to burn though her. She couldn't take it anymore. She wanted his lips on hers so she grabbed his tie and pulled him to her. Their lips molded together and her eyes fluttered closed. His tongue licked her bottom lip seeking permission. Opening her mouth, Skyler moaned when his sinful tongue found hers. Her hands traveled up to his raven black hair and she tangled her fingers to hold him to her.

His arms snaked around to her back and she knew she wanted him. It had been six months since she had taken a lover to her bed and that was the longest she had gone since she lost her virginity. He tore his mouth from her and she groaned.

"I want you," he said, saying the words she was terrified to say. "But I won't take you here in your office." She frowned at him because that wasn't what she wanted to hear, she wanted him naked and inside her.

"You confuse me," she confessed and he stood up. Her eyes went to the large bulge in the front of his pants causing her mouth to go dry.

Angelo placed his hand in front of her and she took it. He smiled down at her illuminating his dimples again. "I am not the type of guy that fucks someone in an office. I want to take my time with you and I couldn't here." He took the hand he was still holding and placed it on his bulge. "I want you, but I also want to do this right."

She narrowed her eyes because what he wanted she didn't want to give. "I don't do relationships, I like to have sex and that is it. My life is too demanding for anything more than simple sex."

"Well then I guess I have to woo you," he murmured, removing her hand from the front of his pants, bringing it to his lips. When he kissed her knuckles he kept his chocolate eyes on hers. "Let me treat you to dinner."

She moved away from him because she couldn't think straight when he was touching her. "That sounds like a date."

"Because I *am* asking you on a date." He grinned at her and she felt things she hadn't in a while. She wanted to wake up in his arms in the morning; she wanted his handsome face to be the first thing she saw.

"I don't know," Skyler responded hesitantly. Angelo moved back to her cutting her off, and when he kissed her hard she forgot the reasons for saying no. When he pulled away she was the one to smile. "Fine. You have one night so make it worth it."

He laughed and hugged her tightly. "If you are there then I know it will be worth it." He reached in his pocket and pulled out a white business card. "This has my personal cell phone number on it, I will leave the when up to you." Quickly, he kissed her cheek, handed her the card and turned around to walk out the door.

She was left standing in her office breathing as if she just finished running five miles.

Here's a sneak peek at
First Glance by L.L. Hunter.
Scheduled to release on Jan. 31, 2014

PROLOGUE

GETTING A CALL to come into work at three in the morning is not a new thing for me. I often expect it. But I didn't expect this.

"This better be important, Jim, if I'm giving up my warm bed for this."

"It is Addy. I can assure you."

"Ugh, why are you so perky this time of morning!"

"I'm a vampire. I sleep during the day."

I shoot ice missiles at my unnaturally perky assistant as he strolls over the fridge to retrieve the reason I was called down here. In less than a minute, he has the body bag on a gurney, wheeling it in front of me, and sliding it onto the metal slab.

"It still gives me the heebie jeebies just thinking about it."

I glance at him in confusion and anticipation and start to unzip the bag. The face that greets me is not what I was expecting, and I jump back with a shriek. Normally, I am fine around dead bodies, being a morgue technician and studying forensic science, but nothing I have seen previously prepares me for this. Lying on the slab in front of me, all pale and cold, is a face more familiar to me than anyone else's.

It's my face.

CHAPTER ONE

I BLINK.

Something is dripping on my face; something wet and annoying. I move my hand to wipe it off but more liquid comes. It's now pouring onto my face, and it is cold. I groan and roll over.

"What the hell?"

"Wake up! Today's the big day!"

"What big day?" I mumble in my pillow, hoping she won't hear me. Fat chance! My roommate has the hearing of a dog.

"I can't believe you've forgotten! You're coming wedding dress shopping with me! You *are* my Maid of honor after all! Unless, you don't want to be?"

I sit up. "What? Don't be silly, of course I still want to be your Maid of Honor." I laugh and toss my pillow at her, which she dodges.

"Great! Then hurry up! We've got to hit the stores early!"

I am not much of a shopper. I'd much prefer to get a wake up call to go to the morgue than one to go shopping for wedding dresses.

"There better be something in this for me, Cory!" I call out.

"There is, don't you worry Miss Paige." Cory pokes her head back into my bedroom and winks. I fight all the power within me not to throw another pillow. *What is that girl up to?*

AFTER THE FOURTH wedding shop, I swear I'm about to start a fight with one of the shop attendants or cut up one of the dresses, and I still didn't have a clue what Cory had planned for me. Did she even have anything planned for me? I was also in desperate need of another caffeine fix.

"Not another shop," I whine.

"Yes, another one. The previous one's sucked."

"Ugh, I need another coffee. I'll meet you back here."

"I swear, Addy, I'm buying you an I.V. bag for your next birthday."

I only faintly hear her as I walk towards the closest café, and I wave her off. While standing in line, I rub my temples and glance at my watch. It wasn't even nine yet. We still had at least another seven hours to spend shopping for darn wedding dresses. It was a nightmare. Where were dead corpses when I needed them? At least they didn't make me try on fugly brides's maid dresses.

"Who's next?" asks the barista. I barely notice it's me he's calling until he insults me. "Hey, off-with- the-fairies girl, would you like a coffee?"

"Huh? Pardon?" I glance up and realize I'm the one he's been speaking to, or rather insulting.

"Oh, she's with us finally."

"Excuse me?" I cock my head to the side trying to figure out why this rude person is saying these things to me.

"I said, would you like a coffee today?"

"No, I'm just standing here getting insulted by a lep-rechaun!"

"Ooh, and she bites back."

"Yes, so watch out." He only smirks, so I add, "First-ly, don't cross me before I've had my full dose of coffee or things get ugly. Secondly, I hate rude people. I can't *stand* rude people. So can you just make me a freaking coffee and we can be done with this. Okay?"

"Gladly. What would you like? I'm not telepathic you know. You *do* have to tell me your order."

"Alright, genius. I'll have a soy latte. Double shot, thanks."

"And can I have a name for that order, or shall I just put off-with-the- fairies girl?"

"I am NOT giving you my name."

"Alright, off-with-the-fairies girl it is then." He writes something on the side of the takeaway cup, smirking while he does it and puts the cup under the machine.

I cross my arms. "Where do you get off?"

"Oh, I got off on the right side of the bed this morn-ing, thanks for askin', Princess."

"I mean, talking to innocent people in such a rude manner. Jackass." He laughs while making my coffee. I watch him with an eagle eye to make sure he doesn't slip cyanide in there.

"I don't normally. You've brought out all my best qualities, sweetheart."

"Don't call me that, smartass. Just make my damn coffee." He doesn't say anything, just smiles as he finishes my order and brings it back to the cash register. "You know, I thought I'd try this place just for a change, but I don't think I'll come back."

"Aww, why not? Was it something I said?"

I scowl and slam five dollars down on the counter and practically snatch my coffee out of his hand. "Keep the change!" I shout as I storm away without giving him another look. I walk back to the bridal store more agitated than I was pre- coffee.

"Where were you? I think I found it," Cory shrieks as soon as I walk in.

"Sorry, the rude Irish guy at the coffee shop was insulting me. He had some freaking nerve!"

"Irish guy? Was it that new place that just opened?"

"Yeah, why?"

She shrugs. "Nothing. Was just wondering, that's all. Is the coffee at least good? Because if the coffee was bad you would at least have another reason to go back and complain."

"It's not bad. Another reason?"

"Yeah, you know, other than to go and ask for his number."

I shove her and shoot her daggers with my eyes. "Cory, he was a complete jackass. No way will I ever consider dating him."

"Come on, Adelaide, you need a date to my wedding. And don't say you'll bring Jim, because that guy is the epitome of a nerd."

"What's wrong with Jim? He's a nice guy."

"He's a nerd. You're not bringing him to my wedding."

"Fine. But I am *not* dating that Irish idiot."

"Whatever you say. Come help me with this zipper."

I groan and set down my coffee with my purse and walk over to where Cory's standing on the pedestal in the latest wedding dress design. When my fingers touch the white satin and lace, I begin to feel faint and light-headed. Then I see something.

My phone rings as I exit the morgue building. I look at the caller I.D. and click answer.

"Hey Cor, what's up? I've just finished work. I'm heading home now."

"Please hurry, Oh my god, there's blood everywhere. There's so much blood."

"What, Cory? Are you okay? What happened?"

"Hurry! Oh my God there's too much blood! It hurts!"

"What happened? Where are you?"

"At home. Please hurry."

Then the line goes dead.

I don't hesitate. I drive straight home, even running a red light on the way. When I reach the driveway I jump out of the car while the engine's still running and hurry to the front door. I find that it's ajar so I gingerly push it open and that's when I see the blood.

Cory is right. There is so much blood. Too much blood. It is everywhere. All over the walls, all over her. And there she is lying in the center of it all in the middle of the living room floor, clinging to life.

"Ad...dy. He's... here." She gasps. I run to her side and kneel down in the pool of blood.

"What? Who's here? Where's Derek?"

"Watch out, he's..." Cory screams and her eyes grow wide, and that's when I lose sight of the world.

I jump back. I must have screamed or done something

369

because Cory spins around and puts her hands on my shoulders.

"Addy, what happened? What is it?"

I can't tell her. She won't understand. How can I tell her I just saw her die, we both died.

"I… nothing. I just pinched my finger in the zipper, that's all. I'll try again."

"You sure? You squealed like you do when you see a spider or a snake."

"Really? I don't remember. It did hurt quite a bit."

Cory exhales and turns back around. "Okay, let's try this one more time."

I almost don't want to do it but I have to. I can't let Cory know what I just saw, not when she's so happy, not right before her wedding. I brace myself and grab onto the zipper again.

Printed in Great Britain
by Amazon.co.uk, Ltd.,
Marston Gate.